ALSO BY SCOTT SPENCER

Last Night at the Brain Thieves' Ball

Preservation Hall

Endless Love

Waking the Dead

WAKING THE DEAD

Scott Spencer

ALFRED A. KNOPF

New York

1986

THIS IS A BORZOI BOOK
PUBLISHED BY ALFRED A. KNOPF, INC.

Library of Congress Cataloging-in-Publication Data

Spencer, Scott. Waking the dead.

I. Title.
PS3569.P455W3   1986   813'.54   85-45600
ISBN 0-394-54356-4

Manufactured in the United States of America

FIRST EDITION

This book is dedicated to Celeste and Asher.

But some man will say, "How are the dead raised up and with what body do they come?"

—I CORINTHIANS

Waking the Dead

1

Sarah Williams left for Minneapolis with our life together in the worst possible repair. I knew enough about the suddenness of things to know that you ought never say good-bye to someone you love without acknowledging that you might be looking at them for the very last time. I broke this emotional law and twenty-six hours later Sarah was pronounced dead and zippered up in a black rubber bag in Minneapolis Community General Hospital.

The police informed Sarah's family down in New Orleans but the Williamses didn't have the decency or perhaps the presence of mind to find me. I finally learned about it on the CBS news that evening, as I sat in our apartment in Chicago, surrounded by the things Sarah and I had accumulated over the three years of living together. The picture that flashed on the TV screen was of Francisco and Gisela Higgins, who had left Chile when the generals took over the government and who had been making the rounds internationally, describing the horrors of the current Chilean regime. As it happened, Sarah had been driving Francisco and Gisela to a church in St. Paul where the parish had given sanctuary to a few Chileans who had fled to the United States illegally. They were in a white 1968 Volvo station wagon, with an indestructible KEEP ON TRUCKIN' bumper sticker in the back—six years hadn't peeled it off, nor had six hundred days of winter in the northern tier, nor, finally, had the blast of the bomb that had been taped to the bottom of the car and radio-detonated when they were just a block from Our Lady of the Miracle. But for me the details came later. I knew something whose terribleness was beyond anything I'd ever known had happened as soon as I saw Francisco and Gisela's faces on the screen and the news reader said, "This afternoon, terror struck a quiet neighborhood in Minneapolis." And then Francisco and Gisela's images were gone and the newscaster went on talking and there was film running. I saw the white Volvo covered in firemen's foam, bare trees, a light April snow falling, and then a reporter standing on the street with a microphone, looking very official and indignant, a big blond boy with a movie star haircut and a fancy winter coat with a fur collar. But my hands were over my ears and I couldn't hear what he was saying. And then there was a picture of Sarah. The same old picture I had seen on her parents' piano in their house on St. Charles Avenue, a picture of her sitting on a wicker chair on their porch with her arms around her knees and a completely happy smile on her face which was rarely that completely happy. The sunlight was in her hair, shining also in the whites of her eyes, the moisture of her teeth, the little gold chain around her neck. My own voice was echoing as I said no over and over and then I hit the Off switch.

I left the apartment without closing the door behind me and without a coat. The late snow that had been falling in Minnesota was now falling through the coarse gray darkness over Chicago. Somehow I seized on the idea that there was something I needed to decide, a course of action I needed to affirm. I don't honestly know what I was thinking; the truth is most of my effort was probably spent fighting going mad.

We were living on 51st and Blackstone. I was going to law school at the University of Chicago and Sarah was working on the northwest side in a place called Resurrection House. We had few friends and virtually no money, so most of the time we had to spend together we spent alone, in the apartment.

I was still strange to the streets I walked that night. The lights in the windows seemed sharp and unfriendly and the families living on the ground floors, whose domesticity I could spy in brightly lit wedges, seemed remote, unknowable. From time to time, I became aware of how cold it was. I looked up and saw the snow drifting past the streetlights. Sometimes my heart seemed not to be beating at all and sometimes it seemed to be beating far, far too quickly. I made my way to 53rd Street and found a bar. I had a few dollars in my pocket and I ordered a beer. I was supposed to be stopping drinking and it didn't quite occur to me that this was a time I could back off that vow. The taste of the beer was too real and its reality made the night undeniable.

The bartender had a large white distorted face, unbelievably grotesque, like something underwater. There was one other person in the bar, a bus driver sitting in front of what looked like a Scotch and soda. There were framed photographs of famous boxers on the wall—that listless automatic decoration they use in bars without any real character. I had some change in my pocket and I went to the phone booth. I was wet, shaking. I dropped the dime in and dialed our apartment and listened to the ringing. And with each ring I thought: My God, it really happened.

Sarah and Gisela had been in the front seat and they were instantly dead. Probably they were each buried with shreds of the other in the casket. Francisco Higgins had been in the backseat, lying down. They took what was left of him to the hospital, where he died two days later. By this time, I was in Minneapolis, too, and I visited his hospital room. He was small in that bed; the equipment was larger than he was. It was a cheerful room, Nordic and up-to-date, with little humanizing touches that were coming into vogue: warm colors on the wall, a child's crayon drawing framed, an orthopedically designed chair for visits.

I really didn't know Higgins. I'd met him only once, at dinner with Sarah and a few of the others the night before the trip to Minnesota. I'd liked him that evening. He was a sort of Chilean government-in-exile, but he had a way of not taking it so awfully seriously, or at least not rubbing your nose in the seriousness of it. I'd liked him then but I did not like him in that hospital room, and as soon as I walked in I realized it was wrong for me to be there. I started to shake and I was having vile, desperate thoughts, my mind jerking this way and that like a snake tortured by a sharp stick. He had clearly been the object of the attack; his wife was a secondary target and Sarah had just happened to be along for the ride. He'd been deliberately attacked, but, in a sense, Sarah's death had been accidental. It seemed inarguable from the beginning that the bomb had been planted by terrorists in the pay of the generals running Chile—the generals who'd held Francisco and Gisela prisoner and who, having succumbed to international pressure to set them free, wanted them silenced. But the last thing they wanted to do was kill an American citizen. Francisco and Gisela were world famous, but it was Sarah's death that became the focus of the stories about the bombing, Sarah's death that made people in America care. And soon Francisco's friends the world over would be making the most of it. They were going to take her away from me and make her stand for something.

Sarah's father was in Minneapolis to accompany the casket on the flight down to New Orleans, where she was going to be buried in the family tomb—burials are aboveground in New Orleans because the loam is too soft to hold the dead securely in their pine and mahogany cocoons. He spoke to the police and avoided the press. He thought the reporters were somehow conspiring with the dissident Chileans to use Sarah's death to disgrace America. He was a large, aggressive man, fit from tennis and the isometrics of his own bad temper, and he came into the cold Minnesota spring wearing a light blue suit, a white belt, and white shoes, as if these were the tribal colors of his better way of life.

A woman from a local TV station focused in on me. It wasn't as if she cared. She was just trying to be original in her handling of the story. I was, at first, the boyfriend of the deceased, and then she promoted me to the fiancé, in time for the ten o'clock report.

I thought I owed it to Sarah to say something but really there was nothing left of me. I'd tried to eat some toast but I couldn't keep it down. It had been twenty-four hours living off the sugar in Scotch. I didn't dare sleep or even close my eyes, and the worst part was I knew that my response to all of this was just in its larval stage, that I had managed to isolate my shock and grief, freeze it back a little, but I wouldn't be able to keep it like that for very long and soon—well, who knew what I was going to feel or what I would make of it? "Whom do you hold responsible for this?" the reporter asked me, shoving the microphone before my mouth.

I thought. I couldn't answer quickly. "I don't know," I finally said. "The government of Chile has a secret police force and they've been known to follow dissident Chileans all over the world in order to silence them."

She waved to her cameraman and then shook her head, dropping the microphone to her side. "That sounds like propaganda," she said. "Can we just keep it—I don't know, keep it personal and immediate?"

"I'll try," I said.

"Good," she said. "It'll seem more real that way."

I sat next to Sarah's father on the flight to New Orleans. Neither of us wanted the company of the other but there was no way around it. His name was Eugene, named after his father. He sold insurance and acted as if this gave him a certain insight and competence in matters of life and death, as if he were a surgeon or a priest. He was successful but not well liked. Sarah was one of his three children—all daughters. He'd named her Sara, thinking it was ladylike, fetching; she'd added the *h* to her name later on. Sarah's mother's name was Dorothy and she was afraid and evasive around Eugene. It was hard to say where her loyalties were. She seemed mostly to care about appearances, and even though it is probably an emotional impossibility to care only for the surface of life, Dorothy seemed to do so.

Eugene and I watched the stewardess demonstrate the safety

features of the 727. It was a rough takeoff, right into the wind. It surprised me how fervently I wanted the plane to crash. Clouds raced past like torn dirty rags. You could hear the engines straining. Then the NO SMOKING sign went off with a little *ping* and we were securely airborne. Eugene lit up a Kool and tilted his seat back. He toed off his white loafers and exhaled smoke through his nose. Sarah's body was in the belly of the plane. Minneapolis was beneath us looking clean, ordinary, distant. Then it curved away, as if the earth in its rotation suddenly jerked forward, and beneath us was the frozen stubble of farmland, and little blue-enameled bumps: the silos. We were flying. We were going to heaven.

When the stewardess came by, Eugene asked her for a vodka and tonic. They weren't serving drinks yet, but she seemed to know he was the father of the woman, the body, below. She seemed also to know who I was and she asked me if I wanted something as well. I said no, just because it was easier. When his drink arrived, Eugene took a bottle of pills from his jacket and shook one out into his hand—he had a large palm and the lines in it had a faint reddish tinge. "Want one?"

I shrugged. "What are you taking?"

"Dorothy's doctor gave her some tranquilizers and I'm taking them," he said. He smiled, as if there was some tragic irony in a man of his enormous strength having to take a woman's medicine.

"Are they doing any good?" I asked.

"I think so. I'm not so . . . jumpy, you know."

I put my hand out and he gave me one. It was the same light blue as Eugene's suit on one half, and dark brown on the other. I put it in my pocket. "I'll keep it for later."

The word *later* had a bad effect on me. Time was moving on, but it was empty now. The word *later* made me realize that my life might be very, very long and that now I would have to live every second of it without her.

"I'm having a nervous reaction to all this crap," Eugene said. "I don't know whether I'm coming or going."

"You're going," I said.

Eugene's intelligence went toward the keen; he regarded what other people said the way a prisoner looks over the walls of his cell, searching for the loose brick, the patch of spongy mortar. Eugene squinted at me. He was forever sizing me up.

"I guess if we knew how all this was going to end up," he said, "then you and I might have worked a little harder on being friends."

"I guess so. And I guess you would have worked a little harder with Sarah, too." I know what that sounds like now, but at the time it seemed like a fair thing to say, and certainly within my rights to say it.

Eugene's eyes filled with tears but just for an instant. "Don't you give me any of your shit, pal. I've forgotten more about that girl than you'll ever know. I changed her diapers and held her hands when she took her first little bitty baby steps."

He took in a deep beleaguered breath and sat deeper in his seat. I could sense the tranquilizer kicking in for him and it made me glad I hadn't swallowed mine. I realized dimly that the expression on his face was meant to inspire guilt in me, guilt over my lack of respect for his loss. But Sarah was in the cargo, directly below us for all I knew, and I could not make a peace that she herself had failed to negotiate. Eugene and Sarah hadn't been easy with each other since Sarah was ten, and I felt I had to keep that going. I suppose it was a way of keeping her alive awhile longer and maybe Eugene was provoking me for the very same reason.

"I'm still waiting for you to tell me what the hell she was doing with that couple from Chile," Eugene said. "Or why she was mixed up with this whole mess in the first place."

"I wouldn't know where to begin," I said.

"Well, I wish she could have come to talk to me about it," he said. "I could have told her she was getting in way over her head."

In New Orleans, Eugene had offered me a bed in his house, but I didn't want to be with them and the prospect of sleeping in or even near Sarah's old room seemed too difficult. I didn't want to put myself through it. I checked into a small hotel called Maison

Dupuy—picturesque on the outside, anonymous within—and once I was there I turned on the TV, the air conditioner, and began to cry without control. It was like colliding with a self who had always been curled within me but whose presence I'd never suspected—just as the self who had once seized Sarah's love had taken me by surprise. I believed in duty, in service, in carefully laid plans, in measured responses and calculated risks, but all of that was gone and what was left was terror and bitterness and a feeling that I was going mad.

It would have been even harder on me except my family flew to New Orleans. My father and mother arrived that evening, with my brother, Danny, and Caroline, my sister. I'd gone out for air and when I returned there was a note in my mailbox that my family was in Rooms 121 and 123. I knocked and my father answered the door. He was reading the *Times-Picayune*, holding it in one hand; he had wire-rimmed bifocals. His hair was duck white, full, wavy, long. His chest was massive and ruddy under his open shirt; he looked as if he'd been body-surfing in the cold Atlantic off the Rockaways. When he saw me, he dropped the newspaper and flung his arm around me, pulled me toward him. "Christ almighty," he said in my ear, in his rich, porous voice—it always sounded as if he ought to clear his throat. I put my arms around him, held on. I saw my mother standing behind him, with her fingertips touching the bed, as if for balance. She had a pretty, round face. Danny used to say that Mom wore her hair like Lesley Gore. It was parted in the middle and had a dramatic flip on either side. She looked reserved, isolated, a little lonely, like a widow. She wore her glasses on a chain around her neck and they rose and fell on her bosom as she took deep emotional breaths.

Dad walked me in and handed me over to Mom, who held my face in her large, soft hands and kissed me on each cheek and then the chin. My parents had always meant safety and loyalty to me and seeing them shored me up. I began to see how I might be able to get through this.

"It's the worst thing that's ever happened," Dad said.

"What can we do?" Mom said. "Do you want to talk about it? Just tell us what to do. We're here for you."

"And for her," added Dad. He'd really liked Sarah. He thought we would get married and give him wonderful grandchildren. He also hoped that she would help me with my career, keep me strong and a little bit hungry. They both believed in absolute right and wrong, and they each had little bulletin boards within their hearts upon which grievances were posted and never taken down. "She was a wonderful girl, Fielding. There's nothing more to say. A rare and wonderful girl."

"Eddie," Mom said, with a note of caution.

"It's OK, Mom," I said. "He's right."

"It's not a question of right," she said softly. It seemed as if it had been years now that half of what she'd said had been murmured to the side, as if the people who really understood her were phantoms, just offstage.

"We weren't even getting along," I said, suddenly putting my hand over my eyes. And then I had a desolate thought: Every misunderstanding, every quarrel, every overheated contest of the wills was now, by dint of her death, destined to become a memory of unutterable sweetness.

"It's still in the newspapers," Dad said. "It's not something that's going to go away. Not just the local papers," he added, gesturing to the *Times-Picayune*, which lay open on the floor, turned to a page of advertisements showing drawings of lawn furniture, "but all the papers. The *New York Times*, the Washington *Post*, and of course your Chicago papers, too." Dad was still a printer, coming to the end of a thirty-year hitch at the *New York Times* plant. Yet no matter how many half-truths and retractions he'd set type for, he still believed almost religiously in the printed word. He read three papers a day and every week or so went to the public library to read out-of-town papers. He subscribed to a dozen magazines and patrolled the used bookstores on Fourth Avenue, often buying books for no other reason but that he liked the look of them.

"Do you know anything more about what happened?" Mom said.

"Nothing," I said. "Just what you know. I haven't been trying to find out."

"There's going to have to be a thorough investigation," Dad said, bringing his hands together and nodding, as if he'd just then decided to conduct the inquiry himself. "This isn't Tijuana or somewhere. They can't just come here and carry on like it was."

"We were a little surprised," Mom said, tilting her head in a way that suggested tactfulness, "to learn how . . . involved Sarah had gotten. We didn't think of her that way."

"It was recent," I said.

"We sent letters to Senator Moynihan and Senator Javits," Mom said.

"A different letter for each of them," added Dad. "You can't appeal to a Javits the way you would a Moynihan. Pat's stuffy, but he's from the streets."

"You'll come home with us when this is over," Mom said.

"I'll tell you one thing," Dad said, sitting on the bed, resting his weight on his hands. "Killing an American girl was just about the stupidest thing those bastards could have done. People are never going to forget this."

"I guess Sarah would be glad of that," I said. I was hearing my voice as if it were coming from a different spot in the room.

"It's a terrible thing to say, I guess," Mom said, coming to my side and putting her arm through mine, sensing, I think, that I might lose my balance at any moment, "but we're going to have to sit down soon and talk this whole thing through. This is going to involve you in all *kinds* of ways and maybe you'd like a chance to figure out just how you're going to handle it." Mom had worked for twenty-one years for a state assemblyman named Earl Corvino, whose motto was Let's Minimize the Impact. Mom had gotten a pretty raw deal from Corvino but she'd learned a few things while she was at it.

That night, I moved into Danny and Caroline's room; I couldn't afford my own room and, more, I couldn't bear being alone. I was still accepting the truth of Sarah's death one cell at a time. With Danny and Caroline, I felt protected; they would know what to do if I suddenly fell into ten thousand pieces.

We stayed up late talking. I remember laughing. I remember Caroline recalling the tricky little current events quizzes Mom forced us to take over breakfast. What kind of plane was Captain Jerry Powers flying on his mission over Russia when the Soviets shot him down. Answer: a U-2. Right but wrong, silly: his name isn't Jerry, it's *Gary*. Like fanatical gardeners working in soil of questionable fertility, our parents slaved over us with a kind of diligence that certainly included love but was not confined to it. And now here we were, the three of us, bound together not only by the normal genetic magic of siblings but by the sort of loopy heroic narrative that binds veterans of a long war. Veterans of the Asian wars wear those satin jackets that say on the back I Know I'm Going to Heaven Because I've Spent My Time in Hell and then have a drawing of Korea or Vietnam. Danny had wanted us to wear jackets that said the same thing but with a picture of our genteel shabby brownstone in Brooklyn instead.

The war of our childhoods had been all the more peculiar and exhausting because it had all been waged quite clearly and endlessly for our own good. And here we were, the sum of their efforts: Danny was a fly-by-night businessman living six golden miles above his means; Caroline was a painter without enough money to buy paint, with two children and a tough marriage; and I was almost a lawyer. Yet, none of us worked the swing shift; none of us carried our lunch in a pail. We'd hightailed it out of our class.

We drank a few bottles of tepid wine and fell asleep. But I was up again before dawn. My heart was pounding as if I were being chased. I lay in bed listening to the air conditioner, to the deep, almost musical breathing of my brother, the slow rich exhalations of my sister, and it seemed that this thicket of horror and loss into which I'd been tossed had always been my life. It was impossible to believe that there had ever been any happiness.

The sun was getting ready to crest and another day without

her was going to begin. And in New Orleans, too: the city of her longing. How she missed the smells of the place, the grillwork, the shotgun houses, the music, the tall icy drinks . . . We ought to have spent more time here. Tears were rolling into the corners of my mouth and I rubbed my face with the harsh, starchy sheet. I got out of bed and dressed in silence. Then down to the lobby, where the night man at the desk was reading *Our Lady of the Flowers* and the porter was walking slowly over the tiled floors, pushing an ammonia-soaked mop in front of him. I just sat there with my hands between my knees, staring straight ahead. A while later, I looked up and Danny was standing there. He hadn't bothered to dress. He was in blue silk pajamas. His eyes were a similar color. His hair was the same light tan as the Minnesota farmland seen from the plane. His face was angular, his mouth a little tense: he never looked tired.

"Are you losing your mind?" he asked, crouching down before me, putting his bony, powerful hands on my knees.

"I don't think so," I said.

"You look terrible," he said. "And you've got to get through this whole fucking day. You've got the funeral. And there's going to be reporters, questions, everything. This is going to be very hard."

"It's just the beginning," I said.

"I know. But let's get through today. Come on. Follow me. I've got something for you." He got up and put his hand out for me. He put his other arm around my shoulders and took me back to the room.

Caroline sat up in bed as we walked in. It was not yet seven in the morning. Caroline slept in her underwear and a black T-shirt. She had brown hair and dark eyes; her jaw was square, her cheekbones high—she would never go pasty like the rest of us. Her looks fit her dramatic personality. "What are you guys doing?" she asked. In childhood, she'd been our ringleader, but life had been tougher on her and now poverty and disorganization made her uncertain.

"I'm going to medicate Fielding," Danny said. He pulled his Mark Cross bag from beneath the bed and flipped it open. Zippered into a little side compartment was a tinfoil packet. My stomach lurched but only for a moment, like a drunk trying to get out of his chair but then giving up. Danny opened the foil packet and inside was a dingy powder, caked on the top, loose on the bottom.

"Are you seriously doing this?" asked Caroline. "I know what that is."

"You've got something else to get him through this?" Danny asked, the confidence blowing through his voice like a stiff breeze.

"And what's he supposed to do tomorrow?" Caroline asked.

"Tomorrow he can flip out. At least half the world won't be watching."

"Is this what I think it is?" I asked.

"Yes. OK now, just take a little."

"Am I going to be sick?"

"Why would I give you something to make you sick? Just don't take too much."

"I suppose you'll be joining him," Caroline said.

"And how 'bout yourself, Sis?" asked Danny.

"Forget it," said Caroline. "In my neighborhood, this is no game. A junkie ripped off Rudy's lunch money last week."

"Well, it wasn't me," said Danny, handing me a piece of candy-striped straw.

And so as I walked into Sarah's funeral it was within the soft armor of two snorts of heroin, each the size of a match head. The service was in a Catholic church, though Eugene was barely Catholic and Dorothy was nominally Episcopalian. It was the same church I'd gone to with Sarah for her grandfather's funeral: St. Matthew's. The whole issue of Catholicism was suddenly very touchy. It wasn't as if the Williamses blamed the Church for what happened, but clearly there were *elements* in the Church they did blame. After all, Sarah had been in Minneapolis to deliver three Chilean refugees to a Maryknoll convent, where they were to be given sanctuary. The Williamses had had it with priests and they'd had it with me. I was not expected to sit in the first pew with the family but had to find a place among the fifty or sixty others who made up the human periphery of Sarah's short life.

To get into the church, I had to make my way past a surprising number of reporters and photographers, not only from our own press but from papers around the world. In the car my parents had been trying to prepare me for the questions—the answers to which they feared would be tied to the tail of my own political future like a string of tin cans—but I could scarcely respond to their promptings. As we got close to the church my body began to sweat like mad and I felt so faint that I lay my head back and the sun came through the back window of the taxi and struck my forehead and eyes like a hot yellow maul. When we pulled next to the curb and into the fractured chaotic shade of a tall magnolia tree, the press clustered around the car. Some of them made a decent attempt to appear respectful, though others were too disassociated, too ambitious to care. "OK, here we go," said Dad, and I realized that in ways he could not quite know or control he was glad for the commotion: he had always wanted to help make history, the way some men forever embrace the ambition to write a novel or paint a great mural, and here at last we were, we lowly four, with the ear of the world cocked in our direction and its great glassy eye blinking at us every hundredth of a second.

"Mr. Pierce . . ."

"Hey Fielding, Fielding . . ."

"One second, one second . . ."

Across St. Charles Avenue, opposite the church, a small knot of people holding placards stood vigil. The signs read SARAH WILLIAMS—VICTIM OF AMERICAN IMPERIALISM, and STOP SUPPORTING CHILEAN NAZIS. Someone had managed to enlarge a picture of Sarah, and this picket sign, outlined in black, was at the front of the group. Someone with a deep, sonorous voice called out, *"Com-*

pañera Sarah Williams," and the others responded: "*Presente.*" Then the deep voice said, "*Ahora,*" and the others said "*Y siempre.*" Sarah Williams. Here with us. Now. And forever.

I had been following Danny's lead through the reporters and into the church, but the chanting across the street had stopped me cold. I had expected the heroin to cancel, or at least slow, my mental processes, but in fact my thoughts were coming fast and loose—yet encased in a kind of dark, soft silk, rendered more or less harmless. It occurred to me that those people across the street were trying to steal Sarah's death away from me and then it occurred to me that that was perfectly all right. If they wanted it so badly, they could have it.

One of the TV reporters took advantage of my slowing down and stuck a microphone under my nose. He was an open-faced young fellow with thinning sandy hair, freckles, a seersucker suit, a classy drawl.

"Who do you hold responsible for Sarah's death, Fielding?" he asked me.

I took a deep breath and everyone then knew I was going to answer the question: they had that radar working. Other microphones craned in my direction. I felt Danny's fierce, bony fingers on my wrist and Dad's hand on the small of my back. I was dimly aware that here was the spot where I was expected to blame the U.S. government for the whole thing, but I couldn't do that, even if I wanted to I couldn't do it. Anyhow, it was all so much more complicated than that. "Me," I finally said. "Myself."

And with that, fifty more questions came hurtling toward me but Danny pulled me hard and Dad kept his hand at my back, steering me through the reporters, who felt nothing about blocking our way with their shoulders, elbows, even their cameras. I thought I heard Dad murmur something to me, something on the order of That's the way it's done, boy, but I wasn't sure. I was feeling the heat.

We were walking up the stairs to the church door now. The reporters had for some reason agreed not to follow that far. I guess it looked bad on film to see them chasing people straight into church, their wires spread out behind them like cracks in the earth.

My family and I sat toward the back of the church. We stumbled over the feet of some people who looked to me as if they came from Sarah's mother's side of the family: I could place those broad, milky faces, those flexible, slightly frowning mouths, the thick wrists, the meaty calves. I sat between Caroline and my mother and they each took my hand. I nodded my head a few times, trying to give them the feeling I was all right, that I was going to make it through this somehow and they ought not worry. My skin seemed suddenly to come hideously alive but I refused to disgrace us by clawing away at myself. I heard a low moan, a strangled bit of weeping, and I leaned forward for a moment and looked at my father, whose face, though uncovered, was contorted in pain. I felt a lurch of anger, even contempt: if I was going to sit through this, then he sure as hell could, too.

I looked around the church, careful not to take in the altar, behind which I knew was Sarah's coffin. Off toward the door to another, smaller chapel, sat Sarah's friend Father Mileski, along with Father Stanton and Sister Anne—they'd all worked together at Resurrection House with Sarah in Chicago. Mileski was pulling at his dark coarse Russian beard and weeping openly. I wondered how a priest could weep so at a funeral; I wondered if he'd lost all faith. Stanton, twenty years older than Mileski, frail, white-haired, with sunken cheeks and mild blue eyes, sat bolt upright and stared at the altar, with a look on his face as if some piece of clerical gaucherie were being committed. Sister Anne's eyes were averted; she seemed to be in prayer, with her lips moving rapidly, silently.

Across the aisle were some people who I guessed were from Eugene's side: mournful ectomorphs with dark angry eyebrows and long tapered fingers.

Bobby Charbonnet was there with his pert, efficient-looking wife. Bobby had lived across the street from Sarah when she was growing up. She had focused all the excoriating heat of her emerging sexuality on him—rapturous mash notes, nighttime unveilings in her bedroom, whose little windows faced his. Bobby had been terrified and it wasn't until he was safely away at the University of North Carolina that he had dared to respond to her—but then, of course, it was too late. His delayed response had provided the emotional balance, and gave Sarah a chance to move away from him. From then on they were friends. He and Sarah had once taken me on a black music tour of New Orleans. We heard the Meters in one bar, Professor Longhair in another, and then visited an old piano player named Tuts Washington in his tiny, redolent house, where we sat with Tuts and watched TV—Vice President Agnew was resigning his office on all the channels.

I looked at Bobby and he finally noticed me: he brought his pale, delicate hand up to his throat and shook his head, and then Nina, his wife, made a gesture to me that I took to mean we would talk later on—though when I thought about it later I realized it could not possibly have meant that. We scarcely knew each other and now it was too late to begin. Sarah's death had sealed her old life off from me once and for all.

At last, I looked toward the front row. Sarah's parents and her sisters were sitting there with the backs of their heads toward me. Sarah's mother wore a dark gray hat with a black veil pinned to her auburn hair. Eugene's bald spot was shimmering with perspiration. Carrie was there with her husband, Jack. A tough-looking duo, they ran a couple of oyster bars in the French Quarter. They'd never had much use for me or for Sarah, really; they'd treated us as if we were not quite welcome customers, with that mixture of courtesy and disdain that can be so painful. Sarah's other older sister, Tammy, was there, finally separated from her awful husband. She turned around. Her heavy face was swollen and blotchy, as if she'd been attacked by hornets. When she saw I was looking at her she put up her hand in a gesture of greeting and sympathy and I raised my hand—how incredibly heavy it suddenly felt—as if to touch her.

From somewhere, organ music was playing: tepid, faintly religious, like spiritual Muzak. I tried to lower myself into the well of my feelings but I seemed to be stuck, frozen in some indeterminate darkness within. It was the drug and I felt a rip of shame, a revulsion with myself. It seemed crummy to have come to her funeral in a narcotic haze. If this was the time to say our last goodbyes, then I ought to have kept myself open to whatever grueling chaos of feeling the day had in store. I tried to move away from the drug, which seemed now to fill me like a wheelbarrow of sand, but I could tell without really trying very hard that it was simply impossible. The music was playing on and on and then it suddenly stopped and I heard snuffling. From beyond the church door, across the street, the demonstrators were still chanting and in that brief churchy silence we heard them, too: *Compañera* Sarah Williams—*presente—ahora—y siempre.*

Shut up and go home, I thought, but without hatred or conviction. I shifted in my seat, settling in for whatever was next. I already had had the first inkling that time was moving on—hideously empty but beginning to pick up new color and weight: those distant voices, the people in this church, my own slow, doped-up heart. I had *already* survived. This loss would forever embrace my life but it would not stop it, and if I look back honestly at those last few moments in church before Father Laroque grasped the pulpit with his angry white hand and began his torrent of clichés, I realize now what I could not quite know or admit then—that I had already begun to adjust to life without her. I was not going to blow my brains out or slit my throat. It seemed clear there was only one reasonable thing to do and that was press on and continue to build my life as I'd been putting it together step by step since I'd been eight years old—the age I'd been when I realized that what I wanted to be was not left fielder for the Brooklyn Dodgers but president of the United States.

2

I persisted for five years, taking little ceremonial Japanese steps toward my goal, when suddenly the hook of fate caught onto my belt loop and lifted me up by my pants. I was finished with law school and had passed through a couple of years' seasoning in a top law firm and now was in harness with the Cook County prosecutor's office. I kept my conscience from slashing my ambition to ribbons by now and again trying to patch one of those selective holes in the net of justice through which the slimiest, best-connected crooks traditionally passed. But now I was being offered a rather dirty deal myself and I was going through all the motions of thinking about it, though I knew in an instant I was going to say yes.

I was standing at the window, looking down at Lake Michigan, which in its frozen state looked like a broken mirror. There was one of those winter storm watches on. The TV stations had all day been featuring those soft-faced fellows standing in front of their weather maps, excitedly drawing concentric circles, vectors, their eyes bright with this vision of some impending meteorological doom—which they themselves barely understood, according to an exposé I'd read a few weeks before, which revealed these guys were no more qualified to explain the weather than you or me. But they were believed—so much so that they even *apologized* for bad weather. A lot of the office buildings in downtown Chicago had knocked off early; traffic was thick below. Yet even at this kingly remove—I was fifty-five stories up—I could hear the morons below hitting their hooters and the sound of all those horns rising up in a hornet's hum of frustration.

It was getting dark fast and now my reflection in the glass was more distinct than anything beyond it. I was dressed in my prosecutorial best, fresh from a day in the law library—gray suit, white shirt, red and blue tie. My hair had gotten a little long. It's harder to look threatening and imposing when your hair is curling over your collar. I needed a shave, too. I was starting to look like the defense. Also, I looked like I needed a rest—a week on a beach, a look at another world, palm trees, frozen cocktails without the liquor, a chameleon's-eye view of all those rich pampered waxed and tanned legs gliding over the white sand. I must have been feeling a little sorry for myself, feeling older than I was.

"You still with us, Fielding?" asked Governor Kinosis.

"I'm thinking," I said, keeping my back to them. "Look at all these people scrambling to get out of town because of a little snow. Makes you wonder what it would be like if we had a guided missile coming toward us."

"Look, that's not what I came all the way over here to talk about," the governor said.

Oh God, what a moron.

I had to concentrate on what was being offered. I had to pay attention not to the Greek but to the gift. I was thirty-four years old, the son of a printer and a typist in what was now becoming an upscale wedge of Brooklyn but which was, in my day, a neighborhood for workers and civil servants. Ambition was seen there as a kind of girlish vanity, but unbeknownst to our hardworking, friendly neighbors, chez Pierce was a hothouse of it. We listened to the news at least three times a day and read the early edition of the newspaper Dad brought home at the end of his shift, doling out sections as if it were the staff of life, and we even had a family constitution, drawn up by me and ratified, after a week of debates, by a three-to-two vote, split by gender. The odd thing was that my parents were on the whole *pleased* with themselves: this drive came from sheer energy, not self-hatred. Dad was good at his work and active in his union and respected as a porch-stoop raconteur and philosopher.

Mom's job was with Earl Corvino, the infamous Brooklyn pol, too senile now to bother prosecuting, and though he ran her ragged it gave her a sense of belonging and engendered in her an absurd sort of loyalty to Brooklyn, as if it were a misunderstood nation. But once the mere business of their lives was taken care of, they still had a lot of pep left over and that psychic heat was turned on us. With their guidance and encouragement I eventually found my way to Harvard. Danny's energy and genius didn't need the validation of a fancy degree, so he settled on New York University, where he lasted less than a year, and Caroline, after two years at the Boston Museum School, ran away from all of us and went to Europe.

After college I went into the Coast Guard and it was then I met Sarah and for a while it seemed as if my life might change its course. But then Sarah died and I continued with law school, and from there I went to work for a man named Isaac Green— who was sitting right next to the governor now, and whose sky-high apartment this was. Isaac had done his best to adopt me, figuring I was a bit of a stray dog—by which he meant my own father could not provide me with the connections Isaac could. Isaac Green's wrenching disappointment was that his own son, Jeremy (a classmate of mine in college), had a horror of his father's world and professed some complicated Sufi-esque contempt for Anglo-American law and was now in La Jolla customizing Ya-mahas. I knew what was happening. It was completely obvious. And after giving the matter some thought, I decided to take advantage of the situation. I came to love Isaac, and it did him good to know there was someone who wanted everything he had to give, who would read every book, shake every hand.

When Isaac had been the proper age to think about a career in politics, it was nearly impossible to elect a Jew in Chicago. The best you could do was stay usefully behind the scenes or get yourself appointed to the bench. But it was dull behind the scenes and, worse, when you sent those *dummkopf* actors out onto the stage the lights got into their eyes and as often as not they flubbed their lines. A judgeship had a certain staid grandeur to it, but there wasn't enough excitement, nor enough money. Isaac had the tastes and self-image of the peerage. He should have been one of those exquisitely comfortable yet compassionate Englishmen talking socialism with Beatrice and Sidney Webb sixty years ago. He needed his season tickets and his eighty-dollar cognacs, but he wanted to do the right thing, too. He wanted his hand on the lever of history, but he wanted it sticking out of the sleeve of a custom-tailored suit.

I was Isaac's political career. He oversaw my passage through law school and then took me into his firm, where I was given more responsibility than I deserved and maybe even a little more than I could handle. While I had been with Sarah, he couldn't quite trot me out at his dinners and cocktail parties as much as he would have liked, but after she was gone he kept my dance card filled, and I got to know some of the unindicted criminals, parochial school snitches, black businessmen, and cement and meat millionaires that make up political life in my adopted city. Then, one day, I was informed by Isaac that the state senator from my neighborhood was retiring (off to Key Biscayne with about three million of the people's dollars) and Isaac somehow could arrange it that I would stand for the vacant seat.

I was meant to jump for it, but a career or even an episode in state government had never been a part of my plans. I was young enough to be grateful for whatever faint power was being offered me, and I didn't want just to say no flat out. To be honest, I didn't have much of an idea what state senators did, and so Isaac arranged for my going down to Springfield, to look around and meet the governor. I sat in on a session. The heated debate was about whether to remove the cardinal from its honorary post as Illinois state bird. The representative from Waukegan was reading in a monotone from a paper, prepared by a "leading ornithologist," in which the cardinal was described as a cowardly bird and then there were statistics about the dwindling cardinal population in Illinois. When that was finally over, someone else wanted to reintroduce a motion to rename a bridge near Moline after a local boy who'd been killed in Da-Nang. And blah blah blah. I was so bored, I seemed to be drowning in it. And there didn't seem one person down on the floor remotely destined for a career in national politics.

I stayed the weekend, hacking around, wasting time. Sunday,

I was invited to the governor's house for brunch. Kinosis's idea of keeping the common touch was inviting state legislators over for buffet breakfast at the state house, where he'd serve big cakey pancakes tricked up with strawberry preserves, and little rib-eye steaks, and Greek salads with black olives, feta cheese, and Pepperidge Farm croutons. Kinosis's daughter Dawn, a sallow, sleepy-eyed girl of ten with lint all over her blue skirt, made name tags for us out of colored construction paper and glitter. "Hi, my name is Fielding Pierce," mine said, and even the governor wore one, being a family man and having, as well, an occupational fondness for anything bearing his own name. (Dawn was the last child left at home; her siblings were already slurping from the public trough up in Chicago.)

Kinosis had little to say to me; he ran through the familiar story of his humble beginnings, how his father ran a business involving buying animal fat from those old Back of the Yards slaughterhouses and selling it to cosmetics companies, who used it for making lipstick. And I told him my father worked as a typesetter and my mother—and this is something I probably should have not said—worked for a pol who reminded me a lot of him. I hadn't realized it before I said it, but old Earl Corvino and Kinosis were definitely a part of the same subspecies. They had the same cold intelligent eyes, the same neon smiles, the same maddening habit of eating off other people's plates. I think I won the humbler-than-thou contest, but as far as Kinosis was concerned I was still an egghead, a snob. He knew I was hooked into Isaac Green and the district I would represent included the U. of C., as well as some of the most awful slums in the city, the sort of ghetto they show pictures of in Communist countries to prove how terrible capitalism is. Kinosis didn't run well with the University people, who found him crude and corrupt; nor did he find many supporters among the blacks, who, despite the urgings of their ward bosses, could not vote for a man who, when he was in high school, had had a fistfight with a black kid and killed him with a punch to the forehead.

After having given it some thought, I told Isaac a week later that I would rather not run for the state assembly. He was disappointed but not very surprised. I explained to him I wanted to move in a different direction and soon after that I left his firm and started working in the county prosecutor's office. Isaac helped with that, and it had also fallen to him to explain to Kinosis that I wouldn't be coming down to Springfield. According to Isaac, Kinosis had taken my refusal as a personal affront and I had what Mom later called my "first political enemy."

But now, Kinosis was sitting in a wing chair, right next to my benefactor, in Isaac's reproduction old English study, with its smells of leather, roses, and the smoke from the fire flashing in the hearth. Just as the weather folk promised, snow was starting to fall. We saw it first up here, like insiders seeing a preview of a new movie. I followed its descent and watched it change colors as it drifted past the Christmas lights below.

"What the hell you looking at out there?" Kinosis asked the back of my head. He didn't sound quite so menacing off his own turf. There was a snag of petulance in his voice.

"He's thinking, Ed," Isaac said. "You don't want a snap decision, do you?"

"Well, I don't want to spend half the night sitting here, either."

"Let me get you another drink, Ed," Isaac said. I heard him get up and saw his reflection in the window, floating over mine. He was wearing a burgundy smoking jacket and an ascot; his thin white hair was perfectly combed. It *was* getting rather embarrassing standing with my back to them. I suddenly realized I'd been carrying this too far and now it was appearing as if I were having some kind of nervous episode, which I was not.

Kinosis had called this secret meeting to tell me he was willing to make me a U.S. congressman, if I had eyes for the job. Of course, those poky old nitpickers who framed the Constitution blocked the governor from exercising his God-given right to appoint whomever he wanted to fill a vacant congressional seat. The best Kinosis could offer me was a quick special election in my district and my name in the Democratic column—that's what he *could* control. And it was a lot. If your name appeared in the Democratic column in a special election, chances were you wouldn't even have an opponent. The Republicans had given up the district as a lost cause a long time ago, and any local pols from the Democratic side, no matter how slighted they felt that Kinosis hadn't chosen them to take over the vacant seat, would probably swallow what I will loosely call their pride and wait for other opportunities. Kinosis ran the party like a marching band and if you there with your little glockenspiel fell out of step, you'd have the guy behind you with the trombone walking up your back.

So a seat was mine if I had eyes for it. And I did. But what took the spin off the whole deal was that the seat I was being offered had just been vacated by a man who'd been forced to resign. Jerry Carmichael. He wasn't much of a congressman, but he'd gotten himself elected five times. He was a cheerful, innocuous sort of fellow, a hell of a lot more inoffensive than a politician ought to be but no more so than they really *are*. He was a congressman from Chicago; he'd gone quail hunting with Dick Daley. He knew his way around. But his connections had now run out on him, or maybe he'd crossed someone, perhaps screwed some construction firm who'd been counting on a new ramp to the Skyway and the zillion tons of cement it would entail, or maybe he'd gotten drunk and told someone what he really thought of them. It doesn't pay to wonder. But something must have gone wrong, because one afternoon there was a picture on the front page of the Chicago *Sun-Times* and the next morning the same photo ran in the *Trib*, and this picture showed a blond, good-looking young guy with enough panic and self-interest in his eyes to show up through the linotype.

The guy's name was Ted Simon and I suppose those who follow politics with the statistical obsessiveness with which little boys follow baseball knew Simon was Jerry Carmichael's $48,000-per-year legislative aide. At least that's what he was before the picture ran: now he'd been reduced to Carmichael's catamite, though Simon was no page, but a burly guy in his thirties. It never was clear why he came out and told the world that he and the congressman were lovers. Maybe Jerry broke a promise; maybe Simon was nuts. But if what he wanted to do was stop Carmichael's congressional career, then I suppose he was a happy man.

Not only did he say that he was Carmichael's boyfriend but it went further—it always does, like when you call the police or contest a will. Because soon Simon was saying he did next to no work, that he knew nothing about the issues or Congress, and hadn't gotten past the tenth grade back in Live Oak, Florida, his old mossy hometown. He stopped short of saying he couldn't read or tie his own shoes, but he made it pretty clear his only real job in the Rayburn Building down in Washington was thinking of interesting things he and Jerry could do once the workday was over.

Carmichael more or less sat tight and I remember thinking that was the right thing to do. He issued a statement that was a little terse, saying Ted Simon was a valuable, respected aide with many friends on the Hill (a brilliant touch, that), who, perhaps from overwork, was having a nervous breakdown. Maybe if it all had stopped there, Carmichael could have survived, but Simon, once unleashed, would not shut up. Next thing anyone knew, he was on "Good Morning, America," seven fifteen in the morning, sobbing into his big freckled hands right there in front of David Hartman and several million American earlybirds, saying he wanted to make a clean sweep of it, that he loved his country and hated his life, and so forth. The press, used to trapping their victims, didn't know what to make of Simon's wild, insistent surrender. After all, who asked this guy about his personal life? And why couldn't he shut up about it? Maybe he was one of those haunted crazies who enjoy confessing to imaginary crimes. And really, was it such a crime? America was getting to be a big boy now, and surely we could understand a little hanky-panky. After all, it's lonely over there in the corridors of power, what with the bomb shelters in the basement and the echo of Florsheim heels everywhere you turn.

So for a while it looked as if the press and everyone else might just be a little reluctant to believe Simon's story, or at least reluctant to act upon it, when suddenly Carmichael emerged from his seclusion and announced he was resigning his office for family reasons, and if that was true he must have had a pretty impatient crew in his family because the resignation was effective immediately. It was a rather pointless Congress anyhow—this was heading toward the last year of Carter, with the country knowing he'd be back to peanut farming and to meticulously blue-penciling his memoirs—but still the quickness of Carmichael's resignation took everyone by surprise. The seat had been open for ten days now and everyone was curious whom Kinosis would "recommend" for the special election; I had been wondering too, without ever entertaining the thought it would somehow be *me*. And now the offer was made and I felt obliged to take it—obliged, that is, to a lifelong ambition that I'd been carrying along with me like an idiot brother whom nobody likes but who now, at last, was going to come into his own. I still knew what a shitty deal Carmichael had been given and that if people were half as good as they liked to think they were, then none of this would be happening.

I turned around and locked eyes with Kinosis. The governor has a formidable stare, uncivilized, voracious. His eyes barely fit in with his smooth, careful face. They looked feral beneath the canopy of his black, carefully arranged hair, which showed the tracks of his comb like a well-tilled field.

"Can I get something straight here?" I said. "Are you asking me if I'd like the job or are you offering it to me?"

The governor looked like he'd never heard such impoliteness in all his life. Isaac stepped in.

"You're his choice, Fielding," he said. "It's all been discussed."

"Jerry Carmichael's got thirteen months left to his term," Kinosis said, yanking his tie loose and popping the top button of his lemon yellow shirt. "I'm going to set the date for the special election, make it January 22, if that's a Tuesday. You can get sworn in the next week. You got any idea what it's like to be a freshman congressman down there in that zoo? They'll yes you to fucking death but no one'll listen to a word you say. Half your staff's going to spend their day working on their résumés because they're looking for a job, knowing you probably won't make it back next term. But Isaac tells me you know the ropes and play the game fair and square, so who knows? Maybe you'll stick. If not, at least you'll be able to tell the world you were a U.S. congressman for a few months. Who was that guy, Isaac? That creep from LaGrange who got himself elected to Congress in '56 and got his ass kicked the next time out, and he's been trying to make a living on it ever since? He opened the House of Representatives Bar and Grill and when that belly-upped he tried Congressional Putt Putt PeeWee Golf Park, the first hole you shot the ball through the doors of a little plaster Capitol building. What was that moron's name?"

"Lou Conway, Al," said Isaac. "He's dead now."

"He is. Well, what a shame." Kinosis's face took on a horrifyingly efficient look of sadness—years of practice of laughing and joking in the back of his car and then, when the driver pulled in front of the funeral parlor, getting out with a look of mourning. "Yeah, Lou Conway. Well," he said, his face changing to threatening as easy as turning the page of a magazine, "if you disgrace me down there you can always become the next Lou Conway."

"You mean dead?" I asked. I felt pride stirring in me, like a patient starting to come out of the ether in the middle of the operation.

"OK, now look," the governor said, putting his drink down on the little bowlegged table next to his chair. He glanced at his gold-encrusted wristwatch, the kind of watch you find on a nattily dressed murder victim stuffed into the trunk of an LTD. He checked the time and scowled. He thought acting as if you were late for your next appointment meant you were a big shot, whereas Isaac had taught me long ago that truly important people went at their own pace and didn't worry who was waiting for them. "I'm handing you something men work their whole lives for," Kinosis said. "And now you've got to give me something, too."

"Ah," I said, raising a finger, "the part I've been waiting for."

The governor took a deep breath and looked over at Isaac, who was at that moment wincing delicately. That wince bothered me, made me think I was maybe playing it a little too fast and loose. "A comedian," said Kinosis.

"He's excited," Isaac said. "Thrilled. Who wouldn't be?"

"How'd you get a name like that?" Kinosis said, leaning forward in his chair, acting as if he'd just skewered me. "Politics ain't for people with fifty-dollar names."

"How many people named Dwight do you know?" I said. "Or Franklin or Lyndon or Woodrow?"

"His father's a typesetter," Isaac said. "He was setting type for an article about Henry Fielding, the novelist—you know, the chap who wrote *Tom Jones*. You remember *Tom Jones*, don't you, Ed? They made a marvelous film of it."

"Yeah, I remember, I remember," the governor said, with a bit of sulkiness. "Look here," he said to me, "I don't need to make a career knowing about you. Just tell me if there's anything about you I don't know or maybe even your pal here doesn't know—and maybe we ought to."

"I don't know how to answer that question," I said.

"Hey, look here," said Kinosis, "I don't like your goddamned tone. In politics you got to like people. That's something you better learn and learn quick. Politics is people, pure and simple. And if you're in this business and you don't like people it's like being a plumber and you're afraid of a little water."

"Come, come," said Isaac, "this is nonsense. There's nothing about Fielding you don't already know. He's a good kid. And clean as a whistle. Good parents, father's a working man, union boy. That sort of thing. And his mother worked for Corvino. Do you know him?"

"No," said the governor.

"A Democrat."

"What'd she do for him?"

"She shlepped," said Isaac with a comic shrug. While Kinosis laughed (at my mother's expense), Isaac quickly added, "He's got a brother with maybe some business problems and a sister who's got a marriage that maybe isn't the best that ever was—but this day and age no one holds that against anyone. Look at our president and his crazy brother Billy."

"All right," said Kinosis, standing up. He smoothed his jacket down and felt the front of it; he seemed disappointed to find a big fat belly beneath it. "I'm not going to make myself sick over this. I'll send you to Washington and by the time you figure out how to find your ass without using both hands it'll be time for a new election and if we ain't friends by then that'll be that." He came up to me. I had five or six inches on him but he knew how to use his shortness in a threatening way, like those little dogs that can get under a Great Dane's stomach and chew it out. He patted me ceremoniously on the shoulders and then turned to Isaac, who had risen from his chair when the governor did.

"You're doing the right thing," Isaac said to him.

Kinosis shook Isaac's hand and gave him a long searching look as he did. "Is tonight Hanukkah, Isaac?" he said.

"That's over already, Ed."

"Well, I hope you had a goody."

"You'll be in town for Christmas?" Isaac inquired.

"Nah. Me and Irene are going to Crete. We know a great little place there that we're never going to tell anyone about. . . ."

They went on for a few more minutes. Isaac was patronizing him, but so subtly the governor didn't know it. It was hard for me to listen. I turned away and went back to the window. The entire city had disappeared. It was just entirely gone and in its place was a thick white curtain of snow.

Isaac had both hands on my shoulders and was looking at me with a smile so sweet and tender that it made me feel fatherhood was a matter of feeling rather than blood. His blue eyes were ablaze with mischief and triumph. "This is a great day, Fielding," he said, in his lively tenor, a voice that had traveled from the West Side of Chicago, through the University of Wisconsin, and now,

after four decades of assimilation, seemed to be plunging through
the veneer of the American idiom and becoming suddenly British
in its inflections—a bit of fanciness for which people sometimes
poked fun at him, though I never saw the harm in it. The empire
with all of its pompous privileges was just about dead and if he
wanted to ape the accent it seemed harmless.

"Why didn't you tell me this was going to happen?" I said.

"It wasn't feasible."

"That's not much of an answer," I said.

Isaac pretended to think about it. "No," he said, cocking his
head and furrowing his eyebrows until he looked like a brilliant
Jewish leprechaun, "it isn't much of an answer, is it. The governor
wanted to tell you himself. He wanted your reaction."

"You still could have told me. You brief me for dinner parties,
for God's sake."

"What are we worrying about here?" Isaac asked. He tugged
at my arm to lead me to where Adele was waiting for us. "Come
on," he said. "You'll join us for an early supper and then we'll
send you on your way. I'm sure you want to go home and tell
Juliet."

Juliet was Juliet Beck. She was Isaac's niece and, for the past
two years, my quasi-fiancée. Our relationship had the eerie comfort of an arranged marriage.

We walked out of Isaac's study into the next room, which was
the library, a dark green room lined with books. The walls were
covered with pictures of Isaac's old friends—Adlai Stevenson,
Herblock, Max Lerner, John Kennedy, Golda Meir, Sidney Hook,
Fritz Reiner, Paul Douglas, Earl Warren, Sam Dash, Archibald
MacLeish, Saul Bellow, Sidney Yates. The books ranged wide,
not just the usual expensively bound rubbish you find on lawyers'
shelves, but collections of Chekhov, O. Henry, Whitman, Twain,
Jewish history, Freud. The library's windows faced northeast and
I saw the curve of the lake, outlined in street lamps. The street
lamps were fading, obscured by the snow.

"It wouldn't be safe to travel now," Isaac said, noticing the
storm for the first time.

We left the library and crossed a long, narrow hall. Now we were in the dining room, with its pink and gray wallpaper, blue tiled fireplace, Chinese rug, and huge rosewood table. Adele was leaning across the table lighting the candles with a long wooden match. The warm yellow-orange light shined up into her face, softened her. Adele was the skeleton in Isaac's closet. She had a powerful intelligence, great beauty, wit, energy, and high spirits, yet whatever she'd been capable of had been left undone and her life had been devoted to Isaac—looking after him, buttoning his cardigans on the coldest days, listening to him, correcting him, making him strong. Hers was the sort of life that made feminists fume and it was no accident that Adele herself was devastating in her critiques of these New Women—she called them the Atomic Girls, and said they wished they were still in boarding school, where they wouldn't have to muss with contraception or worry about the rough play of boys.

"Did the governor leave?" she asked.

"Didn't you see him out?" asked Isaac.

"No. I was in the kitchen helping Mrs. Davis."

"Oh-oh," I said. "Let's organize a search. He's probably hiding somewhere in the apartment." I was at Adele's side and she lifted her face for me to kiss. Her cheeks were warm from the candlelight.

"It all went perfectly," Isaac announced. "As so few things in life do."

Adele gripped my hand and squeezed it hard. Her strength was unsettling; it was like being touched under the table. "So tell me," she said. "Now how do you feel?" Her accent was traveling in a different direction from Isaac's—back to Russia, to sunsets, to the linden-drunk breeze combing the wheat.

"Lucky," I said.

"No. Luck has nothing to do with it. Luck is for Mah-Jongg. This is something you deserve."

Isaac picked up the heavy cut-glass decanter and poured red wine into two glasses and water into mine.

"The only way this makes sense to me," I said, "is to figure

Kinosis tagged me because every other possible replacement offended someone powerful and I don't stick in anyone's throat, being an unknown."

"It's true, Fielding Pierce is not a household word," Adele said. Every now and then, she would come forth with some piece of current lingo and it always surprised me. I wanted to tell her: You don't need to talk that way, Adele.

"We come from a long tradition, Fielding," Isaac said. "And what's at stake here is nothing less than civilized values. This is an age of mediocrity. Synthetic suits and those enormous portable radios. Barbarism. It's all around us, everywhere. Someone told me they make bathroom paper printed up to look like the flag now. Can you imagine? Who can even count how many illegal guns there are in this city alone? Three hundred thousand, at least. This is a desperate time and a marvelous opportunity. You'll shine amongst them, Fielding. Shine. Your honesty. Your toughness. Your respect for decency and enduring values."

Isaac handed me a wine glass filled with water. He kept an eye on me, see. I waited for him to give Adele her glass and then the three of us stood at the end of the table, our glasses aloft.

"To Congressman Pierce," said Adele.

"Hear, hear," said Isaac.

"Everything I've been able to accomplish, I owe to you two," I said, and then we drank. The door swung open. The Greens' cook, a small, arthritic woman named Cordelia Davis, whom the Greens called Mrs. Davis and who called the Greens by their first names, and with whom they had once traveled down to Selma for Dr. King's civil rights march, only to be horrified by the rowdiness of their comrades, came slowly in, her face a cheerful mask, holding tonight's rack of baby lamb on its gleaming silver platter.

3

I had six cases pending at the county prosecutor's, and now that I was leaving I had to put everything in order. I'd believed from the beginning that sooner or later I'd be leaving the CP's office, but now that my time was up I felt unexpectedly nostalgic, almost regretful. I was not a great lawyer but I was good and what I lacked in thoroughness and subtlety I made up for in vigor. I was one of the great browbeaters; I loved to make a rich crook sweat. I had in two short years bagged an alderman, a construction contractor, a refuse-removing syndicate who were dumping their garbage on remote curves of the lakeshore, and a health care clinic that had been taking blood out of poor patients' arms and selling it to a county hospital a few blocks away. There were some cases I had to prosecute that I would have just as soon walked away from, but I let myself do my job even when I didn't exactly relish it, with the proviso that I would not make things worse for myself by pretending that what I was doing wasn't a little off.

But now, suddenly, it would all be behind me. I had a lot of squaring away to do and that meant working late. It was three days after my meeting with the governor and my third night in a row of working late. I called my apartment and Juliet answered.

"I'm late again," I said.

"The phone's been ringing all evening," she said. "I feel like your assistant."

"Take it off the hook, then," I said. "Or just don't answer."

"Oh, I couldn't do that," she said. "There's too much going on now."

"I'm just finishing up. I'll be right home. Have you eaten?"

She said she had, but you never could tell. I didn't count those cottage cheese and scallion snacks as food. I locked my desk up for the night and shoved what was on top of it into my briefcase. I heard the thud of the charwoman's bucket outside my office, the rattle of the icy wind against my dark windows. A moment of almost rapturous loneliness struck in me like a pipe-organ chord. I walked out leaving the lights on. They'd been pasting those Save a Watt stickers near the light switches and they annoyed the hell out of me. I'd be glad to save a watt but first I wanted the Justice Department to haul the oil companies into court for price fixing, creating artificial shortages, cutting secret deals with foreign governments.

Traffic was slow as I drove south toward home. Out over the lake, the weather was chaos. New snow clouds were winging in, yet there must have been something warm in the air, too, because pale stems of winter lightning shot down toward the gray, broken surface of the water, followed by long groans of thunder. Alternating sprays of sleet and snow whipped against my windshield and the wipers left chalky smears that caught the streetlights.

It had become rather a terrible habit of mine to phone Juliet before heading home if my schedule was irregular. Last year I'd arrived a day early from a trip to New York and barged in while Juliet was in bed with a guy named Ted Olden, who had been our doctor. Olden had been dead asleep and Juliet had been propped up with pillows behind her, reading *The World of Our Fathers*. She was naked; I looked at her warm breasts, the book, and the look of absolute horror on her face. I think I said "Glad?" and switched on another lamp, a gray pottery lamp with a big black shade that stood on the rococo chest of drawers with its intimations of Europe, culture, and exile that we had inherited from Juliet's mother. The lamp cast its light onto the chair containing Olden's baggy gabardine suit, the boxer shorts nesting inside the trousers. Juliet tried to shake Olden back to our side of the great divide, but he was resisting her efforts. Speechless, I watched her jiggle his arm, and then, her panic rising nicely, smacking her fingers against his cheek, and then, really cooking now, shouting, "Theodore, for God's sake, get up!" Theodore? I asked myself. Why so formal? We'd always called him Ted. Ted won't renew my dex prescription. Ted's coming for dinner. Did you see Ted's postcard from Glasgow? Olden sat straight up in bed, waking with a little of that old med school snappiness. What happened next is too mundane and disappointing and humiliating to go into. I said nothing I care to remember and the only act of violence I committed turned absurd: I picked up the gray pottery lamp and flung it toward the wall, but the cord was plugged in and the lamp stopped with a jerk in midair and plunged to the floor. I don't know if Olden ever confessed the sordid little adventure to anyone; Juliet and I never mentioned it to a soul. Yet it lived between us and perversely raised the stakes of passion between us for a while. Infidelity has a way of heightening and cheapening desire.

We lived in a bay-windowed brownstone on Hyde Park Boulevard. I pulled into the driveway next to our house and saw Juliet's old green Volvo. There was light coming from our windows on the third floor. I let myself in and stomped up the stairs to our apartment.

Juliet was petite and in perfect proportion. She was certainly the smallest woman I'd ever been with, although the only time I really noticed her tininess was when I kissed her from head to foot and realized how soon it was over. She was beautiful, with black hair and white skin and a blush that looked like windburn in her cheeks. She worked as a restorer at the Oriental Institute and ran a little business of her own on the side called European Restorations. Every once in a while she got to work on a piece from a genuine master—a tattered Holbein, a Whistler watercolor upon which a child had laid a Creamsicle. She loved old things; she revered the distant past and mourned for it like an exile will long for the land of her birth.

She was the daughter of two elderly academicians and she seemed to have been born knowing all the things I had to strain to keep track of—the prices of things, the hidden histories of objects, of gestures and phrases, the proper way of organizing the various tiers of acquaintanceship—whom you send a note to, whom you send flowers, who gets invited to parties of ten, who comes to parties of fifty. I had no confidence in mastering that sort of thing, and now with Juliet to look after them I just let it go altogether.

She had come to Chicago from Paris, by way of Bucks County and Palo Alto, and she had come as an orphan. Isaac did his best to look after her but she was an enigma to him. Really, she was an enigma to everyone and I think she was half a stranger to herself. She seemed to believe her emotional makeup was different from other people's and she perceived herself as a mixture of unnatural tenderness and utter indifference. She was kind to other people but jokey about herself; she treated her own heart as if it were a cartoon character or, at best, as if it were reciting something it had read in a book. Luckily, she had inherited the family keenness for politics and they at least had that point of contact. Juliet knew her stuff from Metternich to ward politics.

When Isaac introduced us, Juliet was at the end of a torrid but herky-jerky affair with a married man—an affair that, on Juliet's part, seemed to alternate between times of indifference and bouts of abject, almost pathetic desire. They were eventually found out by the man's wife and the affair ended—with scarcely a good-bye. Juliet entered into a relationship with me in the same spirit that exhausted businessmen go to the Caribbean—though what sunlight she saw in my heart was a mystery to me. I think she was attracted by my own detachment: she was looking for an emotional duty-free zone where she might pick up some happiness at a lower price.

I let myself into the apartment and Juliet was on the red velvet sofa, paging through a book of Balthus paintings with a look of disapproval on her face. "I hate the twentieth century," she said, closing the book.

"Not me," I said, leaning over her, kissing the top of her head.

"Don't you touch me with your icy fingers," she said.

I had put my cold hands beneath her sweater three or four weeks ago and now she feared my doing it again every evening.

"The mayor's got the snowplows working already," I said, taking off my coat, letting it fall.

"We're supposed to get ten inches of snow tonight," said Juliet. "Uncle Isaac says in Chicago snow is a big political issue."

"How's work?" I asked.

"Fine," she said. "How about you?"

"I don't know. Not so great. Calls?"

"I wrote them down. They're on your desk. There's quite a few."

"Shit."

"Some of them will wait," she said, "but some of them won't."

"I don't think there's anything left of me right now," I said, stretching out my legs and rubbing my eyes.

"You may as well get used to it," said Juliet. "You are ahead of your schedule but you have to keep pace. There's nothing to do about it."

"I just have to do it my own way."

"Well, poor Jerry Carmichael called. Twice. I think it would be needlessly provocative if you didn't ring him back."

Danny once said that my being with Juliet was like a junkie living with a nurse. I moved closer to Juliet, though something within me—a heaviness in my bones—prevented me from putting my arm around her. "I made a resolution today," I said. "I'm going to stop turning the radio onto the soul music station when I give the car to a black parking lot attendant."

"That's a good resolution," said Juliet. She sat there with absolute stillness and seemed to be waiting for me to touch her.

"You've noticed that I do that?"

"Yes. I noticed."

"How come you never mentioned anything?"

"I just figured you wanted the guy to take better care of your car."

"But it's weak," I said.

Juliet shrugged.

"It is." I closed my eyes; fatigue came over me like a thick mist.

"Are you going to make your calls?" Juliet asked.

I slipped my hand beneath her sweater and felt her warm, heavy breast; I laid my cheek on the top of her head, against that rich, comforting bonnet of dark Balkan hair.

Our apartment had three bedrooms. It had once been well occupied by a musical couple with four children. Before we painted the entire place bone white, we lived with the archaeology of the Belsito kids' exuberance: kick marks, crayon skids, dried Play-Dough on the fir floors, roller skate gouges in the foyer. Now the place was as clean and uncluttered as one of those young professionals' apartments in the magazines. The children's bedrooms had been turned into home offices, one for me and one for Juliet. We each had our own phone, our own number; our offices were joined by an old wooden door with a crystal knob that had turned violet from sunlight and which we never opened without first knocking. I walked into my office. It was a white rectangle lined with books. The window looked out at a young oak with its branches thick with snow.

Juliet had placed my telephone messages next to the phone. I looked them over until I found Carmichael's number and then I dialed it, deliberately not giving myself a chance to organize my thoughts. I realized a long time before that in order to be truly prepared for leadership you had to be born to it; the rest of us just had to trust instinct.

"Yes?" Carmichael said, picking it up on the first ring. His voice sounded high and quick, as if he were waiting for a call from the hospital. It conjured his face for me: receding brown hair, aviator glasses, a nose half the size of my thumb, a patchy brown mustache hovering over whistler's lips.

"Hello, Jerry. This is Fielding Pierce."

"Hello, Fielding!" he said, with a friendliness that was unnerving—probably deliberately so. "Glad you called."

"Good," I said. A pause. "What can I do for you?"

"Hey, it's more what can I do for you. I just wanted to help make this an orderly transfer. I realize we're dumping a whole lot in your lap."

"That's all right," I said. A car passed below and its headlights lit the snowy oak; a skin of ice was forming on the window.

"I was hoping you could stop up this evening," Carmichael said, "and we could go over a few things. You'll be surprised how fast this is going to get complicated and I think we better grab this time while we can."

"I'm glad to see you're not overly concerned about this winter storm watch," I said, sitting on the edge of my desk. "I think it's a way of dress rehearsing us for nuclear war."

"Yes? That's an interesting way of looking at it. So you'll come over? I'm just five blocks away."

"Sure," I said. "We should talk." I looked at my watch. It was nine thirty.

He gave me his address on Cornell. I hung up the phone and stood there and felt my heart beating. I felt suddenly enormous. I felt if I stretched my arms out I could touch both ends of my room and then if I stretched a little farther I could reach out beyond. My ambition had always been mixed with a certain unreality, but now that it was starting to be realized a new, deeper, stranger unreality was taking hold.

Juliet was eating ricotta and scallions in the kitchen. I came in dressed to leave.

"I better go see him," I said.

"I'll wait up for you," she said.

I nodded. A turn had been taken in our relationship. Events were forcing our hand and we were both a little embarrassed that the sudden velocity of our partnership was taking us beyond the natural boundaries of our feelings for each other. We were on our way to becoming a public couple and we barely knew each other.

The snow had stopped for an hour but as I drove over to Carmichael's apartment it was beginning again. The new snow was soft, floaty, as if someone had slit the belly on an enormous pillow. By the time I pulled in front of Carmichael's high rise, a half inch of new snow was on the ground. There was a parking space in front of his building, somewhat marred by the presence of a fire hydrant—I parked anyhow, figuring it was nothing I couldn't fix.

I walked into the wind, toward Carmichael's lakefront condo. I could see through the glass doors into the lobby. A tense, athletic-looking black man in a doorman's uniform was pacing about, staring with anger at the video monitors—fancy security system. The TV screens showed only the closed, icy door of the underground garage and three empty elevators, each opening its door to an empty corridor, and closing it again. It seemed the doorman was the only living soul in the building.

"I'm here to see Congressman Carmichael," I said.

"Name?" He didn't take his eyes from the monitors. I couldn't imagine doing his job. What was his mind like after eight hours of looking at those screens?

"Pierce," I said. The lining of my nose had stiffened up in the walk from car to building and now, in the heat, it was starting to run. I wiped it on the sleeve of my coat.

Still glaring at the screens, the doorman picked up a phone and called up to announce me. "Mr. Carmichael's in Ten A," he said to me, hanging up the phone and indicating the elevator bank with an irritable jerk of the thumb. I felt his eyes on me as I made my way on in. After all the lousy publicity, did the doorman assume I was one of Carmichael's lovers?

Carmichael's apartment was at the end of the hall on the tenth floor. I walked toward it quickly; I wanted whatever was going to happen to go down quickly. I knocked on 10 A. There was a braided-rope welcome mat in front of the door; a pair of salt-stained rubbers had been left out to dry.

"Fielding!" he said, throwing the door open to me. He was dressed in a pair of brown corduroy jeans, a blue blazer, and a white shirt: he had a teenager's trim, tentative body. His face gleamed; his skin looked poreless and immaculate. "Glad you could make it." He reached toward me and clapped a hand on my shoulder. "This has been quite a turn of events, hasn't it," he said, ushering me in, taking my coat. "But it's all working out. We're getting it all under control. The governor tells me you've agreed to run and I want to tell you I just couldn't be happier about that."

He was rubbing his smallish hands together as I followed him into his apartment. It was decorated Chinese, with watercolors of pandas and pagodas, gold and blue carpeting, vases filled with dried flowers, lamps with rice-paper shades, low black-lacquered tables. I smelled coffee and furniture polish. There wasn't a book or a paper in sight. At the east end of the room was a picture window with a view of the lake, obscured now by a flashing curtain of snow.

"Lorraine and the kids are in Florida while all this craziness sorts itself out," he said, indicating with a wave that I should sit on the sofa. "Hell of a situation, huh?" He sat down on a chair near me and crossed his legs.

"Yes, it is," I said. I wanted to tell him how repulsive I found the scandal but the danger of sounding insincere brought me up short. I supposed if I'd really found it disgraceful then I would have refused to profit from it. Though I did not think the benefit was wholly personal: I truly did believe I'd be a better congressman than Carmichael. His record was undistinguished, gutless.

"Well, I'm glad you've decided to step in while we work out our options," he said. He squeezed his hands and dropped them into his lap. "Hey, like I said, Lorraine's in Florida—the lucky stiff—so there's nothing to eat. But I've got coffee going. Want a cup of coffee?"

"No, thanks."

"Well, maybe later. It's one of those do-hickey jobs that keeps the coffee warm, so if you change your mind . . ." He gestured toward the kitchen and his blazer opened up a little: to my great surprise, he was carrying a pistol in a fancy tooled holster, strapped Pinkerton-style under his arm.

For a moment, I felt death in that room, like a current of icy water in an otherwise tepid lake.

"Well, with one obvious exception," he said, just as merry as can be, "you'll be inheriting a hell of a staff. I've talked to them, naturally, and most of them have decided to hang in there with you, pal, and give you all the support you need. Unless, of course, after the election you plan to bring in your own people."

"I don't have people yet," I said. In one moment, it seemed

abundantly clear that Carmichael, driven mad from the loss of his office, had invited me to his apartment in order to shoot me. In the next, however, it seemed impossible. Some people just carry guns. My brother, Danny, has a handgun, for example. Eisenhower, when he was president of Columbia University, used to stroll the Upper West Side with a .45 in his pants.

"What kind of gun is that, Jerry?" I asked, casually.

"Oh, this old thing," he said, nudging it with his elbow. "It's ancient. A .38. I really should get rid of it and buy a new one, but I'm always so busy. Anyhow, with all this insanity going on, I'm going to be keeping a low profile for a while. But I don't want you to think you're going out there to get slaughtered. I'll be working with you, behind the scenes. I'll be with you every inch of the way." His merriness was increasing as his motor raced.

"Well, I really do appreciate that, Jerry. Let's just hope it won't be necessary."

His smile broadened; now it was well past all human proportions. This was exactly the grin of a man who was going to shoot someone. "Oh come on, it'll be necessary. No man is an island, right?" Suddenly, all this cheerfulness seemed to exact its toll and his boyish face went slack, revealing an older, more frightened face beneath it. He sat back in his chair and breathed out a long sigh. His eyes lost their focus; his skin went gray. "I've got a rest coming to me and I'm going to really enjoy it," he said.

Just then, the phone rang and he picked it up. "Yes?" he said, and then cleared his throat. "Oh, hi," he said, sitting forward, suddenly animated again. He covered the receiver for a moment and then lipped to me: It's my wife. "Well, how's the sunshine, honey?" He was drumming his fingers rapidly against the arm of the chair. "Hey," he said, "hey hey. Slow down. If they're bothering you, don't talk to them. That's all there is to it." He listened for another moment, twitching with impatience: it had been his hallmark as a public servant—Carmichael loved to talk but loathed listening. "Look, honey. I think you're getting very carried away. If anything, the reporters are on our side. They've been goddamned supportive." He fell into a reluctant silence again, nodding vigorously as he listened to his wife. "Look, Lorraine—" he said at one point, hoping to derail her. But she was used to his filibuster techniques and went right on. (Her picture hung over the fireplace. It was one of those outdoor art fair type of paintings, the kind my sister Caroline says degrades reality by reproducing it so simperingly, as if the Master of the universe was a sentimental fool in love with pastels and big-eyed bunnies. Lorraine Carmichael looked to be an attractive woman: short, Peter Pan–ish hair, a sharp nose, a shy smile. The Carmichael kids were posed with her: a four-year-old in an aqua tutu, a toddler in a candy-striped stretchie.) "OK, OK," Carmichael was saying. "So he's a bad egg. Then change your routine. If he's bothering you at the pool then spend less time at the goddamned pool." Pause. "No. There's no one I can call." He gripped the phone and said, in a confidential, desperate whisper, "Don't you understand? There's no one I can *call*."

I stood up. I had no business overhearing any of this. I put up my palm as if to indicate we could talk later. Jerry waved frantically at me and pointed to the sofa, practically ordering me to sit down and wait. I pretended to misunderstand and continued to make my way out.

"I can't talk to you now, Lorraine," he said abruptly, and hung up the phone. "Fielding!" he called out, springing out of his chair. "Where are you going?"

I was halfway down the foyer, my coat and the door tantalizingly in sight. But I had no choice but to turn around. "It's quite a storm out there, Jerry. I better get home while I can."

"Hey, what's a storm between friends, right?" He was walking toward me, his arm out as if to embrace me. He was making no attempt to keep the jacket closed over the gun. "You're not going anywhere until we drink a toast. OK?"

"I don't drink," I said.

"Hey, come on."

"I don't. I can't." I'd been keeping away from alcohol for four years now, but it still felt awkward to refuse. I had never been a completely out-of-control drunk—I never lost my job, never was arrested. But I was what they call a *chronic* drinker. Or at least that's what I called it. I'd beat back the habit on my own, but it was never very far away.

"Oh," said Carmichael, "it's like that? I didn't know. Well, you better watch your ass down in Washington. You won't believe how they drink down there."

"I'll be careful, Jerry," I said. I turned my back to him as I dressed for the trip home; I could feel him looking at me, felt him stirring. I moved slowly, taking care to wrap my scarf neatly, buttoning my overcoat, flipping the collar up.

"I really do wish I didn't have to be alone tonight," he said in a cheerful voice. "Oh well. I can always make phone calls. Or shoot myself. Ha ha."

I turned to look at him for a last time. "Don't shoot yourself, Jerry. All right?"

He smiled, perhaps a little embarrassed. "OK," he said. He buttoned his jacket and patted the almost imperceptible bulge.

"If you'd wanted to fight this thing," I said, "I would have supported you."

His lips were pressed together, though he was still smiling, and he shook his head no.

"It's a witchhunt, Jerry. You got a shitty deal."

He continued to make that tight-lipped smile and continued to shake his head no. "It's OK," he said. "A little rest. It'll be fine. We'll talk tomorrow, OK? I mean, you know, if possible. Go over some things. We've got a lot in process I want to, ah, familiarize you with."

I felt a flash of affection for Carmichael, yet I knew if I resisted any outward show of emotion I would be glad later. I put my hands in my pockets and fished out my gloves. I put them on, nodded, and let myself out the door.

"This is all going to be just fine," he was saying. "We just got to keep this thing going, right? Keep it going."

When I got down to the street, three more inches of snow had fallen and my old Mercury, spinning its wheels, dug a sooty ice pit for itself. I rocked it back and forth and got nowhere. I was in a cloud of exhaust fumes and beyond that cloud the snow was falling faster and faster. I gave up on the car and got out, figuring it wasn't a very long walk.

I made my way toward home, the only thing moving in the dark, arctic streets. The snow was gray-blue drifts on the ground. I stepped in new snow and sunk once to my knees. The blizzard and the wind were starting to play with my senses. One foot in front of the other. Don't think. Just walk. Like AA. One step at a time.

I'd only gone two blocks when the street lamps blinked twice and then went black. The lights in the windows along the way suddenly disappeared. A spurt of terror went through me and then I calmly explained to myself that it was a power failure. We'd had one in an earlier storm. It had lasted only twenty minutes. I heard a muffled shout from one of the apartments along the way. But I could see virtually nothing. A great stillness settled over this snowy quadrangle of world, a stillness only I disturbed.

And it was then, at that moment in the snow, in that darkness, that aloneness, with the full bewildering weight of the day upon me, that suddenly Sarah was with me—not her face, nor her voice, but just the specificity of her weight in eternity. I felt her in the snow. I knew she was gone, yet I sensed her so powerfully within me and in that fissure between what was known and what was felt, she was real. I felt my insides touched by her tender, ethereal fingers; her breath was in my lungs.

"Sarah," I said, my voice rising like steam, caught by the wind and carried away. Desire can resurrect the dead, loneliness can baffle the intellect. Was she there only because I longed for her? Dead almost five years now . . . It was the fourteenth of December. It was her birthday.

Thirty-one years ago she'd been born in New Orleans, at Touro Infirmary. She'd been lucky to be named Sara. Mr. Williams believed in sprightly, submissive names for girls: her sisters were Tammy and Carrie. Perhaps they'd sensed her fanatical will from the moment of birth: I remembered her baby pictures—a long face with huge cold blue eyes. Spooky little girl. I felt her heart beating next to mine. Was she here because I'd grasped the dream from which she'd tried to persuade me? Had I conjured her to witness my odd triumph? We can love the dead like loving God and Sarah was within me, as frightening as an angel wielding a sword.

I closed my eyes and stumbled on. I felt the weight of the snow in my hair. My trousers were soaked; my bones were throbbing. Sarah rose within me, with her straight dark brown hair, her large forehead, her earnest, demanding eyes, her wide mouth, powerful chin, the articulated muscles in her arms. And though we did not have an easy time of it and were, in truth, falling to pieces by the time of her death, I would have given—I was going to say my right arm, but really I would have given more than that, a great deal more than that, to see her again.

And then, just as suddenly as her presence had filled me, it was gone again and in the wake of her leaving was a startling emptiness, as if the lack of her had just carved out another cavern of aloneness, and it was just me in the night, trudging through the snow on my way home, firmly fixed on this side of the mystery.

I could barely see our apartment building and, once I found my way in, I had to keep my hands on the wall to find my way up the pitch-dark stairway. There was a complete silence, a silence without curves or cracks, except for the noise of my boots staggering up the stairs and my shattered breaths, rattling around in me like frozen lace.

Snow was dripping off me, falling in clumps. It was still warm in the apartment, though the furnace had cut off with the power. "Home," I said, shaking my hands until my gloves fell off. Juliet came toward me, holding a candle. She was starting to unbutton my coat when the phone began to ring.

"I'll get it," she said.

I peeled off my clothes. I could barely see myself in the dim, unstable candlelight. The scented candles sat in their little red glasses, trembling in the little drafts. I flexed my fingers. I hoped there was hot water for a bath. My face was burning and itching as it thawed. I dropped my wet trousers onto the floor and rubbed my hands over my legs. Juliet came back, holding a candle in a white ceramic sconce. The flame lit her up the middle but even in the eerie light she looked calm, dependable, set in her ways. "It was a woman," she said, in a slow, contemplative voice. "I said you weren't home and she said she'd try later. I asked her for her name but she just hung up."

Just then, power was restored and all of our lights came back on.

4

I first met Sarah Williams when I was twenty-four years old, in 1970. I was in the Coast Guard, stationed for the time on Governor's Island. I'd gone through Harvard like a hot knife through butter, learning what I could, making surprisingly few friends, and, on the whole, behaving like a boy building a résumé rather than a life. Now, my master plan ticking away, it was time to fulfill my military obligations in the least bloody way possible— I couldn't imagine a man being elected to any important office who hadn't put his time in in uniform. When I was finished with the Coast Guard, there was a spot waiting for me at the University of Chicago's law school, a spot reserved by the father of one of my few college chums, Jeremy Green's father, Isaac. Isaac and I had met one Thanksgiving and then again at the Greens' cabin in Wisconsin the following summer; Isaac sensed my calculating spirit, liked the way I thought ahead. My own family, while enthusiastic, had its doubts. My father worried that the spot at the U. of C. might not wait for me, worried that in trusting Isaac I was falling for a rich man's idle promises—like Charlie Chaplin used to in those painful comedies, in which he'd be befriended by a slap-happy drunken plutocrat, only to be coldly rejected in the sobriety of the next day. As for my mother, she was passionately against the war in Vietnam and though the Coast Guard was not a combat unit of the armed forces, she was sick with worry that I'd get myself killed. "All Danny had to do was say he was a homo," she reasoned with me, though even as she said it she knew I could never take that route. She tried to get her boss, Earl Corvino, to pull some strings with his pals in the Democratic Party—the party of peace, now that Nixon was in—but he advised her against it. (We all knew he wasn't thinking of anything except saving himself the trouble of doing her a favor—as she aged on the job, the old pol was getting cool and even abusive. He saw his own decay in her graying hair.)

It was an autumn weekend, uncommonly hot, with the sky the color of a spoiled oyster. I went into Manhattan dressed in my whites. I was a skinny thing, then, and with my startled, spiky military haircut I looked like I'd just pecked my way out of an egg. Danny had just begun his business; it was the first year of Willow Books and I was going to meet him at his office. Our plan was to have lunch and then spend the rest of the day getting into trouble. (This was before Danny's appetite for destructive recreation became ravenous: these were the hors d'oeuvres, the mere morsels of mayhem, before the feast of self-abuse began.)

I was one hundred and one percent aware of how rigid and antique I looked walking into the offices of Willow Books in my white uniform, with its blue epaulets and gung ho cap, and my caste mark sewn onto the forearm of my right sleeve—at that point petty officer second class, with the eagle, crossed anchors, and double chevron.

Willow Books had been created by Danny after a visit to some communizing, draft-dodging friends of his up in New Hampshire. He'd somehow ended up at a yard sale in Keene and there found an old book called *The Science of Marriage*. It had been published in 1902 by a man calling himself the Reverend Otto Olson. It was a sputtering, hilarious, rather loony sex manual for who the Reverend Olson described as "gentle people of all denominations." It was what our mother liked to call "a fountain of misinformation." And Danny, cleverly, had an instinct that it would be great fun for thousands of people to read such a corseted, guilt-ridden, Byzantine sexual document. The book was in the public domain; all Danny needed to raise was the cost of manufacturing 10,000 copies. And as he had a knack for making rich friends, he soon was in business. *The Science of Marriage* ended up selling 250,000 copies. Danny's picture was in *Newsweek* and he also appeared on a TV panel, along with five other "hippie moguls," though one bestseller and a hand-painted tie hardly qualified him on either count. But he was in business, nevertheless. He plowed the profits into an apartment for himself, new books to publish, a company car, and rented space in a red stone building shaped like a rook on the corner of 23rd and Fifth. The floors were slanted; the windows throbbed with sunlight. I emerged from the elevator into the little reception room—beanbag chairs, copies of *Rolling Stone*, a huge mural of a willow tree in the moonlight. The receptionist's name was Tamara. Her small, peaked breasts were visible beneath her diaphanous Indian blouse.

"Hi, Fielding," she said. "Kill anyone today?"

"Not yet, Tamara," I said. "Is Danny here?"

Danny had a real appetite for ideas and schemes, but there was a methodology to business, a certain kind of orderliness that repulsed him. He was living well. He would always live well, despite the setbacks to come. Even when we were growing up there was something high rolling in him: he loved bets, dares, and anything impractical. The money he'd made on his best-seller had already evaporated from the heat of his plans and appetites, and Willow, even in its infancy, was living in a state of ceaseless fiscal peril. Sometimes Danny was a week or two late meeting his payroll and turnover was high. I hadn't been to the office in three months and of the eight employees, only two were familiar—Tamara and

Wilson Wagner. Wagner was an enormous redhead from Providence whom Danny called Rhode Island Red, a linguist, translator, an avant-gardist who stayed on because he didn't exactly need the money and because he could still convince Danny to invest in beatnik poetry, each volume of which was published at a loss. Wilson's title was Executive Editor. Danny was Publisher and President. They shared an assistant. She sat in the center room, with access to Wilson's open, chaotic office and to Danny's, which breathed stealth and secrecy, and which was usually locked.

How strange to remember talking to her that day, knowing now, as I could not know then, how deeply I would love her, how heedlessly would follow where she led me, even when it cut against the grain of my life, my plans, even when it defaced the picture of myself I carried within me like a campaign poster.

She looked up at me. A manuscript in a shiny orange box was on her desk. Her hair was half covered by a blue and white bandanna and she wore small turquoise earrings, a red and white striped blouse opened three buttons on the top, in a way that was both casual and chaste. A light on the bottom of her black phone was flashing off and on.

And so we nodded to each other and I said, "I'm here to see the boss."

"Who are you?" she asked. She looked me up and down, unsubtly, trying to see beyond the uniform.

"His brother," I said.

"Oh, yes," she said, with a certain lilt in her voice, an enthusiasm I took at the time for a kind of passing attraction. "He's been expecting you. Go right in."

"You're new here," I said, inanely.

"Yes." The light continued to flash on her telephone.

"Like it so far?" I asked.

"Love it," she said, dismissing me. (Later she would say: "Those *questions* of yours. And in that uniform? You were so *grating*.")

I walked into Danny's office. He was standing at the window, his platinum hair nearly down to his shoulders, wearing a large pink shirt, gray slacks. He was smoking a joint and watching the insurance clerks on their break in Madison Square Park. "Look at this, look at this," he said, turning his becalmed, reddish eyes toward me. "Great game." It was touch football, six on a side, fellows who crunched numbers in the big Metropolitan Life Building, guys suited for a great deal more adventure than their desk jobs afforded them. I came to a window as a tall black guy pulled down a wobbly pass and then stumbled and fell to his knees. "The score's tied at fourteen," Danny said. "Which side do you want?"

"I'll take the side with the ball," I said.

"It's a bet," said Danny.

Danny was my younger brother by eleven months. He used to drive Mom and Dad into exhaustion and despair, though they felt his difficultness was probably connected to some inner excellence, some precocious impatience with the indignities of being a child. They really knew how to put the best face on things. Danny was rebellious, pleasure-seeking, fearless, and accident-prone, whereas I was deliberate, empirical, calculating, and believed in trade-offs and negotiations. Danny taught me about what to want and I like to believe I taught him a little about how to get it. He always wanted to be rich—not for the prestige but for the sheer physical pleasure. He thought of wealth as an eternal massage, as softness, convenience, and ease. He felt that being poor rubbed the spirit out of life, a spirit that could live only in an atmosphere of frivolity. He hated to see Dad counting out his change. What goaded me was our insignificance. Odd the things that make us what we are, the makeshift plows that till the fields of destiny. I remember seeing a newspaper when I was nine years old. I was paging toward the sports section when I came across the obituaries and saw that some fellow who owned a chain of shoe stores had died. There was his picture and a column of respectful details about his life, and it struck me with manic force that if my parents were to die, if all of us were suddenly taken ill and died, not a word about us would appear in any newspaper on earth. Three children, a father who worked as a printer, a mother who typed and filed for the local Democratic Party boss: we were totally expendable.

"What time do you have to be back in the water?" Danny asked.

"Ten tonight," I said.

"Hey, is that another stripe I see on your sleeve?"

"Don't get too excited. They come pretty automatically if you're a good boy."

Danny took my arm and inspected the sleeve. "It's a darned nice feeling knowing you're out there patrolling New York Harbor. Fucking Cong, you know, sneaky little devils. They could be on Fifth Avenue like *that*." He snapped his fingers. He had our father's powerful, capable hands.

"Yeah," I said, but I was feeling a little riptide of self-doubt that took the form of embarrassment. I could usually hold my own in these kidding contests, but standing in his office, feeling the sleekness and acceleration of his life, a life he drove like a hot car, and sensing all those skeptical people outside his door, people who undoubtedly judged me harshly for wearing a uniform, people who had no idea of what my real feelings were and what I wanted to do with my life, I felt awkward and stranded and my confidence shrank within me. And I was feeling something else, something that temporarily dried up any sense of fun in me—Sarah. Sarah, who seemed so patently unapproachable and whose face as it drifted in that tender chamber in which we preserve the objects of desire, awakened in me a need shot through with a kind of wretched hopelessness.

"I can hardly wait for you to get out of that fucking rinky-dink Coast Guard," Danny was saying. "It scares the piss out of me, man. How do you know Nixon isn't going to take the wrong pill and send all you guys over to Vietnam? I think you've outfoxed yourself on this one, Fielding."

"What do you want me to do? Desert?"

"Maybe. Maybe. I've got two authors living in Toronto. Draft resisters, both of them. And their book is coming out in a couple of months. It's going to sell great. A science fantasy thing called *Saturn's Godfather*."

"That's very encouraging, Danny."

"I'm your brother. I'm looking out for you. Remember you taught me the Coast Guard song. Well, my new assistant told me what the fuck 'Semper Paratus' means. Always ready. And I don't like that always ready shit. I get distinct death trip vibes from that."

"Your assistant? That girl out there?"

"Yeah. Sarah. Catholic girl. They know their Latin."

Desire, drunk on its own sense of doom and futility, manifested in me as a kind of nausea. I wanted to grill Danny about her but I thought that if I just shut up and forgot about it, it would go away.

Danny had his hand on his chest and now threw his arm out, like Al Jolson, even with a bend in the knee. "Everybody sing!" he said, in a tinny vaudeville accent.

> *"So here's the Coast Guard marching song,*
> *We sing on land and sea."*

And now I was winging with him. We put our arms around each other and stomped around his office, our feet slamming down with such force that his pictures quivered on the wall—his Andy Warhol print of nasturtiums, the photo of himself and Mick Jagger and a pale English girl with a black eye, his framed xerox of the first check received by Willow Books, his blowup of the dust jacket for *The Science of Marriage*.

> *"Through surf and storm and howling gale*
> *High shall our purpose be*
> *Semper Paratus is our guide*
> *Our fame, our glory, too,*
> *To fight to save or fight and die*
> *Aye! Coast Guard, we are for you."*

And then the door opened and there she was. She was standing at the end of a sunshaft, a cone of molten gold filled with small orbits of dust that fell just before her feet. She was wearing red leather shoes, open at the toe; her long, hard legs were bare and alive with a light blush of hair. She wore a black skirt made of something sheer and vaguely shiny and which, more to the point, stored an abundance of static electricity, a charge that made the material cling to her knees, her thighs. We came to the end of our song and stood there. Danny kept his arm around me, not letting me go, though I wanted to strike a more dignified pose.

"You getting taller or something?" he said to me.

"I'm growing on the job," I said. It seemed a miraculous jolt of inspiration to me and I hoped that one quip would warn Sarah not to judge me too quickly.

"I wanted to show you something," Sarah said, walking in and closing the door behind her. She was holding a thick copy of *Publishers Weekly* to her chest. "You guys are making me homesick," she said. "I used to march around with my sisters like that."

"Sisters like in sister or sisters like in nun?" asked Danny, his voice rich with flirtation, that way he had of snatching a thread of personal information and spinning it into a web of assumption.

"Sisters as in sisters," she said. "Anyhow, these are the spring books in this issue," she said, coming toward us, opening the magazine. She moved slowly, enjoying our attention. She passed over me with a glance and, like a country cousin, I looked down at my shoes. "Arlington Books is doing a book about J. Edgar Hoover that sounds like the one we're doing." She found the page and showed Danny an ad: a picture of the FBI director with a devil's horse and a maniac's grin. The title was *Night Comes to the Potomac*.

"When are they publishing?" Danny asked.

"They come out in March," Sarah said.

"When do we come out?"

"End of May, early June."

He heaved one of those sighs that puff out the cheeks. "Oh-oh," he said, soft as a voice from the next room. "Can we rush it and get ours out before theirs?"

"The author hasn't even turned in the corrected manuscript yet," said Sarah.

"Good," said Danny, seizing upon it. "Let's cancel it and get out of the whole fucking deal."

"Well . . ." said Sarah, and now she was looking directly at me. I wondered why and then I realized she was asking me to step in. Talk a little sense. Be reasonable. How did she know that had always been my job?

"As your future lawyer," I said, "may I ask you one question?"

"What?"

"Do you have a contract with your author?"

"Yes." Edgy.

"Then you'd better stick to it."

"A lot you know," said Danny, walking over to the window. "A contract is a house with a thousand doors. Lots of exits." He glanced out. "Hey," he said. "My team just scored. That breaks the tie and you owe me five bucks."

Danny turned toward us again with a look on his face that announced the subject was closed, and he said it was time to go to lunch.

I knew in an instant I was not going to find the casual confidence it would take to suggest to Sarah she come along, too. I rubbed my forehead with my open palm. Beyond the door, I heard Wilson Wagner's psychotic laugh—big heaving ha-has that dredged up a foam of phlegm with each aspiration. It's odd to consider the small moments in which the soul is in peril: wanting her to join us for lunch somehow attached itself to those few moments when my life hung in the balance—when the Pontiac spun out in the snow and rolled over and over, when I'd been cleaning a gun and it accidentally went off and the light fixture above me rained down a hail of white glass, when, as a child, I came upon a homeless man sleeping near the frozen bushes in Prospect Park and gave him my pocket money, only to be grabbed by the arm, pulled violently toward him, and kissed on the mouth. I looked desperately in Danny's direction and saw he had no intention of inviting her along and then I plunged deep into myself, hoping suddenly to find enough casual nerve to ask her.

"Mind if I join you?" Sarah said.

With a shot of relief, I clapped my hands together and the noise they made was absurdly loud, like bursting a paper sack filled with air. "Great," I said, heat surging through my face like a red tide. "We'll all go together."

Danny looked at me, censure shining like a varnish in his blue eyes. He was telling me to cool it—not because he objected to Sarah's coming along but because he knew how much I wanted her, knew it in an instant, and he didn't want me—well, as he put it later, "Firing your cannons to celebrate and accidentally sinking your own ship."

"We'll go to Max's," Danny said.

The last time I'd eaten at Max's Kansas City I'd found a hair in my salad, but Danny liked the place because they let him sign his checks and though he owed about two thousand dollars, they didn't pressure him for payment.

"It's OK with me," Sarah said, "as long as there's no hair in my salad."

It seemed such a perfect coincidence, I began to doubt its reality. This was before my heart had learned to fear its own heights.

In the restaurant, we took a booth, Danny and Sarah on one side, me on the other. We ate hamburgers, drank tepid Cokes, listened to Marvin Gaye and King Pleasure on the jukebox, and I dominated the conversation. Like a fabric salesman lugging out bolt after bolt of material, I insisted on displaying the entire inventory of my personality. I was ridiculously aware of how to ring certain changes, certain prefabricated ironies: poor boy goes to Harvard and all the little social shocks so entailed; Harvard boy goes to sea and with that a new series of awakenings; the middle child misunderstood by his brother and sister; the man born into the wrong generation, looking for honor in a profession that most of his peers have written off.

"Should I be taking notes?" Sarah asked at one point. But did that stop me? Did it even slow me down?

Finally, with my lunch cold on my plate, and their plates virtually empty, Danny derailed me.

"Could you tell from listening to her that Sarah's from New Orleans?" he asked me.

"Actually," I said, "there's two guys in the Coast Guard with me, both from New Orleans. One of them sounds like he's from the Bronx and the—"

"Hey," Danny said, pointing to my plate, "you haven't even eaten."

At last, I realized I'd been talking nonstop and with that inevitable embarrassment came a thick, consuming silence. I picked up my hamburger and took a bite; I chewed it with my eyes averted.

Danny cleared his throat and turned to Sarah.

"What's going on with you these days?"

"My roommate's boyfriend moved in."

"The Egyptian?"

"Yes."

"Sarah lives with a classmate of hers from Goucher College. This girl is about five feet tall, tiny, tiny, and she goes out with this enormous phony from Cairo."

"He just sits around all day and night," said Sarah. I felt her attention on me and I forced myself to look at her, though I was still embarrassed at how I'd been carrying on. "He wears shorts and a tank top and that's it, except for his Rolex watch, which must weigh ten pounds. And he just sits there, looking incredibly angry, staring at the TV set all day and shaking his head in disgust. But if you try and turn the set off he yells like you just stepped on his toe."

I threw my head back and laughed—God, what a laugh: a talk show host on drugs.

Like progressive parents slowly, gently taking a meat cleaver away from a wild child, Danny and Sarah gradually moved the conversation out of my reach. They talked about the office, about books about to be published, manuscripts recently submitted. I forced myself to be calm enough to listen. Sarah's opinions were quick and tended, I thought, toward the extreme. Sarah was one of those Us and Them people, filled with loyalty for those whom fate had somehow placed around her and bristling with suspicion against anyone who might harm her allies.

She wanted Danny to place a retaliatory advertisement in the *New York Times*, accusing the editors of ignoring Willow Books. "Because we don't buy a lot of ads and because we're small and independent and not part of the good old boy network," she explained. She wanted Danny to make the company into a co-op. "That way we'll all have an equal stake in it and if money's short, no one's going to mind. It'll be ours and everyone will work twice as hard." He looked at her as if she were insane. To me she seemed impossibly, supernaturally alluring. I agreed with almost nothing she said, but it scarcely mattered. I was desperate to know her and I had never felt such crushing self-disdain before: I was suddenly little more than the sort of man who did not know Sarah Williams.

When we made our way back to the office, Sarah walked between us. The sky had notched closer to earth and it was even hotter than before. Sarah cooled herself by plucking at her blouse and blowing down toward her breasts. I didn't know if she was flirting and if she was I didn't dare believe it was with me. After all, Danny was her boss; they shared so much common ground. They were on one side of the fault line that went through America and I and all the old farts and young lunatics were on the other. Anyhow, in the history of our sexual competitions, Danny invariably won out.

I glanced at Sarah from the corner of my eye. We were heading north on Park Avenue; trucks were exhaling plague and taxis were honking. She plucked again at her blouse and now dabbed the mist off her upper lip, blotting it with her forearm. Desire seized me like terror. And then she hooked through both of our arms and we walked French-movie style, with Sarah moving quicker than Danny or me, leading us on.

"You never said how you got the idea you wanted to be a senator," she said to me.

"That would take a long time," I answered.

"Oh? Do we have a long time?" This she directed to the boss, who shook his head no.

Then perhaps later, I chanted to myself, fifty times at the least, but was unable to say it.

The elevator in Willow's building was small and ornate, a little opera house for dolls. It was run by an old man in a blue uniform who chewed gum and fiercely gripped the control lever. I brushed my sleeve against Sarah and she didn't move away. When the elevator jerked to a stop, Sarah asked me, "When do you have to get back to the war anyhow?"

And I said, "Can I buy you a dinner tonight?"

And she said, "Yummy."

That afternoon, I grilled Danny about her. I first off established he hadn't gone to bed with her. Great relief. And then I established there wasn't even a flirtation brewing between them. We sat in his office. Danny had his feet on the desk. He tilted perilously back in his old *Front Page* swivel chair. He smoked a joint and then another; I couldn't keep up with him. Every so often, the phone would ring and Danny would handle the business with enormous dispatch—quick, crisp, humorous, confident voice, wholly different from the slightly slurred, druggy growl he dipped back into as soon as the phone was in its cradle.

"She went to college in Baltimore. Goucher College. She spent her free time running a soup kitchen at the waterfront. One of those old saloons, where strippers used to pick change off the bar with their little labia—now some haven for lost souls. She barely finished school. Her parents cut her off. Apparently, they are monsters. Mama's a lush, Dada's a sadist."

"Money?"

"Nothing special. Her grandparents are loaded but they've already announced they're going to will it to the ASPCA."

We both laughed. I was sitting on the small leather sofa, tapping my feet nervously.

"Is that true?" I asked.

Danny shrugged. "I'll tell you what is true," he said. "She goes to mass. I think that's pretty fucking antique."

"What else?"

"What else? Well, I'm surprised she's having dinner with you tonight."

"Why?"

"I don't know. She's very . . . tight with herself. Friendly—but cold, sexually. You can feel when you touch her. It's like touching a man. It's hard to explain."

"Does she see any men?" I asked.

"She has a boyfriend. A painter. A big rich kid named Peter Blankworth. He wears a beaded headband, filthy clothes. I tell you this guy's about seven feet tall and he carries a bowie knife in his boot. He paints after he drops mescaline and then sells the stuff to friends of his family. Sarah talked me into letting him do a dust jacket for us. It was lousy and I'm not paying him a fucking cent. Sarah's pissed at me."

"So is she pretty close to this guy then?"

"I don't think so. I don't even think they fuck. I never see them touch when he comes by for her. But who knows? People can take you by surprise, sexually speaking. Usually, though, I can tell by knowing someone what they'll be like in bed. Like Sarah. Sarah—"

"Can I bring her back to your apartment tonight and use the extra bedroom?" I asked, cutting him short.

"You know what I'd like to do?" Danny said. "Let's do up a very moderate amount of Methedrine and go over to Fourteenth Street, to Julian's, and shoot a few racks of nine ball. Want to?"

"Come on. Can I use your place tonight or not?"

He squashed out the joint and was going through the top

drawer of his desk, looking for the vial of meth. He found it and held it to the sun, tapping it to see how much was left. "Absolutely not," he said. "If I wanted that kind of involvement in her personal life, I'd be asking her out myself. Anyhow, there's no point to asking. It's not going to be that kind of night."

"She's beautiful, isn't she?"

"Yes. She's completely gorgeous, man. Come on. Are you sure you don't want to snort some of this up and go shoot some pool? Remember what Caroline called it the first time I gave her some? Hitler in five seconds."

That evening, Sarah and I had dinner at Max's Kansas City. We weren't ready to strike out into our own territory; it seemed an extension of being with Danny to eat there again. Our waitress had blue-black hair cut like a choirboy's, Bambi eyes, and sharp little feline teeth. She seemed physically afraid of me, as if the man in uniform who sat before her was the embodiment of war and violence. I think she expected me to leap from my seat and shout, "I smell queers," and start taking the place apart.

"She looks like Joan of Arc, doesn't she?" Sarah said, as the waitress hurried away.

"I don't know," I said. I was feeling out of my element. Max's was still the prescribed hangout for the fringes of the pop art crowd and an assortment of other prosperous and self-proclaimed outlaws of the night, and I could imagine how I appeared to them, sitting in my whites, wearing the dunce cap of duty. "She just seemed like a nerved-out skinny little snob to me," I said.

Sarah looked around—at the paintings on the wall, the smoke hovering near the recessed lights, the booths occupied by men in leather vests talking to women in Japanese haircuts, and I could see in her face she was suddenly viewing it all through my eyes —an act of kindness and generosity that made me want to reach across the table and take her hand.

"Do you want to go someplace else?"

"No, that's OK. This is fine."

"Are you sure?" she said.

"No, come on. You're making me feel bad now. I think the waitress is great, OK?"

"All right," she said. "I'll make date talk. What do you do in the Coast Guard?"

"Right now, we're patrolling New York Harbor. There's a new race of sea monsters being created," I said. And with that, I felt a twist of shame—they were the exact words I'd used on a girl I'd met in a bar down on Chambers Street a few weeks back. We'd ended up masturbating each other in the back of a taxi. I tipped the driver five dollars for not being obvious about watching us and then, back at the base, I came down with one of those flus you can get from engaging in some piece of personal ugliness. Yet the story was true. Several of us had been spotting gar-like scavenger fish near the bottom of the river that could only be described as mutations: oversized heads, massive length, extra sets of teeth.

"Where?" Sarah asked.

"A mile from where we sit. All those chemicals going into the water. The drug companies, the breweries. The fish have to change to survive and the changes are monstrous. They look like serpents. Sometimes they run right into our cutters. Some of them even glow under water."

"Do you think you'll have to go to Vietnam?" she asked.

"No. The war's ending pretty soon anyhow."

"This war's been ending pretty soon for a long while," she said. Her voice darkened, accepting the rich hue of her own morality.

"It's just something I have to do," I said.

"I know what you mean, I think," she said. "I've got one of those, too."

"One of what?"

"A sense of destiny."

I laughed. I assumed she was teasing me and I only wanted to show I could take it. But then I realized she was being absolutely serious with me and as I grabbed the laughter back it was replaced by a virtual swoon of feeling for her. Could it be she understood me?

"What's your sense of destiny?" I asked. And now it seemed all right to lean across the table and lay my hand on her wrist, though just for a moment.

"When I was little, I wanted to be a nun," she said.

"What changed your mind?"

"Puberty."

"So now what do you want?"

"A life of unbelievable adventure and profligacy and then at the last moment—sainthood."

It was my turn to say something clever but suddenly my mind seemed like a pair of feet slipping on ice.

"I want a life that makes sense," she said softly. She took a deep breath and then very slowly let it out.

"That's one of the reasons I'm in the Coast Guard," I said. "I feel this great division in my life, a before and an after, and I don't like it. First, there's the me who was raised by poor parents and then there's the me who sneaks into Harvard and starts hanging out with a lot of prep school guys and everyone has fifty sweaters and ten credit cards. I want my life to be all one piece and being in the service helps tie it together. Now, I'm back with the kind of guys I'm used to, the kind who were supposed to be my friends. It's not like I'm rejecting the other, though. I want to be from both worlds. I need both of them."

"Two lives?"

"No, just one very big life."

"And that's why you want to be a senator?"

"That's not what I want, though."

"That's what you said."

"Well, what I really want is to be president."

"You do?"

"Why are you smiling?"

"It's very boyish, isn't it? It's like wanting to be a fireman."

"What's wrong with being a fireman? Someone has to climb the ladder."

After dinner, I walked her home. It was seventy-five blocks north and six avenues west. We walked on the East Side until we came to Central Park and then we walked through the park to go west. "I force myself to walk through here now and then," Sarah said. "Everyone keeps telling me how dangerous it is but I refuse to let myself be afraid."

"By yourself?" I asked. It seemed a perfect moment to put my arm around her. She moved closer to me and I realized with a start of something like shame that she'd been waiting for me to touch her. If I'd had all the time we deserved, it wouldn't have been so bad. But I had to be back at Governor's Island in a couple more hours. I felt absurd and infantile having a curfew.

"When I was eleven years old," she said, "I got an idea that Frank Sinatra was born to be my spiritual guide. He seemed to know everything. I wrote him letters and when I would read in the newspapers about where he was appearing, I'd try and call him there. Then one day, I decided this couldn't go on anymore. I just needed him too badly to do without him. It was an emergency, a prepuberty spiritual emergency. I learned he was performing at Caesar's Palace in Las Vegas and I made up my mind to get there. I dressed in my sister Tammy's clothes—she was sixteen—and put makeup on so I'd look grown-up. And I went to the airport with about forty dollars—everything I could lay my hands on. There was a flight to Las Vegas that left every afternoon at three o'clock and I thought I could sneak onto the plane and whatever happened after that wouldn't matter because I'd be in the realm of a higher cosmic force."

"What made you think so?"

"Something he'd said on TV. He said the important thing was to make it through the night and whatever helped you—it didn't matter if it was God or gin or another person—that made it holy. I thought he was Jesus—and no one knew it. Maybe he didn't know it, either. I still sometimes think everything would have

turned out different for poor old Frank if I could have gotten to
him and told him he was Jesus."

We came to the road that runs north and south through the
park. Taxicabs streamed by and then the road was empty. We
crossed it, holding hands. A few lights from the buildings on
Central Park West were showing through the haze, hovering above
the charcoal darkness like little spaceships.

Sarah lived in a four-story brownstone with a red door and
red shutters. The buzzer for her apartment read Williams & McCabe,
Inc. McCabe was Patricia McCabe, her roommate; the Inc. was
a joke, a way of holding onto the high spirits of their college
friendship.

I stood next to Sarah as she poked around in her purse, key
hunting, and the awkwardness was as real as grief. "I enjoyed
myself," she said, finding the key—one of six attached to a silver
ring and a little red plastic crayfish.

"Can I see you again?" I asked.

"OK," she said. She covered my eyes with her hand and kept
it there for a moment. When she removed it, she said, "There.
Now you see me again." She saw I was too rattled to laugh. "Sorry.
I did that once a long time ago and . . . it just came back."

I took the hand that had covered my eyes and held it. I looked
at it closely, as if I were a palmist, and then, slowly, giving her every
chance to pull away, I raised it to my lips and planted a soft,
fervent, utterly devoted kiss right on the interstices of her fate.
She raised her free hand and touched me on the back of the neck.

"Can I come up?" I asked, holding her hand, squeezing it.

"Too fast," she said. She shook her head.

"Can't we think of this as a wartime romance?" I said.

She touched my face with her open hand and then, as she was
about to turn away, pinched my cheek. Hard.

I waited at the door as she made her way up the stairs. I
watched her feet disappear and then her shadow came slipping
after. I looked at the doorbells; she lived on the fourth floor. I
walked out onto the street and waited to see her. A window was
bright with soft yellow light; a spider plant in a macrame sling

hung down like a pendant. I waited and waited and then, finally, her face appeared in that window. She looked first to the left, then to the right. Then she saw me standing in the street, my lower half obscured by an old cream and blue Chrysler, a streetlight directly over my head, dropping its light on me as if I were a tenor about to break into song. Now she was unlocking the window, using her strength to get it to budge; and now it was rising, slowly, with a paint-splitting groan I could hear clear down in the street. "Come on up, Fielding," she called, sticking her head out the window, an angel poking through the skin of disbelief that separates heaven from earth.

5

The Tuesday after my meeting with Kinosis, there was a dinner party for me at Isaac and Adele's. They'd put it together quickly. Mayor Byrne was invited, Mike Royko, Marshall Field —people whom the Greens thought it would be well for me to cultivate but who did not, except for the mayor, get too involved with the mess and push of electoral politics.

Juliet and I dressed for dinner. There was still plenty of Congressman Carmichael on the news; as the scandal grew older and moldier a lower order of news reporter began to paw over it, just as the weaker hyenas will have their chance after the strong have had their fill.

Jerry wasn't making it any easier on himself. He'd called yet another press conference. The boredom was getting to him and making him stupid. This day's meeting with the press was held at his office on 53rd Street—a sunny little storefront that had once been a bakery. Carmichael came as a civilian, in corduroy pants, a plaid wool shirt—maybe he was trying to give the impression he was just on his way to Michigan to do a little hunting. His eyes had looked psychotic with grief. "I just wanted to make my apologies to the people of my district," he said, staring into the cameras. "I know . . . I let them down. And that is something I'm going . . . I'm going to have to live with for the rest of my life." He was cut from the moorings of his old life and had no more hope than a dinghy in a hurricane.

I made it myself onto the local news that night, though as a footnote to the Tales of Carmichael. A picture of me flashed on the screen and it nicked momentarily into the memory of seeing Sarah's face on the news. The newscaster was saying, "Insiders report the man most likely to fill Congressman Carmichael's seat is a thirty-four-year-old attorney from the DA's office named Fielding Pierce. Pierce, a bachelor and a political unknown, apparently occupies the inside track with local Dems and Governor Kinosis is expected to announce Pierce's spot on the ballot in the next two or three days."

"Juliet!" I shouted. I stood up and walked halfway toward the bedroom. "Juliet? Come on out. I'm on the news."

"What are they saying?" she called back. Her voice sounded awfully far away.

Now Jerry was off the news and so was I and they could get to what the *real* news was. Today they had *two* weathermen—their usual guy with his huckster suit and fever dream pompadour and a special winter storm consultant from something called the American Weather Watch, who was comparing this series of snow-storms to storms of the past. His reminiscences were illustrated by the most unremarkable old photographs of Chicago in the 1930s, showing people in overcoats trudging through snow up to their knees and arty color snaps of bare trees, their boughs heavy and luminous with ice.

Juliet came in, dressed in what I guess you'd call an evening gown, one of those sheer, sparkling, impractical dresses that seem designed to state: I have a fur coat, a warm carriage, and a powerful male protector.

"Wow," I said. "Where are we going?"

"You want to be a congressman or a senator? Well, this is how it's done. And don't kid yourself, Fielding. This is as much a part of politics as anything else."

"I know," I said. "And please don't think I don't appreciate it."

"Joke?"

"No joke."

She smiled. Juliet didn't press matters once she heard what she wanted. Isaac was an idiot about women; he didn't realize how many edges she had. He had bequeathed her to me, stuffed her in my pocket like a silk handkerchief, with no thought more complex than that she would add a little class to my act. He'd been horrified by Sarah, with her feverish opinions and faded jeans, though he'd been naturally too intelligent and too decent to say a word against her. But fundamentally his judgment was that I couldn't make the long haul by myself. Perhaps I ought to have been insulted. Maybe what I should have done was tell him to find another protégé, another lost boy, another wooden arrow to notch onto the bowstring of his frustrated yearnings. But I felt very cool about the whole thing.

Ambition is the ice on the lake of emotion. If I was offended then it was a highly theoretical sort of offense, a murmur all but lost behind the great raucous noise of the parade. I took out my aggressions where they might do the most good. I put them into work, into master plans. And if that wasn't enough, I could always bomb up and down the Outer Drive with the radio blasting, until I exhausted myself into enough docility to sleep through the night and get myself ready for another day of my crusade—a crusade that had begun, as most crusades had, with the highest ideals and the best intentions but during which I had begun to forget about the fallen torches I had once wanted to retrieve, the terrible wrongs I had once wanted to redress, and now the long bloody trek to Jerusalem was something generated by fuel from a deeper and a darker source: the grade-A crude of ego.

"You've got a spot on your suit," Juliet said, touching my lapels with her skillful long fingers.

"I've got spots on all my suits," I said. "We guys from the underclass slurp our food."

"One day you're going to be very powerful and obscenely rich and you're still going to be saying that," Juliet said, trying to make it sound affectionate and teasing.

"Well, whatever stellar heights I rise to," I said, "I'm still going to be me."

"Save it for the campaign trail, Fielding," she said.

I smiled, struck by the fact that I'd meant to say something true about myself and it had come out sounding facetious, fake. Juliet turned her back to me and asked me to help with her zipper. I zipped her up and then negotiated the elusive little clasp at the top. It must have been a thousand dollars' worth of dress. It seemed immoral, but it wasn't something you said. She had a long, bone-white neck and I felt I ought to kiss it. Then of course there was the possibility of just ripping all of that sheer silk off her and taking her from behind—sex gives us the opportunity to tilt the world that quickly and expose all of the elemental savage hunger underneath. I smoothed away a wisp of black hair and kissed her neck. She made a low sound, as if stirring in her sleep.

And then the telephone. The nerves at the pit of my stomach rose up like pigeons from a square. Juliet moved toward the phone but I stopped her.

"I'll take it in my study," I said.

"Let's not be late," she said, as I hurried. I grabbed the phone on the third ring.

"Hello?"

"Fielding, this storm's going to be in the way." It was Isaac. My nerves settled back down like the contents of a room after an explosion—everything under gravity's spell once again but who could say in what order. "I think we're going to have to cancel the dinner for tonight," he was saying. "They've predicted ten inches for tonight. Ach. This place is a Siberia."

"Well, you know these weathermen, Isaac," I said. "They want to turn every storm into an emergency. I swear, we're being dress rehearsed for nuclear war. Even the language they use."

"Well, yes, that's an interesting way to look at it. But after all, we can't expect people to drive in a snow alert. I'm sorry. I can see you were looking forward to it. The mayor's an absolute bore, if it makes you feel any better. One of the most petty and disagreeable women I've ever known."

"Well, that does make me feel better," I said.

He laughed. I'd said the right thing. "Stay inside tonight. Curl up with my niece and let's hope this storm passes quickly."

We said good night—though each time I was ready to hang up the phone, Isaac remembered something else he wanted to tell me. Would I be able to meet with a few of the key Illinois congressional Democrats next Monday, assuming, of course, the governor got around to making the announcement by then? When was I leaving for New York to see my family? Over Christmas? Couldn't it possibly be put off for some other time? No? Then perhaps shortened? And so forth. By the time Isaac was finished with his requests and reminders, we'd said good-bye fifty times.

"God," I said to Juliet, "try getting your uncle off the phone."

"It's only that he loves you," she said.

"Dinner's off," I said. "Snowed out."

She put her hand on her belly, as if to break it the news. "Well, that's all right," she said. "There'll be plenty more."

"Do you really want to go through this with me?"

"Through what's going to happen? Why not? This is the part we've been looking forward to. You're getting recognition. You'll have a voice."

"But what's in it for you?" I asked.

She looked back at me. I had insulted her but her face seemed to register its unhappiness as if it was something *remembered*.

"I don't mean that the way it sounds," I said.

"I know that," she said softly.

"It's just that a couple of days ago you had your life and I had mine and now all of a sudden we're talking as if . . ."

"You're going to need someone, Fielding. Now more than ever. I had a choice to come forward or shrink back and I chose to come forward. I'm sorry if that makes you feel pressured."

"It doesn't. I'm sorry. I don't know why I'm saying these things."

"You're frightened," she said.

"I guess."

"Your dreams are coming true."

"It must be that. I'm sorry. Come on. Let's drop it. Let's keep our nice clothes on and have an evening at home like a couple in a Smirnoff's ad. A roaring fire. Perfect haircuts. And a big bottle of vodka between them." I laughed a laugh so forced and weird that if it had been beamed into the galaxies it would have kept extraterrestrials away from our planet forever. "The perfect evening, right? Can you imagine? Two people alone drinking an entire quart of vodka? What a mess. Right?"

"Your nervousness is making *me* nervous," said Juliet, holding her hand out to me. I took her hand and she came to me. We held each other in a light, calming embrace. "Would it be OK if I did have a couple of drinks?" she asked.

"Of course it would."

"Are you sure? I don't need to." Juliet was always solicitous about my drinking or, rather, my not drinking. My abstinence made her think I was a sort of behavioral time bomb ticking in her midst and she dreaded yet morbidly courted the person she imagined I would become with alcohol in me, a person at once more brutal, more coarse, and more real than the man she'd been living with.

Juliet was not a drinker the way Sarah was—drink tapped Sarah's aggression, made her teasing, argumentative, confrontational, and sexually frank in a way that took some getting used to. Sarah was slow and reverential about wine, but when it came to hard alcohol she was demonic. She could take long cowboy swigs right out of the bottle; she was fervent, even desperate in her belief that alcohol might untie some Gordian knot of rectitude and self-doubt.

Juliet wandered into the bedroom while I fetched a bottle and a glass. She liked drinking in or near bed; it saved on crawling. I poured out her Polish vodka and she accepted it with a certain resignation, as if I were putting her on a train. I pulled a joint of Colombian pot from my breast pocket—a present from a lawyer named Sid Ablin, who was twenty-seven years old, wore a little black derby everywhere except in court, and whom we called Chainsaw in honor of his ability to cut unfriendly witnesses into small, neatly stacked pieces. He was a good prosecutor, but if it hadn't been for the job he would probably have been in the loony bin.

I lit up and tapped the joint against her glass. "To storms," I said.

She looked over the rim of her glass at me and took a sip.

"Why do we feel like this, Fielding?" she asked.

"Embarrassment," I said. "We find ourselves in a very embarrassing situation here."

"I guess," she said. She lay down on the bed and worked her shoes off and then crossed her feet at the ankles. She held her glass with both hands and slowly brought it to her lips again.

"We were just drifting along," I said, with a sudden, weird surge of enthusiasm in my voice. I was figuring it out and the pleasures of diagnosis for the moment overwhelmed the fatality of the disease. "We've been enjoying each other and you haven't been asking very much of me and I haven't been asking a lot of you, either. It's just been nice."

"I think it's been a little more than *nice*," said Juliet, looking away.

"Yes, I agree. It's been more than nice. But there's always been a distance, a buffer. And when we pass through it we cool off a little and we have to pass through every time."

"Oh, stop."

"I'm not saying anything bad," I said, sitting on the bed, putting my hand on her arm. "We've had it great. People see us, they think, Hey, why can't it be that way for us? Right? Isn't that right? That's something we've both noticed. We've kept it very simple and uncluttered. That's how we've wanted it. It's what we like. It's what we can *do*. But now I'm going to be on the ballot and, let's face it, I'm probably going to win." I paused and waited for her to nod, to make some sign of agreement. "I'm going to, you know. It's almost inevitable. They don't call it the Chicago Democratic machine for nothing. And then I'll be going to Washington. I'll have to start pretty soon working on reelection plans, because whatever the Republicans do or don't do they'll certainly come after me with both guns smoking the next time around. And maybe even someone in my own party will go after my seat."

"I know all this. And as well as you do."

"You don't understand what I'm trying to say."

"I guess I don't. But I hate all this fake seriousness. I hate trying to make everything more important and full of agony than it really is. Why can't we just take it easy?"

Her face looked placid; her eyes were expressionless, as if everything suddenly depended on my not knowing what she was really feeling. Yet I knew this act of concealment was performed as much on herself as on me.

"I'm not talking about taking it easy here, Juliet. Jesus, I don't know what you're thinking about. I'm talking about two people. I'm talking about the two of us. I'm talking," I said, in a much quieter voice, "about the fact that you and I have been able to make out pretty well without getting committed—"

"Is that what our life has been?" asked Juliet. And suddenly her eyes were no longer expressionless; I realized with a sick lurch that she wasn't far from tears.

"What would you say it's been?" I went on, with my prose-cutorial vigor.

"I don't know. From the sound of you, it wouldn't make much difference what I said right now. You can come to your own conclusions."

"No. Not true." I felt suddenly that I was lying and that Juliet could see clear through.

"You don't even know what you're saying," she said. She drained her vodka with astonishing dispatch and held her glass out to me. I poured her another, equal dose. "Why don't we just go to bed?" she said.

"I'm not tired," I said.

"Do you want to make love?" she asked.

"Ah. An interview."

"I don't mean it like that. *I'd* like to."

"Wait up for me then. I'm going to ramble around."

She shrugged and sipped her vodka. The color was creeping across her face, a slow red tide. My own feelings were far from me but at the same time irritating, like the bark of a dog a country mile away.

I went to the kitchen and fixed myself a sandwich. I read the papers and when they were done I just paced the house, thinking thoughts that were secret even to myself. By the time I got back to the bedroom Juliet was beneath the covers and her fancy dress was on the floor, a glittering black puddle. I picked her glass off the night table so she wouldn't have to sleep with the smell so close to her and I turned off the light. I felt relieved. I crept out of our bedroom and closed the door with a click no louder than snapping a pair of pajamas closed.

I went into my study and sat at the desk. It was just nine thirty in the evening. There was a long while to go. I went to the window and watched the snow. I looked down and saw my car, with snow covering it like a soft white echo of itself. I felt trapped—in the evening, in myself, in the unforgiving laws of the universe. I wanted a drink, many drinks, many many many drinks. There was a moment after the first drink when you knew there were more to come, and you could walk through yourself as if through the rooms of a cozy paid-for house and the painters had just arrived to put the primer on and soon everything would be painted your favorite colors. I could remember that feeling very well, but I could not duplicate it or even come close. It was just something to remember and do without.

I went back to my desk and dialed Danny's number back home in New York. He had a tape recorder to answer his phone on the first ring. "You're in Beep City," his voice said and then there was the tone. For all I knew, he was there, listening to the machine to see if it was someone he actually cared to speak to—he could screen his calls that way. It wasn't a matter of unfriendliness. He just owed so much money—to authors, and printers, and freelance proofreaders, and photographers, and lawyers, and credit cards, and to other, less official, more punitive types. At the office, he had his receptionist to run interference for him, but the more enterprising creditors now had his number at home and he had to be careful. Not that he'd altogether lost the talent for conning even the angriest of them into liking him, into giving him more time. And he still had the advantage of being so far into debt with some of them that it made them unwitting coconspirators with him— for if he ever went under for good, then where would they be? No, he could charm and he could maneuver and he could stonewall. But it took its toll, and these days Danny needed the nights to recuperate from the pressures of the day. I could picture him in his tony six-room apartment on East 70th Street, with somebody beautiful at his side, and a bottle of Piper Heidsieck and a Limoges plate full of drugs, putting a finger up so his companion would stop speed-rapping for a moment and leaning toward the Panasonic answering machine to hear who it was calling him this time. I didn't want him to pick up just because it was me and so I hung up without saying a word.

I dialed my sister's number after that. (Beware the lonely man with a telephone.) She picked up on the second ring; her voice seemed anxious.

"Hi, Caroline," I said. "Sounds like you're expecting a call."

"Fielding, where are you?"

"Home. Chicago. Did Mom and Dad tell you my news?"

"Are you kidding me? You think they'd keep it to themselves? They're out of their minds with happiness. Did they tell you mine?"

"Yours? No. What's happening?"

There was a silence and then she said, "They didn't even tell you."

"Wait. Maybe they did and I was just too distracted to take it in."

"Right. I'm sure. Well, you can see how proud they are of *me*."

"What's the news, Caroline?" I said, and my voice settled into that half neutral, half put-upon tone—the voice of a man afraid to give up his ephemeral privileges. I knew Caroline's old gripes were absolutely legit: our parents had failed to focus on her all through childhood, except for occasional bouts of condemnation. Danny they had indulged and me they had encouraged, but Caroline they'd kept at emotional arm's length—fearing her sexuality, doubting her intelligence, treating her as if she were on parole. But I'd never known what to do about it. How could I have made them love her more?

"Let's just drop it," she said.

"I'd like to hear what it is, Caroline," I said.

"And I'd like to drop it."

I leaned forward on the desk and covered my eyes with my hand. I exhaled into the receiver and we lapsed into silence. I sat there in the slowly cooling darkness of my study and watched as the reflection of headlights from a passing car slipped across the ceiling.

"Maybe we can talk when I come home for Christmas," I said at last.

She waited a few more moments and then said, "We'll have time then, won't we?"

"I got your boys great presents," I said.

"They're so excited about seeing their uncle," she said. "And excited for you, too. You'd be surprised. They're little—but they *get* it."

"What do they get?"

"That you're going to go into the Congress and really *do* something."

"Great. Well, after seeing how little I can do they'll probably turn into anarchists."

Caroline was silent for a moment and then she said, "Don't worry. You're going to be all right."

"You know what I wish?" I stood up and picked the phone

up, too. I walked across the room to the window. The snow was falling hard now and way down the block a snowplow was stopped, its orange light spinning around and around.

"What do you wish?" asked Caroline, because I'd forced her hand.

"I wish that Sarah was here." I stood, watching the snow, waiting for whatever Caroline would say.

"I miss her too, Fielding. She was really something."

"You know, it gets better, it gets better, then it's like it never got better at all."

"Is everything OK with you and Juliet?"

"Yes. It's not that. It doesn't matter how happy I am with someone else. It's still *someone else.* I want—I don't know. I just miss her. It's all this snow."

"What do you mean?"

"It's really coming down."

"I know. It was on the news."

"It makes me lonely."

"Soon it'll be spring." I heard her shifting in her chair and then leaning forward. I could see her doing it and I knew what it meant. She was holding me closer, tighter.

"I just wish she was here to see all this," I said. "I don't think she ever believed it was going to happen."

"Can I tell you something?" asked Caroline. "If you were still with Sarah—none of this *would* be happening. And I'm not talking about the whole Juliet-Isaac thing. This has nothing to do with connections. But everything she was about would have taken you away from where you wanted to go. There's no way you could have stayed with a woman like Sarah and had the career you wanted."

"Well, I'll never know then, will I?"

"I'm not trying to be horrible, Fielding."

"I know." I couldn't altogether reject the possibility she was needling me for my apparent success. Caroline was good at that sort of thing: she could make a landlord embarrassed over his Cadillac.

"I'm starting to pretend she's still alive," I finally said.

"But why? Why would you do something like that to yourself?"

"I don't know. I'm not. It's just happening."

"It can't just happen. Something's causing it. Do you feel so guilty about your good fortune?"

"I don't feel the slightest bit guilty," I said. "I just feel her around me. In the snow. It was snowing when she died."

"I know."

"I just feel her somewhere around. The way you can feel it when someone's staring at you. I think she called here the other night."

Caroline was quiet for a few long moments. "Oh God, Fielding. Don't do this to yourself."

"But you don't understand. I don't mind feeling this way. It's OK. It's interesting."

"It's not interesting. It's completely sad."

"I'm not sad. I'm just wondering what will happen next."

We talked for a few more minutes and then said good night. I put the phone back on the desk and made my way to bed. I slipped in next to Juliet and she sensed me through sleep and moved closer to me. Her naked ass pressed around my thigh; I could feel its softness, its cleavage, the dark heat coming from the middle of her. I reached over to touch her. She was oblivious to me. A faint sweetish smell came off of her skin as she metabolized the vodka.

Outside, in the brittle silence of the winter night, some brave soul was walking by with a portable radio. An old song was on. My heart stopped for a moment. It was Stevie Wonder singing "I Was Made to Love Her."

> *I was born in Little Rock*
> *Had a childhood sweetheart*
> *We were always hand in hand*
> *I wore high-topped shoes and shirttails*
> *Susie was in pigtails*
> *I knew I loved her even then . . .*

I sat up in bed. Someone was out there playing Sarah's favorite song. She once played the 45rpm of that song twenty times in a row. We had danced to that song. She had written the words down in a notebook and used them as a reading exercise in the after-school program at Resurrection House.

I had conjured her. I could feel her in the room, no less real nor more visible than the air, the temperature. I looked around, but there was no signaling light, no moving curtain. I held my breath and waited for her touch. Carefully, I folded back the covers and moved toward the edge of the bed. Juliet reacted to the withdrawal of my body heat and she moved toward me, blindly. I stopped for a moment and let her settle down, but when I stirred again she lifted her head from the pillow.

"Don't go," she said, her voice rising up through the heaviness of sleep.

"Just a second," I whispered.

"Please," she said. She didn't sound like herself. There was a rawness of feeling that was foreign to my sense of her and I had a sick, bleak feeling that after all these months, I'd only known her by half.

I leaned over and kissed the warm side of her face and then the cool. I brushed the hair back from her temple. The music was still playing below; I was mad to be at that window.

"I'll be right back," I said, and now there was an exposed wire in my voice. I squeezed her hand and placed it at her side just so. And then before she could say anything I slipped out of bed.

I stood at the window. The snow was still falling, though slower. It was catching the wind now and drifting back and forth on the way down. It fell past the street lamps. It landed on the tops of the parked cars. Across the street, someone was warming up a Saab. Exhaust streamed out of the tailpipe and rose toward the nearest street lamp, where it turned a luminous chalk white. I didn't know whose car that was but I knew where he lived; he was in the ground-floor apartment across the street and had an old blue-and-white Kennedy poster in the window, a memento from Bobby Kennedy's '68 campaign. I looked around. The sidewalks were empty. There were plenty of footprints but none seemed fresher than the others. Nearly all the windows in sight were dark; those that showed light were gloomy and dim, as if Chicago was a city under siege. And the sound of that radio was gone—if it had ever been there in the first place. I pressed my palm against the icy window.

"Come next to me, Fielding," said Juliet. She was sitting up in bed now. She held the sheet modestly in front of her naked breasts. "What are you looking for?"

"I heard music," I said.

"So?"

"I don't know. Going crazy."

"Come to bed," she said. She reached out to me; the sheet dropped away. Her breasts looked full, heavy. The nipples were dark brown. With the sheet in folds over her stomach, she seemed to be rising, an apparition of fertility, from the surface of our wide, cool bed.

"You really are so beautiful," I said, lying next to her, pressing myself close to her, locked into the great earthly logic of sorrow and desire. I pressed my lips to hers and tasted the night's drunkenness, coming up out of her like heat off a highway. It made me want her more. Her hand was on my shoulder and now she was digging her nails into me. Juliet was not a ferocious person nor was she a ferocious lover. It embarrassed her to think of herself as being somehow different in the sexual act than she would be in other parts of her life—if you did not grunt and cry out outside the conjugal bed, she thought, then why should you adopt a new persona for those few minutes of love? She thought that women who made a great fuss over fucking were either very shrewd or insane, and she would have none of it. I didn't mind. The gentleness of her lovemaking seemed utterly in keeping with our quiet, porous life together.

Her mouth was wide upon mine and her hand lunged hungrily for my middle, as if my hardness was proof of predestination. She pressed herself against me, lifting her hips, and I could feel her wetness against my leg. Her heartbeat came right through her chest like a tomtom. It was the drunkenness, of course, and it was the urgency that came from my life's suddenly changing. She could feel me slipping away and it inspired her. I knew she only wanted to pull me into the heat of her need, but just as the brilliance of the moon makes its dark side seem haunted, the quickness of her passion made all of our other nights together seem all the more wasted.

She took my hand and placed it between her legs and then closed her hard cool swimmer's thighs on me. She pushed me flat on my back and straddled me; she was now looking down from what seemed an enormous height. She touched her own breast for a moment, closing her eyes, experimenting. She seemed to be looking within herself for an image of a woman transported—but who was that woman going to be? She was rocking back and forth, without putting me inside. She exhaled and I felt a hesitation, a draft of sobriety blowing through the bright haze of her drunken inspiration. She waited a moment until it passed and then rededicated herself to the pursuit of an ecstasy that was well beyond our reach. Yet we wanted each other and, more, we needed each other. We were not waifs in a storm and I don't know why we felt like that, but we did. Maybe all we felt was failure. We were making love in acknowledgment of our own cautious defeat, and though it was bringing us together I wondered if afterwards we'd ever be able to look each other in the eye. Juliet turned and put herself near my face and took me into her mouth. It somehow didn't feel particularly good but its intentions were and we could enjoy it for that. After a while, she turned around and fell onto my chest. We kissed; fatigue was starting to show in both of us. I rolled on top of her. She raised her knees and placed her hands gently on my back and the specificity of the weight of her touch suddenly made it like every other time. After we were finished, I rolled onto my side of the bed and put my hands behind my head. Juliet curled next to me; her touch was casual, sleepy.

"That was so nice," she said.

"Yes," I said. "It really was." And then, to my great horror and even greater shame, a sob rose up in me, so heavy and round I thought I might gag. I covered my eyes. I would have liked all the life to go out of me just then, all the soft, vulnerable, humiliating, uncontrollable life.

"What did I do?" asked Juliet, anxious, weary, wanting an answer but already starting not to care.

"You didn't do anything," I said.

"Then what's wrong?"

"I don't know. Ever since this thing with Carmichael went down, I've been feeling really spooked." I turned on my side and looked at Juliet's profile as she rolled away from me. "It's the strain," I said. "The ultimate horror of getting what you want."

"You're going to be just fine," said Juliet. "Are you worried about me coming to Washington with you? Because if you are— I've thought about it. I talked to Uncle Isaac about it. I *think* I've made up my mind for a change." She lifted her hands in one of those you-know-me expressions.

"What have you decided?"

"We'll do a commuter thing. And if you get another term then we'll see about something permanent. I think that'll take off some of the pressure. At least I hope so." She looked at me, asking for an answer.

"Is that what's bothering you?" she asked after a silence.

"I don't know," I said.

I never expected Juliet to read my secret thoughts. ESP seemed the very least of her powers; sometimes, if she was not prepared to hear it, she could barely understand what was said to her directly. Yet now she put the back of her hand against her forehead and said, "You're very far away, aren't you."

"Yes," I said. "I guess I am. I'm remembering Sarah tonight. That music. I feel her so close. I'm sorry."

She was silent for a few long moments and then she said, "It really hurts that you're not thinking of me." She sighed. I realize now she was expecting me to say something, to contradict her, to put things back in their familiar place. But I didn't say anything. There was another noise from the street, just a car. Its headlight shined on the icy window, turning it pewter for a moment. And then, suddenly, Juliet shot up. She looked at me with wild, furious, betrayed eyes and she got out of bed. She pulled a pillow and the top quilt off and stalked naked across the room. I knew I should call her back, stop her from going, but I couldn't. It was time to be alone. I wanted to lie there, praying for a visitation. I wanted only to feel the warmth of an impossible light.

The light from the hall raced across the bedroom floor as Juliet opened the door and then with a slam I was in darkness again. I was in darkness and I was in pain and despite all that I believed and could not believe, despite having no more expectations of the miraculous than any other ordinary modern soul, despite all the arguments of common sense and all the cautions of fear, I was waiting.

6

Our first Christmas together—1971. I had a four-day leave and we went to New Orleans. I was in uniform, flying half price. Sarah in jeans, lace-up boots, a black sweater. She was afraid of the flight. She drank down two miniature Scotches and then wrapped her arms around me and pressed her face into my chest. The plane was full. "To die on Christmas with the only man I've ever loved," she said, looking up at me, trying to play it light—but the words frightened her still more deeply and she closed her eyes, shuddered.

Picked up at the airport by Sarah's sister Tammy. Tammy was ample, a little sloppy. She wore a flowered dress and torn red tights. Her honey-colored hair was piled on top of her head. She and Sarah embraced, squealed. Tammy was five years older than Sarah, but seemed deferential, perhaps a little wary. "Come on, honey, I'm triple-parked," she said, taking Sarah's hand, looking me up and down, smiling. We got into her Opel, me in the back with my legs drawn up so my knees were practically on my chin. The car was a wreck; the torn upholstery reeked of marijuana. Sarah's braid hung over the front seat and swayed like a pendulum as we made our way onto Airline Highway. Sarah asked after Derek, Tammy's husband. I rolled down the window and stuck out my fingers. It wasn't particularly warm. Tammy explained that Derek and she were probably going to get a divorce. "He's always on me about my weight and shit," she said. "Anyhow, what are you supposed to do with a guy who sleeps in silk pajamas with his little underpants on underneath them?"

"He's such a skinny little thing," said Sarah, nodding.

"Now he's got a little brown poodle and he named the poor thing Cynthia," said Tammy, almost sympathetically. "And he's started shaving his own chest."

"I'd say the marriage is over," said Sarah.

"I know, I know," said Tammy. She yanked down the sun visor. A joint, fat as a waterbug, was under a taut rubber band. She worked it loose, lit it. Then she found my reflection in the rearview mirror and spoke to me. "All the women in our family are walking disaster areas," she said. "Daddy is a tyrant and all of us are weak-minded because of it. We're just a bunch of *victims*."

"Speak for yourself," said Sarah good-naturedly.

Tammy took a drag on the joint and passed it back to me. Because I was in uniform, I was always obliged to prove my flexibility. I took a drag, though it was the last thing I wanted.

"Sarah was the only one of us who could stand up to him. Once, he was insulting everyone, just saying ugly things, and she scratched him right across the face. Big welts."

"What'd he do about that?" I asked.

"He started choking her and banging her head against the

floor," said Tammy with an explosive laugh that sent the blue-gray smoke billowing out of her lungs.

"And everyone just sat there and watched," said Sarah.

"We were *scared*, honey. Scared. We weren't like you. We didn't grow up thinking we had a direct pipeline to God."

Our first stop was Sarah's grandfather's house in Metairie. A sub-urban plantation: back entrance for the servants, a couple of live oak, wet green grass, a cast-iron darky with a horse hitch in its hands, Greek columns on the porch. Sarah and Tammy called their grandfather Granddaddy, but that was as friendly as it got. He lived alone now—their grandmother had died a year before, curled up in front of her dressing table, a bottle of Bacardi dark rum against her cheek.

"He'll love *you*, Fielding," Sarah assured me. "He'll go for the uniform."

His name was Eugene Williams and he'd never worked a day in his life. He was living on the last of a family fortune (made in real estate) and it pleased him to think there'd be very little of it left when he was dead. It was a kind of neatness, thoroughness, like not getting up from the table until your plate was clean. He kept everything he had in checking accounts, stashed away in banks in New Orleans and all over Jefferson Parish. Whenever he needed money, he went to one of his banks and cashed a check for five thousand dollars. The staff of black nurses who now tended him around the clock got paid in cash.

There were no books in the house, no pictures on the walls. Gold rugs. Salmon wallpaper. Candy corn in a silver bowl. A smell of cooking, detergent, dust, age, and dog. He had eight dogs. Countless cats. A white wicker cage stuffed with finches. An aquarium filled with bubbling murky water, in which little slivers of goldfish darted psychotically around. He'd just lost his raccoon—one of the nurses let the creature out and it made a dash for freedom. This lost raccoon's name was Chapman and little

Chappie's disappearance dominated the old man's conversation. We sat there listening to him while the cats and dogs paraded around us, brushing against our legs. "They don't *think*," Eugene was saying. "How do you let an animal loose like that? No chance for survival, that's the pity. I'm sure Sarah will tell us it wasn't deliberate." He reached down and picked up a white angora cat by the scruff and dropped the surprised cat onto his lap, where he patted it with his large, unstable hand. He was a huge man, even after the shrinkage of age and disease. Lantern-jawed, elephant-eared, he looked like an albino Buddha. He was wearing a brown pajama shirt and gray woolen trousers. He had yet to look in my direction. He just couldn't be bothered with new information.

A large color console TV was on, showing a college football game. Eugene was almost deaf and kept a smaller, black and white TV on his lap, so he could keep his hand on top of it: he could feel the vibrations and interpret them.

"Are you taking this in?" Sarah asked me, not bothering to lower her voice. Tammy glanced at her nervously; she didn't care for the liberties Sarah took. I nodded yes. "Smell this place and look at him," she said to me. "He's the most selfish man in the world and he despises all of us."

The nurse on duty that day was a thin, lopsided black woman named Violet McAndrews. She helped get Eugene ready so we could bring him with us to Sarah's parents' house. She put a sweater on him, a scarf, gloves, a stocking cap. He looked like a dazed, homeless man; he squirmed and muttered insults as the nurse dressed him. She seemed not to mind, but of course she must have. His eyes were opaque; he didn't lift his feet when he walked. For a moment, I sensed his impending extinction and felt a tremor of pity for him. He would die afraid, unhappy, profoundly uncompleted. Tammy had his arm as we walked toward the car and Sarah walked behind, doing a grotesque imitation of her grandfather's feeble shuffle. Tammy bit her lip to keep from laughing. Mrs. McAndrews watched from the window. Eugene, of course, was wholly unaware of Sarah's mean joke. And I was startled to feel what I was feeling—a desire to take Sarah by the shoulders and shake her.

Christmas at the Williamses'. A brick house, ugly, rectangular, looking somehow like a large bomb shelter that had risen from the ground. A cyclone-fenced backyard in which ran two Chihuahuas, Benny and Penny. "Check out Benny's penis," advised Sarah. "Isn't it dominating?" It was true. The dog seemed half cock.

Sarah's father was named after his own father, Eugene. He was well built. Arctic blue eyes, the blue of a high-pressure cold front moving in. He wore golfer's duds: green slacks, lemon yellow shirt. The hair on his muscular arms was dark and wiry. His smile was at once panicky and vengeful. Crushing handshake. A ha-ha voice. He was an insurance agent and enjoyed making provocative statements about himself, such as, "I only play to win," or "My paycheck is my report card." Sarah's mother flirted with me. It seemed automatic, almost dutiful, as if she'd once read about it. Her name was Dorothy. A large woman—the other girls had inherited her spaciousness. She had blond hair, green eyes set wide apart, one of those sensual, unhappy mouths that detective writers call "bruised." She was clearly an alcoholic and I think she recognized in me a kindred spirit. "I'll bet you could use a drink," she said to me, before we were altogether in the house, before we'd even been introduced. Eugene's drum set was prominently displayed, his Music Minus One records stacked on the Sherwood stereo console.

"Hi, Daddy," Sarah said, on her tiptoes, kissing him on the cheek. "Merry Christmas. Are you sane or insane today?"

"Now, don't start in, Sarah," Dorothy said, her voice a mix of warning and despair.

"I am completely insane," Eugene was saying.

"He won't drink the new vodka we got him," said Dorothy.

"It tastes like sewage," said Eugene to me.

"Three dollars and twenty-nine cents per *quart*," said Dorothy. "Does anyone realize what kind of savings that is, over a year? Anyhow, vodka's something you *mix*."

Her parents treated Sarah as if they considered her ill-mannered, obsessed with criticizing them, finding fault. They felt betrayed by her opinions, her inflexibility. They seemed to have little private jokes at her expense, teasing comments that were difficult to resist—even after three months I sort of knew what they meant. There *was* something fanatical about her morality. Her other older sister was there, Carrie, with her new boyfriend, an ex–football player named Oliver, upon whom Eugene doted and whom Dorothy treated as if he'd rudely spurned her advances—she was brusque, impatient, guilt-provoking. Carrie seemed to be campaigning for her parents' approval. She agreed with whatever they said and soon picked up their attitude toward Sarah and adopted it as her own. "Calm down, Sarah," she'd say. Or, "Oh-oh, we'd better change the subject. Look at Sarah's face."

"It's all right," said Sarah blithely. "I already explained to Fielding we were a family of moneygrubbers."

She took me by the arm and asked if I wanted to see her old bedroom. We walked up the carpeted stairway, past the beveled window at the landing with its underwater view of the house next door. Her room was gray and green, with a canopied bed, a little dressing table at which to act out a dollhouse version of grown-up unhappiness. "I'm sorry," she said, closing the door and leaning against it. "I know I'm embarrassing you. It's like this every time I come down. I always act like an idiot." She looked around the room. "Can you believe this place? I haven't lived here in six years and nothing's changed. It's the room of the little girl who died." She toured me around. "Here's my bed. Here's the closet. That's the window I looked out at night. Across the street, that's where the Charbonnets lived. Bobby Charbonnet was two years older than me and I adored him. I used to walk naked in front of the window, very quickly, hoping. Now Bobby's married and running some grain elevators outside town. Here's my dressing table. All my high-school virgin cosmetics are here. Here's Cherries in the Snow." She picked up the lipstick and applied a little on her lower lip, bending slightly at the knees so she could see herself in the dressing table's mirror, one of those old-fashioned looking glasses that look like a slice of bread. "Oh, and here's my Jungle Gardenia." She twisted the cap off—it resisted and then, with a little crunch, came loose. She sniffed. "Jesus. One whiff and I've got acne again."

"You've got to lighten up," I said. "They're just people."

"I know. But that's who I am in this family. If I stopped burning their asses they wouldn't forgive me."

"I doubt that," I said. I put my arms around her. Perhaps I was catching her sense of bad behavior, but there was something powerful and arousing about being with her in that chaste little room, redolent as it was of the teenage Sarah. She pressed herself against me: it would have been gross had it not been so pure, so bright and sharp with need. She guided my hand down to her middle and pressed her vagina against my palm. She had changed into a green silk skirt, elasticized around the waist, full below. She lifted it and put my hand first on her belly and then lower, into her thicket, her moistness, the unadorned biological fact of her. "Put your finger in me. I always wanted you in this room." She made a little gasp as I entered her and she moved toward me a half step, plunging me deeper. "All of that moaning and griping and all that incoherent unhappiness was just my way of waiting for you, Fielding," she said.

And I believed her then and I believe it now.

Night. All the presents had been opened. No one seemed to care particularly for anything they received. Material unhappiness, like the aftermath of junk food, or that numb, cheap feeling you get after watching TV. Sarah and I, as she had warned, were put in separate rooms. Conventional behavior was as close to morality as her parents dared venture—but now I'm talking like her. I was put in a daybed in Eugene's home office: a metal desk, certificates of merit from the Prudential Company framed and hanging on the wall like diplomas. A picture of Eugene and the other salesmen standing beneath a banner that said SAN DIEGO WELCOMES THE GO-GETTERS!!

I lay in the bed, watching the luminescent Westclox, struggling to stay awake. The Coast Guard had taught me to fall asleep as soon as I became horizontal, no matter what the circumstances, but tonight I had a rendezvous with Sarah in her room. At midnight, I rolled out of bed and crept out into the hall. I could hear breathing behind the closed doors. I felt like a criminal. A light was on in the bathroom; the toilet was gurgling. Someone had left the medicine chest open and I saw my reflection in it as I passed. Yikes.

I walked into Sarah's room. Warm moonlight was pouring in through the window. I heard the low note of a riverboat. There was the smell of coffee roasting, millions of pounds of coffee. I whispered her name as I came toward her bed. The moonlight touched her face, making it golden, strange. I saw her eyes were closed and my spirits sank. I wanted her so badly. I came next to her, leaned over her and listened to her deep, unconscious breaths. Then I saw there was something on her chest. A note pinned to the blanket's cool satin border. It said, "Wake me and fuck me. Sincerely yours, Miss Sarah Williams."

The next night at midnight, I sneaked back to her room and again she was sleeping. This time, however, there was no note. Touched by the terror of denial, my instincts began to reverberate, as if threatened by death. I watched her sleep and finally my great need of her and the enormity of desire convinced me of the lunatic notion that Sarah would like nothing more than to wake up to a slow, rippling orgasm. Yes! A surprise party for the libido. (I had something of the sexuality of a sailor on leave. Frequency of contact meant so much to me. I wasn't thinking of the pummeling she took around her family.) I pulled the covers off her and watched her moonlit nakedness. I was a man in a dream. Then I slid down to the foot of the bed and carefully straddled her, opening her legs slightly with the pressure of my thumbs against the tops of her thighs. She moaned in her sleep. Experimentally, to see if I would awaken her, I kissed her belly, and then the disheveled border of her thick, shaggy pudendum.

I put my mouth over her opening and then softly pressed my tongue against her. I slipped two fingers into her and moved them back and forth and now I was conscious of my own body as it was covered by a layer of cold sweat. Paroxysms of desire mixed with a sense that I was committing some indecency. My heart was beating haphazardly, wildly, and I thought to myself: a good death. I kissed her again, again, she opened herself further to me, and then, in a soft, dazed voice, she said, "Daddy?" I jerked away from her in shock and looked up at her. She'd propped herself on her elbows and she was grinning down at me. Now she was laughing and I was laughing, too. "You creep," I said, but that just made us laugh louder. It was that hysterical laughter you succumb to when you're not supposed to make a sound. Her parents were right across the hall. Windows were open; walls were thinner than back home. Our laughter came in gasps. I scrambled up in the bed and lay next to her. We buried our faces in her pillow. I kissed her and she laughed into my mouth; our teeth clicked, my lungs filled with her wine-dark breath.

On the day we were to leave, Sarah and I drove over to her grandfather's for an obligatory visit. She was sullen behind the wheel. "I've been making these little dutiful visits all my life," she said, driving slowly, taking the long way, showing me the sights of her girlhood—St. Rita's School, the riding academy, the boathouse in Audubon Park where she'd first made love, the cemetery where her ancestors were—graves in New Orleans were kept above ground and the thousands of unburied crypts looked like a litter of discarded appliances. "He complains if I don't visit," she was saying. "So I do. I take the easy way out. God, he is such a cold, selfish bastard and he made sure my father was even worse—all the coldness but none of the confidence. And God only knows what *my* father's turned *me* into."

"I never knew my grandparents, really," I said. "People die young in my family."

"You don't know how lucky you are. Why are you looking around like that? Do you want a drink or something?"

"Not really."

"We can stop somewhere if you want."

"No, it's all right."

"You really drink a lot. I never noticed before."

"Vacation," I said, looking away, feeling a mixture of relief and embarrassment.

She was silent for a while. We were driving under magnolia trees with dead blossoms high up in their gnarled boughs. Sky battleship gray. "I'm unforgiving," she said.

"Not if you can say it," I said, though I didn't quite believe it. I had a gnawing sense of her as a fanatic.

"That's sweet of you," she said, smiling, accepting it. "I frighten myself. As lives go, mine hasn't been bad, not *so* bad. But I seem so much angrier than other people."

"You're angrier than I am," I said.

"I know."

"I don't have time for anger," I said, drawing myself up, brushing something imaginary off my trousers.

"You must be very busy," she said.

"No. I just want what I want, and anger won't help me get it."

"Then you should want something else," she said. She gave me her purse and I opened it to find her a cigarette. There was a tube of lipstick, a Zippo lighter, about ten bucks' worth of change and crumpled-up dollar bills, a napkin from Pat O'Brien's, with the inane invitation to "Have Fun!" printed in green. Her Camels were in a red leather case, one of those touristy things embossed with the words *New York City*. I opened it up, lit her cigarette, passed it to her. As I replaced the pack, I noticed, snaked on the bottom of her purse, lying in a brown moss of dirt and loose tobacco, a string of rosary beads.

We pulled into the circular driveway to her grandfather's house, one of those delusions-of-grandeur jobs, as if the house were the abode of minor royalty. "All this *graciousness*," Sarah said, and I couldn't have agreed more—though I realized our shared aversion to that sort of bourgeois fanciness was really very different in origin. I felt privilege as a foot on the back of my neck and Sarah thought of it as a garish shoe she'd been expected to wear, one that fit her badly and offended her tastes. The twice-a-month gardener was there, cutting back the hedges, feeding the dogwoods. Mrs. McAndrews was out with him, passing the time. When we got out of the car, she waved to us. "Your granddaddy's inside watching his TVs," she called out.

"Thank you," Sarah called back. "Poor woman's so desperate for company," she said to me, in a private voice. "Granddaddy treats her like shit. He treats all the nurses like that. His money gives him that right."

We let ourselves in and walked into the den where he kept the large console TV. It was on terrifically loud and there was something in that sound that struck me as ominous, or perhaps there was a scent in the air. We walked in. He was sitting in his camel wing chair, dressed in a baggy white sweater and blue trousers. His back was to us and he didn't turn when we entered. The portable TV was in his lap, blasting away. A celebrity game show was on. Someone was in an isolation booth, trying to guess what his wife had just said.

At first, we thought he'd merely fallen asleep. But his face was too slack, his chest too still. His fingers on the little TV had already stiffened.

"Oh no," Sarah said, in a defenseless voice. Haphazardly, incompetently, she looked for his pulse. I put my arm around her and tried to turn her around, lead her away. I knew he was gone. There was no reason to let her put herself through it. He'd died in his chair and it was a lucky death.

"I'll call Mrs. McAndrews," I said.

"No, no, please." She stood there looking at her grandfather and then, almost shyly, she reached out and touched the side of his bloodless face. She made the sign of the cross and knelt next to his chair. She turned off one TV and I turned off the other; the room jolted into a deep, sad silence. She folded her hands, closed her eyes, and rested her forehead on the arm of the chair.

"Oh, dear Jesus," she said, sobbing. "Please take his soul."

7

Things were moving quickly, though with no particular direction; time was rapid but shallow, like a dying pulse. I was out of my office at the County Court Building. I was invited by the Illinois Democratic Party to a meeting in which I would be named the candidate for Carmichael's seat, but the meeting was called off at the last minute because Kinosis's nephew got into a six-car collision around Carbondale and after that the governor and the Mrs. were off for their winter holiday. There's nothing quite so irritating as overconfidence in others, especially when you yourself are anything but confident. I played squash with a lawyer named Ed Pinto and he hit me on the side of the face with his racquet. The white of my eye turned into tomato soup for a day but then went back to normal, though I still had a queer feeling in my head, as if someone had dropped a freezing little fork in the middle of my brain and left it there. Juliet and I had a decent couple of days and then it was time for me to go to New York to have Christmas with my family. Juliet had left it open whether or not she'd be coming with me, but she settled it by falling into foul spirits and I think I was doing my part to seal the deal, too, because I have no idea what we fought about—though I was in it as much as she was.

All we really needed from each other was a decent good-bye, and we were used to saying good-bye so it ought to have been easy. Yet she felt heavy, almost comatose, in my arms as I brought her close to me for a parting kiss and her lips were cool, hard, and I don't know that mine were any more appealing.

"I'll call you tonight," I said.

"You'll probably forget," she said.

"Of course I won't."

"It's OK. It doesn't really matter."

"Then why'd you say it?"

"It's just that you always do when you go to New York. Forget."

"I'm sorry about the other night, Juliet."

"I know you are. You can stop apologizing now. I mean I really wish you would. There's too much to do. Let's just go on to other things."

"To the business at hand?"

"OK."

I pulled her to me again for another try and this time, as she did her best to return my embrace, I realized how empty and sad my gesture was. My suitcase was packed, shut, and standing at the door next to my stack of Christmas presents. There was the sound of a car's horn honking below. Isaac had insisted on taking me to the airport. It was Christmas morning, before eight o'clock.

Juliet watched from the window as I walked to Isaac's car. I looked back at her; framed by the beige curtains, the glare from the snowbound street obscuring half her face, she waved slowly —or seemed to—and I waved back. Isaac stayed at the wheel of his Continental, dressed in his herringbone overcoat, his Russian hat. He'd be asking no questions about why Juliet wasn't taking me to the airport or coming along for the ride. That would be indiscreet. Isaac was not interested in the necessarily untidy private lives of others.

I got into his car. It smelled of pipe tobacco and that after-shave lotion he got mail order from a little Bulgarian chemist's shop on Portobello Road.

"Juliet says hello," I said as we pulled onto the street.

"She's well?" he asked casually, in a tone that didn't invite an answer.

"Fine," I said softly. I watched the apartment houses go by and tried to think of all those souls inside as my constituents. I wanted them to live better and to *be* better; I wanted them to need me as I needed them. Yet they slept now, with their presents beneath the trees, and if they knew my name at all they probably assumed I was just another jackal running with the pack, another set of sticky fingers in the public pocket, another overgrown jock with a gung ho heart.

"We'll be seeing Juliet later this afternoon," Isaac said. He turned in his seat to see if a car was behind him before making a left turn. He didn't trust mirrors.

"Keep an eye on her, will you?" I asked. "She holds so much in."

"Her father was exactly like that, Fielding. And it always worked itself out." He accelerated and we were on the Outer Drive, following the shoreline of the gray, chunky lake.

"I suppose you're looking forward to seeing your family in New York," Isaac said wistfully. I don't think Isaac very fully understood why I needed my old family, now that I had him and Adele. He saw them as dicey characters. My sister had married a black man and what little Isaac knew of Danny made him jittery head to toe. He must have seen them as bad influences and seen my continuing attachment to them as a danger—as if they represented an unruly sort of life into which I might suddenly revert and fall.

"It'll be good to see them. I just wish there was more time."

"Yes," he said. "But there isn't. You realize that, don't you?"

"Yes."

"The election will be January 22. It's around the corner."

"I know. But how can I lose? There'll be no one opposing me."

"There's a great deal more to do than winning," Isaac said. "After the election, you've got to hit the ground running." We drove in silence for a few moments. A wave of terrifying, senseless hope was going through me. I had just had a vision of seeing Sarah at the airport. I wanted to close my eyes and follow that thought, to worry that inflamed nerve of longing, but I didn't dare. Yet even as I tried to let it pass, it left its traces on me, like a fog can leave shreds of itself in the tops of bare trees.

"So you'll be at your parents' for the Christmas festivities," Isaac said.

"Yeah," I said. "I haven't even seen their new house. Did I tell you? They moved outside the city."

"Ah," said Isaac with a smile. "The great working-class heroes have opted for life in the suburbs."

"You've got it all wrong," I said. "The suburbs are for the working class. The city is too fancy for normal people and it's even spilling over into Brooklyn. My parents' apartment went co-op three years ago and they either had to buy it or get out. Talk about changing neighborhoods. To them, it was a tragedy. So they sold their apartment to a Wall Street couple and took the money they made on the deal and bought a house out of town."

"Very enterprising," Isaac said. "Has it changed them?"

"How do you mean?"

"Well, they've always been on one side of the bargain. Now capitalism's working in their favor. I was only wondering."

"A way of life ended for them, Isaac. Don't you understand? It was like the weight of all the new people with their new money opened up a hole and everything my parents once knew sunk into that hole and now's gone forever."

"Well, they made the most of it," said Isaac. "That's the important thing. Surviving."

When we got to the airport, Isaac glanced at me from the corners of his eyes and said, "There's something I wanted to bring up with you."

"Good," I said.

"Good?"

"Well, it explains why you're going to all this trouble. I could have just as easily taken a taxi."

"It's no trouble, Fielding. I'm an early riser." He was as aware as I was of my tactics and he knew I had, for a moment, deflected him. He moistened his lips and started in again. "I'm a little worried about your family."

"Granted," I said.

"I'm only talking about possible repercussions on our campaign."

"What am I supposed to do, Isaac? Get another family?"

"It's just something to be aware of, that's all. You have a sister with an unconventional marriage and a brother—well, you know, a brother with all the earmarks of a dangerous style of life."

"I think of them as assets," I said. We were falling into pattern with the other cars arriving at the airport.

"Yes. Well, this isn't about how *you* think of them."

"They humanize me, Isaac."

"I think you're quite human enough." He glanced at me to see if I was smiling.

"I don't," I said, and I wasn't smiling. "Anyhow, if the president can survive a beer-swilling brother who makes private arms deals with Libya, then I think I can survive Danny and Caroline."

"And Sarah Williams, as well," added Isaac. "We have to expect that to come up one of these days."

"Yes," I said. "One of these days."

We drove to the American Airlines terminal. Traffic was thick and rude—even on Christmas, I thought inanely, as if the mere birth of Christ could make people stop leaning on their hooters. Isaac was nervously clearing his throat, as if sentiment was congealing at the back of it. It was hot in the Lincoln but he kept his lamb's wool cap on and his white hair was damp with perspiration.

"I don't even know how to thank you, Isaac," I said.

"There's nothing to thank me for."

"Right. And Pinocchio owed nothing to Geppetto."

"Folklore," said Isaac with a shrug. He turned toward me and with a stiff, clumsy lurch of emotion, he put his arms around me and pressed the side of his face against me. "God bless you, Fielding. I know you're going to do well. Just remember: The barbarians are all around us." He put his hand in his coat and pulled out an envelope. "Will you take this? Adele asked me to give it to you."

I looked at the pale green envelope. My initials were written on it. The snow rattled against the windshield like a beaded curtain. There was a solid ring of taxis and buses and cars around the airport. Skycaps were pushing luggage around in their pipe-metal carts, cutting unstable tracks in the wet snow. There were at least a hundred travelers and any one of them could have been Sarah—Sarah in a fur coat, Sarah in disguise, Sarah transmuted by time. I promised myself not to look in anyone's face. I was in the grip of a long and powerful hallucination; I would hide from it.

"What is it?" I asked Isaac, holding up the envelope.

"From Adele," he said. "Go. Your plane takes off in ten minutes. Go."

I clapped my hand on his shoulder and made a determined face at him—lips pursed, eyes wide and steady, head slightly nodding. He smiled back, the light dancing in his eyes.

"Wonderful career," I heard him say as I climbed out of the car. A skycap near the American Airlines door looked questioningly at me and I tried to indicate with a shake of the head that I was too hip, too virile, to be helped. I turned to look at Isaac a last time. The snow was sticking to my hair, my eyelashes. The weight of the suitcase was cutting a groove in my hand.

"I'll call you," I said.

I hurried through the airport, down the carpeted ramp with its metal walls radiating cold and the disinfected odor of the plane at the end of it, and found my seat. The 727 was full. It was Christmas morning and the stewardesses were wearing reindeer pins on their uniforms.

After takeoff, I opened the envelope and saw to my great surprise that Adele had written me a poem.

To a Man at the Beginning

Life is a journey between solitudes.
We are born in aloneness and we
Die in aloneness
We dance on graves
We are solitary as stones
The wind through the window extinguishes the
Last candle
Sorrow is everywhere
Betrayal
A world of death camps and soft fur coats
Human lampshades and exquisite chocolates
A bird on the wing and then the sky darkens
And then there is light
Darkness and light.
Darkness again and
Then there is light, there is light, there is
Light.

Adele Green   December 24, 1979

In New York, I rented a Ford and drove from LaGuardia to my parents' new house in Nyack. They lived on Mayfair Street, a narrow strip of asphalt that pointed straight down at the Hudson River like the barrel of a gun. The river was filled with ice islands, moving slowly like squares in one of those hand-held puzzles. The street was icy and I held onto the steering wheel of my car with both hands, feeling not quite in control.

My parents' house was near the bottom of the street. It was made of fieldstone and yellow wood. With the prerogative of home-owners, they'd put a large Styrofoam snowman on their icy front lawn. Dad's instructions had been to pull into the driveway behind their Impala, but the town plow had left a wedge of hard dark snow in front of the driveway, grille high, and I had to park on the street. Carrying the suitcase and shopping bag uphill, I felt a senile shortness of breath. Nerves. I spit and put my left leg in front of my right, pivoting off it like a gondolier. The sky was coming closer, notching down like a canopy upon which plaster is falling.

I went up the little salt-pocked sidewalk to their house, patted the Styrofoam snowman, looked for their faces in the window. I climbed the three-step porch and rang the doorbell. In a moment, the door opened and they were standing there. I was the socket and they were the plug and now we were together and the lights were on.

"Merry Christmas, Congressman," Dad said, and opened the aluminum storm door to me. I trudged in and dropped the suitcase on the bare, highly polished floor and opened my arms to Mom, who was gliding next to me like a boat sidling into the dock. They both looked superb. Somehow younger, more fit than they had a year before. Mom's hair was cut short, pixyish; her jawline was tight, youthful. She was wearing dark red lipstick and nail polish, a turtleneck sweater and new blue jeans. Dad was in jeans, too, with a blue and green flannel shirt. He'd put on a little weight and it suited him. His hair was bright white and combed back in three gentle waves. His face was pink, healthy, scrupulously shaved.

"Look at you two," I said. "You both look fantastic."

"What'd you expect?" Dad said, furrowing his John L. Lewis eyebrows and raising his fists. "What else we got to do but make ourselves pretty?" He grabbed my valise, making, I thought, rather a show of it, hoisting it up as if it weighed a pound or two.

"Am I the first one here?" I asked.

"Danny and Caroline'll be here soon," Mom said. She was looking at the suitcase Dad was carrying: she had an eye for expensive things. "Nice bag, honey."

"A gift from Isaac," I said.

"I thought so."

We walked into the living room: low ceilings, smooth walls, a mustard-colored sofa, a new red-brick fireplace with glass doors over the hearth. The console stereo was playing, tuned to an easy listening channel.

"We'll take you for a tour later on, Congressman," Dad said.

"Place looks great," I said.

"Well, there's plenty of work to do," he said, pleased. He'd been a frustrated handyman all his life—but he'd always refused to improve property he didn't own, not wanting to be a sucker for the landlord.

"Does anyone want to come out to the backyard with me and plant some tulip and daffodil bulbs?" Mom asked.

"Mom," I said, "it's the dead of winter. There's snow and ice on the ground."

"Her bulbs came late," Dad said. "Mail-order crooks."

"If I get them in now, they can be up by spring," Mom said.

"But the ground's frozen," I said.

"You just do a little at a time," Mom said. "It'll look so pretty when they come up in spring. I really don't want to miss that."

"*Dutch* bulbs," Dad said, with displeasure.

"Dad's on a Buy American thing," Mom said.

"Half the American Beauty roses come from the Middle East," he said, as if that opened the case and shut it. He turned to me. "Did you catch that thing on the news about Jamaica? By next year, we're going to be getting thirty percent of all the plastic bottles used in this country from Jamaica."

"I didn't catch that," I said.

"It was on the evening news," he said. "John Chancellor."

"I don't have my staff yet so there's no one to brief me," I said, with a large accommodating grin.

"That's why you have to take me to Washington with you, big shot," he said, sending his luxurious eyebrows up and down, and then winking. "Since I became a senior citizen—which is what they call us people they throw onto the scrap heap—my mind's been going a mile a minute. I've been reading history, philosophy, all that stuff a workingman's supposed to leave to his *betters*." He pointed at me, as if I might be a part of that mass of jackasses and snobs who'd been underestimating him.

A little later, Dad went down into the cellar to investigate the boiler, which he thought was pumping out heat a little erratically. Mom had work in the kitchen and I followed her in. She opened the oven and peered in at the Christmas turkey, which was draped in a butter-soaked dish towel and sat on the oven rack like a Latin American dictator in a sauna.

The kitchen was blue and yellow, pleasantly old—though our table and chairs from Brooklyn looked a little edgy in their new home. Mom's old bulletin board was there, too. Every day she made a list of things to accomplish and kept it on view as a public record of her dutifulness, even when the end of the day would find only half the list checked off. Next to her list of tasks were assorted supermarket coupons, a flyer announcing a New Year's Eve Get-Together sponsored by the Rockland County Support Group, a bill from the Heigh-Ho Snow Removal Service, an ad from Willow Books for *A History of Altered Consciousness*, an article from *Family Circle* about children from racially mixed marriages, and a postcard reminding her the county Democratic Party was having its steering committee meeting January 6.

"The Democrats pretty well organized around here?" I asked.

She was just closing the oven door. Her thin, almost stern face was flushed from the heat and she dabbed at it with her open hands. "Not like the city, hon," she said. "Sort of amateurs, really. Eddie and I end up running the meetings, even though we're newcomers."

"I'm sure they appreciate it," I said.

"I don't think so. You know how people are."

How people were was her specialty. She narrowed her glance as she looked at me and reminded me of what I'd always believed about her—that she was powerfully shrewd, cleverer than most, able to X-ray artifice right down to the corrupt bones of motive, the cloudy marrow of hidden intentions. She was, after all, a cop's daughter, used to life on the edge. She had a Lutheran's sorrow over human corruption and a street kid's confidence in her own ability to get through it. I never met her father: dead of a heart attack at forty-two, buried in his sergeant's uniform. Grandma was a cloud filled with bad weather, Dutch and German, enormous, disgusted with the world, quietly apocalyptic in her rocker with a blanket over her big, square knees.

"Do you miss New York?" I asked Mom.

"Like crazy sometimes, to tell you the honest truth. Your father loves all the quaintness out here and it's good having our own place to park the car. But it's so goddamned quiet here you can hear your arteries hardening. And it really drives me nuts sometimes being surrounded by a bunch of spoiled broads never did an honest day's work in their lives. You know all those ladies on the TV commercials about to burst a blood vessel because their husband's underpants didn't come out of the wash white enough? Well, they're real, Fielding, and they're living right here. You see them in the A & P huddling around a box of detergent like it was a radio and there was a war on."

"But you're busy enough, aren't you?"

"Oh sure. What did you think I was? Complaining? I'm just getting used to things." She shrugged her small, round shoulders, her way of not so much accepting fate as sloughing it off.

She went to a cupboard and took down seven dinner plates and then put them on the counter. They were red and white with a circular design, like a close-up of Donald Duck's eyes when he is losing his self-control.

"We're kind of surprised you decided to come for Christmas," she said. "There's so little time before the election. We figured you'd be too busy."

"I have a couple of days," I said, with a slight petulance in my voice. But her maternal muscle, never awfully developed when it came to things like little slights and misunderstandings, had by now completely atrophied; she failed to rise to my bathetic bait.

"Well, I shouldn't worry. I guess if you've made it this far you can make it the rest of the way without your mommy telling you what to do."

"They say I'm a sure thing," I said, shrugging. I took a green bean out of the colander and Mom slapped my hand.

"Dad's beside himself with this whole thing," she said. "He hasn't slept in nights." She glanced toward the doorway to make certain we would not be overheard. She was always scouting out her privacy: family members, passersby, people in the next aisle at the supermarket—all potential snoops. "This whole thing has made him real proud."

"You know," I said, "if you think about it, it's kind of depressing. I mean—I thought everyone was already pleased with me."

"Now, I *knew* you'd say it. I knew you'd turn this all around so it would end up hurting your feelings. And you *know* what I'm saying here, so there's just no excuse. All I'm trying to say is how high his hopes have always been."

"Not yours?"

"Of course mine. What's wrong with you today? Golly, Fielding, I'm trying to talk about Dad and you keep trying to turn the conversation back to yourself. What's wrong? Are you feeling insecure or something?"

"As a matter of fact, I am."

"Well, that's one luxury you can't afford. You've got to learn how to take it on the chin and keep coming back for more." She raised a warning finger. "You're a shrewd cookie, you are, and you know how to win."

"I know how but I don't know why," I said.

"Don't be a wise guy," Mom said. "If you don't know why by now you better make up a reason because you don't have the time to be thinking of it now. I think Dad might be giving you some position papers, just things he's written down. I want you to be sure to thank him and let him—" A sudden intake of breath, as if cold fingers had touched her. "Well, that's just wonderful, honey. That's really funny."

I should have been disoriented but I knew this abrupt change meant that Dad was now in earshot. For all Mom's deafness in matters of phones and doorbells and movie soundtracks, she was keen as Cochise when it came to her husband's footsteps.

Dad came into the kitchen wearing a green wool parka, rubber snow boots on over his trousers, unfastened. He looked like a large sloppy child.

"What's funny?" he asked.

"My God," said Mom, with some artificial heat in her voice, "can't two people have a conversation around here without having to explain it all away to someone else?"

Dad shrugged. He couldn't have cared less. "Do you want to take a walk with me?" he asked, the heartiness in his voice bordering on aggression—he had a horror of rejection that included even the most trivial matters. He hadn't been given enough to do in his life, his spirit had been underutilized, and his sense of honor had settled into pride.

"Where we going?" I asked.

"Just down the hill," he said. "I'm going to pick up some cold cuts at Skipper's."

"As if he knows what Skipper's is," said Mom, shaking her head.

"Let me guess," I said. "It's a restaurant. Near the water. Mostly seafood, but steak and chicken, too."

"You see!" said Dad happily. He seemed genuinely impressed with my powers of deduction.

"Political power's made me a genius," I said. "OK. I'll keep you company."

"You don't need to," he said. "I'm fine going alone. I just thought you'd be interested in seeing a little of the neighborhood."

"Yeah, that's fine."

He protested for a few more moments and then we left. We had to tread slowly because of ice on the steep sidewalk. Silver horsetails of exhaust plumed out of Dad's wide nostrils. A wind was coming up off the river, with a little mournful, unstable howl in it. A thousand feet of the Hudson was visible, framed between the edges of two gray and white buildings. A flock of low-flying sea gulls winged across the frame.

"So we've got your Jewish godfather to thank for this," Dad said, as we headed down toward the river's edge.

"I suppose," I said. I still worried that my father would feel belittled over how much I'd accepted, how much I'd needed, from a stranger.

"I guess the best thing that happened to you was when that man's son went hippie," Dad said, smiling. He shook his head, a connoisseur of fate, a cartographer of advantage. My father's radicalism had never led him to the socialist parties of the thirties and forties. He believed in the distinctiveness of the working class and believed there were things a worker felt and understood that no bourgeois could ever hope to. Yet in the end, he felt the working class was a prison and while you were in it you behaved honorably, but if you were truly excellent you never stopped scheming your way out. He himself had never made it out, but now, finally, he believed he had thrown himself against the wall with enough force to allow his children to walk through it as if it was merely gauze.

"I guess that's true," I said. "Though I think it would have worked its way out one way or the other."

Dad shrugged. "Bullshit aside," he said, "you need a helping hand. He's got the connections. The cocktail parties, the old school tie, and all that jazz. Unless you're born rich or you're a first-rate thief, politics is too expensive these days. What choice did you have? How's Juliet, by the way. I thought maybe she'd be coming back with you."

"She's all right."

"Nice girl. A real . . ." He pressed his lips together in a near grimace, the way he did when he considered any of the world's delicate creatures. "A real lady, in the best way."

We walked in silence for a few moments and then, to my great surprise, I said, "Do you ever remember Sarah?"

"What do you mean? Of course. How are we supposed to forget that?"

"What do you think about when you remember her?"

"I remember whatever I remember. The funeral. All the reporters, how you couldn't get a straight story. And then the whole thing just . . . drifting away. Like it never happened in the first place."

"I miss her so much," I said. "I can't walk away from it." The air seemed not to conduct my voice. The words fell dead, as if I'd spoken them directly into my hand. Dad glanced at me from the corner of his eye and kept walking. We were near the bottom of the hill, a hundred feet from the shore of the Hudson. We were coming upon a large family-style restaurant called Skipper's. The sign showed a lobster drinking a frosty mug of beer. We walked across a parking lot; the wind off the river blew snow across the yellow diagonal lines. Above us, a faint circle of sunlight was caught in the bare branches of a tree.

"You just have to keep going, that's all," said Dad finally.

"I know that. I am."

He gestured to me and I followed him around to Skipper's side entrance. It was an aluminum storm door marked DELIVERIES ONLY. Sarah used to say the whole world wants a backstage pass; even Dad liked doing things differently from the general public.

I followed him into the dark, carpeted restaurant, into the scent of lemony rug shampoo, disinfectant, stale beer. It was an enormous place, set up to feed two hundred people. The tables and chairs were nautical. It was silent save for the distant drone of a vacuum cleaner.

"That's Skipper," Dad said. "He does everything himself. A businessman, but he knows what work is."

Just then, the vacuum cleaner shut off and the silence went through the restaurant like a change of light. Dad and I peered into the shadows, through the huge double doors decorated with Santas, past the empty salad bar with its Plexiglas protective shield to prevent diners from breathing on the chick-peas and pickled beets. Skipper was somewhere in there, but we could not see him. I listened for his footsteps and then suddenly we heard his voice.

"OK, asshole, get ready to die," he said, in a voice burbling with rage.

"Hey hey, it's us, Skip. It's me. Eddie. Eddie Pierce."

Skipper emerged from the shadows, holding a very large, very black .45. It seemed that part of being a congressman was having guns pointed at me, just as part of it seemed to include listening to Sarah's pearl ring tapping on the frozen pane of glass separating this world from the next. Skipper had a big gut and white hair, a flushed face. He looked like a loud-mouthed bigot in a bar. He smiled when he saw my father.

"Who's that with you, Eddie?"

"It's my son. The one I've been telling you about."

"Oh-ho, Eddie's boy." Skipper stepped forward, but with his gun still pointing at us. He waved it slowly back and forth like a surveillance camera in a liquor store. "On your way to the nation's capital to give 'em hell."

"Unless you shoot me first," I said.

Skipper smiled and pointed the revolver toward the floor and clicked on the safety. "They got ten cartons of chicken stock and a side of beef. The fucking apes." He shoved the gun into his belt, where it dug into an overhang of gut.

"You want to be careful with those things, Skip," my father said. I could hear by his voice that it was somehow important for my father to make Skipper like him.

"Yeah, yeah," said Skipper. "The whole fucking reason I got this thing's so's the other guy's gotta be careful. Am I right?" He winked at my father and settled his gaze on me. "Am I right, Congressman?"

"I kind of like the idea of gun control," I said.

"Hey, hey, it's licensed," Skipper said, patting the black handle.

"Well," I said, feeling a sudden buoyancy within me, like you feel when you've been driving for a long while and you begin to smell the ocean, "I think handguns have a pretty poor record here in America. When you take all the people who've been shot, you find a hell of a lot more *good* guys have been killed than bad guys."

And so we debated gun control for a few minutes. No surprises, but it felt all right, like loosening up your forehand by hitting a tennis ball against a cement backstop. I held my ground and I didn't make Skipper feel he was having to give up any of his. There rarely seemed a good reason to make someone feel wrong. Even if you could get them nodding in hang-dog abject agreement, the moment you turned your back they'd go off on a chase after the first point of view that reminded them of their own darkest impulses. If you had an audience, you might want to take someone apart, make an example out of him, but one on one you did better to try and make it seem that you were both reasonable sorts, both working the same side of the street. The sentence construction went like this: "I *agree* with you, and that's why we have to—"

Dad was nuts over what he called my "common touch." He thought it came from him and he loved to see me display it. When we'd taken the walk down to the restaurant, I'd assumed my father had brought me along out of simple paternal pride, to show some local lout the oldest son who'd made a name for himself. Yet now that we were here, I realized his motives had been more oddly mixed. He had also wanted me to see Skipper, thinking this man with a face filled with strangulating blood vessels was somehow emblematic of a constituency. Dad worried that I was continually having to fight off the temptation to make myself fancy, and might miss remembering that the reality of life in America grumbled in the bellies of men like Skipper.

"I'll tell you what I'd like," Skipper was saying. "I'd like to see this a country where people take care of themselves again and not everybody looking for a handout. I mean it," he said. "All this freeloading shit makes me sick."

"Are your parents alive?" I asked him.

"My ma is, thank God," said Skipper, with a reverence quick as a blink.

"Does she get Social Security?"

"Sure."

"I guess she's collecting your dad's now, too, right?"

Skipper shrugged.

"How about Medicare? Does your mother get that?"

"All right, all right," said Skipper, throwing up his hands as if I'd been haranguing him for hours. "It's Christmas."

"That's right, it is," I said, and I felt suddenly something going slightly out of control in me: that heat within me that had always seemed like the burn of appetite now seemed something stranger, less controllable. I had a vision of Sarah with her feet up on the radiator, wearing only brown socks and underwear, smoking a cigarette and watching the snow fall past our window.

"Quite a boy, Eddie," Skipper was saying. "If I let him talk to me any more he'll turn me into a Democrat or something."

"Worse things could happen, Skipper," my father said.

"Listen to him," Skipper said to me, jabbing his big thumb in my father's direction. "Don't he know in Skipper's you get meat and potatoes, and not white wine and brie?"

"That was pretty good, Fielding," Dad said, as soon as Skipper was out of sight. "You talked right *to* him. You didn't talk over his head but you didn't just go along, either."

"It's not like I convinced him of anything."

Dad looked at me strangely, as if he expected me to do something from which he would need to restrain me. "You look kind of tired," he said, prompting me.

"I just dropped it, you know," I said.

"What'd you drop, kid?"

"I could have spent the rest of my life trying to find out what happened to Sarah, why it happened, who did it, who let it happen. But I let it pass. It seemed like a lost cause."

"It *was* a lost cause. You don't go down with the ship. And why would you want to? You have things to do." He took my wrist and spoke to me through clenched teeth. "And the chance to do them."

Skipper appeared with a large white plate that held little circles of salami, chunks of cheese skewered by green-tasseled toothpicks, crackers crowned with little kremlins of processed cheese. The plate was covered by a tight skin of Saran Wrap and a red bow had been taped to the top of it.

"Here you go, Eddie. Hors d'oeuvres for eight."

"Looks nice, Skipper. It gets me off the hook. I told my wife I'd help with the dinner."

"My sister's got a Polack pal who made the sausage. Let me know how you like it, OK?" He handed the plate over to my father and then wiped his hands on his shirt, giving his belly a humorous grab and shake. "You like spicy sausage?" he said, looking at me.

"I didn't move to Chicago for nothing, good buddy," I said.

Skipper laughed and I could feel my father's pride beating within his own chest like a swan flapping on a lake, rising, rising, yet not quite taking off. I was, he felt, acting like my Old Self.

Holding the tray of cold cuts before him, my dad walked back up the hill and I followed him, the wind at our backs. I heard the high-pitched whine of tires spinning in ice but when I looked around, I could see no cars with drivers inside them, no tailpipes pluming exhaust. The steam from my father's nostrils flowed behind him, waving like a ghostly scarf over his shoulder. Some unknown sensation went through me, like a marble rolling down a flight of stairs. I had a premonition that somewhere—perhaps back in Chicago, at Juliet's, or at my office, or perhaps right up the street at my parents'—the phone was ringing and it was for me. I could practically hear the phone ringing. I stopped and leaned against a red Impala, trying to catch my breath, find my rhythm. I felt a degrading sort of squeezing pain in the center of my chest—degrading because, even riding the turbulence of anxiety, I knew full well that I wasn't having a heart attack.

"What's wrong?" Dad said, turning around and seeing me propped against the car.

Just resting, I said, though as I noticed he was continuing to look at me and now was coming to my side, I realized no words had come out.

Dad laid the tray of cold cuts on the Impala's icy hood. The plate of meats and cheeses began to slip toward the street and he had to pounce on it with his thick gloved hands. Holding it steady now with one hand, he reached out toward me.

"What's going on here?" he said, his voice swinging like an acrobat between the rings of love and impatience.

"I don't know," I said, in a whisper that sounded a thousand times more desperate than what I'd intended.

"Come on," said my father, "come home, come home." He touched me with a tenderness that was just barely self-conscious. He was handling me, trying to do what was best, but through the calculation shone a true devotion, as bright as a flame behind a curtain. I looked down at his hand on my arm and then covered it with my own.

"I'm sorry," I said. "I'm just . . . I don't know. I'm in terror."

He nodded, as if he knew exactly what I meant. And perhaps he did. He was still holding on to the tray of hors d'oeuvres with his left hand and now it was starting to slide again and he inched closer to the car, reestablishing his grip.

"Can I just say something right now and then I promise I'm never going to say it again?" I said.

"Come on," he said, "you don't have to ask a thing like that."

I took a deep breath. I could feel my nerves settling down, assuming their old, practiced shape, like a room that's been exploded and then comes back together, without a doily or a fork out of place. I had to speak quickly, because soon I'd be too thoroughly my familiar self to say it. "I want to be good," I said. I took a deep breath and tried to think of what I'd meant to say and then I realized I'd just said it. My father was looking at me with some confusion in his sharp brown eyes; he didn't know what he was supposed to respond to.

"You are good," he said. "Maybe too good."

I smiled. "I don't know what I am."

"There's a lot of guesswork in life," my father said. The corners of his mouth lifted in an economical smile. "It's a scary business. Just being alive."

I felt as if he had assumed the weight I'd been carrying—not forever, but just for an instant. He'd given me a moment without it, a moment to feel the outlines of my self without that pressure on it. I stepped toward him and put my arms around him, burying my face into his coat collar. He smelled of coffee and Aqua Velva. His arm went around me like a brace on my back. Our feet were shuffling, trying to keep their balance on the icy incline and as the embrace continued and we breathed together, my father finally took his hand off the tray of hors d'oeuvres and as luck would have it, the bottom had quick-frozen to the hood.

When we got back to the house, Danny's car was parked next to mine, bumper flush. This year he was driving a dark brown Jaguar, which, I noticed, he had dented severely on the driver's door. Danny liked to own extravagant things and he liked to wreck them. He had the anarchic relationship to possessions of those rock stars a decade ago who liked to check into dainty old hotel suites and peel the paper from the walls, flush the sherry glasses down the toilet. Danny had a moth-to-flame relationship with privilege and elegance, but it was a unique species of moth—one that tries to extinguish the flame that lured it. Danny always lived in apartments that were at least twice what he could afford and when he left them they looked like Beirut. He bought himself a ten-thousand-dollar cherrywood dining table and ate pizza off it without a plate. He wore custom-made silk suits and slept in them. He wanted to behave, I supposed, as if the finest money could buy was merely his birthright, that after eons of dozing in the lap of luxury, he was bored. He'd always been like that.

As a teenager, he spent fifteen bucks on a silk tie—an incredible sum, then; it seemed like a thousand dollars—and then used it as a sweatband while he played basketball in a vest-pocket park near Grand Army Plaza.

He had brought Caroline and her boys with him from the city and when Dad and I came into the living room, they were all gathered around the fireplace, where Danny was igniting the newspaper he'd twisted under the grate. Caroline and Rudy and Malik were on the sofa and Mom was just coming in from the kitchen, holding a tray of glasses.

"Fielding!" Caroline said, the first to see me come in. She sounded overly surprised, as if someone had neglected to tell her I'd be here. She sprang from the sofa and came toward me, hugging me close before I could get out of my overcoat. I could feel the cold from my body rushing into her.

"Caroline," I said, feeling her hair against my cheek. "You feel all bones."

"Take the hint," she said, smiling, grabbing the flesh beneath my chin.

"Here's my lawyer," said Danny, rising. The hearth behind him was thick with smoke and then suddenly an orange lick of flame showed in the crook of his arm as he stood there, grinning, with his hands on his hips. "My mole in D.C."

Mother put the tray of glasses down on a side table and brought her folded hands up to her breast. Her eyes seemed dazzled, almost stricken by happiness. It was the first time we'd all been in the same room in a year.

"You look fantastic," I said to Caroline. It was only the truth. There was color in her long narrow face and her hair had been pinned up in a complex, fancy braid, with sprigs of baby's breath stuck jauntily in the sides, half fetching, half satiric. She wore a necklace of what seemed to me, in my ignorance of such things, diamonds, and a delicate red and peach sweater. Caroline had virtually no money, but always managed to look striking and fashionable. She claimed it was a talent she'd picked up while living in Paris. "A Parisian girl working in a factory looks better dressed than an American doctor's wife," she'd once said and since then had pursued a kind of ragtag elegance as if it were an art form.

"God, look at those velvet pants," I said, stepping back, feeling a wave of tension, almost a desire to run outside and breathe alone for a moment. "Fantastic."

"Danny's," she said. "I starve myself to stay his size."

"Hey hey, what have we here?" I said, walking toward the sofa where Caroline's boys, Rudy and Malik, sat. Rudy had his father's dark blackness as well as his large, injured eyes. Malik looked more like a Pierce: tall, not entirely well put together, with curly brown hair and an overbite. They were each looking toward the fireplace, presumably fascinated by the fire, though it was obvious they were only hoping to appear absorbed, out of shyness. I put my hands on each of their heads and felt a twinge of love; they were my only genetic legacy in the next generation.

"Hi, Uncle Fielding," said Rudy, turning around and looking up at me. He was wearing a light blue summery suit and a clip-on bow tie. Malik was dressed more for the season, forsaking formality for function in brown corduroy pants and a pullover with reindeer.

"It's great seeing you guys," I said. I wanted to kiss them but I was afraid they were too old for that now.

"Congratulations, Uncle Fielding," said Malik. He had his father's phlegmy voice.

"Thanks, pal. How's your daddy these days?" We all felt possessive of Rudy and Malik. But I didn't like to pretend they were wholly ours. Eric McDonald was their father, and the other half of their life.

"He's fine," said Rudy. He seemed happy I'd brought it up. I walked around and sat between them on the sofa, with my arm around each. "He said to say hi to you," Rudy was saying.

"He's quite a guy," I said. I was glad my back was to Caroline for that one. She was subject to fits of anguish over Eric, as uncontrollable as a malarial fever. The rest of us had never expected the marriage to take. Too much warfare, from the very beginning. They'd met during Caroline's European travels and even her letters home throbbed with the subtext of their discord. "I tossed Eric's alto sax out of our hotel window yesterday evening. It looked so pretty when it landed in the snow, a little golden curlicue far below in the Tivoli Gardens." Yet Caroline stuck with him, sketchbook in hand, as he and his quartet made their northern European tour, and by the time they hit Paris and the chestnut trees were in bloom, Caroline wrote home on a postcard showing the Eiffel Tower in a sunset, "The reason this card is so corny is I'm pregnant." She came home, finally, when Rudy was two years old and five months after that came Malik and a year after that she and Eric split up for good.

"Look at you," said Danny, fixing me with both his pointers. He was wearing a loose-fitting charcoal jacket; he'd pushed up the sleeves and the pink shirt beneath it. The hair on his arms was wiry, golden; his tendons thick and close to the skin. "You've really done it. Congressman Pierce. Really adds class to the family."

"We always had class, Danny," Dad said. He'd just come in with Skipper's tray and placed it on a side table. "And the best kind of class."

"Yeah," said Danny. "*Working* class."

"You always wanted more than we could give you," Dad said. "But when I was coming up, being a first-rate printer was nothing to turn your nose up at."

"We didn't turn our noses up at it," Danny said. "You turned our noses up for us." He was smiling, but it seemed a pretense at good humor. There was a sharp, boyish urgency in his voice, a vein beating hotly along his temple.

"OK, you two. It's getting on my nerves already," said Mother. With a shrug, she turned to me and said, "They've been fighting all year."

"What about?" I asked. "Noses?"

"That's truer than you think," said Danny to me, with one of those weird, Las Vegas–y bang-bang gotcha gestures.

"Who knows what they fight about?" Mother was saying, casting her eyes about and finally settling on Caroline, who nodded sympathetically. Caroline had always had a spooky fondness for Mother, a love so complete and self-effacing that it could only be unrequited. As a child, she followed Mother around the house, studying her, and Mother's nature had enough steel in it to clang with despair over her daughter's adoring her so. It seemed like weakness, madness. Mom was repelled by anything easy and it was too easy for her to please Caroline. To make it seem more interesting, she began to interpret Caroline's unstinting praise, to search out the secret aggression, the snottiness beneath it, and with that breach of faith their relationship turned tragic. Caroline began expressing her love with a kind of daredevil self-hatred. "Love ya, Mommy," she'd called, slamming out of the house to some adolescent rendezvous. She was part of a crowd of wild girls who went with their boyfriends to a creepy, end-of-the-world-looking place near the Brooklyn Bridge, where in all kinds of weather they swigged Southern Comfort and fucked in the back-seats of Buick Skylarks, Plymouth Furys, Chrysler LeBarons. You could see the Watchtower clock from where they parked, looming over the stark girders of the bridge, counting off the seconds we sinners squander in our spiritual morass. I'm remembering now the milky dawn and Caroline sneaking into the house, like a drunk in the Sunday funnies, with her shoes in her hand, and our mom sitting in the yellow chintz chair, a Pall Mall glowing in her hand, a cup of tea gone tepid near her elbow. I heard the screams from my alcove upstairs and came running down in my Fruit of the Looms. "They laugh at you when they've done with you, you know that, don't you," Mom was hissing and Caroline sat on the floor before her, her head down, her arms wrapped around her knees, as if waiting to be beaten.

Dad was supervising the opening of the presents. He stood at the tree and picked up the gift-wrapped boxes one at a time and called out the name of the recipient. "Caroline, this is for you, from Santa and Danny," he said, giving the box an avid shake next to his ear. (Danny's presents as usual put the rest of us to shame—they were invariably expensive and perceptive. Caroline received an antique Cartier watch from him, I got a French leather briefcase with my initials burned in, Mother got an autographed picture of Franklin D. Roosevelt framed with a letter FDR sent to Mayor Walker in 1930, and Father got a huge history of the

C.I.O. and a specially made pair of glasses for reading in bed.) The boys made out like bandits, though the gifts seemed to embarrass them as much as please them. I knew their father had them in a Muslim school uptown and I supposed they were learning things that made these rituals seem rather foolish. Watching Rudy gently peeling the candy-striped paper off the binoculars I'd brought for him and then seeing the tender but withheld smile he gave to me, I had a quick sinking feeling that in a few years I would hardly know this boy at all. Malik, younger, accommodating by nature, seemed closer to us, but when he came to kiss me after opening my present I made the mistake of holding him too closely and with his bony little chest pressed into me I could feel his spirit leaping back like a toreador evading the horns of a bull.

The presents were open and the living room was a wasteland of torn colored papers. Danny built the fire up to a chimney-charring roar and our father filled his cup with the killer punch Mother had brewed. (I was starting to resent my club soda.) Dad stood in front of the fireplace holding the cup before him. With his large noble head, the rich white hair, his broad shoulders, his ardent eyes, it looked as if he were about to erupt into song. "I want to make the toast," he said. "The first of many." The fire danced behind him and suddenly the heat made him turn around. "It's burning my ass," he said.

We all laughed—but especially Caroline. She had always found our parents strictly puritanical and any deviation from that Gothic picture of them she carried in the most injured part of her consciousness made her giddy.

"And I'm going to make one after that," our mother said.

"Everything in its time and place, Mary," Dad said, with a bow. "To Christmas," he said, in a boom. "To a season of family happiness . . . and sharing . . . and peace." His voice suddenly stopped, as if blocked by an avalanche of emotion. His face darkened, he looked away. There were luxuries of feeling he would never have allowed himself ten years ago, which now he felt were his entitlement, like a pension. "To a new year coming, the first year of the decade. A year which I hope will bring us together many times in happiness." He stopped again and took a deep breath, forcing something down in himself.

"Get a grip on yourself, Pop," Danny said, in a perfectly adolescent way: taunting and embarrassed.

Dad nodded at Danny, acknowledging, even a little grateful for having been brought up short. "I want to make a toast to the kids, then," he said. "To Rudy and Malik. The most . . ." He took another deep breath and now extended his lower lip and shook his head—an old, affectionate gesture, meant somehow to symbolize the fragility of everything that was good and decent in the world. "The most terrific couple of grandsons anyone could ever hope for. And I want to make a toast to my kids, too. OK? To my firstborn, Caroline, who always could wrap me around her little finger—"

"That's news to *me*," said Caroline, in a voice that wanted to be more humorous than it was.

"And who has made us so proud with her accomplishments as a mother and in the world of art. And to our second, Fielding, on his way to the capital, helping to bring a new day to this country, new directions. Like an arrow that's always known its mark or a hammer in the hands of a man who knows how to use it, Fielding has always known where his life was going and though we're proud, none of us is surprised."

He nodded toward me and I grinned back at him, though a part of me felt raw, cheated. I had always been the easiest child, the one to see the world through their eyes, the one who could be counted on to cause the least trouble, and I had been waiting all my life for a moment I realized now would never come—the time it would be my turn to be seen as I truly was, when it would be my turn to make them gasp and worry and radically revise all of the clear, convenient ideas they held about me.

"And to Danny," he was saying. "Our youngest."

"And baddest," said Danny, raising a finger.

"True, true," said Father with a smile.

"And vainest and most preening," said Caroline.

"And most decadent," I added.

"OK, OK, Jesus," said Danny.

"Wait wait wait," said Father, holding his hand up. He wanted to get through this. "His achievements are many. For a son of the working class to live like a prince . . ."

"Christ," said Danny. "Here it comes."

I glanced over toward Rudy and Malik. They were sitting with their hands folded on their laps, their lips pursed. Caroline stood behind them, a hand on the shoulder of each.

"And to have his own business," Father was saying. "With people who look to him for their livelihood. All my children are hard workers, who know the dignity of labor, and the pride of accomplishment and since . . ." He paused and brought the cup closer to his lips, signaling us all that soon we would drink. "Since none of you little snotnoses would be here on earth if it wasn't for me, I think I got the goddamned right to feel pretty good myself."

"OK, OK," said Caroline. "Mommy has to make a toast now."

"I think I'll hold my tongue," said Mom.

"Sounds like fun," Danny said.

Mom looked at Danny and kissed the knuckle of her thumb. We never quite knew the origin or the meaning of that gesture. It seemed to have come from her old neighborhood, but whenever we asked her what it meant she said, "Whatever you want it to, kiddo." She went to her chair and sat down, legs crossed, and took a deep drink from her cup of punch—eggnog, ginger ale, dark rum, Spanish brandy, Old Bushmill's.

And then, watching her drink, and looking around the room at my father, brother, and sister, each with a cup of punch, and listening to the steady, gloomy beating of my heart, as even and desperate as human time, pulling me in its tidal rhythms toward the end of my one life, I felt a sudden desire go through my resolve like a knife slashing through an oil painting: I would have a drink, too.

"Oh, come on, Mommy," Caroline was saying.

"You're dripping on the wall-to-wall carpet, Caroline," Mom said, pointing to Caroline's cup.

I crept across the room and as unobtrusively as possible I served myself a half cup of punch. I counted to myself: one, two, three. And then I took a drink: my heart began to race like a blind bull let out of its dark stall.

"Well, if you won't, then I will," said Caroline, draining her cup and then slapping it down on the sideboard. She gave Dad a seemingly playful little shove and took his spot in front of the hearth. The bark on the logs was popping and hissing; threads of dark gray smoke sparked with orange rose up toward the chimney.

"To Mommy and Daddy, on their first Christmas in the new house," she said, her voice a little blurry with shyness. "To Danny for getting away with it *sans* indictments, to Fielding for being like a goddamned train that always runs on time, and for poor little me for surviving another year. And most of all to Rudy and Malik—*bon voyage!*"

"Bon voyage?" said Dad. "Where they going?"

"With Eric. He's going on tour in Africa—Nairobi, Monrovia, Tunis. And he's taking the kids." If Caroline was presenting this with false equanimity, she was doing a creditable job of it. Her smile was large, firm, her shoulders relaxed. The lids of her large eyes were a sleepless pink—but that wasn't unusual: she had always turned in her bed as if on a spit over the fires of hell.

"That's great, kids," I said.

"Monrovia?" said Danny, shaking his head.

"Liberia," said Caroline.

"I know," he said. "But who'd go there?"

"Speak not if you know not," said Caroline.

"How long is this trip?" asked Dad.

"What about school?" added Mom.

"We got permission," said Rudy. "Our teachers *want* us to go."

"Yeah, that way they won't have to put up with you," said Danny.

The boys didn't seem to have a terrific sense of humor about themselves—but then, neither had we. It's difficult to bear in mind the incandescent sincerity of childhood, the rapturous religion of self.

"You'll probably end up learning more in two weeks than you will a whole year in a classroom," said Dad, adjusting to the shift with fabulous dexterity.

"It's two months," said Caroline. "The Academy will give them full academic credit for the trip."

The Academy was the Malcolm X Academy, on 137th Street and Riverside Drive, a Muslim school where, Caroline feared, Rudy and Malik were being taught to be unable one day to look at their own mother with love, but to see only her whiteness and the cruelty it represented.

"So it's Merry Christmas and bon voyage," she said. "And a time for all the rest of you to promise to look after me because—" She stopped, and gave a portion of herself over to the suddenly amassed emotions. "Because I'm going to be lonely. No. Not lonely. But missing them. So everyone has to make a fuss over me and make sure I'm OK. OK?"

"We might have done that anyhow," Mom admonished. "You didn't have to put it in words."

"Your neighborhood's coming back to life, Car," Danny said. "After-hours clubs, weird places. It's a scene now."

"My neighborhood's a slum," Caroline said. "And I'm too old for that shit."

I happened to look at Dad. He was sitting in his chair, looking down at his feet. He feared one day Caroline would lose the boys, that Eric, the pressures of history, and the steady, persuasive indoctrination of the Muslims would finally make the relationships impossible and she would be a mother in only some half-assed, formal sense and he would cease to be a grandfather at all.

"I'll look after you, Caroline," I said. "If you look after me."

"You going to arrange it so I get a national endowment grant?" she asked.

"Why don't you come back to Chicago with me and help me get set up? I can make you a part of my staff. Pay you."

"Oh no you don't," shouted Dad, truly alarmed. "Are you crazy?"

"What are you talking about?" I said.

"Eddie's right," Mom said. "That's nepotism and many a promising politician's taken a fall over just that sort of thing."

"It's very common to have relatives on staff," I said. "Jack had Bobby and Bobby had Ted." I glanced over at Caroline. She'd drawn herself up and stared at our parents, as if they were betraying her.

"I don't care how *common* it is," said Dad. "It's not right."

"I don't think I could do it no matter what," said Caroline. "All my stuff's here and I'm working three jobs, you know."

"Expendable," said Danny. He was crouched by the cast-iron ring in which a dozen or so fireplace logs were stashed.

"I work in a friend's bakery, I still teach that class at the adult education extension, and I'm back at that exercise joint, leading an aerobics class."

"Come to Chicago with me," I said. "Just for a couple of weeks. There're no classes now and take a vacation from the other two jobs. Stay with me and Juliet."

"What'll I do?"

"You can help me run the campaign. Think with me," I said, going to her side, putting my arm around her. "We can make policy decisions."

"This isn't one of your little games, Fielding," said Dad, desperate with an anger he didn't know how to pursue.

"If it looks like it'll be a problem," I said, "then I won't put her on salary. I'll pay her some other way."

"No, no," said Mom. "That'd be worse. Don't be sneaky."

"I won't be sneaky, Mom. It's going to be fine."

"You think that's something you might like?" Mom asked Caroline.

"Two weeks?" said Caroline. "It might do me good to get away for a while. What do you think, kids? You think your mom ought to help Uncle Fielding get elected?"

"What would you do?" asked Rudy.

"I don't know," she said. "Lick envelopes. Whatever."

"Will you be back when we come back?" asked Malik.

"If I go. I have to think about it. But I'd be back home way before you guys."

"Oh good," I said, squeezing her to me. "You're going to come with me. I know you are. God, I feel better for this."

"Terrific," said Danny, in a low voice, rising up from his crouch with a log of white birch in his arms. "Leave me here to wallow in my own messes." I couldn't see his face to know if he was smiling. He tossed the log into the fire and when it hit the andirons it sent up a burst of sparks.

Danny found his cup and raised it before us. "All right. It's my toast. To the end of the seventies and good goddamned riddance. We'll wipe the slate clean. It'll be like going into Chapter Eleven. All old debts canceled! Tomorrow is ours!" He brought his heels together with a Prussian click and brought his cup to his lips.

We all drank with him and as I took another swallow of the punch I had a vision of four years' sobriety plucked out of me like a splinter. I had never been, at least in my own mind, a falling-down drunk. I had never actually called myself an alcoholic. I was very tender and discreet when it came to describing my own problems and I never went further than calling myself a Problem Drinker—and I had even worked the affliction into a few passable jokes. Of course I worry about my drinking, I said to Sarah. I worry if there's enough bourbon, enough ice. But I'd also known that it had a power beyond my power to control it and that one day it would lay me low. And so I quit before it became a true emergency and I quit cold, with very little prelude and no backsliding. I took another small sip and felt my blood turn, like a crowd of faces at the crack of the bat.

"I have no idea what I'm drinking to," Caroline was saying. "What does that toast mean, Danny?"

"I'm sure if we knew we wouldn't be able to enjoy our drinks," said Mom.

"Wait a second," I said, raising my cup, "let me make a toast." If any of them suspected there was something darker than club soda in my cup, they gave no indication. Their eyes were mild, attentive. It was time to hear from Kid Reasonable.

"To the dead," I said. "The dead." I was home and when you were home you didn't have to think about what you said before saying it. Still, I was flying blind on this one. I raised my eyes toward the ceiling. "To Bobby Kennedy. And . . . and Jack. And Malcolm X and Martin Luther King." The ceiling was freshly painted and I could see the little bumps in the yellow latex, like chicken skin. "And Otis Redding, Sam Cooke. James Agee and Humphrey Bogart, and Edward R. Murrow—"

"Fielding," I heard my father say.

"And to Sarah Williams," I said, my voice as blurred and diffuse as a light in the fog. "May she rest in peace."

The lights around the bridges were barely visible through the thick, slow, cottony snowfall. Christmas night in Danny's Jag and Danny at the wheel—the most sober of the Pierces: his capacity was tragic. I sat next to him, feeling the alternating flashes of sweet drunkenness and total terror. Three drinks and I was blotto, but cutting through the wet sawdust of my mini-stupor was the fear that I had just set myself off on a round of drinking that would somehow end with me in a rented room, drying my underwear on the radiator . . . I leaned back in and distracted myself by imagining an auto wreck. All of those cars we were passing, and the cars that passed us: everyone on the road had been drinking all day and half the night and I was trying to gauge the level of drunkenness and Christmas night despair and plain old everyday Thanatos in all the drivers that accompanied us in our slow, slippery trek into the city. Caroline was in the backseat, sitting between Rudy and Malik, who were both asleep, collapsed against her. Danny was reaching across me, opening the glove compartment, clawing through the jumble of cassettes.

"Steely Dan?" he asked.

"Ich," said Caroline. "Too cold." She was speaking in a monotone, striking a note that experience had taught her would not awaken the children.

"Mom and Dad look so fucking good, it's unbelievable," I said.

"Pop's getting a gut, though," said Danny. "Didn't you see?"

"I think it looks good on him."

"You would. How about Lou Reed?"

"Lou Reed's all right," said Caroline. "Just make sure you don't play the one with the racist lyrics. Mom looks tired, doesn't she? She waits on him hand and foot."

"Lou Reed thinks it's so fucking hip to be a junkie," I said.

"It is hip," said Danny, putting in the Lou Reed tape. "But Lou Reed hates scag."

"He used to sing that heroin song," I said. "The one where he says it's his wife, it's his life."

"That was a long time ago, Fielding. Look, if you're going to be a great congressman, you'd better get a little more current with pop song lyrics. Even Jimmy Carter can quote Bob Dylan. You gotta jump on it, stay on it, be on it."

We drove Caroline to her apartment on First Avenue and 10th Street. Christmas seemed to have petered out ten or twenty blocks to the north of her. By the time we were pulling in front of her building, with its fire escape covered with the new white snow and a blank look of secrecy and desolation in its windows, the Christmas lights were a thing of the past. Next to her tenement, surrounded by cyclone fencing, was a vacant lot littered with the upturned bricks of the building that had once stood there. It looked like a desecrated cemetery viewed from above. I noticed three human forms receding deeper into the darkness of that empty place. The headlights from the Jaguar hollowed out two tunnels in the black snowy air.

I walked Caroline and the boys up to their apartment on the second floor. The halls looked soft, as if you could pull chunks out with your fingers. The light came down from buzzing fluorescent circles. We had to lug all the presents up, so progress was slow. It was nearly eleven at night and the boys were stumbling tired.

"Did you really mean all that about me coming to Chicago to help you for a while?" Caroline asked, as she opened her door. Three locks.

"Of course I did. And as far as I'm concerned you've already promised, so you can't back out."

"Check check double-check American eagle?" she asked.

"Exactly." It was the ceremonial phrase by which we'd sealed bargains when we lived in that distant country—childhood.

"Call me tomorrow, then," she said. "When you guys wake up. We'll do something."

"OK." I kissed her on the cheek. She kissed me back and opened the door. The door opened directly into the kitchen. A table lamp was on, with a flowered shawl draped over the shade. A radio was playing. Signs of life to ward off the desperate. I put my arm tentatively around Malik and then around Rudy, trying to embrace them in a way that seemed somehow casual, athletic, using that code masculine shame has created for affection. And to my great surprise they suddenly clung to me, holding me tightly with their strong little hands. They clung to me, and as I held them close I looked up at Caroline with tears in my eyes.

Danny was resting behind the wheel when I got back to the car. I stepped into the fragrant warmth. He had the radio on; the news was just ending and it was time for the weather. Even on radio, the weathermen were high with a sense of calamity.

"All this shit about snow alerts and winter emergencies," I said. "It's really a way of preparing us for a nuclear—"

"I want you to come someplace with me," Danny cut in. "Are you too tired?"

I said no. If I'd said I was too tired, Danny would unquestionably have offered a drug to perk me up.

"Don't you even want to know where we're going?" he asked me. We turned north on First Avenue. All the stores were dark except for one fruit stand. A fat man in an apron was clearing the snow off a display of oranges with a broom; a city bus was stopped near the fruit seller and the bus driver was swaying from foot to foot and slapping his arms to keep warm, waiting for his oranges.

"All right," I said. "Where are we going?"

"To an Oriental massage parlor, where else?" He accelerated through a yellow traffic light; before us, dimly perceived through the thick snowy night, an infinity of yellow lights stretched out. Danny started to laugh. He'd had, since childhood, a strained, rather sneaky laugh, the laugh of a kid in trouble, and luxury and success had done little to improve it: it was still the laugh of a boy being dragged down the hall by his arm. "Do you remember that line in *Notorious* when Claude Rains comes into his Nazi mom's room and says, 'Mother, I think I've married an American agent'? Well, now I can say, Brother, I think I'm in love with a Korean whore." And with this out of the way, he began to laugh wildly. It was as if he'd conned me, drawn me into a situation far beyond what I'd bargained for, what I could control. It was one of those laughs that sound saved up and thus overripe. Showing his worst side was Danny's dark, simple version of personal honesty: he liked to leave the little packets his cocaine came in crumpled on the desk; he never hid a rejection or a setback; he recounted his shady business deals, his balletic avoidances of creditors, his tax shelter schemes with greedy lawyers representing greedy doctors, as if all of these comprised something admirable, something amusing—a dashing character, a malfeasance that shared an un-expected border with virtue.

"I don't think I want to go to an Oriental massage parlor, Danny," I said.

"For me, Fielding. For me."

"Are you serious? Are you really involved with someone who works in one of those?"

"Be careful, Fielding. This is important to me."

We turned west on 14th Street. It was Christmas again. There were the big fat old-fashioned bulbs, green and red, wrapped like creeping vines around the frozen poles of the street lamps. A city plow was clearing the street. We drove past the Academy of Music, once the opera house in the days of Edith Wharton, now a great musty sagging place whose marquee read GRATEFUL DEAD—CANCELED.

We drove to Sixth Avenue and took an illegal turn north, through the flower district. Palms and bamboo plants and birds of paradise pressed against the steamy windows, bathed in pink light.

"Why are we going there, Danny?"

"I want you to meet her," he said, in his evasive voice. He'd had to develop the skill of making people uncomfortable asking too many direct questions. He glanced at me from the corner of his eyes. The car swerved as the light turned green. "You've got to help us, Fielding," he said. "I'm begging you."

"You haven't asked for anything. I haven't said no. And you're begging already?"

"Yes. I'm begging you."

"Why do we have to go there?"

He looked at me with false, tactical surprise, as if he were seeing me clearly for the first time, as if I were revealing something he'd never guessed about me heretofore. "You're afraid to go there? Is that it? Afraid to fuck up your reputation?"

"I don't have a reputation."

"Don't jerk me around, Fielding. You are so goddamned obsessed with the whole boring deadass master plan that's run your whole life, you won't go with your own brother to meet his girl friend."

"That's a funny way of looking at it," I said. "It's not as if—"

"I am not being funny," Danny said, pounding his fist against the steering wheel.

"OK, OK," I said, patting his shoulder. His temper unnerved me and always had; I'd developed a way of treating it as if I took it lightly.

"Jesus, Fielding. Don't you realize how far out of my mind I must be to be thinking like this. This girl—her name's Kim Hahn. She speaks terrible English. She's a complete square. She comes from Seoul. These Korean shitheads brought her over, promised her a job, and then stuck her into this fucking whorehouse."

"Which you just happen to patronize—from time to time."

"One of our authors brought me there. Ben Lacoste, who did this book called *Oriental Love Techniques*. Twenty-five bucks, they wash you head to toe, walk on your back, do some jiveball shiatsu massage that's really pretty painful and annoying, and then for another fifty they'll fuck you. Tiny little hard beds. All the girls have portable tape players they listen to Korean music on. The place is run by this tiny old woman who never talks. Sits there behind a desk wearing pedal pushers and a fake Madame Chiang Kai-shek black silk shirt. But the place is really run by Korean gangsters and *those* guys—this is something you should know about, Congressman—those guys are plugged into these fanatical Korean right-wing militarists and the CIA and who the fuck knows what else. These are the kind of guys who would kill someone like Sarah for five hundred dollars and a box of rifles. It's a very scary scene and Kim wants to get out, but she can't. Even if they don't cut up her face, they'll have her sent back to Korea—she's here illegally. They smuggle the girls in. None of them are legal. And if she's back in Korea she's in disgrace because everyone knows what these girls get brought over here to do. And if she goes back then I'll never see her again and I'm not ready for that, not yet anyhow. I really like this girl."

"You're in love with her?"

"No, I'm not in love with her," he said, as if he were speaking to some hybrid of a guidance counselor and a duck. "I like her. There's something special—look, I don't need to explain. I like her. She deserves better. She's a fabulous lover, by the way, though I suppose under the circumstances I shouldn't be saying that."

"What circumstances?"

"You sitting there judging me and feeling so pissed off that I'm dragging you into my mess. And what if we walk into this place and it's raided and next day your career's over. Right?"

"What is it you want me to do, Danny?"

"You've got power, Fielding. And I'm your brother." He smiled—a smile that had once been so magnetic, so full of quick spirits and high feeling but which now, having been used so often to ward off disaster, looked a little cunning. "We're two of a kind," he said. "We're both in way over our heads. And one day it'll all catch up to us. We'll run out of luck and we'll be living worse than Caroline without a nickel to our names. But now we're out there together and we should help each other. OK?"

"I don't know what I'm saying OK to."

"You can be Kim's influential friend. You can use your connections and influence and get her a green card, or something that'll let her stay here without having to deal with those fucking gangsters."

"I wish it was that easy."

"Now you sound like a politician."

"I am a politician, Danny."

Danny flexed and unflexed his long blunt fingers on the steering wheel.

"Well, that wasn't how it was supposed to be. You were the one who wanted to make the world better. I always thought the idea was getting into politics so you could have power and end wars and feed people and get the snobs out of our way. But now you're acting like just being in politics and covering your ass is the most important thing and all the other stuff comes second."

"Well, I sure as hell am not running for office so I can get some woman in a massage parlor a green card," I said. I took a deep breath.

"It's not just *some woman*," Danny said. When the streetlights came into the car they turned his hair bone white.

"How long have you known her?" I asked.

"Six, seven weeks."

"A massage parlor. It's so . . . ridiculous. You're taking too many drugs. It's poly-drug abuse."

"Remember what Sarah used to say? We'd be walking through Union Square and we'd see some junkie on a bench with his shoes slit open and flies around his face and Sarah would say, 'How do you know that's not Jesus? How do you know?' That's what Sarah used to say and you loved her. Or are you denying that now?"

"So is this what it is?" I asked. "The woman in the massage parlor is Jesus?"

Danny turned the car west on 30th Street. The plows hadn't been on this street yet; we were driving through three inches of new snow. Snow flew past the streetlights, millions of dotted lines. "She's just a nice person, Fielding. And she makes me feel good. Nothing to do with her professional services. There's something nice about her."

We pulled in front of an old loft building, with a hand-painted address stuck up in the high window above the swinging metal doors. On the second floor, parallel to the street lamp, were the windows for an outfit called Lopez and Portillo Fashion Outlet. The rest of the windows in the building were in darkness. A line of red light bulbs was visible through the busy blackness of the winter night, marking the shaftway along the side of the building. The Jaguar's windshield wipers waved back and forth, patiently clearing off the snow as it fell.

"Here we are," said Danny.

I don't know if what I felt was caution or cowardice, but it was awfully difficult following Danny into that darkened building. There was a row of doorbells outside the door. Danny lit his gold lighter and pressed the button marked 9—the one with the Oriental characters next to it. A woman's voice came out of the intercom speaker. "Hello Merry Christmas," she said. "What you want?"

"I saw your ad," said Danny.

A buzzer went off disengaging the lock and we pushed our way into the small, scuffed, and dirty lobby, which was lit by one nervously buzzing fluorescent bar. There was the smell of raw leather in the air. I followed Danny to the elevator. He pushed the call button and we heard a clatter of chains, as if we'd just roused a ghost. I was thinking firetrap, murderer's lair, immigration raid, public disgrace, laying each fantasy of disaster before me like a Tarot card. We entered the bleak industrial elevator, with the missing panels in the ceiling and a view upward of pulleys and cold greasy darkness, and I added another possible disaster —plunging elevator. The elevator started with a great optimistic jolt but then rose slowly, slowly.

"They're open on Christmas night?" I asked.

"Yes," said Danny. "Shocking, isn't it?" He put his arm around me and then, masking the affection, pretended to put me into a hammerlock. I saw us in the small round mirror in the upper corner: two johns in their overcoats with snowflakes in their hair.

The elevator door was locked on the ninth floor. Peering in at us through the small chicken-wired window was a young Korean woman with violet eye makeup and black curly hair. She saw Danny and brightened. The door was unlatched and she opened it for us. She stepped back; she was wearing a little terry cloth skirt, fashioned like an ice-skating outfit. She had pudgy little toes, the nails painted violet; she was wearing rubber flip-flops.

"Hello, how are you," she said in a lilt that sounded tired and sarcastic, as if she was only imitating the empty things people said to one another.

She led us into a shag-carpeted room where, on black modular furniture, four other Korean women sat, one dressed in a black leotard, another in red sparkly hooker shorts, the third in a kimono (she was squinting through the smoke of a Salem as she smoothed out a rough spot on her heel with an emery board), and the fourth woman in a bikini and leg warmers.

There was a smell of garlic and oil in the air, and the smell of bleach. The windows were boarded up and covered in tattered red velvet draperies. We were standing in front of a desk. There was a large wooden rose pumping out the manufacturer's version of rose scent. A black telephone. A green tin money box. Sitting behind the desk was the woman whom Danny had described to me: the old woman in the Madame Chiang Kai-shek blouse. She was sipping tea from a thick white cup that looked as if it had been swiped from a cafeteria. Her little amber face looked sad, untrustworthy; she seemed to emit a kind of corruption that verged on idiocy.

"You both?" she asked. She had a high, sharp, unstable voice.

"Yeah," said Danny.

"Fifty," she said, opening the money box.

Danny dropped a fifty-dollar bill on the desk.

"Wait a minute," I said. "This isn't what we're here for."

Madame Chiang cocked her head and looked at me. She could tell from my voice something was wrong and she smiled in anticipation.

"Leave this to me," Danny said. "You worried about the bread?"

"Are you paying for me to get a massage?" I felt perfectly stupid. The small-town cousin dragged by his short hairs into the vortex of a wicked good time. The woman in the black leotard and the woman in the short shorts stood up and came toward us.

Danny put his hand up to stop them. "No," he said, to Madame Chiang. "I want Kim."

"Kim? Kim? Who Kim?" she said, shaking her head. She locked his Grant into the box.

"Kim," said Danny loudly. Whorehouses depend on the shame and timidity of their clients for their smooth running, but Danny seemed perfectly at ease and filled with the moral correctness of his own desires. "You know. Kim."

"No Kim. Not tonight." She gestured to the two women, who'd stopped when Danny's voice rose.

Beyond the black modular sofas was an archway sporting a beaded curtain, beyond which the business of the place transpired. And now through the beaded curtain came a young, square-shouldered Korean woman dressed in sheer pantyhose and an oversized man's turquoise shirt, with a young Chinese fellow dressed in a restaurant worker's white fatigues on her arm. His long hair was wet and combed straight back. Hers was shiny, rather short, pulled into a small ponytail held by a red rubber band.

"Kim!" said Danny, with a laugh of relief.

"Oh, *Kim*, *Kim*," said Madame Chiang, as if the problem all along had been in Danny's pronunciation.

Danny waited for Kim to walk the Chinese cook to the elevator and when she turned around she came to him and slipped her arm around his waist. She had little gold star studs in her earlobes; a scent of baby oil came off her. She embraced him simply, quickly, just a touch of her head against his shoulder. I must have been staring, I must have been forgetting where I was, because when the woman in the leotard took my hand to lead me toward the back of the place I was startled.

"Shower and sauna?" she said.

"No, no," I said, more in confusion than morality.

"Must shower first, then massage-y," she said. She had a simple round face, hard dark eyes, a mole at the corner of her mouth. Suddenly, I had a fantastic idea: I'd go back to whichever little room she was attempting to lead me, take off my clothes, and make love to her. Why didn't I think of that before?

Danny was at the desk, talking to the old woman. She was shaking her head. Kim stood behind him, looking at the carpet. Another woman appeared through the beaded curtain, this time with an Anglo in tow, an Isaac Greenish sort of john with a sprig of holly pinned to his suit and an odor of excellent Scotch pouring off him.

"You want drink?" my date asked me, trying to get me a little more involved.

"OK," I said.

"No," said Danny, turning toward me. "Stop. We're leaving." He went back to his negotiations with the crone. He had a hundred dollars on the table and now a hundred more. She accepted them with a shrug, locked them in her box, and then, perhaps as a way of preserving her dignity, walked away and joined the others watching TV.

"We're going to my house," Danny announced.

"You don't buy me," said the woman whom fate or perhaps a hand signal had assigned to me. She looked extremely angry and rather frightened, too. "I stay right here." She called to the old woman and the two of them began arguing in Korean. The silk-clad proprietress was waving her hands over her head, as if the situation was well beyond her control.

"Let's go, Fielding," Danny said commandingly. Kim went back through the beaded curtain and a few moments later reappeared, dressed in blue jeans, boots, a purple leather jacket with a red fur collar. The woman in leotards sat down on the sofa again; none of the other women were looking in our direction. One of them got up and switched the channel on the TV set. The "Tonight Show" was on. Johnny Carson and a couple of his sidekicks were making elaborate bows toward each other, as if they belonged to one of those boozy small-town lodges. And now Danny, Kim, and I were heading for the elevator. It was waiting for us. As we got in, the old woman shouted something to Kim and Kim answered without looking back.

"I have to be back in two hour," she said, as the elevator doors slid shut.

"We'll talk about it," said Danny, jamming his large thumb, with its chewed-off cuticle and weirdly phallic proportions, against the button marked G. The elevator shuddered and began to inch down.

"This is my brother, Kim. This is Fielding."

She gave me her small, light hand and I shook it. I felt enormous, ridiculous next to her.

"He's going to help you," Danny said.

"Hello," she said. "Sorry my English," she added, shrugging.

"That's all right, that's all right," said Danny, rapid fire. His nerves were starting to churn inside my stomach. I could feel the energy going through him, but I had no idea what he was thinking. It was dazzling, confusing, ultimately unsettling, like a passionate quarrel next door heard through the walls, without one word distinguishable. His leg was shaking, one of his first nervous habits, the cornerstone upon which a mansion of nervous habits had been built: the nail-biting, the snuffling, the head tossing, the throat clearing. The slowness of the elevator was torture for him.

We could see the wall of the shaft through the window and we watched it tick by, brick by brick. "Come on, come on," he muttered beneath his breath. And then, suddenly, I realized what his hurry was. He was wondering if a call had been made and if we in fact weren't going to be met in the lobby. When we finally reached the ground floor and the door opened, Danny shot out of the elevator with that controlled hysteria I'd been taught in the Coast Guard, when we practiced taking our posts in case of attack. The lobby was empty. Now Danny just wanted to get to his car, get the snow off the windshield, get the motor running. "Come on, let's go," he called over his shoulder.

"My purse," said Kim, suddenly pressing herself against the back wall of the elevator. "My purse upstairs."

"It'll be there when you get back," I said. "OK? Come on." I took her by the arm. She'd seemed frail to the point of lifeless when we'd shaken hands, but now she yanked away from me with the ferociousness of a whip.

"My purse. I need my purse."

"You'll just have to forget it," I said, taking hold of her again. I knew if I let her go, she'd only go back to the ninth floor, and we'd be locked out, and that would be it.

By now, Danny was practically out the door. He turned around to urge us on and saw I was holding onto Kim and that she was struggling to get away from me.

"Let me go," she said, fear making her voice sound electronic.

"Keep hold of her, Fielding," Danny shouted. He ran back toward us as I pulled Kim out of the elevator. The doors slid shut, and as the car rose, the little chicken-wire window went dark.

"Good," said Danny. "Thank God." And then to Kim: "You want to go back up there?"

She shrugged, looked away.

"Is that what you want? Don't you understand? I'm trying to help you."

"I'm scared," she said, taking a deep breath, drawing herself up.

Danny looked at her and then took a step forward. He put his arms around Kim and she passively let him embrace her.

"Come on, Kim. We're not going to hurt you. We're going to work something out. You're going to be OK."

"I'm scared," she said again.

"Come on," said Danny. "Let's get out of here."

We got into his car and pulled away. He didn't take the time to clear the snow off the windshield and for a few moments we were driving blind: all we could see was the flashing snow on the windshield, ignited by each passing streetlight.

We drove north on Tenth Avenue. No one spoke. Finally Kim turned on the radio, and after playing with the dial for a while, she found a station playing Oriental music.

"I've got one quick stop," Danny said. We were on West End Avenue now. He pulled the car in front of an immense 1920s apartment house, with columns and carved stone figures at the entrance. There was a long shabby awning from the curb to the front door. Through the glass, I could see the doorman, sitting on a folding chair near an electric heater, reading the newspaper.

"What are we doing here?" I asked.

"I just have to make a stop," he said. And before I could object, he slid out of the car and hustled into the building. I watched him talking to the doorman and then he was out of my field of vision.

As soon as Danny was gone, I turned to Kim in the backseat. "I hope I didn't hurt you when I grabbed your arm," I said.

She shook her head no.

"Danny wants to help you," I said.

"Danny very nice. Big spender. Funny."

"He likes you," I said, and then shook my head.

"He classy guy. What your name?"

"Fielding."

She tried to say it, got close. "That's a funny name," she observed.

"I know. I've been getting laughs on it all my life."

"What you do? What your profession?"

I thought for a moment and then decided to go ahead with it. "I'm a congressman," I said.

She nodded, as if this was very believable and made perfect sense.

"Do you know what that is?" I asked. "I'm a United States congressman."

Kim looked out the window. "Danny buy junk here?"

But of course. That was exactly what he was doing, though it hadn't occurred to me until Kim said it.

"I hope not," I said.

"It's OK," said Kim. "As long as you careful."

Danny emerged from the apartment house looking immensely happy. His overcoat was open and flapping in the stiff snowy wind. He gestured to me to take the wheel and I slid over. Danny walked around to the passenger side and got in; the cold came off him and lowered the temperature inside the car.

"Success," he sang. "Success. Success."

"Did you just buy heroin?" I said, slipping the car into gear.

"Poor you," said Danny, shaking his head.

"Poor me because I've got such a low-life brother or poor me because I'm so paranoid?"

"Both," he said.

I drove through Central Park, on the route to Danny's current digs on East 70th Street. Danny was talking to Kim, trying to put her at ease, and at one point he climbed into the backseat so he could be next to her, touch her. Once, when we were thirteen and fourteen and, though he was the younger, his sense of sexual risk and adventure far outstripped mine, I watched through a crack in the bedroom door as Danny worked his raw magic on a neighborhood girl named Sally Margiotta. She was lying on his bed and he was sitting on the edge of mine. Her eyes seemed to be closed and Danny tossed a pillow onto her stomach and asked, "How did that feel?" after it landed. She said it felt OK. Then he tossed it again and it landed lower and he asked again, and again she said it was OK, and now I was going into a kind of twisted-up crouch to see a little better, but also from the weird pain, because desire and envy were going through me like food poisoning. I could hear Danny now, his voice low, resonant— he'd had a deep voice even at thirteen—and now Kim was answering him in a whisper. He said something insistent to her and there was a silence. Then she whispered again and they both laughed secretively.

I'd made it through the Park and was stopped at the traffic light at 66th and Fifth Avenue. A Mercedes limo pulled next to me and I looked in its windows. They were opaque but then one rolled down and I saw that Henry Kissinger and his wife, Nancy, were in that car. Wait! Wasn't that the car in which I belonged?

My God, the West was passing the dying Shah of Iran around like a hot potato. The president was vulnerable. Decisions were being made, deals struck, my colleagues and competitors were burning the midnight oil, and here *I* was, chauffeuring a poly-drug abuser and a Korean bathhouse attendant.

A few minutes later, we arrived at Danny's new apartment— five large, barely furnished rooms on the top of an old building facing the park. The ceilings looked like wedding cakes; there were dark, veiny mirrors over the fireplaces. Danny was making a study of the European fashion magazines: he liked the sort of photograph that showed a woman in a full-length fox coat being attacked by a pack of pit terriers. The magazines went for fifteen, twenty, twenty-five bucks a pop and there were dozens of them strewn across the bare walnut floors. There were gray push-button phones that looked foreign, like telephones from the best hotel in Buda-pest, and those were tucked into corners here and there—perfect for the man who crawls around his apartment but still needs to make important calls. The rent on the apartment was $2,800 a month; Danny was ninety days in arrears.

Kim sat on the floor, with her back against the wall. She stretched her legs straight out before her and looked at the tips of her boots. Danny was in the kitchen, getting a bottle of wine and three glasses, and Kim was stuck with me.

"You like New York?" I asked her.

"Yes," she said, "and Honolulu. But most I like Holland. Beautiful city."

"You were born in Korea?"

"Yes," she said. Edgy.

"It's a long way," I said.

"Oh yes," she said. "Very far." She glanced toward the kitchen and when Danny appeared her face brightened.

"Somebody left a fabulous bottle of champagne here," Danny said. "We are in luck." He held champagne glasses by their stems between his fingers and carried a bottle of Taittinger in his other hand. He sat next to Kim on the floor and worked the cork out of the bottle. He pushed it back and forth with his bully-boy thumbs—the thumbs of a lumberjack grafted onto the hands of a hypnotist. After a couple of wiggles, the cork suddenly exploded off and hit Danny square in the forehead. Now it was rolling back and forth on the wood floor and Danny had his hand over his forehead, where it had struck. Kim was laughing and her delicate hand was covering not her mouth but her eyes.

"Are you OK?" I asked.

"What happened?" asked Danny. He reached down and picked up the cork. "Can you believe that?"

"Are you OK?"

He uncovered his forehead and let me see for myself. There was a dark pink circle where it had hit, with a little blood showing through.

"Ouch," I said.

"Is it bleeding?" he asked.

"A little."

He poured the champagne; only a little had fizzed out of the bottle. He handed a glass to Kim and then reached across with mine. He picked his up and said, "Christmas is over," and took a long drink, draining the glass without stopping for a breath. He quickly refilled his glass.

"This makes me want to pee pee," said Kim.

"I was hoping you'd say that," Danny answered, moving closer to her, putting his hand in her lap, kissing her under the ear. Then he reached up and took a small dish off the windowsill. It was empty and he put it on his lap; he took a packet from his shirt pocket, opened it up, and poured a little heroin onto the plate. He reached back up onto the windowsill and found half a candy-striped straw.

"I'm going to have to insist you have a little of this, Fielding," he said. "Normally, I wouldn't. But normally I don't get this quality shit."

"Pass," I said.

Danny lifted a finger and cocked his head. "I'll get back to you on that," he said. "Maybe you'll change your mind." He put the straw in his nostril and bent over the plate. He snorted up a line of heroin only a half inch long, maybe three-quarters of an inch tops. He closed his eyes and breathed out; you could actually see his muscles relaxing; he looked suddenly smaller, more pliable.

He passed the plate to Kim and she took a little up in her long dark-red fingernail and snorted it. "You make me junkie," she said, giving him a playful little punch on the arm.

Danny carefully took the plate away from her and placed it on the windowsill. Then he put his arm around her and kissed her on the cheek, the eye, the forehead, the hair, and then, finally, on the lips. He pushed his weight against her and she slipped gracefully backward. She opened her legs to him and raised her arms. "You press hard on me," she said, beckoning him forth with her waving fingers.

I stood up. "Where do I bunk?"

"Down the hall. Second door on the left. You sure?"

"Yeah. I'm wrecked."

"Sorry I'm not a better host," he said.

"You're fine," I said. I glanced down at the glass of champagne I'd left on the floor. I'd taken a small sip out of it. The bubbles were still coming to the surface. Leave it there, I said to myself.

My room was small, white, with an interior-facing window. There was a mattress on the floor covered by a red and black quilt. One of those fancy gray phones was on the floor next to the bed. I heard Kim laughing in the front room and then a sound like *oouff*. I closed the door and got undressed. I checked my watch. It was only one o'clock—midnight in Chicago. I could call Juliet and not be so terribly far out of line. No. It was too late. And she'd be able to tell from my voice that I was a little drunk. I lay on the mattress and looked up at the two bare light bulbs in the landlord's ornate ceiling. My body felt oddly warm. I ran my hand over my chest. I closed my eyes . . .

And the next thing I was aware of was this: I reached for the phone and got Information. I asked for the number of a Sarah Williams and, as if there was nothing difficult in this request at all, the operator, a man, gave me the number. I dialed it quickly before I forgot it. One ring. Another. And then she picked up the phone.

"Hello?" she said.

"Hi," I said. "It's me."

There was a silence. I stood up and walked across the room. Couldn't feel the floor beneath my feet.

"Is it really?" she said.

"Yes. How are you? Are you all right? Is there anything I can do?"

"How long have you known?" she asked.

"I don't know. Always. Can I come and see you?"

"Please. Right now?"

"Yes."

"It's late. And the roads are bad."

"But it's our snow, isn't it? It was the snow all along. The snow kept you alive."

"How did you know that?" she asked.

And just after she asked it, I was awake again. My heart was wild. I opened my eyes and looked up at the hundred-watt bulbs above. I felt clammy, a little panicked; my bones felt like wet sand. I forced myself to get up and walk across the room to turn off the lights. The room seemed to jerk a little to the side as the darkness clicked into place. I lowered myself onto the mattress again and pulled the quilt over me. It felt as if I was going to cry but then I thought it would be better if I didn't, and good discipline, too. I stayed perfectly rigid on my back and looked up into the darkness and I told myself to remain calm, absolutely calm, and I said this a number of times until I finally fell asleep—yet even then there was one more dream: Sarah crouched at the end of the mattress like a primitive soul, her eyes blazing, her face intent, watching me as I slept.

8

In all the time we lived with and for each other, Sarah wrote me only once. I was still Mr. Coast Guard, out on my boat heading toward Alaska—a ridiculous mission involving salvaging another Coast Guard ship that had opened itself up like a tin of kippers against the edge of a glacier. Sarah had quit the job with Danny. She had an apartment, half a house really, on Staten Island, and I stayed with her there whenever I could. Mornings, she went to work in Lower Manhattan, doing research for a group calling itself the Catholic Action Project for Judicial Reform. I took a kind of trigger-happy pride in the fact I'd made her interested in the law and chose to gloss over the fact that the group she worked for was busy proving that we lawyers rarely gave the powerless a fair shake. Hell, I had no vested interest. I was no fat cat and had no intention of becoming one. I still believed Sarah and I were united in a belief in the same sorts of things and separated only by matters of temperament and tactics.

These are the words she wrote to me.

Dear Fielding,

It's hard to believe this letter will ever reach you. You seem so far away. I have a map in front of me and a circle marking the Bering Strait where I imagine the *Portland* is by now. If you were going off to fight a war, a good war, then I could be writing this by candlelight and weeping. And then I'd go to church and pray for you. But there's only one war out there and it's a bad one, the worst ever, and even though you've promised me your ship's not going anywhere near Southeast Asia, I can't help thinking at the last minute your course will be changed and there you'll be getting shot at by people who I want to win. It's what you Harvard lads call ironic, right? I love you and I love them and I don't want to take the test and choose who I love more—one of you or a thousand of them. I'd cease to live whatever I chose.

Peter Blankworth came to see me at work today. (No one comes to see me at our little hideaway on Staten Island!!!) After all this time, he suddenly wants to give me the money for what my abortion cost—three years ago! Peter's turned into one of those men who try to make themselves seem interesting by coughing a lot.

Hi. It's late now. I wrote the first part of this waiting for my Progresso clam sauce to simmer up and now it's three in the morning and I'm awake, needing you, and it's a thousand and one monkeys on my back. It's freezing in here. I feel like going next door and waking up the O'Maras. (I know they keep their half of the house ten degrees warmer than ours.) I'm wearing your black T-shirt under my nightgown. Remember? You were looking all over for it before you left. But I had it. Hidden. My guilty secret. I always need something here that smells of you, that special blend of Mennen and sweat and the smell of starch from your Coast Guard sheets and something else, something unspeakably delicate and innocent, like a biscuit browning in an oven. You are my one true lover, Fielding. It amazes (and humbles) me to think that while I was growing up in New Orleans you were growing up in New York, that we were eating and dreaming and growing our hair and getting ready to be sexual and we were still strangers but our fates had been cast and every step we took was only bringing us closer and closer until we fell into that bed and you were inside me and we both knew in a moment that we'd come to the end of the line. We will never be apart. I know this. I know this one hundred percent. We may be at each other's throat or we may be separated by 5,000 miles, but we will never be apart. We are one thing now and that thing is our love, an ideal which arose from us and will outlive us—for real love is indestructible.

You are my darling. Oh Jesus, if you were here right now. The things I would do. You'd be screaming for mercy, pal.

So. Get off the boat. Get off the boat and come home. Please!!! !!!!!!!!!!!!!!!!!!!!!!!

"Here's my dream," she said, leaning over to my side of the bed, her chin in her hand. "Do you want to hear it?" Naturally I did, though my eyes would not open. "You're a young senator and I'm your wife and we're at a big fancy Washington party. Everyone's there—senators, the prez, the secretary of genocide, you know, the works. You're in a tux and I'm wearing a very expensive gown. Low cut, with little spaghetti straps. And all I can think of is I have to keep my hands down, my elbows close to my side, because I haven't shaved under my arms and if anyone sees, your career is ruined."

We moved to Chicago together, a night flight upon which we celebrated the exact second-year anniversary of our becoming lovers. They didn't serve champagne, so we mixed bourbon with club soda. Lots and lots of drinks, but we knew how to behave. She was wearing blue jeans and a red shirt; I was still in my uniform, my last half-price flight. All the lights beneath us seemed enshrouded in mist.

Through friends at the Catholic Action Project, Sarah had arranged for work in Chicago. She was going to run a recreation program at a priory on the northwest side, a place calling itself Resurrection House. When we got off the plane it was ten o'clock at night in Chicago. You could feel the September heat right there in the airport. We already had an apartment waiting for us, the top floor of a three-story limestone building on Blackstone Avenue.

We had budgeted money for a taxi but there was a surprise in store. We were met at the gate by a priest. Father Mileski. He was thirty-three years old. Long black hair, a bushy, apocalyptic beard. He was massive and if he wanted to look like Christ, then it was after the Savior spent a year or two pumping iron. You could see his muscles beneath his black clothes. His eyebrows grew together and his small brown eyes beneath them seemed always to be moving, even as he stared at you. "Sarah?" he said, coming up to us. "Sarah Williams?" He had a deep bass voice, slow movements, a giant oppressed by his own size.

"How'd you guess?" she asked him. I was raised never to admit who I was to strangers, but I suppose that already this man was no stranger to her—she was, of course, mad for priests, especially if they looked like misfits.

"You were . . ." He gestured. He seemed to be struggling for words. He smoothed his beard. "I knew what you looked like," he said finally.

"What a great way to start," Sarah said, taking my arm.

"I thought you'd need a hand," Father Mileski murmured, shifting from foot to foot. "I hope I made the right decision. I have a car. I can take you to your new apartment."

"It's just wonderful," said Sarah. She tugged at me and looked up into my face, smiling. Her eyes seemed dazed with happiness, as if the appearance of this thick and towering priest had somehow anointed us, blessed our beginnings in Chicago with a promise of good luck and purpose. Whatever misgivings she had about tagging along as I followed the tracks I'd laid before I'd even met her were instantly dispelled by Mileski's coming to meet her. Now she belonged in Chicago, too. She was longing to be needed and now she was. Her happiness was so quick and so complete that I was glad for the priest's coming, too.

But as the saying goes: Little did I know.

"You're drinking too much," she said. "It's not funny."

"When was it funny?" I asked. A drunk loves to be hassled when he's pouring; I gave myself a little extra.

"Don't run it around in circles," she said.

"No, no, I'm curious. When was it funny? If we can trace it back, then maybe I can make it funny again." I pointed the bottle in her direction, offering her a bit. An unlikely proposition. It was midnight. She was in her domestic-looking terry cloth robe, the one with coffee stains on the sleeve, the one that always smelled like buttered toast.

"Are you nervous?" she asked. "Are you having trouble sleeping? School?"

"Yes, yes, yes, everything." I took a drink. It felt as if I'd sloshed a little on my chin, but when I felt it with my palm I was dry.

"Don't do this to me," she said, in low, even voice.

"What am I doing to you?" I asked, with a cool grin, Johnny Darkness off on a toot.

"I don't want to look after you this way. It's a pain being the girl in her bathrobe telling the boy to be careful."

"Then don't."

She stepped toward me and knocked the glass out of my hand. There was bourbon on my shirt, ice cubes in my pocket. The glass rolled back and forth on the little Oriental carpet and then off the edge and onto the gray wooden floor.

"How very persuasive," I said.

"You talk like a college boy," she said, turning away. "You didn't talk like that when you were in the Coast Guard."

"I can't do very much right with you, can I?" I said. I picked up the glass, took the ice out of my shirt pocket and put it back into the glass, and then poured myself another drink. It felt as if I were winning an incredible victory. The cold wet spot on my shirt touched directly onto my heart.

Father Mileski became her best friend and I found myself in the cosmically stupid position of becoming jealous of a priest. There was a lot of attention that year being paid to priests leaving their orders to marry. Nuns were going on talk shows to announce they planned to have children. I never really suspected her, but I pretended to, trying, I see now, to cover up a deeper, more painful jealousy: a meeting of souls that excluded me. They worked ten, twelve, sometimes fourteen hours at Resurrection House, while I sat around with sharpies and sellouts and ambitious up-from-under boys like myself, studying contract law, the warp and woof of the Constitution. It was hard to compete with the emotional rush of life at Resurrection House, with its crises, its incandescent moments of passionate friendship: the little boy who finally talked, the rapacious landlord forced to cough up a little heat, the shootout across the street. My conversation seemed anemic next to what Sarah and Mileski—Steven, now, by his own insistence—talked about daily.

Their clients were largely Mexican. They had small, smooth faces, stiff blue jeans, socks with bright silver threads. There were a few furious white holdouts who used the settlement house because there was basketball, a Coke machine, but the whites in that neighborhood were Appalachians and as distrustful of the Catholics as they were of the browns and blacks.

Sarah lost weight. She developed purple half moons beneath her eyes. Her breath stank of cigarettes. Something savage entered her lovemaking and at times this vehemence was hypnotic, catching, and at other times it was merely scary. I am remembering her now on top of me, thrusting up and down, wildly, like an angry man, with her fingernails digging into my shoulder so that when she was finished and took her hands away she'd dug eight little frowns into my skin.

One night, she brought Mileski home for dinner, along with a new addition to the priory named Father Stanton, and Sister Anne. Stanton had come to Chicago from Rhodesia and his nerves were shot. He'd seen torture, fire fights; the headlights of his Land Rover skittered over the thorn bushes, behind any one of which could be lurking a man with an automatic rifle. He'd lost favor with both sides—with the blacks because of his color and with the whites because of his sympathies. He was tall, with gray hair, large ears. He was a shattered man. His hands shook; sometimes he opened his mouth to speak and nothing came out but a dull, gagging noise. Sister Anne taught English at Loyola but put in her twenty hours a week at Resurrection House. She was a large-boned, red-faced woman with thick, steely hair, a man's jaw, pale eyes that split in two behind her rimless bifocals. Stanton brought a bottle of red wine; Sister Anne brought a salad of green beans and chick-peas. Mileski came with a package of sugar doughnuts. Stanton was attempting to tell us about sidewalk etiquette in Salisbury—how the blacks would have to leave the pavement if a white person was using it. We drank the wine, with me leading the charge. Sarah sat next to Father Mileski and when she wanted him to comment upon something she patted his leg. Suddenly, the very unlikelihood of their becoming lovers seemed proof of its inevitability: Sarah liked nothing more than a nice stiff swim up-stream. She was a sucker for painfully unconsummated love affairs. (I was remembering that window in her bedroom back in New Orleans and those steamy charades for the boy a million miles away across the street.)

Sister Anne was asking me what contribution I could make to the priory and its work, once I had my law degree.

"You've got some of the oiliest, most corrupt lawyers in the city working for the diocese," I said.

"Yes, but what we're trying to accomplish is something very different," she said. "We're a church inside a church." And now her eyes narrowed and behind the thick, distorting spectacles they looked like those flat little fish the light shines right through.

"Are you Catholic?" she asked me.

"Half," I said.

"You can't *be* half Catholic," said Sister Anne.

"Watch me," I said, and drew an imaginary line with my finger, starting at my forehead and going down to my belly.

"Don't argue with him," said Sarah. "He likes it too much." She got up from her seat next to Mileski and sat on the arm of my chair. She did a takeoff of someone shaking her lover by the shoulders.

"So, Steven," Stanton said, finishing his wine with a manly flourish, and then crossing his legs, "what are we going to do about getting these two decently married?" His accent was Rhodesian, fancy yet blunt.

"It'll happen," said Steven. He had a modish sense of fatality, a strain of passivity that he could carry because of his sheer physical power.

"She has a genius with children," Stanton said to me. His teeth seemed to lack a protective enamel; they were bruised from just one glass of burgundy. "She's just so lovely with them. It's a comfort to see it."

"I don't think I'm her type for that sort of thing," I said. I really did say this in a high style and I'd meant it to be somehow amusing—as if I were so confident of Sarah's and my perfect love that I could play at trashing it in public. But they didn't know me well enough to get the joke and I probably didn't deliver it with half the aplomb I'd intended. My heart began to race as my words hung like smoke in that small, poorly ventilated room. Our dinner guests in black looked at me with their exhausted, sympathetic, yet strangely cool eyes—for, of course, they were not thinking how I would survive the awkwardness of this moment so much as they were wondering if this sack of blood they saw before them held within it a soul destined for heaven or for hell.

A Sunday at the lake. We were at that place people in Hyde Park
call the Point, a promenade of huge, colorless rocks encircled by
the gray, slightly sinister busyness of Lake Michigan. It was a hot
summer day and people were sprawled out on the rocks like lizards.
Sarah and I were with Father Mileski. He wore a brief, iridescent
bathing suit, such as a swim racer would wear, and his legs looked
massive, like brown, furry trees. Sarah was wearing a pale green
bikini that was a little small for her. She kept fiddling with the
elastic around her legs, tucking her pubic hair in at the sides. I
was the only one who wanted to swim. There'd been talk in the
papers about the water's being polluted, and though the city insisted the problem had passed, it seemed that Sarah and Mileski
stayed dry for political reasons.

I watched them as I trod water; they were each propped on
an elbow, talking away as if they hadn't seen each other in weeks.
When I returned, I leaned over for a towel and saw Sarah's eyes:
they seemed to be holding back torrents of tears. I asked her what
was wrong. I crouched down and put my hand on the side of her
face.

"Nothing," she said. "Steven was just reminding me what Jesus
said to the Pharisees."

"You're kidding," I said. Then, trying to cover the callousness
of my incredulity, I asked Mileski what in fact Jesus had said.

Mileski shrugged modestly and seemed reluctant to go into it.
"This was when the Pharisees wanted to curry favor with him.
And Jesus explained why he was going to keep his distance and
he said, When I was hungry you would not feed me and, you
know, when I was naked you would not clothe me, and . . . and
when I had no place to live you offered me no shelter. And the
Pharisees said, Wait a minute. We never had a chance. We never
saw you hungry or naked or without a place to live. And Jesus
said, Every time you saw a hungry man and didn't feed him—
that was me. And every time you saw a naked man and did not

clothe him—that was me. And every time you saw a homeless man and did not give him shelter—that was me too."

I looked down at him. The sun, like a dumb animal, was trudging toward the west and it was slightly behind Mileski now. I had to squint to look in his direction. A half dozen wisecracks gathered within me and the pressure of not saying them felt like the suppression of an enormous sneeze. What if it really was that simple, I thought to myself. What if all we were required to be was *good*, what if there really was a guide, a standard upon which to measure our actions, and by doing so we could serve both heaven and earth far more valuably than we could ever hope to through a life of calculation and compromise?

Sarah rolled onto her back and put her hands behind her head. She crossed her legs and I looked at the bottoms of her feet, pale and creased as ancient hands, and I felt a warm river of sentiment going through me, and then I thought: They're right. We must *do* something.

That night, I was sitting at my desk, reading the *Harvard Law Review* by the light of a green glass lamp. I could hear the dull roar of the shower and when Sarah stepped into the spray the difference in the sound seemed to suggest the exact shape of her body. The pipes clanged and then she moved away from the spray. The water hit the tiles in an undifferentiated rush and when she stepped forward again she carved in silence another replica of herself. A few minutes later she emerged from the shower. She was naked except for a yellow towel she'd wrapped around her hair like a rooster's comb. Her body was blotchy from scrubbing. I glanced up and then went back to my reading. I don't know why I was being so difficult. It was my awful way of flirting, daring her to court me. She came to me. She leaned over my back and put her arms around me. "I want to have a child," she whispered into my ear.

Like a man in a trance, I rose from my chair and turned to

face her. I put my arms around her and held her. Silently. Head-lights from passing cars arced across the room. We were breathing together and she pressed herself against me. "Just do it, OK?" she said. "There's nothing to talk about."

I carried her to the bedroom. She was not a small woman but she felt light to me that night. I placed her on the bed and she put her hands behind her head and watched me as I undressed. She parted her legs and then brought them tightly together. "I want you so much," she whispered. My erection was enormous, absurd. I threw myself onto the bed, kissing her, feeling her, making her ready. I slipped right in; she seemed larger than normal but her great silky spaciousness was somehow more erotic than any slight skid of resistance. I was inside her as far as I could go. She opened herself wider and pressed me tighter against her. A moan of pleasure hummed at the back of her throat, and as I began to move I was falling through a trapdoor of sensation. It was the first time I'd ever made love with such mortal purpose, the first time it seemed possible that the whole history of the world could be altered by one ejaculation, and I was overwhelmed by the newness and gravity of it—this loss of my real virginity, this coupling that made all the others seem trivial.

Sarah felt my swelling and she clasped me still closer. I put my mouth on hers in a large indistinct kiss and just before my semen and its innumerable genetic messages were about to flash out of me I felt the heels of her hands, hard and panicked against my chest. "No," she said, frantically. "Stop. Please stop." Quickly, guiltily, I pulled out of her. An ache went through me; the air seemed heavy, an alien atmosphere. Sarah drew her knees up and closed her eyes.

"Did you come in me?" she asked. She reached over and felt my cock, running her finger over the tip. "Sorry," she said, trying to laugh. "I thought . . . I just can't do this."

I didn't know what to say. An hour ago, I hadn't even thought about a child, but now I wanted one with a deep irrational hunger. I lay back on the bed as she slipped out of it. She went to the bathroom. I could hear her washing herself, like a whore. When she came back to the bedroom she asked me if I wanted her to put in her diaphragm so we could make love anyhow. I said no. Did I want her to give me head, jerk me off? No. No. She shrugged and picked up her clothes, carried them out of the bedroom. That was it. I listened to her footsteps, heard her pants zippering up. Then there was silence, a long, long silence. I got up, out of bed. I walked into the living room and she was gone. There was a note. She needed to walk, to think. She'd be back in an hour or two. She signed the note with Love. I sat on the sofa with the note in my hands, reading and rereading it. Then I stood up and poured myself a drink and turned on the TV. It was the little black and white GE television that used to be her grandfather's. His hand-print was worn into the enamel on the top of it.

9

At the last minute, the goddamned Republicans thought they could make an issue over the fact that I was an out-of-towner, a New Yorker no less, and they decided to put a man into the race against me.

They chose a fellow named Enrico Bertelli, a Chicagoan by birth, a resident of the district for forty-one years, the owner of a little Hyde Park coffeehouse called the Golden Portal, where you could have cinnamon-flavored cappuccino and listen to Vivaldi coming through the KLH speakers. Bertelli was barrel-chested, white-maned, light on his feet, vaguely bohemian—berets, Argyle socks under his sandals, paisley ascots. He was so godawful lovable you wanted to tell your troubles to him, you wanted to sit at a little wobbly table eating sourdough rye and cheese and listen to him spout the philosophical clichés that professors used thirty years ago to get freshman girls to give them blowjobs: life is so tragic, we must make beauty, peace, love—lower my pet, lower.

It was a brilliant piece of casting; I had to give the Republicans credit for that. If there was going to be a resentment vote against me, Bertelli was a perfect magnet for it. A charming old dodo without a political bone in his body, Bertelli could count on the fifteen percent of the district that was somehow Republican and after that who knew how many cappuccino lechers and hometown boosters he could rustle up as well. It didn't seem he was actually going to defeat me, but suddenly I had a race to run.

The Republicans announced him four days into the new year and Kinosis's boys, with their customary tact, at first tried to say it was too late, that the ballots for the special election were already on press. But a finger to the wind hipped the gov that people weren't exactly thrilled to have their right to vote taken away by a printing press, so the next day he made a big show of announcing that *new* ballots would be made up, this time with a name in both the Democratic and the Republican column.

Kinosis was irritated that now an actual campaign would have to be mounted in my behalf, but Isaac was thrilled. "I didn't particularly care for you slipping into Congress *completely* unnoticed," he said, calling me with the news. "With someone running against you, people will have an opportunity to hear you speak. You'll be building a constituency."

I was at home with Juliet. Our version of a cozy winter afternoon: she at her desk and me at mine. She was reading a book about infamous art forgers which I'd gotten her for Christmas two years ago, but which she was just getting to now. I always had the idea that Juliet, if the world ever got really screwy, could be an art forger. She was so meticulous and knowledgeable, and heaven knew a little elegant larceny might be just what we needed—as a couple, that is. Of course, when Sarah drifted toward the receiving side of the law I went rubber-legged on her and refused to follow. When it was time for her to start taking serious risks, risks that finally, and literally, exploded in her face, I was nowhere near her. Was I like that moral coward in the Camus novel who looked the other way when a woman leapt off a bridge and who then spent a drunken, misty middle age wandering Amsterdam, looking for another leaping woman so he could behave better next time?

I told Juliet about the Republicans' nominating Bertelli and she closed her book, while keeping her place with her thumb. "It looks like I'll have to work a little harder for this than I first thought," I said. Juliet furrowed her brow. She was wearing a red sweater with little pearlized buttons, a black skirt, high boots: it astonished me how well she dressed for hanging around the apartment reading a book about art forgery.

"I think it's just as well," she said, after a silence. "It'll give you a chance to mobilize a staff. And it'll bring you a lot more attention this way. People will have an opportunity to hear you speak."

"Your uncle's very words," I said.

A flush of color, sudden as a hawk's shadow, went across her face.

I acted as if I hadn't noticed. I shoved my hands in my pockets and started to pace. "I'm going to have to take what staff I get," I said. "And that means a lot of tired old hacks from the organization. Fuck it. It doesn't matter. When the election's over and I have a little breathing space, I'll start choosing my own people. All I really need now is people to answer telephones and get things printed up."

"You're going to need a lot more than that," said Juliet. "You're going to need a press secretary, media adviser, some sort of legislative aide to help you work on your positions . . ."

"No, I'm not. I'm not going to need that. I know what my positions are. I know what I want to say."

"Now you're just being silly."

"This Bertelli. He's a nothing. He's like a write-in candidate, you know, like voting for Tiny Tim. And he's a lecher."

"Are you going to use that?" asked Juliet.

"No. But maybe we'd better get married so I can run on the morality issue. What do you say?" I truly thought this was a funny, or at least a *frisky* crack. I hadn't meant it to be taken seriously. But the corners of Juliet's soft, deep-lilac-colored lips drew down.

"I don't think you're in proper shape to marry *anyone*," said Juliet, with a sincerity edged with vehemence.

"I was just kidding," I said, as if this could put me back in her good graces.

"Uncle Isaac thinks we *should* get married, you know," said Juliet, flipping open her book. It was a cold, cloudy day; the light in the room was brackish.

"He wouldn't dare say that to me," I said.

"Well, with me he's not so shy. With Mommy and Daddy dead, he assumes that right."

"And what did you say?" I asked. I leaned against the door frame and folded my arms over my chest.

She thought for a moment and then shook her head. "I don't remember," she said. "I don't like talking about these sorts of things. It makes everything so explicit and ugly. I think these things are just supposed to happen and it's awful when you make a fuss about it. Like those jerks in California applauding for the sunsets."

"Well it would be pretty awful if we got married and then I lost the election anyhow."

"Yes. I suppose we would feel like fools then."

I breathed in, breathed out. I felt heavy, cluttered with junk. "You should turn the lamp on when you read in here," I said. "The light's so bleak."

"Why would it be so awful if we got married, Fielding? I mean, just as a point of information."

"I meant if we got married for the sake of the election and then I lost anyhow. That's all I meant."

"Why does that make my stomach hurt?"

"Look, if it was me saying we ought to get married, it would be you saying what I'm forced to say. This is the system of checks and balances we've worked out."

She shook her head and looked away from me, into the uninviting darkness that gathered at the far end of the room. "You're making me feel cheap."

"Cheap? You could never feel cheap. You're just confused that you're asking a low-life like me to marry you. And you—"

"I am not asking you to marry me. You're being unbelievably cruel."

"OK. I'm sorry I said it."

"Are you having any more of those . . . episodes?" she asked me. She wanted to make eye contact with me for this one and because she was sitting and had to look up, her eyes appeared a little crazed for the moment.

I waited good and long before answering. It was a shitty question, but I knew sooner or later she'd have to ask it. I probably deserved it for going on about it that night of the radio, for not going to the extra bother of lying.

"Episodes?"

"Yes. Like before you went to New York."

"Oh that." I waited another moment and then said, "Yes." I suppose I'd meant to put her in her place, to stiff-arm her for coming after me like that, but the thing backfired on me and the case of my admission, and hearing it, hearing my voice putting that weird signal out into the world, sent up a storm of longing in me—and a second storm of fear. I've always done passably well in masking my feelings, but at that moment my face must have looked no more stable than a broken egg.

Juliet stood up at her desk. I could see she wanted to come to me. I don't know if it was instinct or feminine training, but my distress awakened in her a desire to shelter me from my own misery. She opened her mouth to say Are you all right? but there were other forces in play by now. We were in a complicated situation and she was letting it dawn on her slowly just how over her head she was. This was supposed to have been something rather easy, this arrangement between the two of us. But now she was living with a man who, for all she knew, might start chasing after cars in a day or two. And she was also living with a man who loved someone else with the openness and lack of common sense that we dare only with unattainable lovers.

Juliet had taken me on, knowing that in a hundred ways I was the wrong sort of man for her—I'd slept too close to a noisy childhood radiator; been too shifty and mean through school; developed a kind of flipness and even a hardness that made me a little coarse and obnoxious to someone as delicate, as cultivated as Juliet. I mean, I still thought it was funny to open and close my mouth and wave my arms around when she watched the opera on TV, and even when I was on my best behavior, acting so proper and under control that it could give you a pounding headache to behold, there was always something a little off, like a Russian playing jazz. But Juliet had allowed herself to go this far and perhaps she thought that at thirty-four there was no easy turning back. I don't know what exactly was going through her but it was no one thing. And like a three-penny nail quivering in the invisible net strung between the positive and negative poles of a magnet, Juliet could neither come closer to me nor get further away. She could not even say whatever it was she wanted to say. She just looked at me, with her eyes pulsating betrayal one moment and compassion the next, and soon it was me going toward her, coming closer and closer and she drew herself up to receive me, and then finally I had her in my arms and was holding her close, whispering, "I'm sorry, I'm so sorry," into the fragrant folds of her soft white neck.

Sunday there was a brunch at Isaac and Adele's and I was introduced to the people who'd be running my campaign. Juliet and I arrived before the others. Juliet was sensing in me a return to a somewhat businesslike attitude and for this I guess we had the Republicans and old Bertelli to thank. And if I was going to start acting a little more like my old self, then Juliet could, too. Though she was moodier, and more disorganized than I was emotionally, she was still perfectly capable of doing a profit and loss calculation, and had, it seemed, come to the decision that I was essentially the same person I'd always been, one, and two, that I was about to be getting to the serious part of my career, which would surely be interesting, and three, that whatever possessed me to rub her face in the ashes of the dead was probably just a reaction to my sudden fortune and would surely pass, if it wasn't exactly passing already.

Juliet was helping Adele and Mrs. Davis in the dining room, whereas Isaac and I were sent into his grand Tudor study. There seemed some primitive superstition involved here, as if we were not supposed to see the dining room table, with its place settings and goblets and linen-covered bowls of bagels until it was completely prepared and the lunch was to begin, just as a groom is not supposed to look at his bride while she dresses for their wedding.

"These are animals, you know that, don't you?" Isaac said to me, leaning forward in his club chair and patting me on the knee. He was giving me a little rebriefing about the people we'd be meeting today.

"Me too," I said.

"No. These are different kinds of animals. The kind that push over garbage cans for their meal."

"Those are called raccoons, Isaac. Raccoons are cute."

"Don't quibble, Fielding. I'm trying to help you through this."

"Well, I guess it's the least you can do. Right?"

He looked at me queerly. Isaac gave me a lot of leash, but he didn't like to take any nonsense. He believed in contracts, both written and unwritten, and ours stated that he would train me, guide me, give me access and acceleration, whereas I would continue to listen to him, respect him, carry the torch he was handing over to me.

"I never do the least for you, Fielding," he said. "I do only the maximum."

"I realize that," I said, sitting deep in the chair, stretching my legs out before me. I checked my shoes. I'd stepped in a bit of

snow between our front door and the driveway and my black shoes
were stained near the sole by a pale lacy fringe of ice and salt.
"But," I said, with a sigh, "I can't help wondering what Kinosis
owes you. He doesn't really know *me* and it doesn't seem he much
likes me."

"Granted," said Isaac, cutting in, trying, I suppose, to bring
me back to my senses.

"So what's the deal?" I asked. "I think I better know, don't
you?" I wanted to grill him on this one; I wanted to stand up and
poke my finger against his chest.

"If that was my thinking, I would have said so," replied Isaac,
with one of those old-fashioned wan smiles.

"I'm under a lot of pressure here, Isaac. I have to get things
straight."

"What kind of pressure, Fielding?" he asked, three perfect
wrinkles appearing in his forehead, like a trio of gulls. We'd long
ago taken that extra twist and turn to where it was impossible to
distinguish his paternal concern for me from his ambitions.

"Internal pressure."

"Trouble with the New York family?"

As if that wasn't the only family I had.

"No, no. None. They're thrilled for me."

He shrugged, as if doing me the courtesy of not puncturing
the fantasy. It was really so incredibly disagreeable of him, but it
wasn't as if he could help himself. "Then what sort of pressure?
Everything OK with you and Jule?"

"Hey, we're getting pretty man-to-man, aren't we?" I said,
with a bright smile that he was smart enough to know meant Watch
It.

"I'm trying to help you through what I fully realize is a difficult
period of transition. First you want to talk and then you don't."

"I want to talk about why Kinosis is putting me on the ticket."

"It's a very complex debt, Fielding. It's an accumulation. The
primary reason I haven't gone into a great deal of detail about it
is that frankly it would take me hours, weeks, to unravel the whole

thing. As you know, the governor is not a brilliant mind. But he listens and it's better than having a Republican down there. A Democrat is simply beholden to a more cosmopolitan constituency and has to answer to a greater variety of people. Kinosis comes to me from time to time for advice. Asks me to look things over. I tickle his vanity, if you want to know. He appreciates it. And since you're probing, I may as well tell you it is an *exhausting* task. Nothing takes its toll like emotional labor."

"That's what my father used to say."

"Oh?" said Isaac, raising his eyebrows—flat, furless little creatures that looked like white makeup painted over his eyes.

"Yeah," I said, pretending I could not decipher the message in Isaac's eyes, which were cloudy but bright, like pieces of quartz dipped into icy water. "My father always said he'd rather lug trays of type than answer a question from the boss."

"What was he afraid his employer was going to ask?" inquired Isaac.

"That's not the point," I said. "Emotional labor. That's what we're talking about." Something directed my attention toward the window, a change of light, as if a hand had suddenly passed in front of the sun. The window darkened, giving me a shaky, out-of-control sensation in the pit of my stomach. The darkness seemed to hover there like a curious bird, and then it lifted and the sharp winter light was back.

Isaac rubbed his palms together, his signal that it was time to proceed with matters. "All right," he said, "let me tell you who'll be here. It's a mixed bag, to be sure." Isaac reached into the inside pocket of his suit and withdrew a discreet leather notebook. In the past year, his memory was, as he put it, "starting to go on the fritz," but his response to this was completely practical, straightforward. He simply began writing everything down and he did so without drama or effort—just like quickly rinsing the cup after finishing your tea. He opened the notebook and pursed his lips.

"Mostly Party regulars," he said. "People we've discussed over the years."

"You mean hacks," I said, smiling.

"Yesterday they were hacks, Fielding. Today, they are dear friends. OK?"

"OK. Let's hear it."

"Rich Mulligan."

"The bloodsucker."

"Please. No comments. Let's just get this done. Tony Dayton. He'll be helping run the campaign. Roman Kurowsky."

"No."

"Yes. He's a congressman, a Democrat, his district abuts ours."

"He's an insane pig."

"Fine. OK. Lucille Jackson. Dr. Henry Shamansky—"

"Wait a minute. *Doctor* Henry Shamansky. I know this guy, Isaac. He's a sociology professor, for Christ's sake. He runs the Independent Voters of Illinois. He wears corduroy suits and has muttonchop sideburns. I am not calling him 'Doctor' Shamansky."

"Call him whatever you like, Fielding." He squinted at his notebook. "Goodness. I can't even read my own writing. Yes. Oh yes. Sonny Marchi."

"You've got me on that one. Never heard of him."

"A real live wire. Criminal face. He's married to the governor's daughter Cynthia."

"Yes. That's right. I remember your telling me about him. You said he was a baboon."

"Yes. Well, Kinosis can't simply give us a gift. He'd put a string on his dime before dropping it into a pay phone, if he could."

"This kind of stinks, doesn't it, Isaac?"

"Not at all. What we have here is something completely marvelous. You are going to Washington. This is what we wanted, remember? This is what *you* wanted. And for all those lovely reasons."

"I still feel that way," I said, with a twinge of defensiveness. Did he think I'd forgotten? What Sarah despised in political ambition was its habit of becoming a tautology: I want to win because I want to have power; I want power because you're nothing without it.

"Then be realistic," said Isaac, as if this was enough to settle the issue.

I nodded. And it did make sense. Then and now. If I could actually house the homeless, say, then the person who climbed into that warm bed would not care if Congressman Pierce had to smile when he felt like snarling in order to put that bed in place. No, my abused scruples would not be the pea beneath the mattress. "Who else'll be here?" I asked.

"A woman named Kathy Courtney."

"Don't know her."

"She was Carmichael's press aide for the past four years." He paused, let me digest. "Very capable. Comes from New York."

"Very loyal of her to be working with me."

"I don't think loyalty has much to do with it, one way or the other. Carmichael had seventeen people working for him. Five here in the district, twelve in D.C. What do you think they're doing? They're working on their résumés, that's what. And if you keep any of them on, they'll continue to work on their résumés and be on the phone and having lunch with anyone who can help them find the next position."

"Then I won't keep any of them on."

"That's one solution. Of course, you'll be spending most of your time interviewing people for staff positions . . ."

"OK. Go on. Kathy Courtney."

"She knows the press. Here and in Washington. She's organized. Energetic. Celibate."

"Celibate?"

"An observation," Isaac said, shrugging.

"What does she want to do for me?"

"She wants to be your press aide. She wants to stay on. And in the meanwhile, she can keep you keyed in to Carmichael's unfinished business. All the people waiting to hear from him who might not know he just got caught with his trousers down."

Congressmen with their pants at their knees, celibate press aides. All of this was pretty raunchy material for Isaac. The excitement was really getting to him.

"Shall we?" he said, rising. He had my father's vanity upon getting up from his seat—*never* push off on the arms, *never* grunt.

The brunch. Adele served food she normally wouldn't think of putting on her table: strawberry-flavored pancakes; rasher upon rasher of curly, glistening bacon; pitchers of orange juice made from concentrate; a baked ham with pineapple rings impaled on it. Isaac claimed to be on a diet and stuck to coffee and Coffee Rich. Adele had long before perfected a way of appearing to eat without actually letting food pass her lips. I, of course, succumbed to the siren song of Free Food and ate heartily—so much so that at one point Juliet put her hand on my wrist, in what might have appeared to be an affectionate gesture but which was really one of those subtle, firm signals, such as an expert trainer can give a mad, snarling dog. I grinned at her and put down my fork and then began slugging down orange juice. It occurred to me that two weeks on the campaign trail ought to have me looking like Taft.

But I was doing more than coating my nerves with carbohydrates; I was trying to chart my course through these swift, shallow waters. I was at once an outsider and the center of attention. Tony Dayton sat on my left, smoking a Winston which he held with four fingers and which he ashed into his food. He had dark injured eyes. He wore a flashy houndstooth jacket, a pin on the lapel that said JAZZ!! He glanced over at me and saw something worried in my face. "Don't let it get you down, old buddy. I'm your new best friend."

From the outset, Isaac controlled the conversation. He talked about my qualifications, my strengths, my possible weaknesses, as if I weren't in the room. "We've got a fresh young face," Isaac was saying and no one but Lucille Jackson even glanced my way.

Lucille Jackson was the only black at the meeting. She and her husband owned a few funeral homes in the ghetto; they were old-fashioned Negroes, with processed hair and Cadillacs. Lucille regarded me with her arms folded over her enormous bosom. She had an extravagant frown, like a sumo wrestler. Her crucifix rested in her cleavage, sinking into a sea of hot fudge. Lucille's reputation was that she could deliver 100,000 black votes but as my eyes met hers I suddenly didn't believe it. She was just like most of the others, a part of a process she barely understood, and this hocus-pocus about votes delivered was just like a witchdoctor clapping his hands before a thunderstorm and then convincing everyone that his hands caused the rain. I may not have had the friends I ought to have had west of Cottage Grove but I knew enough about what was going on there—the average age, the unemployment rate, the cost of a bag of heroin—and I could campaign there with or without her.

Tony Dayton was going to manage the campaign and his great concern was how much money the Party was giving us. "We got to at least make this look like a campaign and not some dance down by the union hall," he said.

And then Rich Mulligan, who was thick with the civil servants and had control over the precinct workers and the loudspeaker trucks, went nostalgic. "Ten years ago," he said, looking at his fingernails, "we could run a decent campaign for ten thousand bucks. Now it takes a goddamned million."

"This is the reality of the modern world," said Shamansky, and his voice was so sonorous you wanted to argue with everything he uttered.

"I don't get it," said Sonny Marchi. He combed his oily hair forward; he had the keen eyes of a poacher. I couldn't figure how a well-off girl like the governor's daughter could have married him. She must have been kind of tragic herself. "We got the votes, right? I mean, hell, vote early and vote often. Am I right?"

There was an uneasy silence as the knights of the round table decided who would do battle with the hedgehog.

"There's already so many ruffled feathers," said Mulligan, "I think what we need to do is coast and the way you coast is you stay in neutral. And in terms of the bucks, we can get enough ink for free. Reporters got nothing to do this time of year. Am I right, Kathy?"

I looked across the table at Kathy Courtney and felt a quick intestinal tug: I saw Sarah's face superimposed over her own for a moment and even when sanity erased the vision, the moment left a trace of itself. Kathy Courtney had short red hair, a strong, stubborn face. She wore a blue silk blouse, a prim string of pearls. Her voice was husky. "You're right about that, Rich," she said. "The newspapers and the TV boys are ready to run with anything we give them. And I wanted to mention something else here. And that's that we can count on Jerry Carmichael's full cooperation. I don't know if we want to have him actively involved but he is willing to do whatever he can for the good of the ticket."

"That's very good of him, Kathy," said Henry Shamansky, nodding sagely.

"It's what I would expect from him," said Congressman Kurowsky in his pious, aggressive drone. He put his hand over his heart, a gesture that seemed to mean not so much that a solemn oath was being taken but that something snaky was being said and that his heart was being shielded from it, much in the way you cover a child's ears to prevent him from hearing something confusing or frightening.

"Jerry always tried to do what was right," said Kathy Courtney, her voice coloring with feeling.

It was at that moment I realized this meeting could easily go to its conclusion without my opening my mouth. I was letting them turn into me a tag-along and it struck me that this had gone on just long enough to lull the lot of them into a false sense of superiority.

"OK," I said, "let me cut in here before things get too far along." I rubbed my hands together to tell them this was something I was looking forward to. "First of all, I want to thank you for giving up your Sundays and coming here on such short notice. I really do appreciate it." That seemed to cover the point I most wanted to make: they were here for *me*. Next, I wanted them to know that even if they didn't know me, I knew *them*. "It's very encouraging to a rookie like me," I said, letting them see my smile, which I knew they knew was manufactured, but that was part of the deal, "to know that someone like Rich Mulligan will be helping to get out the vote. I've always thought that when the history of ward politics is written, Rich'll have a chapter all to himself." I looked around the table. They were all paying attention and it made me want to laugh. There's a wonderful kind of terror in learning how easy it is to control people.

"And it's good to see Henry Shamansky here and know that the Independent Voters of Illinois will be behind my candidacy. I realize Henry's been having his own problems with the internal workings of the Hyde Park I.V.I. and I especially appreciate your being here in what must be a difficult time." I moved my eyes away from him because I didn't want to see his face fall. It would blow it all if I gloated.

"And of course, it's good to see Congressman Kurowsky and I welcome his support, too, though I have to say I'm a little surprised. But who knows, right? Maybe Roman's coming around and we'll be voting together against senseless weapons systems and for a federal jobs corps."

"Don't go holding your breath waiting for it, sonny," he said. And I laughed at this before anyone could, so it would be my joke—not his. I owned the meeting. I looked over at Isaac; he was sitting back in his chair with his steepled hands tucked beneath his chin and when he felt my gaze he nodded.

"And of course," I went on, "I'm very glad to see Lucille Jackson, especially because this election's going to be won in the black neighborhoods of this district. And *not* because we have registered Democrats there but because I intend to offer programs and a commitment to the poor and discriminated-against people of the district that will make sense and give them a real reason to support me." I paused. "Mrs. Jackson," I said, "I remember what you said to a reporter from the *Defender* three years ago. You said, 'Politicians who make promises and then walk away are like muggers.' Well, I've spent a while throwing crooks into jail and I don't intend to become one myself.

"I'm glad to have Tony Dayton working with me. I've followed quite a few of your campaigns, Tony, and I think we'll find a way to work together that will be good for both of us.

"Which brings me to the point I most wanted to make right here. And that's the idea of coasting into this election in neutral. I realize we've only got a short while and two weeks isn't time to raise a lot of complex issues. But I don't intend to sneak into Congress. I want the people who vote for me to know who they're voting for. I don't think we should be all over the map, cranking out position papers like a bunch of amateurs, but I want to pick one or two issues, and hit them hard."

I could feel hate vibrations in the room but I couldn't quite locate their source. It was probably Kurowsky, who could undoubtedly diffuse and project his feelings like a ventriloquist can make his voice come out of the sugar bowl.

"How are we supposed to agree on what issues in the time we've got left?" asked Tony Dayton.

"We won't have to agree on them," I said. I shrugged as if nothing could be simpler. And then I said in a perfectly friendly voice, as if I was merely taking on an extra responsibility so the others would not have to work so hard, "it'll just be up to me."

Like a man who's put on a pair of artificial wings and then accidentally catches a wind, I felt the familiar world growing distant beneath me, and the azure into which I was heading, now that it was reachable, seemed utterly cold, even hideous. Everyone around me was a stranger and the strangest of them all was this man running for Congress, this grinning fake with a sudden clutch of underlings, this new self that seemed to survive only by eating in large bites all of the selves that had preceded it.

It was then, however, Monday, the day after the brunch at the Greens', that Caroline called from O'Hare Airport, to announce she had arrived and where the hell was I. It wasn't that I'd forgotten she was coming to Chicago, but the fact had been lying at a distance from me, like a tool you need but cannot reach. I was home alone when the call came, sitting around in a pair of brown and gold pajamas, eating emperor grapes and reading yesterday's papers. I was sinking into self-reproach and my confidence was shot. The election was in two more weeks and there were a lot of things I ought to have been doing that were perhaps a touch more pressing than wearing pajamas and eating grapes, but that was all I could manage just then. Like most self-invented people, I'd always felt I was a two-destiny guy, the one being the life I'd been born to and the other being the life I desired. Now, with my heart feeling so defeated, there seemed nothing to do but slowly sink back into the vague and insufficient fate most organically deserved. But hearing Caroline's pissed-off voice snapped me to.

"Do you want me to take a taxi down to you?" she asked.

"Yeah, I guess so. God, Caroline. I'm sorry. I have it written right down here in front of me," I lied, pointing at nothing. "And I have you coming in at four o'clock."

"OK, OK, thanks for the lie. I'll be there when I get there." And with that, she hung up the phone.

I hung up the phone. Idly, I picked up the *Hyde Park Herald*, our neighborhood weekly. I paged through it looking for something about the campaign, but it was all book fairs and bicycle thefts. I finally got to the classifieds at the back of the paper and started to read them. I never read the classified ads and I didn't stop to wonder why I was reading them now. But under the personals, I saw the following notice:

F.—Can't stop the music.   S.

Very calmly, I stood up and found a scissors. I cut the ad out and placed it in my wallet. I felt a burst of insane joy, but then it was gone. Don't think about it now, I told myself, but I was on fire with it, like a lover with his first real secret.

I got cleaned up, dressed. It wouldn't be fair to Caroline to appear much less than full of energy and purpose. It was, after all, with the hope of somehow being galvanized by my current that she'd made the trip; if what she wanted was bruised fruit and an unmade bed, she could have stayed home.

Generally, it had been Danny to whom we turned when we needed to feel the acceleration of risk, the reach of great expectations—Danny with his schemes, his palatial, unaffordable apartments, his Japanese and European friends with tongue-twister names and exotic tastes. And before Danny, it had been Caroline who'd been our avant-garde—with her boyfriends on BMWs, her far-flung continental tour, her cryptic letters home written in calligraphy on salmon-colored paper, her dreams of immortality on the walls of cool museums, her marriage to Eric McDonald, the screaming, terrifying miracles of her sons' breech births. Now it was my turn; Caroline's boys were in Africa with Eric, her own ambitions had been beaten down to the root by the stampede of necessity—the necessity of motherhood, the necessity of loneliness, and above all, the necessity of material want; it's hard to be a genius when you're holding three jobs.

A battered taxi pulled in front of the house and I yanked my window up to shout hello. Caroline got out of the cab wearing a full-length black nylon and down coat and black earmuffs. She had a travel bag hoisted onto her shoulder and a plaid suitcase heavy enough to need both hands to hold it. She leaned back into the cab to say good-bye to three people who were sitting in the backseat and then the taxi pulled away, sending up two fans of dirty street snow.

"I'll be right down," I called out to her.

"I got it, that's all right," she yelled back.

I stood up straight; a buzz of emotion went through me. Hearing my voice calling out and then hearing hers—it was the sound of the past, those yells and signals, those deliriously impatient calls that fluttered like birds in the high, airy cage of childhood. I ran to the front door and headed down the stairs. I made it to the locked, beveled glass door before Caroline made it up the porch steps and I opened the door for her. The wind blew straight in at me, parting around her body like white water around a stone.

"Hurry, I'm freezing," I said.

"What a town," she said, with a last effort. She let go of the handle as I took her suitcase from her. I dropped it on the welcome mat and put my arms around her. The outside of her coat felt like dry ice against my shirt.

"Mmmm, you smell so good, Fielding. I guess you're not using that Old Spice after-shave anymore." She rubbed her hand up and down my back. It seemed rather a nervous gesture; perhaps I was holding her too tightly.

I stepped back and closed the door behind her. "That's right," I said. "I haven't since you sent me that French after-shave cream that comes in a tube. You spoiled me."

"But you wouldn't touch it," she said.

"It hung around and finally I tried it."

"Ah," she said, pinching at my stomach, "you fancy little devil."

We made our way up the stairs. It was odd how heavy her suitcase was. "What do you have in here, anyhow?" I asked.

"It's been so long since I've gone anywhere, I've forgotten how to pack. So I just put everything I own into it."

"God."

"Afraid I'm going to stay too long?"

"Don't be funny. If you knew how much I needed you here, you wouldn't . . ." Wouldn't what? I didn't know. Believe it? Stay? I lost the thread. When I glanced back at Caroline, she was looking at me a little strangely.

"You're OK, aren't you?" she said.

"Yes, I'm OK."

"Good. I've been getting enough craziness from Danny. I need a rest."

Caroline dumped her stuff in my study, where she'd be sleeping on the convertible sofa. I looked at the room through her eyes: it seemed to hover uncertainly between sterility and disarray. The bookshelves were neat, dust-free; the Chinese rug from Marshall Field was perfectly square, a cheerful blue and gold with a Chinese character woven into the center—though who knew what the ideogram meant? Perhaps it was a Mandarin obscenity. My desk, however, seemed to be emblematic of a mind gone mad. There were caved-in stacks of papers and journals, little scraps of paper with phone numbers, unread magazines, empty coffee cups, cuticle scissors, my leather-bound journal opened up with two pens stuck in it, a Sony tape recorder and a clutter of cassettes, a handout from the Jehovah's Witnesses which I was too superstitious to throw away. And beneath the desk were the papers that had already been shed, scraps and notebooks and court transcripts that had been forced to the ground by the newer arrivals. The desk was the way station between my crisp public self and the inner self that was slowly caving in.

"Do you realize that if you become a world-renowned statesman, this desk, just as it is, will be worth a fortune?" Caroline said. She was opening her suitcase and unpacking a couple of her dresses before they wrinkled further.

"Then let's wrap it up and ship it off," I said. I was watching her as she fumbled with the hangers. I'd never known her to seem so nervous.

"Are we going to go over to your campaign office?" she asked.

"If you want. It's just getting started."

"I want to. I really want to make that the focus."

"There's plenty of time."

"No. I'd like to start right away. If you get beaten, I don't want Mom blaming me."

"Ha ha?"

"Yes, ha ha," assured Caroline. "But I would like to get going. I don't even know what you want me to do. But I need to be busy. Anyhow, I'm excited. Aren't you?" She sat down suddenly and put her arms up on the back of the sofa. She smiled and held her head at an angle, as if she were going to be photographed.

"You're so pretty," I said.

"I'm thirty-six years old next month," she said.

"Go into politics," I said. "*Fifty* is considered young."

"Well, it doesn't work that way in my business, which is being a struggling artist living in a slum. For that, you're supposed to be twenty."

"When I'm in Congress, I'll see what I can do about getting you a grant," I said.

"I know you will. But for now, how about feeding me?"

We went to the kitchen and for the first time since her arrival, Caroline mentioned Juliet.

"Juliet still living on cottage cheese and scallions?"

"She's branched out a little. She likes turkey breast now."

"How lusty of her," said Caroline. She was standing next to me, peering into the refrigerator. There was bottled water, freshly squeezed grapefruit juice, a bottle of honey and vinegar salad dressing from Maine, a pound of turkey breast wrapped in cellophane, little jars of Scottish jam, a wedge of butter from a kosher dairy store, a tub of Breakstone low-fat cottage cheese. "You've got yourself a fancy girl, Fielding," Caroline said. "Looks like Danny's icebox."

"We can go out to eat, if you want. That's what I usually do."

"So I see," she said, looking me up and down.

"I weigh eleven pounds more than I did in high school, Caroline."

"So who said you were an Adonis in high school?" She swatted the refrigerator door closed. "Don't mind me," she said. "I'm fanatic about being slim. It comes from living on First Avenue and seeing what happens to the women there when they get past thirty."

"First Avenue? How about where we grew up? It seemed like everyone weighed two hundred pounds."

"Not the real Irish ladies, though. They were like sticks. With flashing eyes."

"Like Mrs. O'Mara, Bobby's mother."

"God, what a witch," said Caroline. "I can't imagine her giving birth. I think Bobby must have come out like a painful shit."

"And was content to remain one," I said.

Caroline's face brightened; she seemed surprised at what I'd said, the way people show amazement when a priest makes a frisky little jest. "I thought you liked Bobby O'Mara," she said.

"Me? Bobby O'Mara?"

"Yes. I thought you did. But then I thought you liked everybody. Didn't you?"

"No. Of course not. What kind of idiot likes everybody?"

"Right. That's what I used to ask myself."

I breathed in deeply, as if her teasing wit had an aroma. Caroline had always had what Mom called a black tongue. The passage of time spoils most of our favorite jokes. Where's the fun in sinking your teeth into the egos of your enemies when their egos have been cut in half by the passing years? And what's the percentage of telling jokes at your own expense, when it's already been demonstrated that others see your faults far more clearly than *you* ever could. Caroline's nasty sense of humor had kept her aloft through a misunderstood adolescence and had propelled her through art school in Boston and on to Europe: she seemed to ride herd over time and experience, high on a dark horse of her own venom. She was loyal and God knows she was kind, but she had a lunatic's habit of telling the unpleasant truth and making it funny. I had pitied the boys whose sexual habits she would satirize for us, pitied them for the words they would ask her to whisper and the secret places they would beg her to touch. But they never knew. Caroline didn't want to hurt them; she only wanted to make her own life more palatable, to season it with her sense of humor, just as Sarah used to carry a bottle of Tabasco sauce in her purse, to secretly spice the bland northern food.

Caroline and I took my car and drove over to the Amazing Zucchini to have our lunch. The Amazing Zucchini was owned by an old law school friend named Victor Tomczak. Victor hadn't been much of a student and tended to bring up the rear in most of the classes, but he was a terrific hustler and could find profit like a heat-seeking missile. He had a string of restaurants now and they all had joke names—Paul Onion, the Veal Thing, Pizza My Heart. This one had a sign of a zucchini (with an Italianate mus-

tache) tied up in a chain, with heavy padlocks around it, à la
Houdini. It was a businessmen's spot by day and a junior exec
singles' pickup joint by night. I was hoping Victor would be there,
and I was in luck. He was sitting at a back table with his Chinese
cook, going through a Florsheim shoebox full of receipts. Victor
was a big man. He called himself the gentle giant because he
worried that his size frightened people—especially women. He
had light curly hair, round, staring blue eyes, a cherub's chaste
smile.

"Fielding!" Victor shouted.

He got up so quickly, he lifted the lozenge-shaped table with
him. The cook lunged to keep the stacks of receipts intact, but
Victor paid no mind to the little tabletop drama. He clapped his
hands together and then squeezed them hard, as if in Caroline and
me he'd just seen the main course of a sumptuous human feast.

"I'm finally going to get my hands on some of your money,"
he said, striding toward us. He made it across the restaurant in
five strides and then he did something that never failed to squeeze
out an ooze of fright in me: he threw his arms around me and
embraced me with what I suppose was thirty-five percent of his
strength. I patted his back, like a vanquished wrestler hitting his
hand against the canvas. He broke away from me and looked me
up and down. "You're going to have lunch?"

"That's the general idea," I said. "This is my sister, Victor.
Caroline McDonald. Caroline, this is Victor Tomczak. A good
friend from U. of C. law and the owner of this and other fine
metropolitan eateries."

"I guess that's kind of a waste of education," Victor said, taking
Caroline's hand and blushing.

Caroline gave Victor what seemed to be a smile with a touch
of the come-hither in it. When I was a boy, with a monk's fringe
of hair between my legs, Caroline's flirtatiousness could ignite
volcanoes of lust within me. She had had a kind of frankness about
her body, like a creature raised in the wild, and it gave her a
towering advantage over anyone remotely her age. A dozen times,

no, a thousand, Danny and I had ransacked her room, archaeologists that we were, searching for pieces of the sexual puzzle. We never found a thing—not a condom, nor a sky-blue diaphragm case. One thing: a copy of Erich Fromm's *The Art of Loving*, but that simpering secular sermon had no more smarts about the gritty, grunting deed than had Danny or I.

Somehow, Caroline had perfected a magic act of revelation and concealment: we heard in every corner of our lives the echo of Caroline's sensuality, but we never could find the source. In the end, Danny was to know her more deeply than I: he'd been with her when, abandoned by Eric, she gave birth to Malik. She had gripped his fingers; he had looked down into her huge suffering eyes turning white as the brown rolled back, lifted her hips as the nurse pulled out the blood-soaked sheet and tucked in a fresh one. Their siblingship had naturally deepened after that long July afternoon, with a red smoldering sun perched on the grainy ledge of her window in St. Vincent's Hospital. Danny presented a cleaned and swaddled Malik to Caroline, who had just raised herself up on her elbows, with her huge, milky breasts shiny with sweat and the hair plastered to her forehead, while I was in Chicago, laying the tracks that were supposed to take me through life. And because I was on my own when their love deepened, my relationship with both of them seemed from that point on a little callow. If it had been Danny in this restaurant, he would not have scowled inwardly when Caroline held onto Victor's hand an extra moment. Danny had lost a certain acuity of vision, traded it in for something softer and more encompassing, he would not have bothered to notice the extra moment of hand holding, or the way she disguised her own need to be touched like someone who wants to sneak out of a room will cough to cover the door's tattletale squeak.

Victor brought us to a table near the back and collected a few of the empty Perrier bottles turned into vases for miniature carnations and placed them before us.

"This'll make it festive," he said, and then stepped back and rubbed his big hands together.

"Aren't you going to join us?" Caroline asked.

"Oh no, no," Victor said, as if he'd been offered riches beyond his worthiness. "I've got to get back to my receipts."

"Well, maybe later," Caroline persisted.

"Yes!" Victor said. "Later! I'll bring over strawberry shortcake when you're finished with lunch."

"Nice guy," Caroline said, when he was gone. "Like someone from home."

"Yeah? Where's that?" A waitress appeared with a plastic basket filled with pumpernickel raisin rolls.

"Home is a shifting place," said Caroline, watching me grab for a roll. "It's wherever we long to return to. Right now, for me, it's . . ." She closed her eyes, pressed a thumb and forefinger on her wrinkled, mauve eyelids. "DeKalb Avenue."

Caroline's story had always followed a simple line: the oldest daughter, meant to share a mother's duties, misunderstood, mistreated, denied the dignity of high expectations. Dad had a keen instinct for fair play when it came to his class, but fell short when it came to his daughter; it galled him that the people who built the towers and paved the roads weren't considered the kings of the earth, but as simple a thought as a woman's owning outright her one and only life seemed to him ridiculous, bohemian, fatal. I had always assumed that for Caroline even the heights of hedonism were covered in the scrub and crabgrass of vengefulness. It seemed she never had a love affair, never brushed on a stroke of mocha mascara, never wriggled into a pair of flaming pink pantyhose without half a mind on our parents.

"You know what I can't get over?" she asked me, leaning forward, picking a curl of thread off the lapel of my tweed jacket. "How each of us so exactly fulfilled Mom and Dad's expectations for us. I mean, Christ, they should have worked in the circus and trained tigers to jump through flaming hoops. Do you realize what kind of *willpower* is involved here? It's monstrous."

"You think they wanted Danny to be a seat-of-the-pants businessman? They probably know about the drugs, too. You think they wanted that?"

"You're getting the details right but the story wrong," Caroline said. "Just like a lawyer. You know when you isolate details and ignore the overall picture, it's pornography. They wanted Danny to be successful. They always thought he had a knack for business and they were quick to tell him so. Remember? Even when he was ten, he was selling Christmas cards, magazine subscriptions. Not only business—but it was really like being in the *publishing* business. Mom always praised Danny for his expensive tastes. Don't you remember how Daddy used to drink his coffee and stick out his pinky when he held the cup? He'd say, This is how the ritzy folk do it, and it was supposed to be a joke, like we were supposed to laugh at how silly and weak and fancy the rich were, but the idea was there: we were all supposed to rise. They liked to think they *chose* to live a simple life and what better way to prove it than to have their three children turn out to be complete successes?"

"We were supposed to be the paths not taken?" I said.

"Now you're catching on," said Caroline. "Why don't you stop munching those rolls and we'll order lunch?" She tilted back in her chair and signaled for the waitress. We ordered Irish stew. Caroline ordered a Harp beer to go with hers; I went for the ginger ale. I glanced back at Victor. The cook was shouting at him, slapping down the receipts one after the other, the way players do in those incomprehensible Third World card games.

"With me, the message was different," Caroline was saying. "Partly because they didn't give a shit what I actually *did*. I mean, it never occurred to Dad that women had complicated lives— except emotional complications. And Mom just figured I was as tough as she was and I'd work it out myself. But, hell, look at her life. Typing for that cretin Corvino, who stunk of amaretto and Camels, and who treated her like she was some idiot sister-in-law lucky to have a job. God, it used to make me so angry whenever I'd go over to the office and see how Corvino talked to Mom—"

"I know what you mean," I said.

"You felt that way?"

"Yes. A lot."

"Then how come you decided to be the computer-age Earl Corvino? You'd think you'd want to get as far from politics as possible."

"There's no way to get *away* from politics. The most you can do is close your eyes and pretend it isn't happening or it doesn't matter. And then you let all the worst people do it for you."

Caroline shrugged. "If you use that kind of logic, then maybe so-called nice people ought to become cops and prison guards, too."

"Maybe they should. It's not like what the world needs most is another sensitive English teacher. Anyhow, it's not the same thing. If you're a cop, all you can do is arrest someone or not arrest them. In politics, you're dealing with a wider range of choices."

"OK. I don't know why I'm on your case. I want you to win. I came here, didn't I? I'm just teasing you. But you piss me off when you think this whole thing is something you made up. You don't realize you're just doing what Mom and Dad decided for you."

"That's what families are like."

"If you're lucky," said Caroline. "I wasn't given this kind of choice. The only message I got was don't be a lower-middle-class housewife in an apartment house somewhere in Brooklyn. Beyond that, I had to make it up as I went along—and look what I did."

"You did great."

"I'm glad you think so. I've got three jobs and I'm a sneeze away from welfare."

"You went all over Europe. You've got Rudy and Malik."

"I notice you're not including Eric in my list of accomplishments."

"I could. He's a great musician. Jazz is the most significant American art form. And quack quack quack."

"Exactly. Quack quack quack. He's taking the boys away from me, heartbeat by heartbeat."

"Don't let him."

"I'm doing my best. But Eric's persuasive and he has so much on his side. That school they go to."

"Take them out of that school, then."

"I can't do that. They love it there. And they love their daddy. And they love being black. It's a losing cause for me. And I'm too tired to fight."

"No you're not. You can't let them drift away."

The waitress came with our meals. I started right in on mine but Caroline didn't even glance down at hers: it was a form of exercise, a way of keeping the heel of her hand firmly planted on appetite's forehead as it lurched for her and tried to engulf her in its frantic embrace. "Mmmm, they've got those little carrots in this," I said.

"Oh good," said Caroline, in a manic imitation of enthusiasm, "those little carrots. Things are really starting to pop now." She peered into her dish. "Yes. You're absolutely right. I see one. A . . . little carrot."

"OK already," I said. I felt her sarcasm's sting, but it was not a bad sensation: it felt like something I could trust. "I think it's demented not to show some enthusiasm for your food. And spoiled, too. Half of human history is about getting enough to eat."

"Yes. And the other half is about eating too much," said Caroline. She reached across the table and patted the back of my hand: there there. "And aren't you telling this to the wrong person? Isn't this what you meant to say to Our Lady of the Cottage Cheese?"

"That's a lost cause. Besides, she has problems. She's delicate."

"Naturally."

"Well, I'm not going to sit here defending my girl friend's digestive tract."

Caroline took a drink of her beer. "You're going to win this election, aren't you?"

"I ought to."

"Ought to? I don't like the sound of that. Things that *ought* to happen rarely do."

"It's a Democratic district. The Democratic Party is more or less supporting me. The guy I'm running against isn't much."

"I heard he has style," Caroline said.

"Style? Where'd you pick that up?"

"On the plane. The woman I was sitting next to lives in your district. An old beatnik. Abstract earrings, turquoise turtleneck, gray ponytail. She said this guy, the fellow from the coffeehouse—"

"Bertelli."

"Yeah. She said he has a kind of charming European style."

"Well, what does that mean to you?"

"To me? It means he wears socks under his sandals and pinches you on the can."

"Exactly. What else did she say?"

"Are you ready to hear it?"

"Of course. It's my *job*."

"Well, she didn't know I was your sister."

"That was very cagey of you, Caroline. What did she say?"

"I don't remember her exact words, but she sort of lumped you with the bunch who kicked Carmichael out of office. She thought it was kind of Nazi of everyone."

"Oh Christ. I can't believe this."

"Well, she *was* a beatnik, Fielding. You've got to make allowances."

"It makes me sick. I thought I was going to be the most liberal member of the Congress and people see me as the Moral Majority candidate. Things are very fucked up in this country. No one listens."

"It's the exercise craze," said Caroline. "People enjoying jumping to conclusions."

I paused and watched Caroline take another drink of her Harp. When I want to drink, I get a foul, desperate taste at the back of my throat; I swallowed it back. "I'm glad you came here," I said.

"Well, I don't want you to lose this election," Caroline said. "If you don't make it, that does it for the lot of us—but if you do, then maybe you'll ignite something in Danny and me. We need a winner here, Fielding—"

"You hate talk about winners and losers," I said.

"I'm trying to get into the spirit of the times."

"Wait until you meet the people in my campaign. It'll make you wonder if totalitarianism might be a better idea."

"Believe me, I expect the worst. After watching Corvino doing a tarantella on Mom's back for fifteen years."

"It's more of the same. Fat-asses looking for a free ride."

"So how am I going to fit in?" asked Caroline.

"You will, that's all. You just will. You have to. I need someone I can trust."

"Are you in control?" she asked.

"In all ways but one," I answered.

"Yes? Which one?"

"I'm losing my mind," I said.

"In your case, it sounds like a good idea."

I put my fork down and folded my hands on my lap.

"Something's wrong," I said.

Caroline lowered her eyes. Disappointment? Embarrassment? Or was she just giving me room to come forward?

"It's about Sarah," I said.

"You were talking about her a lot in New York over Christmas," she said.

"I'm going through something very hard now, Caroline."

"Missing her?"

"No. Something else. Feeling her." I fell silent. A feeling of catastrophic fatigue came over me, as if sorrow, like the sands of Jupiter, filled me from head to foot.

"What do you mean, Fielding? You mean as if she was alive?"

"I've been getting telephone calls. Messages. They come in when I'm away. From Sarah. And I don't know how this happened, how I could have fallen prey to it—but I've been believing them. I've been believing she's alive. That she's—I don't know—come back from the other side, or that she never died, or that there's a secret about death that's never been known and now it's coming to light. It's useless to try and explain." I was noticing the distress in Caroline's face. I lowered my voice. "I feel her in the snow."

"Oh God, Fielding," said Caroline, reaching for my hand and squeezing it. Her fingers were icy. "You poor thing." Her pale brown eyes filled with tears.

"I miss her so much," I said, my voice breaking like a little white bowl.

"She was an amazing woman," Caroline said. "I can understand how you could think she'd—well, you know."

"Desire turns us into idiots," I said.

"Thank God," said Caroline.

And then we were silent. Coming from behind me, I heard the furious sound of Victor's cook holding forth in an unbroken stream of Cantonese, punctuating his harangue with clumps of receipts slapped onto the table. Caroline cut a piece of her lamb in half and let out a sigh as she brought it to her mouth, as if the fork was very heavy or she was just about to become a vegetarian. I felt something cold in the pit of my stomach; I knew she was about to say something and I wasn't sure I wanted to hear it.

"I once thought I saw her, Fielding," she said in a soft voice. She carefully placed her fork on the edge of her plate.

I don't know what I said just then. Something like Really? or Who? or maybe I said, You mean Sarah?—but I already knew and I was already watching it happen, like you watch something slip from the edge of the table, an egg, and all you can do is stand there, gesturing silently, waiting for the fatal little crunch to jolt you back into time.

"Yes," said Caroline. "A couple years ago. It was too crazy to mention. But it looked so much like her. I was on the corner of Forty-fourth and Fifth Avenue. I turned west and I saw her coming out of this Japanese restaurant. She was with an older man, very thin, a guy in his sixties. I shouldn't say *she*. This woman. The woman who looked so much like Sarah. I was so unnerved. I wasn't even subtle. I just said, 'Sarah? Sarah?' And she looked right at me. Her eyes just jumped on mine. You know that way she had? So passionate it was—*assaultive?* It makes you step back a little. And the look on her face. She seemed so . . . *caught.* As if it was a bust, you know? She put her fingers over her lips. She looked frightened, except for her eyes, which kept coming at me. I was too surprised to be frightened, or even mystified. It was as if the fact of her death slipped my mind for a moment, and the only surprise was seeing her on Forty-fourth Street when I thought she was someplace else. Then it struck me. And I did get scared. It was December 8. I remember that. The day before Rudy and Malik came home from school with a very complicated theory about the bombing of Pearl Harbor—"

"Please," I said.

"Sorry. I was just remembering. Anyhow, I don't know what else to say." She made a helpless gesture. "I called out to her again but this time she—oh, I shouldn't say *she*—the woman, the woman who looked like Sarah—took the old man's arm. He was wearing a black wool overcoat. And they started walking west, full speed ahead. I was too stunned to follow, right away. But then I did. It was crowded and the wind was coming right off the river. It wasn't a heavy snow but it stung my face. Then she turned around. I think I'd startled her and she wanted to know if I was still following her. And when I saw her face again, she looked different. It didn't look like Sarah. Not really. So I stopped. Turned around. You know, forgot about it."

"You saw her," I said. "You saw her."

"Fielding," she said, and then she said something else. I could see her lips forming the words, could see the tip of her tongue darting back and forth, saw the furrow of her brow, the earnest gesture—but the meaning and sound of her words was beyond me, a window placed so near to the top of the dungeon of the moment that it was hopeless to try and find it. I took a breath and I heard the effort behind the inhale, a rasping, desperate noise, like someone panicking in deep water. Next was my heart, slamming out a hideous, heedless, doom-drunk double time. Caroline stopped whatever she was saying and looked at me with terror in her eyes. She reached toward me but I could not feel her touch. I tried to swallow, but it seemed there was a stick at the back of my throat. I clawed loose my tie and then tore open two shirt buttons and placed my palm on my chest. I was afraid to take another breath: I didn't want to hear that strangled rattling noise. And then I heard an overwhelming groan, as if a dying beast were perched on my shoulder: it was the death rattle of a monster and for a moment the restaurant shimmered before me and the next moment I was gone.

Caroline called out my name and the next thing I knew she had me on one side and Victor grabbed me on the other. They pulled me to my feet. I could hear my voice but had no idea what I was saying. I had a compulsion to move, as if death had just swooped down and, barely missing its target, was getting ready for another pass at me. My head was bright with pain where I'd struck the table. Lunch was mixed with the blue willow shards on the wooden floor. Everything looked pewter-colored and as if it were about to melt. I focused on the cook. He was standing at his table with a handful of receipts, stroking his scraggly beard with his thumb and forefinger and looking at me with absolutely no trace of emotion in his eyes.

10

Our apartment was small, lacking in charm: we were always dead broke. It needed the touch of a woman who could spin gold out of straw, someone who knew where to gather wild flowers or buy gorgeous bolts of Indian fabric for a few dollars and change all that dreariness into something light and lovely. But Sarah was not that sort of woman. We lived in those four rooms like spies in a safe-house. It was all very collegiate. None of our dishes matched; we didn't own a saucer; our silverware had been left behind by the previous tenants, who'd probably decided it was worth less than the box they would need to pack it. There were French doors between the living and dining rooms, but students had been living there for so long that the dining room had for the past decade been a bedroom and the glass panes on the French doors had been painted red and black. Our bedroom had gray walls with green trim: it was the one room we'd painted ourselves. Our king-sized mattress was on the floor. The mattress was so hard, with so little give, and Sarah had so little meat on her bones, that often the skin along her spine was mauve and rose. She never wanted sex to be easy; the idea of a groggy, comforting fuck was an absolute horror to her. I sometimes wondered if it was a form of prudery, this fantastic importance she gave to practically every sexual contact. Sometimes it used to drive me mad. You could not just roll on top of her for a quick lay. I once woke up from a terrible nightmare (a pit, a length of unraveling rope, etc.) and pressed myself against her. The hot, hard flesh of her ass, the Chanel No. 19 on the nape of her neck pulled me away from the night horrors and into an edgy eroticism. I put my hand between her legs and reached forward, up to her center and into her. "Don't," she said in a furious whisper. Making love without ceremony was like going to high mass in dirty clothes: you had to make an effort, you had to acknowledge a certain transcendent importance. It was not, as far as Sarah was concerned, meant to be simple or overly relaxed. There had to be yearning and a certain unreasonableness of desire. The quintessential Chicago fuck in that gray and green room: me on top, supporting my weight with my hands, no parts of our bodies touching except hips, genitalia, tops of thighs. I came in and out of her very, very slowly, the sweat crystallizing along my backbone and turning to salty ice, our breaths twinned and rasping, and the fronts of our bodies yearning to touch—yet every time I started to lower myself onto her she would somehow indicate I should not. The strain was killing—my shoulders, my biceps, my forearms, my wrists and fingers. I felt as if I were going to explode at any moment and, at the same time, as if I would never have any relief. She was moving beneath me, steadily, with a grueling, mindless force. And then, slowly, it would start to get chaotic and her breaths—or were they mine?—would start breaking in two and in the crack would come high-pitched, hungry, desperate sounds, something between begging and encouragement. And now my body was longing to touch hers with a true mania of need, as if the feel of our chests and bellies joining would release me from an exile, and when we were finally coming (it always took a long time, thank God) and I was emptying into her and she was rushing into me, I lowered first my mouth and then my chest and then my stomach and she wrapped her arms around me in an indelible way that withstands the wash of time. And always will. And always, always, always will.

Resurrection House was just one part of St. Christopher's Church on the northwest side of Chicago. The church itself was stolid, built with dark bricks, and the stained-glass windows ranged from dark purple to brown. Sarah's friend Steven Mileski was one of two priests who presided there; the other was a soft-looking, short, overweight, dark-haired, brooding-eyed, thin-lipped, high-voiced Mexican named Father Emanuel Lopez. Father Lopez's great advantage was his Spanish—more than half of the parishioners were Mexican—but he had a horror of those who lived in poverty, imagined their resentments and snaky little schemes for revenge, even hated to have them in his church, where he imagined them thieving away for the sheer sport of it—stealing Bibles and taking them home to rip out the pages to use as toilet tissue, pocketing the votive candles so the bumpy red glasses could be transformed into tequila cups. When he spoke from the pulpit, Father Lopez's eyes shook: he was determined to catch one of those weeping brown old women dressed in stiff black dresses and soft brown sandals in an act of vandalism, even as they knelt before him with their eyes closed and their faces tilted down like sunflowers dead on the stalk.

There was the church and then there was the church basement. And it was here that Mileski reigned: what a demon for the good deed that man was. He ran what he called community outreach programs—for alcoholics, for those teetering on divorce, for battered wives, battered children, for the lonely, the infirm, and even for those who had some artistic talent. He believed in something he called community sharing, which was, as far as I could tell, a sort of mass confession in mufti: Mileski sat straddling a gunmetal-gray folding chair, with his big, furry arms resting on the back of the chair and his apocalyptic obsidian eyes clicking from face to face as friends and neighbors at first haltingly and then eloquently and finally obsessively described their fantasies and sins and looked for consolation in the sounds of their own voices. Mileski's beard came down to his heart; his tar black hair fell in his eyes. His neck was so thick, the pressure against his white collar was intolerable and he wore his shirt open: chest hair geysered up like foam on a beer. He was careful to keep a steady flow of hints; it was critical to him that he not be mistaken for a run-of-the-mill priest. He was young and he was hip. He made jokes like this: The pope's favorite song is "Papa's Got a Brand New Bag." When asked for advice, he'd say, "Well, as a priest and an official representative of the Church and its doctrines, what I *should* say is . . ." And then he'd proceed to give a quick, unattractive gloss of current doctrine, phrasing it in such a way that his own points of diversion became obvious.

Next to the church was a playground and here Mileski coached basketball, touch football, and soccer, which he learned in his year abroad in Cracow. He was resonant of voice and so self-confident it took your breath away: he was like a lunatic in a play, thumping his chest and proclaiming Nothing bad can ever happen to *me*. To recruit a center for the St. Christopher's basketball team, Mileski played one-on-one with a tall Appalachian boy named Reuben Martin and after a fierce game to forty, after which Mileski was drenched with sweat and unable to speak through his huge rapid phlegmy gasps, not only was the vanquished Reuben Martin willing to join the team but he'd also, as part of the wager, agreed to take instruction in Catholicism.

And next to the playground was Resurrection House. It was a little blue and white frame house; it had once been the rectory for whoever was St. Christopher's priest, and no matter how many beanbag chairs and funky posters they put in that house it retained its monastic air. Resurrection House was Mileski's invention: he wanted a place where the homeless, the afraid, where all souls on the loose might gather. There was always an extra bed, always something to eat, always someone to talk to. Mileski ran it with the help of a boy named Hector Guzman, who was then drafted and finally killed in Da Nang. Now Sarah was there, working with Mileski when he was available, working on her own when he was not. It was social work in the old Church tradition. For years, the neighborhood had operated as a kind of way station for newcomers to Chicago, taking them in, letting them get started, and then letting them disperse to somewhat better circumstances as the next wave arrived. But all that had changed. The better circumstances—the jobs, the public housing—no longer existed; the neighborhood became angrier, denser, terminal. "We've really got our work cut out for us" was how Mileski put it, and Sarah, as far as I could tell, concurred. You had to be mad to think that a church could alleviate the suffering of that neighborhood. But like two brave souls trying to bail out a sinking ship with teacups, Sarah and Mileski kept the doors of Resurrection House open for anyone who needed shelter—for the night, the week, for all of eternity.

It was there that Sarah learned a domesticity I never thought she was interested in or capable of, and which I, perhaps out of jealous, found wildly incongruous with what I thought were her best qualities. She was forever pushing around an old Electrolux, stripping beds, bleaching sheets, and that pop bottle filled with wild flowers which our own gloomy quarters could easily have used was placed instead on the Formica table of Resurrection House's always crowded, always redolent kitchen.

I asked Sarah why she was doing nun's work, but to her it seemed the best of both worlds—or perhaps she was only humoring me. "By day, I can do good works and by night I can sip Calvados and fuck my brains out." But there are truths so partial they become lies and I'm afraid that was one of them. The fact was that more and more she came home unable to talk about anything outside the galaxy of human misery in which she orbited by day. "It's so sick," she said to me, "so unbelievably distorted. The Church thinks Mayor Daley is closer to God than the people Steven and I are serving. And if Christ walks among us today, the Church thinks He probably has a butler and a Mercedes." Can we talk about something else? I asked. She paused. "OK," she said. Another pause. And then: "How's school?"

Thanksgiving, 1974. Sarah's sister Tammy came up to stay with us. She was still not divorced from Derek—Derek of the silk pajamas, the poodle named Cynthia, and the shaved chest—but she had lost a great deal of weight. "I swear, that little sonofabitch ain't going to leave *me*. I'm going to get good and foxy and then I'm going to leave *him*." She was in Chicago, she said, to have a real Yankee Thanksgiving and, in fact, the day she arrived we had the winter's first snow. The only window we had that looked out onto the street was in the bathroom and Tammy sat for hours on the edge of the tub, watching the snow fall. "She's cracking up," Sarah whispered to me. "It's kind of scary."

"I keep telling myself, she's your sister," I said, shaking my head.

"She's not this southern at home," Sarah said.

"I mean, really, watching the snow?"

"I know, I know, it's not as if she hasn't seen it before. Daddy gave her and Derek a trip to Aspen for their wedding present. Maybe that's what she's doing in there. Remembering it."

"Derek," I said.

"I know. I *know*. We all take after our mother in our horrible taste in men." Sarah slipped her arm around me and leaned against my side. We were in the kitchen making Thanksgiving dinner, a turkey jambalaya. A thousand times we'd begun to sing, "Oh jambalaya/crayfish pie filé gumbo," but never took it any further. There was a jug of Inglenook on the table, a store-bought pumpkin pie near the sink. Our domestic life struck me as purely conceptual. Perhaps it was the light in that apartment, that soiled, overcast, dull glare. The rituals of cooking and sweeping and plumping up the pillows on the old flowered Minnie Mouse sofa and chairs was to real housekeeping as a little string fence around a garden in the wilderness is to real farming.

Our guests for dinner were Father Mileski, Father Stanton, a poet who was a friend of Stanton's named Madeline Conners, and a teacher named Bernardo Gutierrez, who had recently been smuggled out of Chile and was now living in hiding in Chicago. Gutierrez was a surprise; he arrived with Madeline Conners.

Madeline Conners was a small, stocky woman; her hair was pale brown and her watchful face with its worry lines and sharp blue eyes was cast into innocence by an extravagant mask of pale freckles. She was nearly forty, had traveled the entire world, and worked grinding lenses occasionally to raise money to self-publish a book of her poems. She smoked her Camels like a convict; the ember came so close to her full, cracked lips that you couldn't help staring at her. Madeline had been living in an apartment not far away, taking care of it while its owners were in Taiwan buying toy prototypes. Now they were coming back and she was getting ready to move again—this time out to Silver Spring, Maryland, where her brother lived and where she could put in a couple of months' work at an optics factory and ready her new book for the printer. Bernardo had been living with her in what I sensed was a roommate relationship but he was reluctant to move out to Maryland with her.

Gutierrez was a large, melancholy-looking man. He was in his forties, an exile. While President Allende was in power in Chile, Bernardo had quit his post at the university and gone to work for the new government—writing press releases, trying his hand on speeches. He was an economist, suspicious of rhetoric, constitutionally averse to sudden excitement. But he was capable of clarity and could simplify complicated economic issues; he was given a lot to do. After the Chilean generals disposed of Allende and his regime, Gutierrez went into hiding. One by one, and, finally, dozen by dozen, everyone he knew was under arrest, missing, dead—often found in rivers with their eyes burned out, their genitals sewn into their mouth. Bernardo hid in a church outside of Valparaiso, where his sister was a nun. Eventually, he was sneaked out of the country.

"Why did you come here?" I asked him. "I'd think you'd be angry at the United States."

Gutierrez pursed his lips when he listened and nodded his head. He folded his surprisingly delicate hands over his taut round belly.

"Perhaps I'll go to Cuba," he finally answered, with a sigh.

I looked over at Sarah. His answer somehow gave the impression that I had asked him to leave my country.

"Maybe someday you'll go back to Chile," Sarah said to him, raising a glass. "When this nightmare ends."

"I didn't mean you *shouldn't* come here," I said, feeling awkward, irritated. "I just thought you wouldn't want to, seeing how tough we made it for your president."

Gutierrez stared at me. I had always flattered myself into believing there was virtually no one with whom I couldn't easily communicate, but whatever sympathy and solace I was attempting to show the Chilean was somehow slipping into the fissure between Spanish and English, like a dog that falls into a stream and scrambles out looking like a weasel. I saw in his eyes that my saying "how tough we made it" meant that I considered myself a part of the forces that had engineered the coup: like so many deeply committed people, he took an opinion for a desire.

We served the jambalaya. Madeline carefully separated all of the turkey out and left it in a mound on the side of her blue willow plate. Tammy, who'd been uncomfortable at first when the church people arrived, feeling it meant she would have to be on her best behavior, and who then shifted to another sort of discomfort—the discomfort of a good citizen offended by the seditious disloyalty of her tablemates—seized on the opportunity of the jambalaya's arrival to become still more southern. She was all my mys and ooo wees and she was shaking her fork at Sarah, saying, "You done yourself proud on this one, Sister." Mileski ate heartily; it astonished me to see the Friar Tuckian heap he'd piled on his plate. He had asked us to join hands before the meal and we did: I held Madeline's hard, dry hand and Tammy's soft, nervous one. We closed our eyes and silently reflected on our good fortune. Tammy seemed to be giving my hand an extra squeeze; I had a demented apprehension she was flirting with me but then realized she was trying to make contact with an ally: she was appalled by the company and assumed I shared her feelings.

"Quite a bizarre holiday," said Stanton, in his Rhodesian accent. "What we're celebrating is a gang of rapacious Protestants who came here and stole a country."

"What I would have loved to have been," Mileski said through a mouthful of jambalaya, his thick mustache dripping wine, "was one of those priests who came over here about the middle of the nineteenth century."

"Was that a good time?" Sarah asked. Her face was bright with pleasure—already.

"Well," said Mileski, smiling, "you might say so." He kept his napkin next to his plate and wiped his hand on it without lifting it. "You see, the Church came over with the flock, and the flock was in the cities." He looked at me and winked. "Working their tails off." Back to Sarah and then, with a wave of the fork, the table. "Things were more or less together. The Church administered to the Catholics at hand and pretty much tried to keep up the ways of the old country. And helping the immigrants fit into the whole American trip. But when the *west* started opening up—" Mileski grinned and shook his head. "That was a whole different story. Suddenly, you had Catholics in . . . Nevada, Oregon, you had Catholics picking grapes all the way out in California. And no one to look after them."

"No one to keep them toeing the line, you mean," said Sarah. Good-natured.

Mileski bowed toward her, gladly conceding the point. I half stood up, refilling all the glasses. I realized I was doing a lot of that. Stanton was already looking a little lopsided and Madeline Conners' eyes were pale red, like the inside of hot-house tomatoes.

"There weren't enough priests in America to send them out of the cities. So the bishops had to take emergency measures." Mileski glanced at his plate but decided to continue with his story before taking another bite. He filled his fork and then laid it on the side of the plate. "They had to *import* priests from Europe and send them after the American Catholics. Not a bad solution, you might say. But the problem was that the only priests they could lure over here were priests who had fallen on hard times. We're talking about priests who'd become total juicers, priests—" Mileski started to laugh. "Priests who were maybe a little strange in the head. Priests who'd gotten themselves caught in some pretty embarrassing situations. And when they came over here and they got themselves sent out into the wilderness—well, some pretty strange things went down. As far as the bishops were concerned it was terrifying."

"And this is what you're nostalgic for?" asked Sarah. She indicated to me it was time to pour a little more wine for Father Stanton.

"Those are my *roots*," said Mileski. "That's my pastoral tradition. You realize how sublimely crazy this Church has got to be to let a Polack like me put on a collar."

We were all getting drunk, though I wondered if the alcoholic oblivion I was headed toward was anything similar to the expansive ease and relaxation the others seemed to be drinking their ways into. I drank as if to keep an appointment in Samara, first quickly and then slowly and then quickly again. Mileski seemed to drink in order to expand, whereas Sarah drank to quicken her responses, to play at spontaneity. Stanton drank to escape memory and Madeline Conners drank simply to relax. Tammy, as far as I could tell, drank to wash down her food. And the Chilean Bernardo Gutierrez, I saw, drank to make his fear bearable.

"When do you think you'll be able to get those generals out of the presidential palace and give Chile back its democracy?" I asked him.

Bernardo moved his eyes in my direction. His gestures were slow, careful; he drove the engine of self as if it were falling to pieces. He dabbed his lips with the edge of his napkin and then took a sip of ice water. "I expect to return to my country very soon," he said.

"The rest of South America has to rise up," said Sarah. "Argentina, Peru."

"Wait a minute," said Tammy, quite unexpectedly. "Those places down there are *always* having revolutions. They have a new president every *week*, don't they?"

There was a silence with a spine of disapproval. Madeline Conners finally said, "That's what the press would have you believe. But that's largely propaganda. No reason to fall for it, ah . . . ah . . ."

"Tammy," said Tammy.

"Tammy," said Madeline, nodding.

"This guy you were working for," Tammy said, pointing at Gutierrez. "How long did he have it?"

"Have it?" asked Bernardo.

"You know. Power. How long was he in?"

"A little under two years, unfortunately," said Bernardo.

"Until our guns and money got him out," said Sarah.

Tammy shushed Sarah with a wave. "That's not the point," she said.

"Yes it *is*," said Sarah. Although I couldn't see it, I knew there was now a line of blank space between her body and the seat of her chair. Her sense of argument was different from my own. My instinct was always to leave the other person with the impression that not very much separated us, whereas Sarah's intelligence and outrage seemed always to widen the gap. If she was arguing with you about women's fashions she would end up suggesting you were sympathetic to rapists; if you didn't care for the Rolling Stones she would prove to you you didn't really like rock and roll. She leaned across the table toward Tammy and said, "Don't tell me you've never heard of the CIA. You know, the age of innocence was over some time ago. Our government depends on people not caring and looking the other way."

"According to you," Tammy said, in a deliberately weird, sweet voice, "no one in the world cares—except you." Her hands dropped into her lap and she squeezed them together.

"Just tell me what you think our government *does* in countries down there," said Sarah.

"I don't know," Tammy said, as if she'd been asked to describe the function of some disgusting part of the anatomy.

"That's right," said Sarah, shaking her head. "You don't know."

"Well, does that mean we're the bad guys and the rest of the world is hunky-dory?"

I had to admire her willingness to stay in there and take it, though I did wish Tammy would merely relinquish the point. She scarcely cared anyhow; she was taking the abuse with nothing to win.

"Ask Father Stanton what our country is up to in southern Africa," said Sarah. "Or ask Bernardo. Bernardo isn't even allowed to *be* here. He has to live his entire life underground, as if he were a criminal."

Obediently, Tammy looked across to Stanton. The handsome, silver-haired priest was slumped in his seat; his fine blue eyes seemed to be drowning in a mist. "I must admit," he said, "the Americans weren't of awfully much use."

"When I travel," said Madeline Conners, "I sometimes tell people I'm Canadian. I just can't take the embarrassment, you know?"

"Sometimes we don't know when history will choose us," said

Bernardo softly. His eyes rested on Tammy with a mothlike delicacy. He clearly wanted to put her at ease; he was offended by the Nordic aggression of the others. "Before President Allende, I cared very little for matters of politics. I tended my own garden." He touched the rim of his glass with his fingertips. "I miss those days. It was a good time. But then—" He shrugged. "Life changes. We change. It's how it goes."

"Goddamnit," said Madeline Conners, running her fingers through her short, wiry hair, "it makes me so *angry*, Bernardo. I don't understand why you're not coming to Maryland with me."

He shrugged and gestured philosophically. "I can't," he said. "That whole province of the country is very dangerous right now. Washington is filled with—very dangerous men."

"We should know," said Mileski, in an abundantly cheerful voice. "We put them there."

"He means killers," said Madeline. "Chileans from the junta tracking down anyone from the old regime who might speak out and tell the truth."

"Well, if you know that," said Sarah, "why are you asking him to come with you? What if something happened? He's *our* responsibility."

"Precautions could be taken," said Madeline.

Tammy pushed her chair back and got up. She drank the rest of her wine while standing and then asked, "Is there a telephone in the kitchen, Fielding?"

I said there was and felt relief she was taking herself away for a moment. By the time she returned, the focus of the conversation would have shifted a few more times and she'd be perfectly safe, free to continue her dinner and her vacation away from Derek. I listened to what Stanton was trying to say, but he was seriously drunk now and his accent was going opaque.

Tammy's asking me if there was a phone in the kitchen seemed odd. She had used that phone twice already. She'd called home with Sarah and they'd both spoken to their parents and their sister. She knew perfectly well there was a phone in the kitchen. It struck me that she hadn't been asking me a question at all—she'd been making an announcement.

"I'll get another bottle of wine," I said, getting up.

"Bring the one we brought over," said Mileski. "We're mellow enough now so it won't burn too much to drink it."

"Steven," Sarah said, "why do you buy that crap?"

"I believe if it's too pure an enjoyment, it becomes a venial sin," Mileski said, just as I was leaving the room and pushing my way into the kitchen.

Tammy was sitting on a three-legged stool with the telephone directory in her lap. Though the kitchen was a wreck, she'd made herself a cup of instant coffee. She seemed to have been waiting for me.

"What's up?" I said.

"How can you stand it?" she asked me, her voice, despite the weight of the meal and the wine, shaking with feeling.

"We all have our opinions," I said. "Points of view. Mine's not very far from theirs."

"You're just saying that because you love her. You were in the service. You're . . . regular. These people are just a bunch of crazies."

"I don't know, Tammy. They're doing what they believe in. You have to respect that."

"I'm calling the FBI," she said.

"That's a terrific idea," I said. "It's a call we should have made long ago."

"I'm serious, Fielding. And so are *they*. That guy from Chile is in the country illegally. I mean, why do you think our government didn't want him here? Because of some old library fines? I mean, Sarah might think I'm just an overweight featherbrain— well, I don't even want to think about her goddamned opinions of me. I may not read all the right magazines or sit around having the right conversations with all the fashionable people. But I do know that the reason our government didn't want that little beaner in our country is he's a Communist." She grabbed the phone off the wall and then leaned over her lap, squinting, trying to make out the number in the directory.

I wasn't thinking as clearly as I ought to have been. I didn't have the mental stamina to argue with her and so I just walked across the kitchen and yanked the telephone wire right out of the wall. Like a gangster. The finality of the gesture formed a pleasant cloud of sensation within me. I stood there holding the beige wire and I smiled at Tammy. She was holding the dead receiver next to her ear; it took her a couple of moments to process what had just happened. And when she did she put her hand over her eyes. The veins on her neck stood out. I went to her side and put my arm around her. She had a wonderful, fresh-baked scent. She didn't resist my touch. I held her to me and stroked her hair. I thought she was acting badly but I couldn't help but understand what was making her feel this way. Sarah was rough on her and those priests frightened her. She felt she had stumbled into something dangerous and wrong. And in fact she had her own political feelings: she'd voted twice for Nixon and in college had worn a Goldwater button. "Take it easy," I murmured to her. "You don't want to be like this."

"They have no *right*," she said.

"Of course they do," I said. "But it's OK. Come on, Tammy. Sorry about the phone but . . . you know we've all had too much to drink."

"I want to go home," she said in a small voice.

Good, I thought, but didn't say anything. I held her a little more tightly. Just then, the kitchen door pushed open and Sarah came in, empty-handed. She saw us—Tammy with her face against my chest, me with my arm around Tammy—and stood still for a moment. "Ooops," she said, and then quickly turned and pushed her way out the kitchen door again.

Christmas we spent with a chaos of radical Catholics but I got Sarah to myself for New Year's Eve. We bought a half pound of

Scotch salmon and two bottles of Mumm's and rented a TV to watch *Casablanca* and then the celebration on Times Square. There was a readout on the bottom of the screen showing the seconds going by, as if we were going to be launched like a rocketship into the ether of unused time. We finished the champagne and I went into the kitchen and came back with a half bottle of vodka and another cheaper vodka, about a quarter full. We are really tapped out, I said. "It's no wonder," she said. "Every night you stay up late studying, you end up drinking half a bottle of something." I'm doing *very* well in school, I countered. "I'm sure you are," said Sarah. "But what about in bed?" A slow pulsating chill went through me and I just managed to say, What's that supposed to mean? "I hate to be gross," she said. "I hate when people talk about sex technically." But tonight is a special occasion, I said with a drunken wave. The weight of what was going to be said was already on my chest like a rock—the cornerstone in a soon-to-be-constructed temple of grief. "Come on," she said. "Everyone knows drinking is terrible for you." You never seem to mind it in Stanton and Mileski and that crew, I said, truly grasping at straws. "It's different for celibates," she said. She reached up for me, took the bottles out of my hand, and pulled me next to her on the sofa. She draped a leg over my lap and put her arms around me. Tell me the worst, I whispered. "Sometimes you just can't get rock-solid hard like you used to," she said, "and it's not because of me and not because of you. It's the fucking alcohol."

That night, in a competitive sexual fury, feeling as if my eroticlife was on the line, I made love to her. I made a ceremony out of pouring all the vodka down the drain and then the vermouth, the retsina, the little bottle of Pernod, and, finally, the bottle of Smirnoff I kept in my desk. The landlord was in a magnanimous mood and the radiator in our bedroom sang with steam, though it was two in the morning. I made love to her and then I made love to her again and then again after that. She felt so soft beneath me; she gave herself over with a selflessness that was almost meek, but which held within it her enormous sensual drive, the fierce, radiant power of her genitals. Finally, we lay next to each other. The radiator was silent now; the wind and snow there blowing against the window and cold entered our room thread by thread. Sarah took my hand and placed it very gently over her wet and open center, as if she were inviting me to touch something newly born. "Yikes," she said. I kept my hand there; I could feel the heat rising out of her. Then she whispered, "I'm not going to be able to take this, Fielding. I think you'd better start drinking again."

The next day was open house at Isaac and Adele's. Sarah and I arrived at three in the afternoon. Mrs. Davis was working that day and she'd gotten her skinny, wild-eyed daughter Lucille to help her out. It was not a large party; the Greens liked to retain an aura of selectivity. The partners from the law firm were there, but none of the junior lawyers. I was meant to feel immensely encouraged to be invited and I did. I was the only law student, though the preening, argumentative Wasps who were my teachers were there in abundance. Senator Percy came for a few minutes —two cheese puffs, a cup of punch, a few Nixon jokes, and out: he probably had twenty parties at which he needed to appear that day. Senator Stevenson was in the Caribbean—Isaac and many of the others referred to him as Adlai's boy, as in, "I suppose Adlai's boy is getting sunburned on that boat of his." It seemed to make them feel comfortable to miniaturize him.

Sarah had met the Greens before. Isaac had once taken us to dinner in New York and when Sarah and I first came to Chicago Isaac and Adele had us over twice. It was not, as they say, a good mix. Despite their having lived in Chicago for forty years and mucking about in Chicago politics for most of that time, Isaac and Adele still thought of Catholic girls as tough little numbers in knee socks and green blazers and that Sarah was from the south made their approach to her all the more anthropological. "What was it that Robert Penn Warren once said?" wondered Adele, and it had pretty much gone in a lockstep down from there. They would never have been so crude as to suggest Sarah wasn't a suitable match for a boy of my potential, but it was clear that was how they felt—and Sarah knew it, too. It didn't embitter her toward them; she accepted their judgment and, really, had not even the faintest desire to be the sort of woman who'd make a good wife for a would-be politician. The image of the little woman with a handbag that matched the shoes sitting next to the podium was as close to her emotional style as being a farmer's wife rolling out the dough and canning the zucchini, or a professor's wife serving tea and arrowroot cookies to the great man's newest nubile disciple. Sarah's view of marriage: I'd rather *have* a wife than be one.

I was drinking club soda and lime, feeling toweringly tense and virtuous and Sarah, in a gesture of transitional solidarity, was also teetotaling. She wore black silk trousers and a light blue shirt; her hair was dark brown, shiny, twisted into a complex French braid. This was not a party for beautiful women and she looked odd and vulnerable amongst the others of her gender done up in boxy brocaded dresses, with their stiff, immovable hairdos and their faces pink, shiny, and hard. These were brilliant, plotting, vivacious behind-the-scenes women, women who seemed to have sublimated all of their personal ambitions and half their sexuality in order to help their husbands along. Sarah felt shy. She kept close to me and said, "Don't work the room, Fielding, just stay with me." It seemed like a lousy time to get even for all the times she'd ignored me in church basements or let me languish at the table while no one's holy eyes engaged me. I decided to be big about it.

There was a little fellow named Oswald Ellis who taught economics at the University of Chicago and he and Sarah got into an argument about the new government in Chile. The generals who deposed Allende were, for a series of odd reasons, highly influenced by the University of Chicago's department of economics, which, under the influence of free-marketeer Milton Friedman, had somehow thrust itself into the vanguard of Chilean reaction.

And so, as it happened, Oswald Ellis, with his little shoulders no larger than buttermilk biscuits and his bow tie hovering against his throat like a monarch butterfly, was not only expert about matters Chilean but also passionately engaged. He was regaling Sarah with torrents of statistics, and as he described it, Allende and his socialist henchmen were to the halls of commerce what a gang of psychotic teenagers would be to the Art Institute. "Don't you talk to me about human rights," he snapped at Sarah, "don't you dare talk to me about that. It is *not* a human right to hand a perfectly stable and democratic nation over to the forces of chaos. Nor is it a human right to turn a viable economy into a laboratory for a bunch of old-hat, disproved Marxist ideas." Sarah, for her part, didn't know half of what Ellis did about Chile but the force of her convictions kept her in there, slugging it out with him. She had learned by heart the names of dozens upon dozens of Chileans who'd been tortured or slaughtered by the junta, and so when Ellis would recite figures about tin mines and anchovy harvests, Sarah could counter with, "What about Jorge Guzmán? What about María Sandro?" And Ellis would throw up his hands in an Ach! This woman is impossible! gesture. I didn't want to let their argument get any louder or more unfriendly and so I stayed at Sarah's side.

Isaac came over to us with a slender, dark, very attractive but withdrawn young woman, who was wearing a formal-looking red dress that left her opaque olive shoulders bare. "I want you to meet my niece, Juliet Beck," Isaac announced. "Darling," he said to her, "this is—oh, you've met Oswald already. Well, *this* is Fielding Pierce and this is Sarah Wilson—"

"Williams," said Sarah, pleasantly enough.

"What's that you're drinking?" I asked Juliet, who would one day remind me those were my first words to her, though she could never recall having met Sarah.

"This?" she asked. She looked at her glass. "Sweet vermouth and soda."

"Great color," I said. "It looks like one of those drinks people used to order in movies. They always, I don't know . . . made me want to drink." I laughed and Juliet's attention touched me lightly, the way one might touch something in a store while browsing to kill a little time.

Sarah and I stayed at the open house until the evening. The apartment was thick with what people generally call the dull roar of ego but I was as sorry to go as Sarah was anxious. Still, I didn't begrudge it; we'd be home in half an hour and perhaps then we'd go straight to bed. The thought of entering her created an odd, voluptuous tension in me, like a suppressed yawn. There was a noise at the back of her throat when I put myself into her, a clicking sound, as if a lock were being tripped, a lever allowing me access to a deeper layer of being.

It was eight below zero yet snowing nevertheless when we left the Greens' apartment house, with its gaslit canopy and liveried doorman—the old fellow saluted us good night, on the assumption that if we were guests of any tenant we were by definition *his* social superiors. Sarah and I had left our car at home—it had no heater. The tires were bald. We had to take a bus home to the South Side and as it happened one appeared right away. It looked like a movable green gelatin capsule hovering in the slaty, snowy night. It would take us just a block from our apartment house but it was a long ride and, on that New Year's night, a creepy one.

The dozen or so passengers we shared the ride with each seemed cast onto the bus by dint of some personal tragedy or character flaw. I tried to see them all with Sarah's eyes, tried to believe that each of those lives was at least as valuable and dramatic as our own, that each of those souls held within it the iridescent, weightless seeds of saintliness, that who we were cast amongst were not only God's children but possibly God himself. We all ran the risk of the Roman soldiers who had no idea whose flesh they tore on Calvary. How could we say that that man with the cast on his foot and the corona of dark stubble over his face was not Christ?

It offended Sarah's sense of tact and her vanity to ask you what you were thinking but my thoughts left their mark on my face and I could see by the way she gazed at me that she was wondering. She took my hand and then put her hand and mine in her lap. She was wearing an old fur coat she got years ago at a St. Vincent de Paul's; it was strictly a college girl's idea of campy elegance but it was the warmest thing she owned. Her face looked lined in the steady polluted light of the bus. It was all right; she was not the sort of woman whose beauty depends on her freshness or any trick intimations of innocence. Maybe five years before she could have gotten away with sleeping thirty hours a week but now she couldn't. Her eyes looked stricken, trembling on the cusp between darkness and light, prophecy and sleep, and Sarah herself described the half moons beneath her eyes as papal purple. I realized now I had presented to my mentor and his clique a woman on the edge and I knew enough of how they thought, the sort of emotional ac- countancy and odds-making they came to as automatically as breathing to know that all of them had made the following mental note: If he goes up, he'll do it without her.

"Your friends are all a little tougher than they look," Sarah said.

"They're not really my friends," I said, too quickly. "I don't even know most of them."

"Isaac and Adele?" she asked.

"Most of them," I said. "I don't know most of them."

She shrugged. Outside, the buildings dropped away and we were riding past the railway yards; the snow blew past the red warning lights. "It's your world," she said. "It's where you're going."

"I don't like the sound of this," I said.

"It's just a fact," said Sarah. "You had this all mapped out long before you met me and nothing's going to change it."

"Do we want to change it?"

"Let's face it," she said. "We're both tyrants and we'd love to change each other."

"I don't want to change you," I said, but even I could hear my voice was not convincing.

"Of course you do, silly," she said. She chucked me under the chin and said, in a voice you'd use on a baby St. Bernard, "you big silly."

"Come on, Sarah, cut it out."

"You are the incarnation of your family's ambitions and I'm the incarnation of my family's fears," said Sarah. Now her voice went into a clear, soft alto, as she turned definitive.

I thought for a moment and then said, "So what?"

"Well, it's tough when one's die has been cast. Your father's name is Ed and your Mom's name is Mary and they called you Fielding. Doesn't that tell you something?"

"Nothing I didn't already know. I accept I was meant to succeed. I accept the torch that was passed to me."

"Yes. But can you hold onto it and me, too?"

"I've got an answer for that one," I said. "Yes. I can. I will."

We were silent then. There was a weird element of fun in all of this, as if we were pretending our friendship had reached an impasse and this is what we'd be saying if it had. But we were, as Sarah once put it, walking on thin water and the sense of indestructibility that lovers live with had passed some time ago— this little psychodrama was cutting a little too close to the bone. It was one thing to pretend that we were at a crossroads and that Sarah was getting ready to say good-bye, and it was quite another thing altogether suddenly to realize it was half true and getting truer. Neither of us had ever admitted that the path the other was on was real. Perhaps we'd secretly and stupidly believed we were suddenly going to change, the way you do when you're very young, when you're Elvis one week and Gandhi the next, not knowing that as you grow older the horse goes slower and the plow cuts deeper.

I took an examination in contract law and then went out drinking with Victor Tomczak and another vaguely up-from-under comrade, a woman named Gloria Busterman, whose father was a fisherman on Long Island. We each felt like little soldiers crouched within the Trojan horse of our public selves and it thrilled us to be getting away with it. I took leave of my resolve to be sober but limited myself to drinks I didn't enjoy—in this case, beer. We were all awfully happy, but we were quiet about it. We were drinking at a University hangout called Jimmy's and it was afternoon; most of the other drinkers were people with rather little to celebrate and we didn't want to rub their noses in it. We toasted each other with conspiratorial clicks of the glasses—a dull atonal ping because the mugs were thick.

After, I walked home, six blocks in the snow, and walked up the stairs to our apartment with eggshell care because there was an inch of snow in my hair and I didn't want any of it to fall off. I looked like a gingerbread man whose head had been dipped into a bowl of stiff whipped cream and I didn't want Sarah to miss how incredibly adorable I looked. I held onto the banister and took careful little steps. A small clump of snow fell off as I fished for my keys but I stooped down, picked it up, and stuck it back on. Then I zombied into the apartment, toward the light in the bedroom.

And there I was with a headful of snow, looking at Sarah, who was just out of the shower, her face red and blotchy from hot water and scrubbing, wearing a yellow terry cloth robe, with her hair wrapped in a towel, leaning over the bed while she packed her big blue and tan suitcase.

"Where have you been?" she said, looking up at me, her eyes flashing messages of anger, concern, secretiveness.

"With Victor and Gloria. Where are you going?"

She picked up three neatly folded turtleneck shirts from the bed and placed them into the suitcase, next to a black dress with red piping. "I'm not supposed to tell anyone, but I'm going to tell you," she said. "We're going to Chile."

I nodded, as if this made sense. The heat of that apartment got to my snowy crown and as I nodded it slipped off me and hit the floor in a mass. I unbuttoned my overcoat and I felt something that surprised me: an acute, burning sense of embarrassment.

"We'll be gone about two weeks," she said.

"What's the deal?"

"We're going to help get some friends out of there," she said.

"How are you going to do that?" I felt my nerves go taut and the arrow of my anger notched in.

"It's all planned. It's not difficult and it's not at all dangerous." She folded in a pair of white trousers and then placed her blue and yellow sandals along the side of the valise. She smiled at me, but she was suddenly a shadow behind dark glass. I was barely seeing at all. I thought as a child and ached as a child and wanted to scream bloody fucking murder as a child. Control yourself, I thought to myself. I could taste the drink I wanted in the back of my throat; could just about hear the lucky chatter of the ice.

"When's all this supposed to go down?" I asked.

"Tonight. We're flying down to Miami and from there we're taking Lan Chile straight to Santiago." She walked into my arms; I held her and she pressed herself against me. I knew she was doing it to be kind, to cool me out. She had as much interest in embracing me as she had in reading a magazine; I could feel her heart pounding and it wasn't passion for me that accelerated that guileless muscle. She was on a mission, she was living up to her fondest vision of herself.

"If I thought you'd change your mind if I asked you to, then I would ask you to," I said.

"Why?"

"Because I don't want you to go. Because it *is* dangerous. There's enough danger and horror in the world. You don't have to buy a plane ticket to go out looking for it."

"It's going to be all right."

"Who are you going with?"

"Steven. And a nun from California called Sister Angela."

"What's your cover? What will the generals think you're doing down there?"

"I can't talk about it."

"Even to me?"

"I just can't."

"Well, that draws the line, doesn't it? You think I'm on the wrong side of this or something? Christ, Sarah."

"I promised, that's all. It's all very complicated. We're on Church business. There are people inside the country who know what we're up to and they'll be covering for us."

A few minutes later, Steven Mileski arrived, with Father Stanton. Mileski was wearing one of those Russian caps and he looked like a massive, good-natured Rasputin. He wore his beard outside his black overcoat. Stanton seemed nervous, unstable. "The horror never stops," he said, more than a few times. He was muttering and his fear pushed me toward my own. Mileski was feeling expansive, curious about the trip, looking forward to the sun.

"If anyone comes snooping around," Mileski said to me, putting his arm around me, making me feel like the team shrimp being coached to go up to the plate and hope for a base on balls, "you'll want to dodge all of their questions. Good thing is you've got a talent for that—you know, the verbal tap dancing."

"Thanks for the advice, Steven," I said. "It's really helpful."

He smiled at me, winked. He seemed to want to indicate that he knew how I was feeling and that if there were more time he would have been more than glad to talk it through with me. We were in our living room. Sarah's suitcase was next to the door; her fur coat was draped over it like a big friendly animal. The phone rang. It was Danny in New York saying he was being sued by a printer in from Pennsylvania and Willow's lawyer wouldn't give any more advice until Danny paid his legal bills. I said I'd get back to him a little later and when I turned around Sarah was embracing Father Stanton and Stanton was patting her on the back. His hand looked so terribly gentle and frightened against her red sweater.

"We have to go," said Mileski and now for the first time I sensed the uneasiness beneath his cheerfulness.

"The plane doesn't leave until seven o'clock," I said.

Mileski and Stanton glanced at Sarah, as if my knowing the time of their flight constituted a break in security.

"There'll be a lot of traffic on the Dan Ryan," said Stanton.

I don't know why it made me smile. There was something so American about talking about highways and traffic jams. Stanton noticed my smile and smiled back.

"Not to mention the storm," said Mileski. "God's come through for us and given us a lot to put our shoulder against."

"Yes," I said. "He's *such* a help."

Mileski came up to me and looked into my face. It was a horrible thought, but I could not help but reflect that if moved he could certainly crush my head in his hands. But all he did was slap a resounding hand on my shoulder. "We'll bring her back safe and sound, Fielding," he said. "You have my word."

Despite myself, I felt a wave of relief and gratitude go through me. "I know you will, Steven," I said, my voice suddenly thick.

"Will you pray for us then?" he asked.

"Yes," I said, "I will."

He checked his watch, which was buried in the thick black hair of his arm. "All right," he said. "We're off." He made no move to leave however. His massive chest expanded as he took in a deep, sensuous breath. "You know," he said, "the people we want to help all have souls surely destined to live with God. But we're going to deprive him of their company for the time."

My emotions were lagging behind events; it was just then that it struck me that a great deal more was going on than half my bed's being vacated. Whatever I thought of this mission, their courage was finally undeniable and I realized in a lurch of the heart that I was at last present at the moment I'd always craved, the moment when time is given its color and weight, the moment when history swishes its long armored tail and begins to crawl down another path.

"What can I do to help?" I said.

"Cover for me," said Sarah. "If anyone asks where I am. Especially my family."

"I know, I know," I said. "Is that all? I'd like to do something."

"Do you have any money?" Mileski asked.

"Not really. Twenty dollars or something."

"Then give us twenty dollars. We're way short."

I shrugged and went back to the bedroom, where my wallet lay on top of the navy blue dresser, encircled by an arc of hot yellow lamplight. I opened it up: two fives and eight ones. I took them all and went back to the living room. Sarah, Mileski, and Stanton had joined hands and were kneeling on the floor, their heads bowed, their eyes closed.

"My goodness," I said, "I can't leave you kids alone for a minute." I don't know where that wise-ass crack came from. Perhaps from a dark little knot of resentment. But as soon as I'd said it an overwhelming sense of emotional hunger and helplessness went through me and I covered my face with my hand—too late. I was already crying.

Did I want to kneel with them? Or was I fully realizing that the woman I loved beyond all reason was heading now behind enemy lines and what we had here was no argument, no mere moral assertion, but a full-out risk of life? Yet perhaps the cause of those red hot tears was simply a desire to be a better person, to have the foolish strength that would allow me to ignore all of the odds and all of the conventional wisdom and throw myself toward the light, no matter how dimly I might perceive it. I waited in silence for their prayer to end and when they stood up I said, "Take me with you."

Sarah looked to Mileski and it was he who answered. "You will be with us, Fielding. We feel your love right now."

"No, I mean really. I speak better Spanish than either of you."

"Sister Angela speaks it perfectly," Mileski said. "And I'm not half bad."

"Just take me with you, all right?" I pointed to Sarah. "What do you say?"

She was silent and then she walked across the room and put her arms around me and placed her head against my chest. "I'm so happy right now, Fielding," she murmured. "I want you to believe in me."

"I do," I said. My voice sounded weak, desperate; it had to work its way around a throbbing mass at the top of my throat.

"Everything's arranged for this time," Sarah said.

"We have to go and I mean immediately," said Father Stanton. "Sister Angela will be awaiting you in Miami and it surely won't do to miss your plane."

"Come to the airport with us," Sarah said to me.

And so we drove north in Stanton's Plymouth Fury, with its smell of evergreen air freshener, its terry cloth seat coverings. The heat was on high, Mahler was on the radio; we were in a world of our own because outside it was all darkness and ice and the insane brightness of headlights, the cryptic kiss-off of red taillights. The priests were in front and Sarah and I were in the back. I held her close. She was trembling; I didn't know if she was cold or frightened and for some reason I could not ask. I just held her tighter. She gripped my hand and squeezed it so hard it ached.

Mileski was talking about the trip, hoping they'd have at least a day or two to hit the beach. I couldn't tell if he was just acting bluff or if a quick bronzing was really on his agenda. Stanton, reduced to mother hen by his staying behind, only cautioned Steven to be careful and to come back as soon as possible.

"Do you think what I'm doing is wrong?" Sarah whispered to me.

"No. Not wrong." I stopped. I didn't really want to say anything more. We could have argued until the plane took off; we could have argued in our minds every moment she was gone.

"Then stupid?"

"No. Of course not. Not wrong. Not stupid. I just wish you weren't going." A part of me was virtually screaming This is not the way to get things done. This is not how the world works. This is nothing but a ridiculous adventure. And I think Sarah sensed it.

"I just want to forget all of the things that separate us," she said. "You're my lover, the only man in the world I want to love."

"You're mine," I said, holding her still closer, talking into her hair, breathing in the soft comforting aroma of her scalp.

"I'm getting scared," she whispered.

I closed my eyes. I had a ferocious urge simply to say, Then don't go, but I let it pass. I put my hand against her face; she brought my fingers to her lips and kissed them one by one.

The sound of a low-flying jet. You could feel two hundred wide-eyed souls passing directly overhead. The green signs pointing the way to the airport. The snow flying past the gooseneck street lamps. The Mahler was over and now a tonic water commercial was on. An English accented voice, very pompous, talking about Schweppervescence. Sarah leaned against the back door and crossed her legs. She looked very prim, ordinary; her animation had gone underground. The lights from a passing car wrapped and unwrapped around her face like a bandage.

They had only a few minutes to make their plane to Miami. Stanton drove up to the Departures curb of United Airlines. There was a line of cars behind us that seemed to stretch two or three miles. Getting out and going in with them was out of the question. Stanton put his arms around Father Mileski and kissed him on the cheek, the forehead. The men embraced. "God be with you, Steven," Stanton said and then he took hold of Mileski's beard and squeezed it in his fist and made a deep, wild animal growl. I kissed Sarah and tried to press myself against her, but it was difficult while sitting down, with our thick winter coats on. Then Stanton turned around in his seat and reached back for her. She embraced him and kissed him on the cheek.

"God be with you, Sarah," he said.

"Wait," I said, "I'll get out with you." I wanted to touch her again; I wanted us to kiss standing up so every part of our bodies could connect. I grabbed for her valise and dragged it out after me, on the traffic side of the car. The wheels of taxis were rolling over the rock salt and it sounded as if they were driving over broken glass.

The United sign looked particularly blue and red in that snowy night air. The lights in the pavilion illuminated the snow. Porters were pushing carts piled high with luggage. There was a gaseous, doomy feeling, a whiff of fate gone berserk in the air. The other travelers looked wide-eyed, apprehensive. I suppose no one likes to fly in storms, though by Chicago standards the night really wasn't so bad. Mileski was carrying a small maroon canvas bag with a tan strap; in his other hand he had an old leather briefcase, bulging. He stood back as Sarah and I embraced; he seemed shy, a little embarrassed. I'd never known a kiss to feel so inadequate. We smiled. I put out my hand and she shook it.

"I'll be thinking of you," I said.

"I'll be thinking of you, too," she said.

"Good luck," I said.

"Thanks. I'll see you soon."

"OK." I paused, shrugged, smiled. "Well . . . God be with you, then."

"Thanks." She glanced over at Mileski. Mileski saluted me and then they were off. If that plane was going to leave on time, they were going to have to hurry. They were practically running. The doors opened automatically and I stood there, watching them penetrate and then disappear into the crowd inside. I turned back to the car; Father Stanton was sitting immobile and upright as the cars behind regaled him with their horns.

I slid into the front seat next to Stanton and we pulled into the furious ooze of traffic. The radio was off and we were silent. I could feel his attention on me but each time I glanced at him, his eyes were forward. When we were finally out of the airport and moving south I said, "I appreciate your going out of your way like this, taking me home."

"I couldn't very well deprive you of your final good-byes now, could I," he said, so promptly that it seemed he'd already had this conversation in his mind.

"I had no idea this was going to happen," I said. It struck me just then how nice it would be to be part of his flock, or any flock really, to be able to empty the garbage of my heart into an incense-smelling box and be done with it. Yet I realized I didn't really want to confess; I merely wished to complain.

"She's a brave girl," Stanton said. "Terribly courageous."

"I wish you wouldn't talk about her like that," I said. Stanton turned toward me; I could just barely see his eyes in the darkness of the car. "Sorry," I said. "But you make her sound in such grave danger when you call her brave. It scares the hell out of me."

"Yes, well, it's always peculiarly more difficult to stay behind, now isn't it. For instance, I was posted in a little mission in the bush, far away from the world I'd come to know in Salisbury. And one evening it became, shall we say, urgent to transport two young blacks out over the border and out of harm's way. There were three of us there, three whites, that is, and I was chosen to stay behind and look after things while the others made the trek to the border. Well, I don't think I've ever suffered so much in my entire life. I lay there in my bed and listened to the insects eating the leaves in the banana trees and I quite literally thought I was going to lose my mind. Well, along about eleven the next morning, my friends returned. The mission had been absolutely without incident; they'd stopped off at a neighboring village for a large breakfast and had brought back a little spider monkey as a pet for the children who frequented our nursery program. I vowed to myself I would never stay behind again. Simply too trying."

"Yet you're staying behind now," I said.

"Yes."

"Are they really going to be safe, Father Stanton?"

"Would you like a truthful answer?"

I didn't think much of that question. How do you answer it in the negative. There's something sadistic in people who ask that.

"Yes, I would," I said.

"They are walking into the lion's den and there *is* danger. But the lion is very fat and entirely stupid and frightened as well. I expect they'll have less trouble than you or I will, waiting for them."

The snow was almost stopped. I saw the red wing lights of a climbing jumbo jet. I wondered if that was Sarah's plane. She was somewhere out there, cutting through the clouds, riding some high icy current, speeding away from me.

"Our Sarah reminds me of a woman who I think is a genuine American saint, a woman named Dorothy Day. Are you familiar with her?"

"A little. The *Catholic Worker*."

"Yes. A woman whose fiery temperament prevented her from truly embracing the life of the Church, but who chose instead to goad the Church on to a sense of daring and responsibility that the meeker Catholics might never otherwise have imagined. Sarah is such a principled, passionate young woman. And so fearless. You must feel fortunate to have been chosen by such a soul."

"I guess it's all how you look at it," I said.

"I've wondered why you don't marry," said Father Stanton. "Please don't misinterpret me, though. I certainly recognize the sanctity of love outside the bonds of marriage. And I realize many young people, what with the war, and Watergate, and all of the hypocrisy of institutions, feel that they'd rather not be involved with marriage."

"I suppose we will marry one day," I said. I felt a tremor of hopefulness go through me as I said these words. Perhaps it was what Stanton had intended. "You know, when we met, I was in the service. And now law school. We've always been dead broke."

"You'd like to have more money before you marry?" asked Stanton. When he smiled, his eyes sunk behind folds of flesh.

We drove in silence for a while. I watched the neighborhoods go by, the two- and three-story brick houses, with initials on the storm doors, low wattage bulbs burning over the porch stoops, and I thought that one day I would go into each of those houses and ask the people inside if they would give me the power to make decisions about their lives and the idea seemed more than absurd—it seemed wrong, ghastly. It seemed venal.

"The extraordinary thing about our Sarah," Stanton suddenly said, "is she has no perception of herself as a good person, or even a particularly *moral* one. She lives on the surface of her anger, her outrage, and I think she remains wholly unconscious of her enormous spiritual power and discipline that exists directly beneath that shell of outrage. She is one of those incredibly fortunate individuals who can follow their heart and do just what their impulses dictate—and they will always be on the side of God."

"And you know what side that is?" I asked.

"Yes, I do. And so does Sarah."

And, I thought to myself, she gives great head, too. I turned away from Stanton and watched the city go by: a railroad trestle with walrus tusks of icicles hanging from it; a grocery store with a Polish sign and a picture of a Coca-Cola bottle over it; a vacant lot filled with junked autos and on one shell of an old car stood a wild dog, its eyes flashing red in the lamplight, its muzzle thrust up toward the moonless sky.

Dad retired and there was a party for him. "Even my goddamned boss is coming to this party," he said to me on the phone. He sounded amazed, delighted, even a little scared. He couldn't even put up a screen of disdain, as he did when Mom wanted to celebrate his birthday. He tried to keep it at arm's length. What was being celebrated was not himself, not Edward Pierce, not Eddie, not Dad, but a piece of history.

He had gotten his first job as a printer in 1936. He had set type for the *Daily News*, the *Daily Worker*, *Collier's*, the Book-Find Club, he had printed up invitations to the weddings of Rockefellers and Astors, he had set copy for the first public offering of Polaroid, he had printed up civil defense instruction booklets, and the owner's manual for the Edsel. He had minded his p's and q's and now it was all coming to an end at this party they were throwing for him at the Hotel St. George, which Danny was springing for with who knows what ill-gotten gains. Invited were co-workers, family, friends, union buddies, and even a few of the fellows from management, guys who were not so unlike himself and with whom he could now bury the hatchet of class struggle for an evening of hot casseroles and whiskey right out of the bottle.

We'd gotten the invitation weeks in advance. This enormous

lead time was my father's idea. He imagined people's social schedules as somehow very dense and complex and felt you could not invite someone without at least two months' notice. Sarah and I had been planning to go but now she was in Chile and I was reluctant to leave Chicago, lest she return and find me gone. But the party was on a Friday, eleven days after her departure, and since she said she would be gone for two weeks, I took the chance and flew east for it.

The Hotel St. George was in Brooklyn Heights, not really our kind of neighborhood. It seemed a mixture of well-off widows and young gays. But it was awfully pretty, even in the old snow. The hotel was cavernous and, though later it would be turned into apartments for successful people, the people living in it then were old, many of them on public assistance, most of them with failing health.

Dad's party was in a reception room on the ground floor, a salmon and blue ballroom with an art deco chandelier and an old mauve carpet that had been delicately patterned by the ten million footsteps that had gone over it through the years. Dozens of tables had been set up and each had a bottle of Canadian Club on it. The *New York Times* had chipped in for a trio and they were set up at the front of the room, a piano, bass, and drums: dapper men in tuxedos, with white hair and sly bachelor airs about them. (Later in the party, Eric McDonald played with them: he looked like an African prince standing before the trio, playing with a sweet, full vibrato out of respect to my father and the guests, though Eric's usual saxophone style was slashing, atonal. He paced back and forth, his stiff tusk of beard looking windblown and a touch Satanic as he played "Strangers in the Night" and then "Solidarity Forever." Dad was delighted: it made him feel a part of the twenty-first century to be serenaded by a black relative. Malik was just barely walking. Rudy danced with Mom.)

The party had begun at six and by nine people were going up to the microphone to deliver speeches in Dad's honor. Mr. Glass, the owner of Pinetop Printers, where Dad worked before the *Times*, spoke of Dad's professionalism, called him the Lou Gehrig of Lower Manhattan because Dad was never sick, but he couldn't say anything about the work Dad did because Glass had inherited the company and knew nothing about it. Danny spoke and said Dad taught him about effort and he also taught him that if you don't look after yourself no one else would. "He gave me the guts to take chances and the guts to say what I'm going to say right now—Dad, I love you." We all cheered, though it seemed a little crazy to make such noise after something so private. Caroline wouldn't speak. "Oh, he knows what I think," she said. "Anyhow, I always embarrass him." But a guy named Dave Southworth, who was an international vice-president of the Typographical Union spoke and he detailed Dad's long years of service to the union. "It's rank-and-filers like Ed Pierce that make the labor movement strong," Southworth said. He was a big, sleek man, with his black hair combed straight back, and I couldn't help noting how careful he was to designate my father's status as rank-and-file, knowing, I suppose, that quite a few of us there felt Dad could have run that union a lot better than its officers. I got up and said something, too. Mom's old boss, Corvino, had appointed himself master of ceremonies and when he called me up he put his hand on the back of my neck and announced, "Now he's a lawyer, huh? Remember this one with his shorts hanging down and the mouth full of beans?" I could feel Corvino's Cornell class ring at the base of my skull; I looked down and his little hooflike feet were in black patent leather pumps, such as Gene Kelly might have worn.

"I tell everyone," I said, "that I was born rich and later when they find out I was raised in five rooms in Brooklyn they wonder what I'm talking about. But the people in this room know what I'm talking about because most of you know what my brother and sister and I have been given. Something indefinable, nothing you could put into a safety deposit box." I paused for a moment; I'd had no idea I was going to be so rhapsodic, to swing for the fences like that. "I know for myself, when I become a lawyer, I will nail my various diplomas and certifications of worthiness on the wall.

But the credentials will be . . . incomplete if I do not place above them a picture of my father. Because most of what I know about justice I learned at his knee and the drive that sent me into law school—and Caroline into painting, and Danny into publishing —comes also from our father. You know, even in a perfect democracy, there is not a perfect democracy of spirit, and tonight we are saluting one of the great *aristocrats* of the spirit." Oh yes, I could have run for mayor that night. I did go on some. And at a certain point, I realized I'd been at it for five minutes and risked losing them all. So I ended with a quick, self-deflating joke: "OK, Pa? Is this what you wanted me to tell them?" And the laughter was quick, generous . . .

"What a beautiful speech, Fielding," Mom said, linking her arm through mine. She had a highball, a lit cigarette. Her eyes looked wild and her fancy hairdo was coming apart. "You really had them in the palm of your hand. You could've had them doing anything you wanted. God, it was beautiful." She walked me around the perimeter of the hall; her legs looked dark and skinny in her tinted stockings. "And did you see Corvino listening to you?" She glanced over her shoulder and then took a sudden right turn, yanking me along. "The poor man was *green*. He looked like someone just ran over his pussycat."

We had made our way around the room and now she led me to the bar. I hadn't jinxed my stopping drinking by telling anyone about it. All the bartender was serving was cold beers and ice; the whiskey was in bottles on the tables. Dad was there at the bar with Southworth from the Typographical Union, each of them fetching a paper bucket of hollow ice cubes. Southworth was trying to talk Dad into spending a few days with Southworth's son, who taught sociology at Queens College and was putting together an oral history of the New York City trade union movement. I could see Dad didn't like the idea, thinking it would turn him into an old-timer, droning on about the old days. "I don't care a hell of a lot about what's already happened," he said. "The best is yet to come, right?"

Mom got some ice for her table and put her arm around Dad's waist. "It's a crying shame Sarah isn't here," she said to us.

"Wait wait wait," said Dad. "Think of the expense." He was lightning fast in explaining away possible slights: he couldn't bear to feel overlooked.

"She's away," I said. "Otherwise she would have come."

"Away?" asked Mom, narrowing her eyes a little. She tended to believe that when something was irregular it was amiss and, as unattractive as this was as a way of thinking, life had a way of proving her right.

"She had to go home. Her father's feeling poorly." I hated fake sickness excuses, thinking they were very bad luck, but Mr. Williams was a jerk and I didn't mind the risk.

"Well well," said Dad. "To hear her go on about it, she wouldn't spit on her father if he was on fire. See? Middle-classers patch it up once they get older."

"You think that's what it is?"

"Sure. He's an executive, right? Think she wants to get cut out of his will? Believe me, your mom and I have seen it happen a million times."

"I think his will's probably worth a hell of a lot less than your union pension," I said.

Dad laughed, as if he'd just unexpectedly won something.

"Look at these goddamned ice cubes they give us," Mom said, peering into the bucket. "They're melting already. I better get back to my table with them."

"I'll be right along, Mary," Dad said. "I just want to talk to Fielding for a second."

We watched in silence for a moment while Mom made her way back to their table and then Dad put his arm around my shoulders and we walked to the side of the hall. The trio was playing an airport cocktail lounge version of "Age of Aquarius" and now people were juiced enough to make idiots of themselves on the dance floor.

"That was a nice speech," he said to me, his voice cool, analytical, intimate only in its assumptions. "The way you delivered it. The pauses. The eye contact. But can I tell you something? And I'm only saying this because you're so good and if you're that good, why not be better. OK? First of all, you made it seem like I raised you myself and all the stuff I gave you, like your mother had nothing to do with it. If you were running for office not a woman in the room would have voted for you. And the other thing is maybe you get a little too personal. It's OK with family and all, but if you're going to be a leader you have to get used to the idea that no one ever knows you, not really knows you. You think if people really knew Kennedy they would have gone out and voted for him? A gangster's son who used the White House like a . . . a cat house, who thought he was a thousand times better than the common man? You got to be just like a clean white sheet and people can color it in with what they want to believe. That's why the Eisenhowers win and the Stevensons lose. You just have to—" And here he squeezed me close to him. We were exactly the same height but there was a hardness to his body that mine lacked, a steel spring tension, a stubbornness. "You just have to be real strong," he said. "So strong you'll want to blow your brains out, but you won't. So strong that people can call you a dirty cowardly lying sonofabitch right to your face and it won't make the slightest bit of difference."

"What if I don't want to be like that, Dad?" I asked.

"Then you'll be making a big mistake. You'll be ending up like me."

"Is that so bad?"

"It ain't enough. You'll be tearing your hair out when you read the newspapers or watch the evening news because the world'll be run by people not half as smart as you are and you let them have it. And these people, Fielding, they're not only dummies, not only a bunch of Little Lord Fauntleroys, guys you and your brother would have eaten for breakfast back in the neighborhood—but they're *bad* people, too. They think that working people are dogshit. They take all the decency out of everything. They'd sell the moon and the stars and all the little planets in between." He patted my lapels and leaned back to get a better look at me. "Look good, boy. Strong. You're doing it for all of us."

"I'm doing the best I can, Dad."

"That's right," he said, nodding with sudden enthusiasm. "And that's all it takes."

I felt at that moment a sudden tremor of unease, the sort of inner weather that usually obscures more than it reveals. I felt Sarah near me, not in this room but in my life. She was reachable again and I only wanted to speak to her, to hear her voice.

I made some mumble of an excuse and went out to the hotel lobby, where I found a phone booth. It stank of urine when I closed the door. I called our number in Chicago, making the call collect. By now, I was in a frenzy of anticipation. I knew if she didn't answer then I would have to find Father Stanton and from there I'd be on my way to Chile. Like a man awakening from a long, disorganizing illness, I wondered suddenly how I could have been so stupid, so weak, so easily swayed as to let her go on this mission. The phone rang once, twice, three times. And then, just when it felt as if my nerves could not be tightened another notch, she picked up the phone. I could tell from her voice, even as she said hello, that she was crying.

"I have a collect call for anyone from Fielding Pierce," said the operator, who'd probably heard worse than mere crying on the phone. "Will you accept the charges?"

"Yes."

"Sarah!" I shouted. "You're back."

"Oh God, Fielding. Where are you?"

"I'm in Brooklyn. It's my father's retirement party."

There was a silence and then she began to sob. I stood there and I didn't know what to say.

"Sarah?" Softly.

"I thought you'd left for good."

"I'm on my way home, Sarah. If I leave right now I can get the last plane out."

"Oh, Fielding. I'm so scared."

"Are you all right? Did anything happen?"

"I'm OK. Are you really coming back?"

"Yes. Are you all right?"

"I'm all right. It all went well."

"Are you sure?"

"I'm here."

"Can you wait up for me?"

There was a silence of sorts; I listened to the watery electronic *shhh* of the long distance cables. Then Sarah said: "If I can't wait up, I'll pin your instructions to the blanket."

11

This was just the time when it was beginning to get tough running as a Democrat. There were a couple of hundred unshaven Americans held hostage in Iran, the Russians were running their war games in Afghanistan, and the president was appearing on TV direct from the White House wearing a woolen cardigan because oil prices were too high to turn up the heat in the Oval Office.

Bertelli was trying to make this work in his own favor, talking about getting America back on track and acting as if I were the incumbent, just because my party happened to be in power. Chicago, thank God, was feeling the disillusion with the Dems less than most places—we still ate our kielbasa, rooted for the Sox, and voted the straight ticket. There were, according to Isaac, about two hundred thousand registered Democrats in Chicago who were either dead or had not yet had the privilege of being born. You could count on their ectoplasmic loyalty. In my district, however, with its large numbers of University types, the vote was less predictable: you never knew what those goddamned chrome domes were going to do. They read the columnists and subscribed to the fine-print magazines and had those old leather-bound books from which they could draw horrifying historical parallels.

The non-chrome-domian parts of my district were poor and black. And though the old Democratic organization still operated out in Woodlawn and under the El tracks on 63rd Street and up and down Stony Island and out toward Cottage Grove, it was getting harder and harder to bring out the vote. Not many jobs, lots of freaky crime, hopelessness glowing like radiation out through the window grates—it was awfully difficult to get someone in the ghetto to pin on a campaign button.

Just then, my district was falling under the influence of a slight, hunchbacked, demagogic Baptist named Ebenezer B. Andrews. The Reverend Andrews's church was always jammed and from the pulpit he railed against abortion, describing it not only as a sin against God but as the state's attempt to further oppress the blacks, by keeping their numbers in check.

The Republicans and Bertelli were hip enough to know about Andrews and clever enough to strike a bargain with him—and with no previously existing alliances in the community, they were free to do so. And Bertelli, that old goaty libertine, in whose pretentious little bistro a thousand and one abortions had been decided upon (or "opted for" as they said in coffeehouseland), anoints himself as a defender of Chicago's fetuses and with that sneaky little hop and a skip he catapults himself into an alliance with the most vocal and well-organized subgroup in the ghetto. It was absolutely astonishing! I had already lost the gays; now I was in danger of losing the blacks.

I needed to paste together a base of support quickly, but without an incumbent to run against I found myself casting about for an issue and coming up empty each time. I had a speech I'd been practicing since high school but it was, I realized now, inappropriate for the office I was seeking. I would have to wait for a crack at the White House before trotting out my rhapsodic rhetoric about a better world, a braver people, the rebirth of human decency. I needed to scale things down: after all, you don't get a job as a lab assistant by promising you can cure leukemia. My advisers weren't having an easier time than I was. My exiled predecessor had won his terms simply by being a Democrat and by staying friendly with some of the real estate interests. The Party was willing to throw a little weight in my direction, but whomever else Carmichael had cut deals with had yet to come looking for me. For the time being, it seemed, the democratic process was outpacing corruption and I was all alone.

I didn't know what people wanted to hear and that would have been just fine—but I didn't quite know what I wanted to say, either. All I could come up with was this: I am fairly smart; I am more honest than dishonest; I didn't go into politics to line my own pockets; I promise to work 365 days a year to do what's best not only for the district but the country, not only for the world but the universe. But I wasn't drunk enough on my own sudden fortune to dare suggest this as a line of attack to the moral misers who were running my campaign. It would have seemed like sheer preppy vanity. They would not have known what to do with it —or me. And since the election was only days away and I had no support of my own, I was beholden to them.

I spent a day working with Lucille Jackson, driving around in her husband's stiff-mobile, with its overwhelming nightmare scent of roses and embalming fluids. I spoke in an ornate living room to a ladies' civic club, to a bunch of retired men at the Joe Louis Social Club. I strolled the stark icy streets beneath the rotten latticework of the 63rd Street El and I pressed the flesh in taverns (while the impulse to join the voters in a drink went through me like electric current through a white rat). The best thing that came of the day was meeting Albert Monroe, whom I began to cultivate with the hopes he could end up doing me a lot more good in the ghetto than Lucille Jackson.

Monroe was twenty-two, an ex–Blackstone Ranger, poor, fast, sharp, with sure political instincts. He liked me and wanted to work in my campaign; he kept pace with me all day, cueing me in when I needed it, enduring Lucille's hysterical glowering eyes, because she knew he was cutting in on her harvest, and enduring, as well, the bitter cold January day, because his coat was thin and beneath his red and white Nikes his feet were bare. If I won, I planned to bring Albert on staff.

I didn't get home until nine in the evening. Juliet and Caroline had had dinner together in the kitchen and since they had little to say to each other, no two women had ever looked happier to see me when I finally arrived. I ate quickly and then went to take a bath, hoping to relax and take the pain out of my legs so I'd be able to put in a night's work.

As I soaked, I closed my eyes and dreamed of Sarah. With Caroline around, I could talk about her from time to time and it seemed that by speaking her name I had interrupted the magic that had been bringing her to me unbeckoned. Now I had to conjure her. I remembered her in the tub in her house on Staten Island, sitting in three inches of tepid water because there was a drought alert and she was crazily scrupulous about obeying that kind of civic-virtue law. She dipped a fat brown sponge in the water and squeezed it over her back, but the soap clung to her skin anyhow . . .

There was a knock on the door. I sat up in the water. "Yes?"

It was Juliet. "Tony Dayton and Mulligan are here to see you?"

I looked down and saw I had an erection; the head of my penis peered out of the water like a periscope. I slid down until I was below the waterline.

"Send them in," I said. I felt it would strengthen my command if I had them come in and speak to me in my bathroom.

Tony and Mulligan came in. Tony had a poster rolled up and tucked under his arm. Rich carried a manila envelope, upon which someone had penciled a column of numbers.

"Your posters came off press an hour ago," Dayton said. "You wanted to see them right away?"

"Unfurl it, Tony." I felt beneath the water; I was soft again and so I could sit up a little straighter.

Tony rolled out the poster and held it up for me to see. The whole thing was bordered in a bright, upbeat blue. The top lines read FIELDING PIERCE   DEMOCRAT   WORKING FOR YOU. Beneath that was a picture taken of me a couple of days before during an I.V.I. meeting. I had taken off my suit jacket and rolled up my sleeves and was pointing toward someone in the audience, as if acknowledging a question. (In fact, I'd been asking the fellow to stop interrupting me; it had been a heckler from the Hyde Park Gay Activists Alliance, asking me about my part in the Carmichael affair.) In the photo, I looked open to the tough questions, confident, available, vigorous, et cetera. There was even a smoky haze over the image, suggestive of a healing apparition rising from the battlefield. It was a shock to my underfed physical vanity that the Democrats were trying to make an asset of my appearance.

"Like it?" asked Tony, happily, certain I would.

"Do you?" I asked Rich Mulligan.

"Sure. It came out good," he said, with a shrug that seemed to mean he couldn't have cared less.

"How many did we run off?" I asked.

"Three thousand," said Tony.

I waited, let them try to guess what I was thinking. Then I sunk deep into my bath again and said, "Then we'll go with them." The truth was, I was thrilled beyond decency to see the poster; it was beyond what I had hoped for.

"Just one last thing," said Mulligan. "It turns out that was a good idea you had about a luncheon thing for all the precinct captains—"

"Yeah," I said, cutting him short. "And let's spend some money on that. Where are we having it?"

"Hyde Park Hilton," Mulligan said. He kept his words to a minimum as a form of resistance.

I closed my eyes for a moment, as if to think it over. "OK. What are they going to serve?"

Mulligan and Dayton glanced at each other, little commiserating bats of the eye. "*I* don't know," said Mulligan. "One of the girls'll take care of it."

"Look," I said. "I've got an hour to help fifty precinct captains feel good about humping their asses off to send me to Washington and if we invite them to lunch and serve them slop, what good will it do? Have them prepare cornish hens. One for every plate.

It doesn't cost any more than chicken but it looks like a big deal. And have them stuffed. Say, chestnut stuffing. And rice pilaf. And a fresh salad. They make a dressing there, their own kind of Thousand Islands dressing. It's good. Make sure they serve the salad with that."

I checked their faces to make certain they were sufficiently repulsed by my attention to detail and then I quickly submerged myself in the bath. The water exerted a pleasant, firm pressure against my eardrums and when I sat up again my hair was plastered over my forehead. "Hand me a towel, will you?" I asked and then completed the night's work by stepping out of the tub and coming toward them stark naked, my hand extended, waiting for the towel.

The next morning, Tony Dayton was over for breakfast. Juliet had left early to see a damaged Ingres drawing in Evanston and to bid on its restoration and Caroline was already at the campaign headquarters on Woodlawn. Tony was over to show me yet another product of his propaganda mill, this one a leaflet with the suddenly familiar slogan: *Fielding Pierce Democrat Working for You*. We were sitting at the kitchen table eating a breakfast of coffee and sweet rolls which Tony himself had brought over in a paper bag. Tony was palpably nervous as he gave me the leaflet to look over.

"You know what you've got?" he said. "A great name. It's actually kind of black. And of course it's white. It's hip without going high-hat and it has a swinging kind of honesty to it."

Below the slogan was a line of stars, meant to suggest patriotism. And then came my vital statistics. My schooling, my military service, my time in Isaac's firm, and my years as a lawyer in the Cook County prosecutor's office. It all looked just fine. And in fact it looked familiar, to the edge of déjà vu, since this was the way I'd written it out mentally a thousand times before.

Below my résumé, there was another line of stars. And then,

below those, in bold type, the words *My Credo*. And then, in quotation marks, a paragraph from some automaton purporting to be the candidate himself.

"A lot of what I'd like to say about what I believe can be put into four very simple words: I am a Democrat. I see myself in the tradition of FDR, Truman, and John Fitzgerald Kennedy. I believe in the greatness of America and the greatness of this, the 28th CD of Illinois. The people of this District deserve a strong and vigilant voice in Washington. The people of the District need someone to speak up about their concerns. 1. A fairer share of the federal pie. Right now, we are getting only nine cents back out of every dollar we pay in to the federal government. There's much to do in our neighborhoods and we need the funding to get the job done. 2. A strong America and a safer world. We must pursue the spirit of Camp David throughout the world. 3. My experience as a prosecutor has taught me that violent crime is truly the plague of our times. We need an Omnibus Crime Bill to rid the streets of violent crime. 4. Bringing down those interest rates. I will work with those in Congress who are fighting to bring inflation under control. Inflation is the cruelest tax of them all. 5. An open mind and an open door. Above all, I will make myself available to the people of this District and be guided by their wisdom. A leader who does not *listen* is not really a leader."

I put the page down and Tony's eyes were waiting for me. "So? What do you think?" he asked. He shifted in his seat.

"I've got problems with it, Tony," I said. I saw the disappointment in his face and I tried to soften my remarks. "I mean, a lot of it's fine. Some of it's awfully good. But there's problems."

"But you basically liked it?" he said. "I mean, on the whole?"

"Well, I don't know. I have kind of a hard time with . . ." I looked down at the page. "You know, with saying I believe in the greatness of the people of the Twenty-eighth CD of Illinois."

"You *have* to say that, Fielding," Tony said, very quickly. "That's just a point of departure. Like, do you think Charlie Parker wanted to play 'How High the Moon'? Of course not. But there were interesting chords for him to solo off of and it was nice to play something the audience recognized, so they could see how he was changing it."

"Do you know Eric McDonald?"

"Not personally. But I think he's a talent. Very postbop, but not crazy atonal. Why?"

"My sister Caroline married him."

"You're kidding me." Dayton's small, blunt fingers went into his dark little beard, that obsidian arrowhead.

"No. Anyhow, they're divorced."

"Well, how's that for getting the worst of both worlds, right? The racists will hate her for marrying a black and the blacks will hate her for not making it work. In other words, less said the better. So tell me, babe. What else do you want to say about the leaflet? I'd like to get fifty thousand of them run off by tomorrow. Rich Mulligan tells me he can get a couple dozen precinct workers out and we'll have them in every mailbox in the district."

"Well, I have a hard time with this credo. I mean the whole thing. Or maybe it's just the idea of it, Tony. Usually, you know, one writes one's own credo."

"Not if one doesn't have the time, jazzbo. I didn't think I put anything in it that you couldn't live with."

"Well, how about this belief in the people of the Twenty-eighth CD. That's embarrassing."

"It's just bullshit. No one pays attention. I mean, if someone sneezes, you say God bless you. No one stops the show to figure out if you really meant it."

"Did anyone else see this?"

"Yeah. Of course."

"Who?"

"The whole shebang." And then, suddenly, Dayton's affability vanished. He took a Salem out of his shirt pocket and held it with four fingers, making no move to light it. He leaned forward. "Everyone's seen it and everyone likes it, Fielding. You want to hang this up over a few words? Well, I can't let you. Please. You got to be reasonable, jazzbo. If something screws up—I take the heat."

"What's my schedule for today, Tony?"

"We got you at the Hyde Park Synagogue at eleven to talk to the golden oldies, then Lucille Jackson's introducing you to a few of the black precinct captains. Then we're supposed to get in touch with Kathy Courtney. She's got a dinner lined up for you with some reporters. Maybe even get Royko in on it."

"Good," I said, "my schedule's not so bad today. I've got a little time to take a whack at this credo thing on my own. How would that be? I'll poke around with it for an hour or so and see if I can come up with anything."

"You mean do the whole thing over?" asked Dayton, as if he were Michelangelo and I'd just told him I wanted track lighting for the Sistine Chapel.

"No, no, of course not. Not the whole thing."

"You mean just a word here or there?"

"Look," I said, suddenly irate, "it's my credo. I think I ought to write it myself."

Well, it was ridiculous, it was a time waster, it was miles beside the point, but Dayton could only relinquish. He left at nine in the morning, saying he'd meet me at the synagogue at ten forty-five. "Don't be late," he said. "You know how punctual the Jews are."

"That's a new one on me," I said, seeing him to the door. He was zippered back up in his down jacket. He'd slipped rubbers on over his tasseled loafers. He looked like a very lonely man.

After he was gone, I sat at my desk with the leaflet. Then I got out a legal pad and a nice Mont Blanc fountain pen Danny had given me a couple of Christmases before. I wrote at the top My Credo and then immediately began drawing crazy little faces, the same ugly, long-nosed, beetle-browed profiles I'd been drawing since I was in second grade and which had, for a few weeks, seemed the harbinger of artistic talent but which quickly atrophied into an annoying compulsive doodle.

I dashed off a dozen of these profiles and for a moment they looked like an arc of devils floating over the sappy headline. I started to write. *Democracy is a fight that is never fully won. The enemies of democracy thrive on complacency.* Big fucking deal. All right. *Is America fated to become the pitiful, helpless giant?* No, no, no. That's what you say when you're in SDS and you're bellowing through a bullhorn at a bunch of your middle-class pals on the steps of the Humanities Building. *America is a dream that each dreamer must dream anew.* Yes, well that ought to bring out the boys in the white jackets and butterfly nets. How about a few specifics, jazzbo? OK, no more pitiful giants, no more democratic dreamers. I'm not doing an evening with Walt Whitman; I'm supposed to be running for what we call political *power*. So let's strut our stuff, yes? *A critical choice faces the people of the 28th Congressional District.* No. It's the other way around. *The people of the 28th Congressional District face a critical choice.* OK. A fresh piece of paper. Forget the heading: too intimidating. No more ghouls in profile. Let's just get it down in blue and yellow. One. *I believe* . . . But what? That for every drop of rain that falls a flower grows? Yes. Exactly. Another sheet of paper. *After years of abuse by people in office, in which government has seemed for sale to the highest bidder, the American people have now become disengaged not only from their so-called leaders but from the very idea of politics.* Hey, wait a minute. I actually believe this. OK, let's keep it going. *Robert F. Kennedy, in his last campaign, said that he wanted to make politics an honorable profession again. For my generation in particular, the idea of politics and political office has fallen into disfavor. It is considered dishonest, futile, and even passé. Yet there is a growing awareness that if we do not serve, if we do not struggle for progress and fairness in the political arena, then the most critical decisions of our time will be left for others—the men and women who truly are self-seeking and cynical and who fill the void left by decent people's retreat from politics.* I read this over and then read it over again. The rhetoric was goddamned irresistible. Then suddenly, the phone chimed, like a sane voice, and I grabbed for it immediately. It was Caroline, calling from headquarters.

"Hey, guess what," she said, "we just got ten thousand buttons. Blue and white buttons with your name on them. Isn't it weird?"

"Let's at least try to feel professional about this, Caroline," I said. "Anyway, listen to this. I just wrote it and I want to get it over to Tony Dayton. Got the time right now?"

"I'm working for you, sweetie."

I read her my credo and after I was through she was quiet enough for me to hear someone open the door on her side of the line.

"I'll tell you something, Fielding," Caroline finally said. "I've gotten to know Tony in the past few days, and he is not going to go for it."

"Caroline," I said, standing up so quickly I almost pulled the phone off my desk, "when you tell me you've gotten to know Dayton pretty well you are deliberately creating the impression that you've fucked him."

"I'm going to write that last remark off to high stress, Fielding. I like the credo but I don't think it's what you need for your campaign right now."

"What do you mean?" I asked in a very thin voice—one I could slip like a note beneath the great slamming door of my rage.

"I think it's very nice. And it really does remind me of you. I mean, I can really hear you saying it. And I think that's important."

"But."

"But what's it got to do with the price of potatoes? You're the one who first told me about this district. You've got old people eating dogfood and fifth graders copping skag and little blue-haired widows afraid to go outside and I don't know if they want to hear about whether politics is an honorable profession or not."

"I know what they want," I said. "They want someone to promise he can make it all better—but I can't. I can't do it and I can't promise it."

"You can promise to try, though. This credo sounds more like an argument you'd have with Danny. Or with . . ." She let her voice trail off—nothing strategic about it. She just realized what she was about to say and she kicked the plug out of the wall.

"Or with who?" I asked, but knowing.

"With Sarah."

"OK," I said quickly. "I'll forget it. Wait'll you read what your boyfriend's hacked out for me. It'll make mine sound like Kennedy in Berlin."

"If you refer to Tony Dayton like that again, I will have to comb your face with my fingernails."

"Caroline, can I tell you something?"

"What?"

"I'm awfully glad you're here. I knew I needed you but I didn't know how much."

"That's nice of you, sweetie."

"I mean it. I really do love you. And I'm . . . I'm just glad you're here." Oh my God, I thought, what am I doing? I felt emotion welling up.

I dressed and made my way to the Hyde Park Synagogue, where I was introduced by Rabbi Einhorn, a tall, stocky man in a luxurious Italian suit. Einhorn had rich silver hair, blue eyes, and an adulterer's smooth voice. "Our old people are most anxious to hear your views, Mr. Pierce," he said, right in front of them. We were in a rather small room; there were perhaps twenty retired congregation members, part of the temple's Senior Citizen program. I hadn't developed a standard speech yet. I figured retired people would be upset about inflation so I talked about inflation. I figured they'd be worried about crime in the street and so I was very tough on crime in the street. In no way was I conscious of creating feelings within myself so as to make myself more attractive to others. It was merely a matter of what to highlight—or so I told myself.

Dayton was in fairly high spirits; he was pleased with my performance. We stopped for lunch at a businessmen's joint on Stony Island called Flickers, where Tony played King Pleasure singing "Moody's Mood for Love" several times on the jukebox.

From there, we made an impromptu stop at a CYO neighborhood playground, where I ran that old liberal ploy of playing basketball with a couple of black kids. They had shoveled and swept the asphalt court but a light dusting of snow had fallen over it and as I dribbled the big butterscotch ball it made grainy indentations in the new snow. (I thought of Father Mileski playing one-on-one with that kid for the wager of his immortal soul and I remembered Sarah's immemorial fingers linked through the cyclone fence, as she watched the game.) I passed out campaign buttons and Dayton and I moved on, driving his white Cutlass over to the University of Chicago bookstore to ask the manager personally to hang my campaign poster in the window. The manager refused and then changed his mind when I told him my brother was the publisher of Willow Books. (There was a display of *Shamanism and Science* near the cash register.) The manager said he'd do it as a professional courtesy and on the way out of the store Dayton laid his hand out for me to slap, as if we'd just pulled off an incredible coup.

From the bookstore, Tony brought me to a small shopping center called Harper Court where we just strolled around in the blowing, stinging snow and Dayton mindlessly collared passersby and brought them over to meet me. It was awfully half-assed, but it still took its toll. Figuring the average handshake exerts forty pounds of pressure, then I pressed flesh to the tune of eight thousand pounds.

At the end of the day Tony was to deliver me to Kathy Courtney, my press aide. Although she worked on the South Side she lived north and we took the Outer Drive up toward her apartment. We passed a playground next to the lake. Cadmium lamps lit the empty space; the wind blew the swings back and forth. I closed my eyes and drifted off and I wouldn't even bother to say I dreamed of Sarah except that as I jolted awake again, for the first time I realized I hadn't had a night's sleep in two weeks during which she hadn't come to me in a dream. And that, oddly enough, with Tony beside me and a night of more campaigning before me, was when I finally became certain that she was alive. I felt the truth of it as firmly as an embrace. And it was real, at least as real as that red light throbbing somewhere out there over the lake, out toward Indiana, at least as real as the shadow Dayton's car cast of itself on the roadway, that shadow that kept pace with us but never quite caught up.

We turned off the Outer Drive and headed toward Michigan Avenue, where Kathy lived in one of the posh new high rises. A freezing rain pebbled against the roof and you could hear the tire treads running their pattern, turning around and around like the drum of a mimeograph machine. Tony lit a Salem and savored the first drag as if it was to be enjoyed like the finest wine.

"You did good today, Fielding," he said.

"We're going to have to talk about scheduling," I said. "There was too much time between things and too much of it seemed aimless."

"We had cancellations. These things can't be helped."

I didn't bother to answer.

"I think we'll get sixty percent," he said.

"Well, good."

He took another voluptuous drag of his Salem. And then: "How do you find working with me?"

"I like it fine, Tony. I always know you'll be there, at least."

"Good," he said. "Will you do me a favor then? Don't keep it a secret."

"But I just told you."

"Come on, You know what I mean. I'd like you to tell your boss."

"You mean the American people?"

"Yeah, right."

"Who do you mean, Tony? Isaac Green? He's not what I'd call my *boss*."

"Then why'd you say his name?" Dayton pretended to gun me down with his fire finger.

"I'm psychic. Anyhow. Isaac's just a well-meaning lawyer. What do you care what he thinks of you?"

"I can see the way he looks at me he thinks I'm a lightweight. And we were involved in an aldermanic race three years ago and maybe I made a couple of mistakes and our boy went down for the count. Guys like Isaac hold a grudge."

"Well, if I win, he'll love you all over again," I said.

"Just do me the favor, OK? That guy's got more juice than an orange grove."

"You think so?"

"Are you kidding me? Why do you figure the governor's doing your man favors—because maybe Isaac once got him tickets to *Porgy and Bess*?"

"I think he likes Isaac because Isaac's got class."

"Kinosis cares as much about class as he cares who plays bass for Oscar Peterson. The governor's a mule, God bless him, and he only moves when you hit him with a stick."

"All right. I'll bite. What's the stick?"

We were stopped at a traffic light. Off to the side, a couple of women were in the front window of a dress store, stripping down the mannequins.

"I don't know. But it's something big. How many people in this state feel the governor owes them a favor? But he picks *you* to take Carmichael's office, a guy with little experience and a couple of fast strikes against him." He glanced at me to see how I was taking it. The car behind us sounded its horn as soon as the light turned green. Tony put the car in gear and said, "I'm referring now to the crazy family stuff and the old girl friend involved in all that protest business."

"No one's mentioned it," I said.

"No one's had to. That doesn't mean it won't come up. But the point is, Kinosis must know all this and still he nominates you."

"Because I'm the best. And I'm going to win."

"He doesn't *care* who's the best—whatever the hell best is supposed to mean." He gave me a confidential look and added, "The governor has very relativistic morals."

I closed my eyes. A feeling of exhaustion came over me with the power of a trance.

"All I'm saying," Dayton went on, "is some guy like Isaac who's owed so much—I'd just like him thinking very groovy thoughts about me."

We pulled in front of Kathy Courtney's apartment building. It was seven thirty and we were right on time. I was going to meet her in the lobby and we'd take her car over to the restaurant. I turned the heater in Tony's car on high and put my hands in front of the blower. I always felt it made you seem like a loser to come in with cold hands.

"I'll tell you what, Tony," I said. "Let's win this election. Then I'll talk to Isaac about you. Right now, I wouldn't know what to say."

"I want you to say something *good*," said Tony, with a grin that seemed to suggest a certain complicity on our parts and which annoyed me so much I felt for a moment I might hit him.

"Yeah," I said. "Well, right now it's a mixed bag."

"But—"

"Yeah, and one other thing. It would only make matters worse if you ask Caroline to talk to me about this. I'd find that very irritating." I had my hand on the door, ready to leave. I could see Kathy in the brightly lit lobby of her building, dressed in a bronze down parka, black lace-up boots. When I looked back at Tony I realized I'd pushed too hard. I didn't want to lose him and so I reached over and patted his arm.

"I wouldn't be going through all this if I didn't think I could make a difference," I said. "It's just that time's so short and there's so much ground to cover. I guess sometimes I act a little like an ass." I smiled and he smiled back and as I slipped out of the car I thought to myself: That ought to hold him for a while.

"I've got something I've been meaning to tell you," said Kathy Courtney. "It's just something strange but I think you ought to know."

We were in her car heading toward Rush Street, where we

were going to have dinner with the reporters. She drove a tan Peugeot rigged up with a German sound system and I had a box of her cassettes on my lap, going through them, looking for something to play. She had odd musical tastes: Anne Murray, Captain and Tennille, Helen Reddy. Music to relax you, whereas I had a weakness for music that dripped a little acid on your wounds.

"Go right ahead," I said. I noticed the flirtatious lilt in my voice, puzzled over it, forgave myself.

"I knew Sarah Williams. I went to school with her."

"School?" I said, automatically, as quickly as you'd throw your hands in front of your face if you felt someone was going to slug you.

"Yes. In Baltimore. Goucher College. I was taking political science courses. I didn't really know that many people. Everyone else was studying medieval history or poetry. But everyone knew Sarah."

You don't really have to listen to this, I told myself. We were stopped at a red light. The car next to us was filled with dark teenagers. The interior was wreathed in smoke; they were passing a joint around; I could see the glow of the radio dial.

"I don't even know if I should be saying any of this," said Kathy, her voice small and gloomy.

"It's fine," I said. I waited a moment, let her relax. And then: "Does Jerry Carmichael know this?"

"Jerry? No. Why?"

"You used to work for him, that's why. Who else knows?"

"I don't know who does."

I could feel my questions squeezing her. As a county prosecutor it was my best skill. Once I had been interrogating a cement contractor we were trying to turn and the guy had been insisting on his innocence for six days. Finally, I began really pouring it on and he got so rattled that when he started to rub his eye he poked his finger right through his glasses. With a lap full of lens he came over and we used him as a key witness in exchange for immunity on just three of the eight counts against him.

"Well, you've obviously told someone," I said. "You're in the information business. It's just a matter of remembering, Katy."

"I'm sure I told a lot of people. After."

"After what, Kathy?"

"After she was killed." She looked over at me with frightened, wounded eyes and the appetite for the interrogation just left me. I covered my eyes, but that was no good: there was something waiting for me in the darkness.

"Tell me about her," I said.

"I don't know what you want," said Kathy. A patch of light from the headlights of a turning car went over one eye, down her full cheek.

"Just talk to me about her," I said, my voice slipping away from me.

"She was very funny. I mean in school." Kathy lapsed into silence. "I don't know what you want to hear."

"Anything," I said.

"She was a riot. All over the place. Making trouble. She always wore a trench coat and sunglasses and when someone said she was a spy Sarah said she really *was* a spy. You know. College."

"College," I said.

"And then she got involved with those poor . . . I don't know, kind of scary women down near the waterfront. That shelter she helped start. After that, no one saw much of her. I don't know how she passed her classes."

"She was a fast learner," I said. "She did everything fast. And totally. She went through everything as if it didn't count unless you did it to its furthest extreme."

"I think you're right about that," said Kathy cautiously, as if suspecting I might be trying to lure her into dangerous territory.

"And then she got caught on the wrong side of history," I said, and at that moment I don't think I was altogether aware of whom I was talking to. It was just between me and the darkness in that car.

"When I heard, I just couldn't believe it," said Kathy. "To me she always seemed like such a lucky person."

"Were you pretty good friends with her?"

"No."

"Why not?"

"I don't think she knew who I was. I was a wallflower, a typical Catholic schoolgirl with my wool socks and hideous complexion. We were in different worlds."

And then I couldn't say another word. I was remembering getting the news, remembering the long flight to Minneapolis on Northwest Orient and the stewardesses strapped into the very last seats gossiping back and forth, laughing, sharing some private sketch, some piece of hilarity, and me thinking Sarah will never laugh nor hear the laughter of others, all of this is going on without her. I was remembering the following spring without her, the little clay pot of paper-whites coming into bloom in the bedroom window and the thin line of sweet aroma they pumped out, like a note on an organ left on forever. And I was remembering the phone calls and the letters and the dry desperate interviews with the scattered left-wing magazines that still gave a shit about what had happened to Sarah. And I was remembering the calls from Father Mileski that I avoided, and the trip to D.C. to talk to Agent Donahue, a sallow, softening cop in his forties with two pictures in his little office—one of J. Edgar Hoover and the other a child's drawing of a blue smiling face with the inscription "My Daddy is the Smurfiest. Love, Sean." (I looked at the FBI files, the eight-by-ten black and white photographs were glossy and oddly old-fashioned, as if this were something that had happened a long time ago. The white Volvo was broken in half; it rested in a meringue of firemen's foam. Arrows had been drawn on with grease pencil, indicating where the bomb had been placed, where the impact had been absorbed. There were pictures of the bodies, but I couldn't very well look at those.)

I was remembering everything. I was remembering much too much: I was a man unconscious in the hull of his boat heading toward the Angel Falls. I was remembering now the walk home from Carmichael's apartment and how close she was to me in that storm and then her call as soon as I was home. I was at the cusp of something and I didn't know if it was madness or enlightenment, collapse or transcendence—and it didn't seem to matter which it was. It must have felt like fever when people first began to believe that the earth was not flat, did not end, but curved endlessly around and around upon itself. You could stare at the ocean for a lifetime and see the hard edge at its terminal point and then one day that edge is gone and in its place is a curve—sudden, inexplicable proof of infinity. Perhaps we would one day see death that way, too. Perhaps I was already seeing it. Maybe the dead wait for us to need them before waking—or maybe it is not them at all, but we who do the waking, peeling away the scales of our tragic view of life and death and stepping into a vision at once ecstatic and terrible. Without a total and final death, then consequence becomes infinite. What if an unkind word, a moment's dishonesty, the twisting of a child's arm lasts not just for that moment, not even just for your entire lifetime, but extends itself clear across the arc of time?

We were parked across from the restaurant. I don't know how long I'd been sitting in silence, but Kathy just sat with me, breathing as I breathed.

Finally, she said, "We're here."

I nodded. "You go in," I said. "I'm just going to sit and get focused again."

The way I'd put it set her at ease. She quickly checked herself in the rearview mirror, patted her hair, tugged at the ruffled collar of her blouse. "OK," she said, and opened the door. With the engine off, a thin skin of ice was already forming on the windshield. She got out carefully; there was ice on the pavement. She looked in at me for a moment and closed the door as quietly as possible, like a mother letting herself out of the bedroom of a difficult child, praying the brat won't awaken.

The name of the restaurant was Alan's Rib. These adorable restaurant names seemed to have reached epidemic proportions. It was full of chrome and mirrors and gray carpeting. I looked around for Kathy and couldn't see her. There was a smell of burned fat in the air, quiet jazz from the speakers. Then I saw her, standing at our table, waving toward me. Earth to Fielding. I walked leadenly toward her, smiling in what I hoped was a reassuring manner.

Kathy was with a stout woman with a birthmark on her face. Her name was Sandra McDuffy and she had a Sunday morning public affairs show called "Chicagoland Now" on WGN. My other pal for the night was a guy named George Broderick, from the *Sun-Times*. George was in his late twenties, with a blow-dry haircut and a sack of oats under his vest.

Kathy was nervous and seemed overanxious to please. "I hope everyone's hungry!" she said, as if she'd been long at the stove preparing a meal for our pleasure. As I settled in, it struck me that her tone was all wrong: she was acting as if she needed to make a sale, whereas my instinct said we ought to treat them as if we were doing them a favor.

We ordered drinks. Broderick raised an eyebrow when I asked for a club soda. We chatted back and forth for a while and I did just fine on automatic pilot. I'd been at this business only for a short time but it seemed suddenly, crushingly, that I'd been going through this bullshit all my life.

I could almost feel it happening, like a tremor in the earth— the evening began to turn.

"Is Congressman Carmichael participating in your campaign?" George Broderick asked me. He'd taken a drink of his stinger without removing the swizzle stick and the little red tip had left an indentation on his cheek.

"Let's put it like this," Kathy said, heading me off. "Jerry's still pretty exhausted. Naturally, he doesn't want the seat falling to the Republicans, but family considerations are going to have to come first."

"Jerry's a hell of a campaigner," Broderick said.

"Oh, he loves it," said Kathy. "He just comes to life."

Sandra McDuffy fished her maraschino cherry out of her Rob Roy. She placed it on the napkin and when she saw I was staring at her she smiled. "Do you remember me, Fielding?" she asked.

I didn't. Not yet. But the question and the tone of her voice tripped a lever in me. "I can't . . . ah, can't quite place you."

"You see her on TV all the time," said Kathy, trying to cover for me.

"Oh no, no, I don't mean that," said Sandra McDuffy. "Fielding and I met a few years ago, just when I was starting out in the news business. But you don't remember?" She stopped and held her face up, as if posing for a snapshot.

"Not really," I said. There was a loud burst of laughter from another table; I fought the impulse to turn in my chair and see who was so fucking happy.

"Minneapolis," Sandra said. She saw the confusion in my face and was crestfallen. "Oh, I'm sorry. It was a terrible moment. I suppose you don't remember. Silly of me."

"Minneapolis," I said.

She explained to the others: "It was my first job. I was like Mary Tyler Moore working for the little news department at WJM. Only I didn't have a Lou Grant as my boss. The guy I worked for was a total nightmare. I mean, the worst. And because I was a *woman* he had me on the miscarriage-at-the-zoo beat. Ugh. The worst! But then this incredible thing happened. One of the biggest stories of the year broke and this reporter named Doug Swenson, whom my boss absolutely *doted* on—I mean to the point of total ridiculousness—got an attack of phlebitis and before I knew it, I was on the story. It was such an amazing stroke of luck."

"What was the story?" George Broderick asked. Professional courtesy.

"Well, maybe Fielding better tell you. He was a *participant*."

Like spectators in a very slow tennis match, the eyes of my tablemates shifted toward me. I took a sip of my club soda and with a little imagination it tasted like gin.

"The woman I was living with was in a car. The car was attacked."

"Oh, come on," said McDuffy. "As if that was all there was to it." She was sitting to my left. I could smell her perfume; her eyes flashed with that weird skittering light people have who are thinking ten minutes ahead of you. She took the story away from me as if it were a flag and now *she* was going to lead the parade.

"They were a bunch of Chileans," she said. "And they were all mixed up with these liberation-type priests. They were sneaking out of Chile and coming here. Just the story of these poor people from the mountains of South America waking up one morning and finding themselves in St. Paul in the winter is worth time on any newscast. But it was even more than that. It was like a spy-versus-spy thing. You've got the left-wing Chileans over here and the American priests giving them sanctuary. And then you've got the right-wing Chileans hunting them down. And then you've got a girl like Fielding's old friend getting herself caught in the middle. I must say, my heart goes out to them. Gutsy types, really gutsy."

"Save us from the *past*," said Kathy, rolling her eyes, throwing it away.

"You know why you didn't remember me?" Sandra said, poking me again. "Because I've lost a lot of weight since then."

"You look great, by the way," said Kathy. "What are you on? Scarsdale?"

"No. Nothing like that. Just eating less. And drinking bottled water."

"But I do remember you," I said, in a just audible voice. "I remember your eyes and the sound of your voice and the way you pushed the microphone into my face."

"Women aren't supposed to be aggressive," Sandra said to Kathy.

"Were you involved with the Chileans, too?" Broderick asked me.

"This is such old news," said Kathy. "Fielding really had nothing to do with it."

"But you must have known them," persisted Broderick. "What were they? People from the old Allende days?"

"Yes, they were. I did know them."

Sandra McDuffy looked questioningly at Kathy, who shrugged, as if to say this was the first she'd heard of any of this.

"This is really a new dimension on the whole thing, isn't it?" Broderick said to McDuffy.

"Yes and no," she said. Cagey.

"I guess what I'm supposed to say here," I said, "is whether or not I was working with the Chileans. Well, the truth is, I wasn't. It was something Sarah did."

"Sarah Williams," McDuffy said to Broderick. "His friend."

Broderick nodded. His hand went into his vest; he grabbed a couple of inches of flab and squeezed with all his might.

"I heard some interesting stuff about old Bertelli today," said Kathy.

"This Chilean thing," Broderick said. "I think I remember it now."

"Of course you do," said McDuffy. "It was huge. Francisco Higgins. Gisela Higgins. They were like South American jet-setters. Very glamorous, very left. Not necessarily Communistic or anything. But, you know, part of that whole sixties, Latin American revolution thing. And it *seemed* like the generals and whatever down in Chile had sent a hit squad up here to do the Higginses in. But nothing ever was proved. Whoever put that bomb under the car—"

"They were *bombed*?" asked Broderick.

"Golly, George," said McDuffy. "Where were you in 1975?"

"I was in London, going to school."

"Well, you were certainly out of touch. Yes. The car was bombed. And whoever put the bomb in place got away, just like that. Most people think whoever it was got out of the country. There was the usual talk about conspiracies, you know, the CIA giving the bombers safe passage. And then there were the theories that the left planted the bomb, figuring Francisco and Gisela were worth more as dead martyrs. That the whole thing was a way of embarrassing the new Chilean government."

"That's a pretty far-out idea," said Broderick.

"It's what you call bullshit," I said.

"Do you see your candidacy as a way of carrying this fight forward?" Broderick asked me.

"Now be careful, George," said Kathy. "He wasn't a part of that whole thing to begin with."

"OK," said Broderick, "let me put it differently. If you're elected, do you intend to—"

"Provocative," teased Kathy, wagging her finger at Broderick and smiling.

"Just looking for something to write about," said Broderick, acknowledging her smile with a shadowy grin of his own.

What was I waiting for? Why didn't I clear the table with a sweep of my arm? Had I traveled this far for this? It seemed the path got only narrower and my steps only more careful. What did my tablemates see in me that told them they could talk about the day in Minnesota like this? Did I seem that anesthetized to the horror of it?

Just then, I heard the hollow *thock* of a cork being pulled from a bottle of champagne. I turned in my seat toward the sound. A waitress in black slacks was pouring the champagne for a small bald fellow in expensive clothes. He was with a young, trapped-looking woman. He glared at the champagne as it filled his glass. The candlelight caught the fizz of the wine and made it look hot and angry.

And then, in that last moment, with the net of my attention still cast out into the restaurant, then, with the border guards of intelligence lighting their cigarettes, gazing at the stars, not at all doing their job of stopping anything from crossing over the line between heart and mind, it was then that I saw her, Sarah, just getting up from her table at the side of the restaurant, near the black and chrome bar. There were three other people at her table but she was the only one leaving. She was wearing a black sweater, gray pleated trousers. There was a look in her face of an anger that was at once immense and familiar. Her jaw was tight; her gestures were quick, almost slashing. She pulled a purple wool coat off the back of her chair. She glanced back at the people at her table and shook her head in disgust and then set off, with the overcoat draped over her broad, square shoulders.

"Hey, *hey*," said Sandra McDuffy, pushing her chair back. I had somehow knocked over my goblet of club soda and it was running off the edge of the table and into her lap.

"Sorry," I said, getting up. I watched the back of the purple overcoat go past the bar toward the door to the outside. The piped-in music changed: "Do You Know the Way to San Jose?"

There was a little commotion at my table. Napkins were thrown over the club soda. Kathy Courtney was talking a mile a minute and George Broderick sneaked two antacid tablets into his wide flexible mouth and then looked around with a weird sort of guilt in his eyes as if it were against the law to take Tums. I knew I was making a very big mistake and I knew I had just a moment to cover it.

"This is very strange," I said. "But that . . ." I pointed toward the door just as she was pushing her way out. I turned back to Kathy and the reporters. They seemed uncomfortable and, realizing that, I suddenly realized that whatever I told them would come as a relief. People would rather believe anything than the chaos of an unraveling mind. "I'll be back as soon as I can. But that woman who just left has some statistics I've been trying to get hold of and she's . . . she's very hard to reach."

I groped for my coat but all I felt was chair. Maybe it would be better to leave without it; it might mean I was coming right back. I made what I could only assume was a reassuring gesture and then made my way across the restaurant and toward the door, telling myself with every step that I wasn't doing anything I couldn't somehow fix later on.

The wind was blowing hard like a shoulder against the door but I pushed through. My pant cuffs danced wildly around the tops of my ankles; my tie went straight back over my shoulder; the cold wind was like steel against my belly. The snow was flashing past the streetlights. My heart seemed to be inching around my chest, like an old frightened man walking in the dark. I looked up the block. There was only emptiness. The neon lights of a shop window hung in the web of blackness for a moment and then disappeared, then reappeared. I looked the other way and there she was, near the corner now, where the light governing north-south traffic was red and the westbound traffic moved in a quick grinding blur. *Turn around*, I thought, hurtling my inner voice at her. But of course she did not. Her figure looked dim, unfocused. Snow was getting in my eyes and the sound of the wind whined chaotically. I began to run.

I felt agile and quick. I seemed to be gliding toward her. I raced past the little nut store with the shelled nuts basking in bins beneath infrared lights, past a funky rip-off clothing store called Yesterday Today and Tomorrow, past a dark little bar called Mister Sister. The light changed and she was walking quickly across the street. I could see by the way her elbows and shoulders were moving that she was finally buttoning her coat. I opened my hand as if her warm belly were beneath my palm.

And then, suddenly, I stopped. How could it possibly be Sarah? What sort of displaced suicide was I committing? I stood on one side of the street and watched her walk away and I was telling myself to turn around. But of course it wasn't as simple as that: there are moments when precisely what life requires is that you let go of everything you've believed to that point. And the problem becomes knowing when those moments are. From the time this campaign for Carmichael's office began, I had shared the most tender, undefended center of my heart with Sarah. She had come to me in sleep; I had heard her voice humming in the wires. She would not go away; she only got closer. And now standing on that corner with the snow coming faster and faster I had just one more moment to make what I suddenly realized was the most important decision of my life: Was I losing my mind or was I really going to have another chance with her? Put like that, the choice seemed oddly simple and clear. I called her name and started to run after her. My old and everyday mind was like a light on the shore and the rest of me was a ship sailing out toward the invisible curve of the sea.

She knew I was following her. Her step quickened. She glanced back over her shoulder and then quickly turned away. A shop-keeper had thrown chemical rock salt onto the pavement and her boots crunched over it. In the middle of the block, she stepped onto the street, crossed, and made it to the other side. A bus was coming at a good clip, its windows lighted and green, exhaust pouring out of it like a black bushy tail. I knew if I let that bus pass it would erase her; I darted in front of it, my wimpy shoes almost failing to negotiate the slimy, icy skin of the street.

"Sarah," I said, now that I was behind her again. Only one hundred feet separated us. She didn't turn around. She started to run and I ran after her. In the movies, a chased woman invariably trips over her own feet but she was sure-footed, more sure-footed than I. The cold was starting to congeal in my chest. Thoughts broke off in large vaporous chunks.

She began to run in earnest, full out. I shouted at her to stop; my voice, pinched by the cold, sounded desperate, repellent. I tried to run as fast as she, but I could not overtake her. I could barely keep up. She was close to her destination; I could see it in the urgency of her stride. Then the storefronts gave way to the obsidian spears of a high iron fence. Behind the fence were the barred windows of a parochial school and then the swell of large oval stained-glass windows thrust out into the night like the breast of a great bird. The iron fence flashed by. I saw her running up the steps to the church. A wedge of light appeared in the dark snowy air as she opened the door and then disappeared as it closed.

I went in after her. But there was ice on the steep cement stairs and I lost my footing. I broke my fall with my hands, but my shin cracked into the edge of a step and the pain flew into me like a flock of small frightened birds flushed out of the underbrush. I cursed to myself but tried to keep moving. I was on my hands and knees. My eyes were closed and I made myself keep going. I more or less crawled up to the top of the steps. My left leg was bleeding and so were the heels of both hands, though only slightly. I stood up and grabbed for the door. I heard a low animal moan and then realized it was me.

I pushed through the vestibule, through the double doors, into the nave. The church was dark, warm, and the shadows trembled so it made everything seem unstable. The pulpit was empty but here and there in the pews I could make out a bowed head. I stood at the back of the church breathing heavily, my hand gripped tight on the smooth back of the last pew. A woman with a black scarf over her head was lighting a votive candle with a long wooden match; she blew out the match and folded her hands to pray. I looked for Sarah. My eyes stung from the smoke and the sudden change of temperature. I squeezed them shut for a moment and when I opened them again I saw her near the altar. In front of and to the side of the altar there was a stone corridor leading to a small chapel off to the left side. She glanced quickly up at the crucifix and then darted into that corridor. I could hear the heels of her boots clacking against the floor. I ran down the central aisle. From the corners of my eyes, I saw here and there an old woman on a kneeling bench, whispering her prayers into the knuckles of closed hands.

The little chapel was dark. Only two votive candles burned like large red eyes in the shadows. There were no pews, just a basin filled with holy water and a statue of Mary enclosed in glass behind a Communion rail. It was a wooden statue, painted blue and peach and white; there were cracks in the wood near the eyes and two of her fingers were missing. And except for that statue, I was alone in the chapel. "Sarah?" I said, in a voice just above a whisper. I was quiet; all I could hear was my dry, rapid breaths. "Sarah?" I said, louder this time, and then again, louder still, and again, and again and again. Each cry sent up a satellite of echo that went round and round the vaulted ceiling. I looked for the door through which she could have left—but there was nothing, no way out. I picked up one of the votive candles and paced the small chapel with it. I was saying things, calling her name: I'm not really sure what I said. And then I saw a narrow wooden door. I opened it and the wind came rushing toward me. The flame of the candle pressed against the glass and went out. I tasted snow on my lips. I was on a grillwork balcony; an iron staircase led down to a back alley illuminated by a large buzzing street lamp. She was gone.

I walked back into the chapel. Closed the door. The candle fell from my hand and shattered on the stone floor. I was not large enough to support what I was being asked to bear and as I admitted this to myself what strength I had left fled from me. I didn't know what to do and the truth is I didn't exactly know what to feel. I rested my weight against the Communion rail and stared at the wooden statue of Mary. "Goddamnit," I said, and then I reared my head back and said it again, screamed it this time, and as the echo subsided I heard footsteps coming toward the chapel, hurrying along. "Who is making this disturbance?" said an anxious voice with a British inflection.

I turned and there was Father Stanton, his hair completely white now, his blue eyes immense and offended. He was dressed in pajamas, slippers, a dark woolen robe. Someone must have awakened him and told him a madman was in the church. He seemed not to recognize me for a moment, but then in a flicker he did. He stepped back and clasped his hands together. "Fielding, my God, what's wrong? What brings you here?"

"I don't know," I said, and then staggered toward him and grasped his hand with all that was left of my strength. What cold fingers, I thought as I fell before him.

"I don't know," I said.

He looked at me. I could see enough of his eyes to notice the alarm. I stepped back so he would not be afraid.

"Did you want to speak to me?" he asked.

"I don't know why I'm here," I said. "Where am I?"

"You are in a church," he said. His voice sounded suddenly sharp, annoyed. "And you've created a disturbance. You frightened a woman in prayer. This church is a sanctuary, Fielding. You should know that."

"I want to talk about Sarah," I said. I closed my eyes; I felt his hand taking mine. I felt my strength leaving me like the last light in a room as the door swings shut.

"What do you want to say about her, Fielding?" said Stanton softly.

"Is she alive, Father? Please tell me."

I waited for his answer. I could hear his soft, calm breaths. Finally, I opened my eyes. He was still holding my hand, looking at me with enormous pity.

"She is alive in the hearts of those of us who loved her. And beyond that, there is something greater. She is with God."

I took my hand away from him. "I followed her into this church, Father Stanton." I tried to set my face so I would look strong. I wanted to look very, very strong after saying a thing like that.

Father Stanton came toward me. His image seemed unstable, like something reflected in a very old mirror.

"Fielding," he said, shaking his head. He put his arm around my shoulder and I just stood there, accepting his mercy and staring off into the darkness.

12

Sarah was back from Chile and I was racing home to her from New York, where I'd been celebrating my father's retirement. I got the last plane out and it was empty except for the crew and for me. I remember feeling in my isolation like a president on his own private jet and somehow that felt better than feeling what I really was—a man racing back to his lover with the knowledge growing within him that he was losing her. I was stubborn but I was not a fool: now that she was back from her mission into the steely heart of Chile, I knew that Sarah would need me that night and the next night, too, but I also knew that she was turning and that she was ready to steer her life in a direction I could not possibly follow. It seemed to be just a matter of time. That we had found each other in the first place and managed to stay together for so many, many months seemed in the roaring darkness of that flight home to be a perfect happy accident and now the laws of emotional entropy were asserting themselves. Sarah and I, I thought, were like rockets that had been shot up from the launching pads of childhoods a thousand miles apart. The trajectories of our flights had crossed for a time and we had flown in tandem—but now suddenly our paths were diverging. I could see Sarah cutting her way through space, even as she—or was it I?—got farther and farther away.

In truth, I felt humbled by her bravery, both horrified and awestruck over the choices she was making. It was a terrible blow—this feeling she was becoming, in her own eyes certainly and even to an extent in mine, my spiritual superior. It was a feeling I had carried within me in one form or another all of my life.

In college, I knew a boy who took mescaline five times a week. In a short while he was talking about theories of human electrical energy, angry molecules in the air, hot spots in Harvard Yard, but even as I witnessed his degeneration—the Frosted Flakes in his knotted beard, the staring empty eyes—I could not help but feel a nagging suspicion that he had discovered something I needed to learn and would never be able to. It was akin to what I'd always felt about Danny, who conducted his affairs on a high wire without a net, and it was what I'd always felt about Caroline—with her easy grace under pressure, and her ability to toss out her most tender feeling like a red rose off the side of a ship. For a time, I had felt Sarah and I were exact spiritual equals—conspirators, really. The usual: laughed at the same jokes, noticed the same oddballs hiding in the crowd, were easily aware of the imperfections and even the unavoidable residue of innate human rot that lay at the bottom of every motive, every gesture. We were not angels; we would let the phone ring no matter what brokenhearted soul might have been calling. And we were perfect lovers for each other, too. We went at it with the same sense of risk. We both longed to cut loose from the self we wore like a regulation uniform out into the everyday world. With me deep inside her, Sarah writhed and clutched and it seemed the bones in her face opened a little. I mean her face changed, it truly changed, and I saw a Sarah no one else knew, not even herself, except through me, and this simple, elemental, spacious knowledge bound us: it was the most real and unadorned thing I had ever known and she knew it about me, too. We were each other's pathways into ourselves and we were young enough and vain enough to care about that.

But it was an era, a time of our lives, and returning home to her that night I realized it was coming to an end. It had probably been changing long before that night, but this was the first time I could let myself see it—up there in the darkness inside that little pressurized tube, with the nozzle of light pouring out of the overhead reading lamp and onto the book that remained closed in my lap. I knew that our embraces would be different, and with that knowledge came a deeper, sadder knowledge—that they already had changed. We were not only holding each other, but holding on to each other, and I covered my eyes and squeezed them shut and there was a thud, a little jolt, but that was only my book slipping off my lap into the darkness that swirled like smoke around my feet.

We were awfully glad to see each other but it wasn't long after her return from Santiago that we began to fight. They weren't only the ordinary fights that lovers have. We were discovering the places in which our paths were dividing and each discovery made us a little more desperate, a little meaner. Behind both of us was a pit of sanctimony. I had all the dreadful assumptions of male supremacy luring me back—that LaBrea of wounded pride and obsession with my own path. And Sarah had behind her the equally alluring trap of feeling absolutely that she was no longer speaking just for herself but for God.

The only time after her trip to Chile that she held me as tightly as I wanted her to was a few weeks later when she awoke from a nightmare. It was just past daylight and she rolled toward me and put her hands on my shoulders, her leg between my thighs, her breasts flat and hard against my chest. She was wearing a pajama top and she was naked beneath that. Her pubic hairs were matted and hard around her opening. As she stirred, the scent of our having made love the night before also stirred, as if it had been trapped beneath the bedclothes like a cloud. "Please wake up," she said. "Please." She was cold with panic. Her eyes were immense and seemed devoid of any human intelligence. Her breath was brackish but it would be wrong to say merely I didn't mind when in fact I liked it: all signs of her reality, the overpowering truthfulness of her body, struck a chord of gratefulness and desire in me. I felt a twinge of regret each time she bathed.

"I was in a chair," she was saying. "And then the chair fell into something, a hole in the ground, the floor. I guess I was in a house. It was so quiet. Just—I don't know. Just so quiet. When the chair started falling I thought, Oh-oh, they got me. But I didn't think it was serious. I figured I could get out of it. But then I realized if I got out of the chair I'd be in blackness, nowhere, and I would still keep falling. So I just held on and there was terrible noise, like a train coming into a station, like a subway, getting louder and louder, and I wanted so much to hold my ears but if I let go of that chair then I'd be sucked into space and that's when I realized what had happened. I was dying."

"Yikes," I said, caressing her face. I could feel how much she needed me just then and my heart was pounding. I wanted somehow to seize this moment and use it as a rudder to change our course.

"Yikes? After all your studies with the great Harvard professors, this is what I get? I want to know what you think it means."

"Your dream?" I held her closer still. A little umbrella of air suddenly opened between us where she moved her stomach away from mine. I slid next to her again. "I think your dream means you think your life is dangerous but you don't know how to get out of it."

"Is that what you believe? Honestly?"

"Honest injun."

"That's a disgusting phrase."

"Sarah, it's seven o'clock in the morning. I can say anything I want to."

That evening we went to Resurrection House for a dinner in honor of Francisco and Gisela Higgins. Francisco Higgins had been part of the Chilean delegation to the United Nations and then Chilean ambassador to Mexico during the Allende regime. After the coup when the generals took over the government, Higgins had been arrested, along with thousands of others. He was beaten, tortured, yet later he maintained he was among the lucky ones. There was an international protest on his behalf and the generals had him released from the prison on Dawson's Island. He was expelled from Chile, along with his wife, who had been under house arrest all of that time. They moved to Cuba, then to Romania, and then to Mexico City. Now they were in the United States, following a lengthy battle with U.S. Immigration. Both Francisco and Gisela had accepted positions with something called the Christian Ecumenical Conference on Latin America. They had an office in a building in Washington that was filled with tiny foundations. They were in Chicago now on their way to Minnesota, where Francisco was going to speak at the university about the Allende experiment and after that they were both going to give a talk at a church in St. Paul called Our Lady of the Miracle. What I did not know was that Sarah would be going with them.

On the way to Resurrection House Sarah and I stopped at a little peeling wooden shack over which loomed a large painting of a primitive-looking hot dog—a hot dog fit for a Katzenjammer Kid. We bought twenty hot dogs, each wrapped in waxed paper along with a pickle and a handful of soggy fries. The mustard and relish showed through the opaque paper like a deep bruise. Though all he was serving was hot dogs and Pepsis, the old fellow who worked the counter wore a chef's cap. His eyes were small dark bullet holes, his face misshaped and unshaved. He looked like a madman pretending to be a famous cook.

"What a crazy-looking guy," Sarah said as we carried the sacks of frankfurters back to the car. We were parked beneath a street lamp and snow poured past the light.

"What if he is Jesus?" I asked.

She stepped on my toe. Hard.

I wasn't used to Sarah's other neighborhood at night and as we drove through the narrow brown streets, with the boarded-up windows, the Salem ads in Spanish, the unexpected vacant lots, the unseen but palpable sense of contested turf, I felt a wild swing of impatience. I may not have been raised in the lower depths, but I knew more about treacherous neighborhoods than Sarah did: her courage suddenly seemed like a kind of willful, perpetual half-blindness. She may have been leagues braver than I was, but my caution was born at least in part of experience and her courage was born at least in part of sheer inexperience. The horror of Sarah's childhood was that her father was a moneygrubber, that her sisters were synthetic, thoughtless, that her grandparents had slave-master mentalities. It was a lot to recoil from—but it prepared you for a life of poetry, not for a life on the streets.

"It's very grim around here, Sarah. I hate the thought of you walking these streets at night."

"I'm careful."

"I'm sure you're not. There are at least a thousand guys in this neighborhood who could rape you and not feel the slightest remorse."

"That kind of thinking makes me sick. And it's so *annoying*. You can see where it leads. With the world in flames, I'm not going to decide to be a shut-in."

"I'm not asking you to stay home. It's just a matter of accepting reality."

"Why is it always a certain kind of person who asks you to accept reality?" Sarah asked.

"Is that what you think I am?"

"No. I'm sorry. I don't know why I said that. It was dumb. I just don't know why you're saying things like that. You know this is where my work is. It's not going to do me any good to be afraid all the time. And I don't want to feel like an alien."

"I only want you to be safe."

"It's not enough. Not when I want so much more."

"I don't know what I'd do if someone attacked you."

"Male fantasy time. Anyhow, the truth is, people around here know who I am. And whatever else you might think about them—"

"I don't think anything about them. What are you making me out for?"

"Whatever else, they're very religious. They think of me practically as if I were a nun."

"There's a case right now, right here in town, about two guys who attacked a nun, a fifty-eight-year-old nun, kept her prisoner in an abandoned building, raped her innumerable times, and then cut off her fingers and carried them around in a little box, showing them to their friends."

"Why did you have to tell me that?"

"Because it's true, it happened."

"I think the kind of work you're going into is much more deadly than whatever I'm doing," Sarah said. "It just warps your view of everything. Deals, crimes, bargains—I don't know how you expect to remain a human being."

"I'll leave it to you to keep me straight," I said.

I said it quickly. We seemed to have established a pace: tough talk, bang bang bang. But suddenly Sarah broke the rhythm. It made everything a little more awful when she stopped to consider what she was going to say: off the cuff, anything could be overlooked, but in the silence I knew that what she said next was really going to count. "That's more than I can do, Fielding. I can't accept that responsibility."

"Then I'll just have to change *you*," I said, making it fast again.

She looked at me and then shook her head. And then she looked away. I took a deep breath; the car stunk of hot dogs and mustard.

The hot dogs were in honor of Francisco and Gisela. They adored Yanqui junk food. During the Allende years, Francisco and Gisela had come to Chicago—Francisco to lecture at Roosevelt University on Chile's Path to Democratic Socialism and Gisela to open an exhibition of Chilean weavings. They had somehow been served a meal of Carl's Vienna Hot Dogs and this time they'd sent advance word that they were looking forward to the same type of meal.

Before Allende, Francisco had been a lawyer, dividing his practice between plutocratic friends of the family and *los pobres* from the tin shantytowns on the outskirts of Santiago. Gisela was a cellist. She had studied for years with Pablo Casals and a recording she made years before called "The Romantic Cello Music of Spain" continued to sell: it attained the status of moody, left-wing make-out music.

It seemed just a matter of time before Francisco and Gisela's visas would be revoked. There was law prohibiting the entrance of Communists to our shores, and though the Higginses claimed to be non-Communist, it was really a matter of semantics. They were manifestly a part of that worldwide keenness for change and retribution against which our country stood poised. They made the rounds, addressing university groups, church organizations, visiting with Chilean refugees who had managed to get into America and also with those who were here in secret. They played cat and mouse with the FBI, who followed them practically everywhere.

Francisco and Gisela were already at Resurrection House when Sarah and I arrived. Father Mileski was taking them on a detailed tour of the facilities, which Mileski called "our physical plant." The Higginses were dressed as if for a night listening to Duke Ellington at a smart supper club, and from the looks on their faces I guessed they were ready to leap out of their skins from the boredom of it all. Mileski was pointing out the little handmade tables, the smeary do-it-yourself glazing on the thin, icy windows, and delineating which pink blankets were donated and which we picked up cheap at warehouse sales. "It's all spit, paste, and tape, putting a place like this together," Mileski was saying, and the Higginses nodded vigorously at whatever he said, as if a certain vehemence of agreement could end the story.

Finally, Gisela broke from the tour by engaging a neighborhood woman in Spanish conversation. Bernardo Gutierrez appeared. He was with a new woman now that Madeline Conners was off grinding lenses in Maryland. His companion was named Kirsten; she was heavyset, in her twenties, with a Nordic braid down her back. Bernardo embraced Francisco passionately, but there was something reserved, tentative, even suspicious in Francisco's response. Then Bernardo rushed toward Gisela to grab her hand and bring it to his lips. He sobbed, "Oh comrade, comrade, what they have done to us." Over his bowed head, Francisco and Gisela traded worried glances but Francisco shrugged and then nodded and Gisela put her hand on top of Bernardo's head, giving him solace.

I helped Sarah set a long table; there would be ten of us for dinner. A Mexican woman named Maria was working the kitchen. The kitchen was filled with smoke, but Maria looked contemplative, patting the tortillas and humming to herself. Upstairs were the three Chileans whom Sarah and Mileski had spirited out of Santiago—Pablo Estevez Martínez, who had published a small left-wing newspaper called *La Barricada* before and during the Allende presidency, and his sister and her son. *La Barricada* had had a circulation under a thousand and Estevez Martínez was its sole contributor. In other words, it was nothing more than a personal broadsheet for his own opinions and reactions—a movie review here, a poem there, a scathing piece attacking agricultural inefficiency. Yet after the generals' coup, *La Barricada* was banned and its publisher went into a self-imposed internal exile, hiding out in the countryside and then finally taking refuge in the home of his sister Seny. Pablo was ecstatic, manic really, now that he was out of Chile. He kept a bulging notebook for his jottings in his dark gray sports jacket and at night he dashed off essays on everything from American TV to American weather to the rhythm of the American walk.

His sister and nephew, however, were in terrible shape. Resurrection House was dusty, chaotic, the strangers were numerous and opaque: even those who spoke Spanish spoke it in the Mexican way, and the difference made home seem further away than ever. The neighborhood was scary. Seny and Gustavo, her son, could barely sleep—waiting, if not for the Immigration agents then for Chilean thugs, and if not for them then for some neighborhood lunatic to come in through the skylight with steel tips on his lace-up boots, broken glass in his hair. Even when they slept they seemed haunted by the cold steel dreams of the Northern Hemisphere, whose unfamiliar constellations lurked behind the ominous gauze of industrial smog.

When the Chileans came down to dinner, they were withdrawn and respectful around the Higginses. Even effusive, argumentative Pablo seemed sheepish: old class distinctions clicked in and he took his place. They seemed to trust Sarah. Somehow her involvement in their situation made them confident. She seemed to them what she had always seemed to me—a lucky person, not walking the fault line like Francisco and Gisela, nor complacent with a false sense of security like the priests. She was lovely and quick and altogether American, and they stayed near her as if her bones and background were a safer sanctuary than any church could provide. Sarah set the hot dogs down on a cracked oval platter; Maria brought the tortillas and meat in a pot covered by a damp dish towel. Sarah sat next to me and took my hand beneath the table. I was about to respond by pressing my leg against hers until I happened to notice that everyone else was holding hands, too.

"Thank you for this day and for this meal, O Heavenly Father," said Mileski. "Thank you for opening our hearts to the cause of freedom and may we use the calories you put before us to do your work."

"Amen," said Gisela abruptly, even a little sharply. Mileski's eyes clicked in her direction. He made a small, tight smile that was all but hidden by his beard; the whiskers around his mouth shifted like grass will when something unseen suddenly slithers through.

"Amen," said Mileski. He reached across the table for the pot of tortillas; Maria had twisted paper napkins onto the pot handles so they could be touched.

"Has your Church spoken to you about your activities?" Francisco asked Mileski. The platter of hot dogs was passed his way and he accepted them with a surprised smile, as if he was just that moment noticing them.

"I hear the rumbles," said Mileski.

"I'm surprised they allow you to continue your activities," Francisco said.

"Right now," said Mileski, "it's easier for them to pretend none of this is happening. I'm floundering and they know it. If I ever get it right, then the ax will fall."

"I wonder, Steven," said Father Stanton. He sounded as if he was trying to recreate an argument they'd already had for the benefit of us who had missed it. "The Church is in transition. Not only here but worldwide. She desperately wants to find her way through troubled times."

"In Chile," said Gisela, "they dance cheek to cheek with the murderers."

"A *terrible* thing," said Bernardo. There was something in how he said it—the speed of the response, the slightly inappropriate gusto of the reply—that made something shift in me. I looked over toward Bernardo and he avoided my eyes.

"The Church cannot exist," said Mileski, through a mouthful of food, "unless it can position itself as an alternative to life. Now the elders of the Church may love the capitalist state—but the Church's first love is itself. And if people are going to rise against their leaders, the Church does not want to be caught on the wrong side of the conflict. After all, all those poor people—those are our *customers*."

"Very cynical, Steven," said Stanton. "Very cynical indeed." He glanced at the rest of us, with an eager expression, as if he wanted us to pay attention to his favorite part in a piece of music.

"Well, I don't want to be cynical. Though I can't deny that

in my own mumbly-bumbly way, I am serving the interests of the Church, even as I challenge her."

"That is precisely because," said Stanton, wagging his finger at Mileski, "the concept of Jesus Christ is inherently revolutionary."

"Do you really think so?" asked Gisela, raising an imperious eyebrow.

"Oh yes, really," said Sarah. "And Steven does, too. We all do." Her face flushed; she had that look of absolute vulnerability laced with a love of adventure she had the night she opened her apartment window and invited me in, that first night—it seemed to have happened fifty years ago. She held the edge of the table but still swayed back and forth as she spoke. "You could interpret the Scriptures as the most revolutionary document ever written," she said.

"You *could* interpret it in a hundred different ways," said Gisela very coolly. "And I dare say people have."

"Now, Gisela," said Francisco, with a wink that made it clear he was in complete agreement with her.

"And what about you?" Gisela asked, turning suddenly toward me. "Another good Catholic?"

"No," I said. "Not at all."

"Well," said Gisela, as if this were an enormous relief.

"*Momentito*, darling," said Francisco. "If it wasn't for some brave churchmen, we would not be here and our friends Pablo, Gustavo, and Seny would be in prison, or dead. Or worse."

"Not to mention *me*," said Bernardo.

"Yes," said Francisco, very dryly. "Not to mention you."

"Yes, of course. I know that," Gisela said, dismissively. She turned her attentions back to me. Her eyes were peacock blue; her hair was black and lacquered, swept back, impermeable. I felt very young in her gaze, as if her intelligence cast a light on all that was unformed within me. "Have you been to Chile?" she asked me.

"No. But my partner has." I pointed to Sarah.

Gisela smiled in a slightly patronizing way. She picked up her glass of beer and tapped her ring against it before bringing it to her lips.

"These hot dogs are *fantástico*," said Francisco. "You never could find something like this in a socialist country!"

"So what *do* you do?" Gisela asked me, lifting her chin.

"I go to law school."

"Ah. A student."

"Fielding has his mind made up to go into politics," Mileski said.

"When you put it like that," said Sarah, "it sounds a little odd." She furrowed her dark eyebrows; there was no feeling on earth quite like being protected by Sarah. You felt immense, immortal. She spoke to Gisela. "Fielding is going to be a senator. And you can take it on my good authority that he will certainly be that."

"Well, of course," said Gisela, "you are his . . . ah, his ah . . . his *girl friend*. You are of course a great authority." Her smile looked suddenly girlish; her laugh was high; it was almost as if she wasn't being malicious at all. "So now," she said to me, "you are a member of the student class. And then you will be a lawyer. And then on to the great United States Senate."

"Yes," I said. "Exactly. One two three."

"With so many of your politicians showing their corruption to the world," Gisela was saying, "I am surprised to see someone from the youth who chooses to follow their example."

"No sale," I said, smiling. "Do you really expect me to say I want to go into politics because I want to be some corrupt sonofabitch selling electrodes to the Paraguayan police and arresting peace demonstrators in front of the White House?"

"Vanity, what vanity," Gisela said.

"I think what my wife is saying—" said Francisco.

"You're not my interpreter," said Gisela.

"Please, darling, permit me. What Gisela means is when you enter a corrupt institution, you become a part of it. The system is larger than the people who go into it. It makes its own use of them. That is a historical inevitability."

"Then what you say is leave politics to the worst of America," I said.

"Everything is politics," said Gisela. "Calling your elections and your motorcades politics is part of the sickness of this country."

"Give me some credit, please," I said. "I'm saying we have some fairly worthy institutions and some pretty unworthy people running them. If we leave it to the most greedy and dishonorable people to run things, then we're doing exactly what they would like us to do."

"I never thought I would live to see Fielding sweat," Mileski said from the head of the table, reaching for the pot of tortillas.

"I'm not sweating," I said. "I'm only trying to figure out a way of responding to all of this fucked-up half-thinking without being totally rude."

"Fielding," said Sarah.

"No, no, no, that's all right," said Mileski. "This is church property but it's not a church. Let him go."

"He has no right to speak to *Compañera* Higgins in such a manner," said Bernardo.

Gisela gestured to him, as if making a signal to a dog she wanted to return to his little mat near the door. She said to me, "Please don't worry about your manners. After living beneath the heel of United States imperialism, I am not very sensitive to things like manners."

"Of course you are," said Francisco. "And you always will be. You will always be elegant, and always correct."

"Oh, please stop trying to make everything better and pleasant, Paco," said Gisela. "I am exhausted by your spirits. The politicians of this country sat on their hands with tape over their mouths while Nixon and the CIA and American big business waged a secret war in Chile. And here we have a young man who is obviously aware of all this and yet he chooses to become a part of the very system—the *very system*, you understand?—the very system that put my husband in prison and broke his legs and forced me to live like a convict in my own home. I find it very curious and pardon me but I must investigate."

"So I'm Exhibit A," I said.

"An American legal term," said Gisela. "Why did we come to live in this slaughterhouse, Paco?" she said to her husband, touching her brow like a diva.

"Yes," I said, before he could answer. "Why did you? I'm sure the Algerians would have been more than happy to have you. Or winter in Sofia. Why not? I guess you came here for the hot dogs."

"We celebrate what is best about your country, sir," said Francisco.

And then I made what turned out to a disastrous choice—though to call it a choice at all is to imply I actually thought about it, when in fact it was more of an instinct, or even a mere physical whim. I turned slightly in my seat to make contact with Sarah. I wanted to feel the strength of her frequency but as I looked toward her she bowed her head slightly and looked down at her plate. It was only a slight movement but I felt it as a betrayal, or a prelude to betrayal, with all of the terrifying melodies of the onrushing abandonment compressed and foreshadowed. I realized that in the unpleasant banter between Gisela and me, Sarah's heart had gone out to Gisela and it was redefining our relationship as any other infidelity would have.

"I'm sick of having to apologize for being an American," I said, more or less to Gisela.

"*North* American," said Mileski.

"Pardon my insensitivity," I said, with my hand over my heart. My voice sounded strange, heavy. "I just can't help but notice that when people run toward freedom they have a way of washing up on *North* American shores. Let's face it, this country is the best dream human beings ever had and even as it fails, even as it goes wildly off course, it *still* is the best we've been able to do in the whole fucking history of the planet. We've got the best people, the best music, the best weather, the best legal code—"

"You can't be serious," said Father Stanton, with a hopeful smile.

"I am totally serious. And I am so sick of hearing facile, undercooked—"

"I don't think what Francisco and Gisela have to say can be called facile, Fielding," said Sarah. Her voice was soft, porous; she had placed her hands on the tabletop and was lifting her fingers one at a time. "I think their experiences in Chile have taught them something about *our* country that we all need to know."

"As if we didn't know it before," I said. "We always knew our government plays rough. All governments do. My God, we're the richest, most powerful country in the world—how do you expect us to act? How naive are you? But when you compare it to a country like Chile—I mean, in Chile even the leaders of the opposition come from the upper class. A person like me would have no chance anywhere else. My family, my parents were . . . *nothing*." And I said the terrible, reductive, half-false word with such vehemence, propelled it forth with one of those terrifying gusts of breath that come from the very well of character, that hearing it startled me—and *moved* me, beyond description. I felt the fire in my cheeks, my eyes. The table and the faces around it seemed very distant for a moment and I swallowed, tried to regulate my breathing, as if all that passionate respiration were filling the sails of the self's vulnerable little skiff and sending it out toward the edge. I kept talking to cover my own fear.

"Everyone in our family has been a face in the crowd. You see those old sepia prints of picket lines or policemen's balls or kids playing in the shadow of the Manhattan Bridge and it's not necessarily my grandparents—but it might be. It might as *well* be. And now I've got a brother running a publishing company and a sister who is a terrific painter, and—look, I don't want to use myself as an example of what's decent about this country, but let's say I do earn political office—that has to mean something."

My eloquence was precisely the kind that embarrasses people, but I was too far gone by then to interpret correctly what those blank to sheepish expressions meant: I assumed they were overwhelmed by my passionate logic, when in fact they were only uncomfortable—and a little irritated, and a little amused. It was up to Mileski to be the one to react: "This reminds me of the patient who describes his symptoms as signs of his good health."

"That's ugly, Steven," said Sarah.

"Yes," I said. "It is. It reminds me of something Sarah would say."

"Fielding," said Sarah, "you're in this conversation all by yourself."

"I am in this room by myself!" I said, slamming my hand against the table. "I am choking on the collective sense of superiority."

"We don't know what you're talking about, Fielding," said Sarah, and it seemed clear at that moment she was speaking to me across a chasm and she was surrounded on her side of the divide by her new friends, her new faith.

"Come on, you two," said Father Stanton, and though he tried to sound cajoling, a ridge of nervousness went through his voice.

"No, no, Timothy, let them go," said Mileski. "There's no way to stop the water."

They say that generals, military geniuses, can, in the bloody pitch of battle, come up with a new plan that is at once radical and brilliant. It seemed to me that I needed just such a plan: I needed to end this battle between me and Sarah and I needed to end it instantly. Even a surrender would have been better; something fragile was being trammeled beneath our feet, a delicate root system that would be awfully hard to reclaim if we did it much more violence. And so I stood up and as calmly as I could I said, "Whatever is happening right now, Sarah, let's not do it here. I'm going home. To our house. Are you coming with me?"

"Don't power trip, Fielding," said Mileski.

"Shut up, Father," I said, much, much too calmly: you just can't say things like that while pretending to the world that you're not dying inside. "Are you coming home, Sarah?" I asked her again.

There was silence in that room. We were certainly providing the evening's awful entertainment. Sarah was not meeting my gaze. I noticed that Seny was staring at Sarah, with a curious, peaceful expression on her face. Finally, Sarah looked up at me. Her eyes were filled with tears. "No," she said, "I'm staying here."

I took a deep breath and shook my head, as if giving her time to come to her senses—but, in fact, I was too confused to move. Just then, Seny leaned across the table toward Sarah. She pointed to herself and then to Sarah. And then she said something in Spanish to her son. Gustavo nodded and then translated for us Yanquis. "She just noticed that she and Señorita Sarah are, you know, the same size hands and everything, the same body, and weighing the same. Looking alike." He smiled and shrugged. "I'm sorry, but she speaks no English. She doesn't know what we are talking about here."

They were to leave for Minnesota the next evening. I took the day off from classes and Sarah stayed home, too. We lied to each other and said we wanted to work out our differences, to put our house back in order, when in fact our anger with each other had awakened a kind of awful perversity and what we really wanted to do was use the stick of our intelligence to wedge into the crack in the earth between us and to open it further and further—until the other could suddenly see the emptiness below and panic.

Our method was to say the worst and let it hang there, hoping that the other would be so frightened by the implications that he or she would have to rebut it. Sarah might say, A part of you has always known that a woman like me would never really fit into the sort of life you want. And even as she said it I could sense within it the outright plea for me to say it wasn't so. But time and again I would deny this intuition and deal, instead, with the painful, truculent surface of whatever she said. And so instead of saying, No, what I have with you is much more important than any other thing I could possibly want, I would say, If you weren't so fucking ashamed of me, if you and those ridiculous priests didn't think you had a perfect right to sit in judgment of my life . . . And then this would become a part of the vapor between us, undispelled, until the vapor became a fog and the fog became impenetrable, and we began to feel the only way we would ever see clearly again was to turn away from each other.

She packed the larger of her suitcases while I paced the bedroom, making remarks and then falling silent.

"Now you're starting to act as if I was leaving you forever," Sarah said, looking up from her packing.

"Well aren't you, really?"

"You're making it seem like doing what I think is right means I don't care about you."

"You're quoting Mileski to me? Is this really happening? I mean, has it really come to this?"

"Fielding," she said, shaking her head. "You just don't get it. And I don't know why I try. Because you never will. All you see is what you want."

I stopped pacing and for some reason squatted down on my haunches, like Paleolithic man before the little flicker of fire.

"What are you doing down there?" she asked.

"Resting," I said.

She smiled and I knew the smile was involuntary and that in itself ought to have touched off some confidence in me, a memory that our connection was probably strong enough to carry us through this—but I didn't let it. I shook my head, as if her very smile was a symbol of emotional distance, another betrayal.

"Why are you packing so many things if you're just going for three days?"

"I'm bringing stuff for Seny, too. All she has are little summer blouses and, I don't know what you call them—cocktail dresses."

And then, I had the terrible inspiration to rush across the bedroom, fling the valise onto the floor, where it burped up a few underclothes and then slammed shut. I was pressing Sarah down onto the bed and covering her mouth with one of those awful, authoritative kisses. She was surprised enough, and sympathetic enough, and certainly confused enough just to lie there for a moment, instinctually opening her mouth to the fierce pressure of my lips. But as I pressed harder down onto her I could feel her slipping away. It was a lost cause; grief and anger hadn't burned up enough of my intelligence for that solid emotional fact to escape me. But I powered forward. I put my hand beneath her sweater. Her breast was icy, the skin moist; I realized she was in terror— but I could not say what the source of the fear was. Was it me? Was it the impending trip? Was it feeling us falling apart?

"I want you so much, Sarah," I said.

"Then OK," she said, "we'll make love."

I closed my eyes. I allowed myself a sigh of relief that came out like a sob. I buried my face in the folds of her neck, inhaled the warm scent of her hair.

"Do you really want to?" I asked.

"Yes. Of course. But please let's hurry."

"No. I don't want it to be like that."

"Fielding. Please. We're barely getting away with this. Don't make conditions."

"OK, OK. I won't." I lifted myself up and started to take her sweater off. I pulled up from the bottom but she squirmed away from me.

"Don't. I'll take my own clothes off. You get yourself undressed."

"You see? I knew it. You don't want to make love. You're patronizing me."

She lay there in silence. Her sweater was pulled up to her breasts and she tugged it down, smoothed it out. "You're right. I don't want to make love."

"Then why did you say you did?"

"Oh, God. Do we have to talk about that, too?"

I rolled onto my back and covered my eyes. I felt the bed move as she left it and then I heard her feet touch the floor. I listened to her walk across the room and then I heard her open the suitcase and replace the things that had fallen out. She was usually meticulous when it came to packing; she had travel anxiety and fear of airplanes and she bargained with her terror through slavish preparations. Anyone who folded her socks so beautifully, she thought, was not likely to take the one plane in ten thousand that isn't going to make it. But now she was just shoving the things back into the suitcase. All she wanted was to get out of there as quickly as possible.

"We'll be at Our Lady of the Miracle by tomorrow afternoon," Sarah said. I heard the click of the valise's clasps and then a little *oooff* as she hefted the suitcase up to see how heavy it was. She placed it back on the floor. The radiator was starting to whistle and the pipes—caked with dust, enshrouded in the hasty history of a dozen sloppy paint jobs—began to clang. "Pablo, Seny, and Gustavo will be staying there. The priest there—he's an incredible guy. He lived in Guatemala for a year. He's not at all political. He's just a workaday priest—but he knows giving aid to those whom the state will crush is the duty of a priest."

"Don't make it seem like such a clear-cut situation," I said, with my eyes still closed. I wasn't to look at her again, but of course I could not know that. I thought I'd be able to when I wanted to. I hadn't learned how out of control things can be. "You make it seem like anyone with an ounce of decency is smuggling Latin Americans into this country and giving them sanctuary. When you know you people are just a tiny minority. You know, most people just think you're all crazy."

"Most people?" said Sarah. "Or you?"

"Most people. And me." I waited for her reply to that one. I had the bizarre misconception that I was somehow backing her into a corner and that she would finally have no choice but to spring forward. I even imagined her shaking her head, realizing how miserable I must be to say something so mean, realizing that I was only speaking out of a fear of losing her. I could imagine her approaching my body and my blindness, of reprieving me from my self-imposed exile with a kiss, or even just a touch. But then she picked up the suitcase and walked out the door. She had no reply. I hadn't forced her hand. The game was over.

13

After I left Father Stanton's church, I went back to the restaurant, with some inchoate notion that I could somehow rescue the evening. But Kathy and the reporters were gone; though there were still some people in the restaurant, the chairs at what had been our table were upended.

The next day I campaigned with my loss of judgment from the night before banging like an unhinged shutter within me. I didn't dare look at the newspapers, for fear of reading something about myself that portrayed me as a madman, a flake, a touchy little newcomer riding his own feelings like a greenhorn in the rodeo. Tony knew I had blown it the night before, but our schedule was full and he only alluded to it once, fearing he might otherwise throw me further off my game. In fact, as the day wore on, my manner started to even out and all in all I did the best campaigning of my political life, finally getting my four-minute speech down to two and a half and adding a little swagger to my remarks about fairness, so they sounded less poetic and more like common sense. Dayton's theory of campaigning was that it was more important to appear pleasant than correct, and while I recognized the wisdom of this, I was coming to realize I did better when I was most open about my ideas. Talking about what I wanted to do in the Congress gave me better contact with the voters than I could achieve by just trying to make myself likable. Trying to be jovial, I tended to come off like some idiot on a game show, but when I talked about taxes and job retraining and the military budget, I sounded to the voters like someone they might trust.

My four o'clock stop was at the campaign office, where Caroline and the others had thrown together a Meet the Candidate event. We got a decent turnout. Henry Shamansky was there, since his classroom was only a couple of blocks from the office, and I was aware of him hanging back near the coffee urn, munching on powdered sugar doughnuts and elaborately dusting his fingers off after every bite. He seemed to be studying me. I was talking to a sweet old woman with ribbons in her hair and girlish pink lipstick. She was upset about nuclear power stations and though I agreed with her on the whole, my assent sounded a little metooish and so I just folded my arms over my chest and listened to her. Finally, Henry Shamansky came over to me and said, "I wonder if I might have a word with you, Fielding." I excused myself and we went off to the side, near the literature table, where the empty-headed leaflets extolling my virtues were stacked. Henry looked me up and down and took a deep breath. "You know what?" he said. "You're *good* at this. You really are."

Since Henry was the campaign's official intellectual, I didn't know if he considered being "good at this" as proof of my shallowness. At any rate, I didn't want to thank him for at last realizing something about me he ought to have accepted from the very beginning. If this had been two days before, I might have said something like, What'd you expect? But there was enough going wrong without my causing more trouble and so I just nodded, smiled, took it like a man.

And as I was standing with him and the woman who wanted to talk about nuclear power plants got caught up in a conversation with Adele Green, who'd shown up with her own tea bags because our drekky coffee gave her the shakes, I saw through the storefront window Kathy Courtney's tan Peugeot pull in next to the curb. And then a moment later she was climbing out of the car. She wore a blue cape with a black lining. She carried a briefcase; her fingernails were cherry red. And I was confused to feel at that moment something I had never felt in her presence before—a desire bordering on mania to hold her in my arms, to make love to her.

I bolted from Shamansky and intercepted Kathy before she could make it into the office. I was in my shirt sleeves; my tie caught the wind and whipped over my shoulder.

"I'm sorry about last night," I said, taking her arm.

"What happened to you?" she asked, her voice a little unfriendly.

"It doesn't matter. How'd you get out of it?"

"I don't know if I *did*. I tried, though. But really, Fielding—that's too much."

"I know, I know. It . . . it was very complicated. Look, I want to talk to you."

"Well, let's go in. It's freezing out here."

"No, not now. I mean, I want to talk to you later. I'd like to come to your house after this."

"After this you've got about six more things."

"Then after that." I moved my hand up her arm a little and squeezed. "I think we really ought to know each other better."

"Call me," she said. "Call me tonight when you're coming to the end of your schedule."

"OK, I will. You'll be home?"

She smiled. Her mastery over me at that moment was complete, though fleeting: my soul was in her hands but it was streaking like a comet. "Why would I ask you to call me if I wasn't even going to be there?" she asked.

But it went nowhere. The next time I saw Kathy I asked her why she hadn't been there when I called and she said she'd been home all night and the phone never rang once. And by now my desire had dwindled to curiosity.

I was sitting in a parked car in front of the Woodlawn Association of Retired People, five minutes early for a three o'clock meeting. Tony was at the wheel with his eyes shut, since we'd been at it since five that morning. I took out my notebook and wrote: I wanted to spend the night with KC because she had gone to school with S. To fuck her until she turned into S? Yes? No? Why?

Tony suddenly opened his eyes and said, "What are you writing?"

"Nothing," I said, tearing the sheet out of the little notebook and shredding it into halves, fourths, eighths.

The next morning, I was in bed with Juliet's warm, still body pressed against me and her arms wrapped tightly around my chest. I was dimly aware of her and I had a battered ship's gratitude for its anchor. It was not quite seven yet and the phone was ringing. I felt Juliet's warmth receding from me and she got up on one elbow and reached for the phone.

"I'll get it," I said, coming to so quickly that it seemed a part of consciousness had been awake all through the night, waiting for this call. I lunged for the phone before Juliet could hear the voice on the other side. "Hello," I said. My voice sounded husky, unfamiliar.

"All right," said Danny. "Now, I don't want you to panic but I'll be in Chicago in two and a half hours. I don't want you to meet me at O'Hare. I've arranged a car. And I've got a hotel, too. We'll be—well, I'll tell you when I see you. I just wanted you to know I was on my way."

"What time is it?" I asked.

"Hey, I knew you were going to say that. I guess my antennae are up. Good sign."

"Who is it?" whispered Juliet. She lay heavily back in bed with her arms behind her head.

"Danny," I said.

She rolled her eyes, as if his name implied some comic disaster.

"Are you on your own?" I asked him.

"No man is an island, bro."

"That's very nice. Never thought of it. Call me as soon as you're in?"

"Definitely. Where will you be?"

"Call the campaign office. If I'm not there, Caroline'll be."

"Isn't this completely weird?" Danny said. "The three of us

together again. In Chicago. I wonder if McFate is dealing from the bottom of the deck."

Over coffee a while later, Juliet said, "What's your schedule like tonight, Fielding?"

"I don't know. Why?"

She blushed deeply, the color rolling from her throat up to the hollows beneath her eyes, thick as a carpet. And it's true what they say about the little *clink clink clink* of the spoon in the coffee cup in moments like these. "I'd like to put some time aside to have a talk," she said, her voice squashed beneath a cargo of motive.

"About what?" I asked, with an edge. I smiled: no harm intended.

"I just think we need some time to get back in touch."

"OK. How out of touch are we?"

She shrugged. She took the spoon out of her cup and licked it clean before placing it on the table mat.

"Sick of me?" I asked her.

"Is that a diagnosis or a wish?" she asked. With that, she stood up and looked at her wristwatch. It was a little early for her to be going to work; I wondered if she only wanted to leave with the last word.

When she went, I watched from the window as her car pulled out of the driveway and into the street. It was one of those extravagantly sunny winter mornings, as if all that low trembling gray had just been wrapping paper and this perfect blue dome was the gift inside. The sun blazed in the chrome around her windshield, covering it all with hot light. I could see only a glimpse of her, like one of those faces you imagine you see in the fireplace when you've been drinking. She was on her way to Evanston to pick up five Whistlers from a gallery—smoke damage after a fire last week. I suppose people fall in love with people whose work calls for attention to detail because they imagine that somehow the person will lavish that same care on them. Well, Juliet never looked at me as closely as she did at one of those damaged canvases and if she had I'm not sure I would have liked it or if she would have liked me.

When I walked back into the kitchen, Caroline was pouring her coffee. She was dressed in orange satin pajamas; her face looked as if she'd slept with it pressed hard into a very firm pillow.

"Danny's coming to Chicago," I said, holding my coffee cup out for her to fill.

She handed me the pot instead and sat down. She rubbed her face with her hands. "When?"

"Today."

"Did you ask him to come?" she said, mumbled into her hands as she rubbed away.

"No. Why should I?"

"Because you think I'm fucking up," she said. She folded her hands in front of her and gave me her hard look. It went like this: Tell me the worst because I can take it and I need to know and later I will destroy you for saying it.

"What are you talking about? I didn't ask him. He's just coming." I sat next to her, borrowed her spoon. "Are you? Are you fucking something up I don't know about?"

"I think I'm in love with Tony Dayton, Fielding."

"Take two aspirin, get back in bed, and call me in the morning."

"I'm sorry. I know it makes you crazy. And I feel bad, too, because you called it and I denied it."

"And I suppose he's in love with you, too."

"He's very sweet."

"Please, Caroline."

"Well, he is. He's so *needy*."

"And that's attractive to you?"

"It's not. It's just how he is. I'm sick of opacity; I like to be with someone so transparent. In two days, I knew a hundred things about Tony. I was married to Eric for years and all I ever learned was that he was an angry victim of American racism and that he thought talented people were an aristocracy."

"That's ridiculous," I said. "You've just reduced it to that. You knew hundreds of things about Eric when you were together." I counted them off on my fingers. "You knew he was nicest to people after he'd trashed them behind their backs. You knew cold hurt his teeth so much he was in awe of people who put ice cubes in their drinks."

"Not *awe*."

"You knew he thought if you loved someone too much it made you weak but it didn't stop him from loving you, when he did, and you loved him for it, when you did."

Caroline came over to me and put her arms around me. "Oh, Fielding," she said. "I love you. Thank you for remembering all that stuff about me. We're so lucky to have each other. And I really am glad Danny's coming. You're bringing us all together again."

"I don't know why he's coming here. It sounded from his voice something was fucking up."

"He'll land on his feet. Fielding?" She smoothed my hair back. "Oh-oh."

"I just have to tell you something. Tony told me not to, but I think you'd want to know. You know how he's so marvelous with figures and everything? Well, he's been doing his own sort of informal polls."

"And?"

"And you're slipping, that's all. It's not like being behind or anything, but you're slipping."

"We'll win this, Caroline. Don't worry. I'm sure of it."

"You can't be sure anymore, Fielding. We all have to work harder."

"We're working hard right now. I went to eighteen different places yesterday. My throat is killing me; my right hand is so swollen I can't even get it into my glove."

Caroline touched her forehead with three fingers. "We just have to concentrate better. More singleness of purpose. We just have to put everything else out of our minds. Everything. After the election we can be as crazy as we want."

"No one wants to be crazy, Caroline."

"OK. OK. You know what I'm saying. I want you to win. And after you do, I want you to tell everyone that I helped you." She smiled. "That's not asking too much, is it?"

"You're learning from Dayton," I said.

I didn't get home until nine that evening. I pulled into the driveway and stayed in the car, with my forehead against the steering wheel. It was a clear night, ghostless. The last sliver of moon was tangled in the top of a tree across the street, like a boomerang caught on a branch. I had been campaigning for thirteen hours and I would have been pushing on still further had I not been spared the night's final Meet the Candidate Coffee and Sweet Roll Endurance Test. (The host and hostess were having marital difficulties and they tracked down Dayton to tell him the atmosphere in their apartment was "a little too thick.") Tony had done his best to embarrass me into asking him over for a nightcap—"or a cup of tea, whatever, man, let's just sit down and unwind." I had a pocketful of phone messages, none of which I could respond to this evening. I could barely remember where I had been or *who* I had been: it was as if my soul and the time allotted to it on earth had been spread out like bird seed and then a flock of starlings had landed upon it, each taken a beakful, and then exploded into the sky.

There was only one thing left to keep me going, and it wasn't love, nor was it service, and it sure as hell was not a vision of a more decent world: I just wanted to win this election, as if the person I could be, with that accomplished, was just waiting for me, like a new suit of clothes laid out on the bed.

I crept up the stairs to my apartment. Mrs. Arlington, our neighbor, had taken to lying in wait for me. Twice already she had gotten me into her apartment, with its brown walls and cab-bagy smells and the piano filled with framed family pictures which she kept in rigidly neat rows like tombstones. Mrs. Arlington was involved in a long controversy with the Social Security Admin-istration and now she had chosen me as her new advocate. According to her calculations, Social Security owed her ten thousand dollars in back payments and she had obliged me to inspect the folders of correspondence she had generated. "Jerry didn't do a goddamned thing about this," she'd said, drilling her finger against a xerox of a letter from Carmichael's office which promised to look into the matter. "You don't know what a relief it is knowing you'll be out there, putting this right."

And then I was on the landing to the third floor and I heard Danny's laughter through the door, followed close behind by Caroline's. They had always seemed to laugh in harmony, like two singers who can sound like a quartet. I had never been able to laugh as openly as they and somehow this slight leadenness of spirit had earned me a respect at home that neither of them had ever achieved. What parent with two unruly children would not praise the sobriety of the third? I had an impulse to knock on my own door, as if I might be intruding.

Danny, Caroline, Juliet, and the Korean woman, Kim, were in the living room and Danny was making the rounds, filling everyone's glass from a jeroboam of Dom Pérignon. Caroline was in leotards with red and blue wool socks pulled up to the knee. Juliet was sitting at the end of the sofa with a shawl wrapped around her; the tips of her ears and her nose glowed red. Kim sat with her legs tightly crossed, wearing a short, metallic dress; her calves were as round and hard as apples. They all looked at me as I came into the room and they were as suddenly quiet as a switched-off radio.

"I'm either very late or a little early," I said, shrugging off my overcoat, unwrapping my maroon scarf.

"Do you have enough willpower to have just one glass of this champagne with us?" Danny asked, holding the bottle aloft.

"I have enough willpower to have no glasses but not enough to have one," I said. "Just stay right there. I have some vintage seltzer in the fridge."

By now, Danny was next to me. He was just a half inch taller than me but I was used to hugging rather small women and as we embraced he seemed to tower over me. He smelled of smoke and something oddly chemical. "You remember Kim," he said, stepping back.

"Of course," I said.

"Hello, Fielding," said Kim. "How is everything?"

"Everything's fine, Kim. It's nice to see you." I had a dim sense that Juliet was throwing me desperate glances and it seemed best not to engage her eyes just then. "Everyone please just stay here for a second," I said. "Don't say anything interesting and I'll be right back."

I retreated into the kitchen; I was surprised how unsettled I was. My stomach felt as if it were trying to climb up my chest and out of my mouth. I filled a glass with ice and opened a bottle of Canada Dry seltzer—no salt, no calories, no side effect more harmful than a belch. The fizz danced above the rim of the glass. I leaned forward against the kitchen counter and took a long drink and I felt a hand on my back. I didn't respond right away; I just felt it and let it be anyone.

"I have to talk to you," Juliet said, in a voice just above a whisper.

I put the glass down on the counter and turned to face her. "We're being rude to our guests," I said.

"I can't stay here," she said. "Tonight. Whenever."

I felt a surge of panic, but it was nonspecific. "What do you mean? Where are you going?"

"A friend's."

"Who?"

She backed up as if I'd breathed fire on her. "Polly."

"Well well," I said. I picked up my seltzer; my hand was shaking. Somehow that seemed just fine. "Are you coming back?"

"Of course I am."

"How nice."

She touched my arm. "Fielding," she said. I could see in her eyes how fine she was feeling. She'd been in an awfully shitty position in our house for a long while and now she was recouping some of those small losses. "I'll come back tomorrow," she said.

"Anything special you'd like for breakfast?" I was letting myself say whatever occurred to me. I knew I would regret every syllable, but somehow it seemed to be this moment's destiny for me to say wounded, wounding, moronic things. And as I spoke, I could all but feel my hands going around her throat, feel the weight of our bodies as we fell to the floor as I continued to choke her, feel her nails digging into my eyes as she tried to push me away, see the carnations of spittle blooming in the corners of her mouth as she cursed me to my face and finally told me what she had felt about me all along.

"I'll be home after work. Polly's got an Ingres drawing and the left side is completely foxed—"

"No, no, no," I whispered, putting up my hand. "I don't think even the most strenuous codes of politesse require I listen to this kind of stuff."

"I've been waiting for you to come home. I was supposed to be over there two hours ago." She sighed and shook her head and she simply had no idea how bizarrely merry her eyes were. She was not really free of the languor and pointlessness of our love affair yet, but she was beginning to move, that she knew, and this whiff of emotional freedom was flaring her nostrils. She looked radiant. And I was not so sunk beneath the weight of my own life not to be a little happy for her.

"You know what I think?" she said. "I think if you win this election and go to Washington and I don't go with you—in three weeks you'll barely know the difference."

"And do you know what I think?" I said.

"No. What?"

"I think you're right."

She swallowed hard and nodded her head, as if to say: There. And then she did something that surprised me more than it hurt. She slapped me across the face with what I suppose was all her might. Her face went scarlet. She was immediately sorry she'd done it and she pushed that regret down because she felt, on the whole, I deserved to be hit—not just once, but again and again.

"You don't have to worry about this spoiling things between you and my uncle," she said. "There's nothing I can say to him that will either surprise or disillusion him. He knows you're a hungry, cold, self-serving little nobody from nowhere. And he's known it all along. *And* it doesn't make the slightest bit of difference to him."

"Can I ask you a question?" I said.

"Yes. But I don't feel obliged to give you any answers."

"Fine. That's fair. What I want to know is—this morning, when you were saying you wanted us to talk tonight, is this what you wanted to say?"

"No. I just wanted us to talk. I wanted to try."

"I don't think I want to try, Juliet. This whole thing between us is just effort."

"I don't think you know what you want right now, Fielding."

"Well, there's no point in arguing that, is there," I said. I made another try at the seltzer and now my hands were steady. A wonderful psychotic calm had come over me.

She looked at me for a long moment and her dark eyes radiated pity. She reached up and touched my face. "You're blotched," she said. "I'm sorry I hit you."

"I'm sorry I didn't hit you back," I said, and thank God there was no mirror in that room so I don't have to remember the big ugly smile I gave her right then.

I waited in the kitchen until she had enough time to leave and then I went back into the living room. "Oh good, you're here," said Danny. "I've got hot news and I want you to hear it. You know, of all my addictions, inside dope is the greatest."

I sat on the sofa next to Caroline. She put her hand on my knee for a moment and I nodded my head. Then I reached over and took her champagne glass and took a nice swallow of it.

"Ah good," said Danny, "a chance to see my brother go down the tubes."

"What's the hot news?" I asked, leaning away from Caroline as she reached for her glass.

"Well, you're the perfect person to tell this to," said Danny, walking over and filling my glass. He gave his glass to Caroline and he took the one Juliet had left behind. "There's an FBI undercover investigation going on right now. And guess who they're investigating."

"You," I said.

"No," said Danny. "IRS, DEA—but *not* FBI. Guess again."

"Whoever planted the bomb that killed Sarah."

"Oh Christ, Fielding, rest it with that."

"Bomb?" asked Kim. She drew up her thin, hard legs so her knees touched her chin. Her face was a perfect oval, her hair thick as a whisk broom.

"Then just tell me," I said, finishing the champagne. My body writhed in disappointment over the parsimonious alcohol content of the bubbles. I wasn't remotely drunk; I'd broken my promise for nothing.

"Congress itself," said Danny, with the same triumphant smile with which he once years ago presented to us the box of Trojans he'd found in Dad's underwear drawer.

"The FBI is investigating Congress?" asked Caroline.

"I'm sure," I said.

"That's right," said Danny. "I'm going to be publishing a book called *A Paranoid's Guide to Conspiracy Theories*. My author's this big pumpkin-head lunatic who lives on Tylenol with codeine and he's into everything—Howard Hughes, the Ellsberg break-in, UFOs, Chappaquiddick, every fucking assassination since Lincoln. Anyhow, he's been publishing articles in all these little Yippie papers and these guys in the FBI *love* his stuff. They respect him and they get a kick about reading about themselves. And they're his social life. I mean, he actually hangs around with them and now and again they let something slip. Anyhow, he told me that some time in the next month or two about twenty members of Congress and even a couple of senators are going to be arrested. I mean really busted and busted hard. The FBI has been filming these guys taking briefcases filled with cash and pretty soon the whole country's going to be seeing these straight-bag guys in suits and ties pretty much selling themselves, the people who elected them, I guess really the whole country, the American way of life. It's not going to be as much fun as Watergate but it'll be just as big. You know, in what it *reveals*."

"You seem very pleased with it," I said.

"Hey, when the mighty fall . . ." said Danny with a shrug.

"Well, I don't know how mighty congressmen are. I guess next to regular working-class guys they are. But the way you describe it, it's not guys from Dad's union who are setting these congressmen up. And *somebody* is. And maybe that somebody is completely powerful and has a vested interest in demeaning the Congress, in turning us against our elected representatives. Don't you think that could be it? If anyone wanted to wreck the Constitution, a perfect beginning would be to convince people that Congress was just another form of organized crime."

"When Fielding starts talking about the Constitution," Danny said to Caroline, "you know it's going to be a long night."

"What laws do you pass when you go there, to Washington?" Kim asked me. She felt the conversation about to take a mean turn and she wanted to steer it toward more neutral ground.

"Good question," said Danny.

"Oh, you're so patronizing to women," said Caroline. "You're worse than Eric."

"Me personally?" I asked Kim. I put my glass down and felt the relief and disappointment of a man talked in off the ledge: what will I do with the rest of my life? "I don't guess I'll be passing *any* laws. In the beginning, you just fit yourself in and build a base. You make friends. Try not to make too many enemies. You learn the ropes."

"Ropes?" asked Kim, though I don't think that was all she hadn't understood.

"What Fielding is saying is this," said Danny. "He goes to Washington. He's sworn in. And he keeps his mouth shut."

"Very nice," I said. "I appreciate the vote of confidence."

"You're being just terrible," Caroline said to Danny. "I don't understand what you're trying to do. If this is how you feel, I don't see why you bothered to come here."

"What if I told you I came here for my own safety," said Danny.

"I'd be terribly impressed," answered Caroline.

"Well then, there you have it," said Danny. "I'm in a bit of *agua caliente*. It's funny how one thing leads to another."

"What are we talking about here?" I said. I felt something turning inside me, shifting and going hard, as if the vapors of ambition and caution were finally turning into a distinct and separate self.

"I made a slight error in judgment," said Danny, raising one finger and smiling his ravishing smile. "And that was treating a drug dealer as if he were a printer. You see, with a printer or a proofreader or a jobber, you don't get eaten alive if you don't pay up."

"But with a drug dealer you do," I said. "As if you didn't know."

"Well, hope springs eternal," said Danny.

"Yeah," I said. "For a junkie."

"Fielding," said Caroline. "Get a grip."

Danny saluted in Caroline's direction and then turned back to me. "It all started with Kim, taking her out of that massage parlor Christmas night. They were furious. And when she didn't go back the next day, they made it clear they wanted her back."

"They?" I said, sharply.

"They," said Danny. "Yes. They. The Koreans. The goddamned Koreans are completely insane."

"Korea man very proud," said Kim to me, in a rather patient voice. "They think—oh-oh Kim run away and we say OK, then all the other girl maybe run away, too."

"They're looking for her?" Caroline asked.

"Were," said Danny. "But then I got smart. Or *thought* I did. And I cut a deal with them. They'd leave Kim alone, leave me alone, and I'd go into business with them."

"What kind of business?" I asked. "These are not nice people.

They're tied in with all kinds of paramilitary types and crime bosses."

"I know they're tough customers," said Danny.

"Do you?" I asked. "What kind of business were you doing with them? And please don't tell me it was publishing."

"It was kind of a drug thing," said Danny, and I must have been putting more pressure on him than I thought because his voice faltered for a moment.

"*Kind* of a drug thing?"

"Yes. Well. A drug thing. It was amazing how amateurish they were. I mean they had the supply thing worked out well but they were lost in the dark about demand. They didn't even know how much the shit was *worth*. I thought it was going to be a lot easier than it turned out."

Certain spontaneous calculations could not be avoided at this point. There was one thing I could trust in Danny: he never made any situation seem worse than it was. If he said he was having a few little tax problems, that meant two gray suits from the IRS had just come into Willow's offices and grabbed the Olivettis. If he asked if I had a minute to answer a couple of legal questions, that meant he was being sued by six authors and a dozen type-setters and his own lawyer wouldn't even return his phone calls because the check Danny had sent him as partial payment on last year's retainer had bounced higher than Danny himself had gotten with the drugs he'd blown all his real money on.

"Are you OK, Fielding?" Caroline asked.

"Yes," I said. "Of course. Feeling the drink is all." I put my hands over my face and rubbed my eyes.

"It's probably what you need," said Danny. "It's like loosen up or snap."

"Oh shit, Danny," said Caroline. "Really."

"Look," said Danny. "Life is vicious and life is fast. It's full of swindles and tough luck and the whole thing is so fucking hard I don't see why people have to stay completely straight and sober through it. These things are here because we need them."

"Maybe your brother worry," said Kim to Danny. "You know, with our troubles going and making more troubles for him."

"I think you've hit the nail on the head," said Danny.

"Nail?" said Kim.

I stood up. I felt something pressing down on me, as if I were trying to stand in a cell with a five-foot ceiling. I pointed at Danny. "I don't want to get involved with your messes right now. I think it's either very stupid or very sadistic for you to come here now."

"Wait a minute," said Danny, with that relaxed, enticing smile. "You're taking this too far. It's not that big a thing. It's going to work out."

"I'm carrying too much," I said, and to my immense horror my voice broke. Oh God, the stink of self-pity. "In case no one noticed, Juliet is no longer in this apartment. I don't even know when or *if* she's coming back."

"We know, Fielding," said Caroline, in a tone that was meant to be soothing. "We weren't going to say anything if you weren't."

"I don't think she was leaving because of Kim and me," said Danny.

"I didn't say she *was*," I said. "She's leaving because I haven't spoken to her in three weeks and whatever I said before that didn't carry us through." I stopped and took a deep breath. I didn't want to hear that desperate note in my voice. "She left because we didn't really belong together in the first place."

"Well, we could have told you *that*," said Danny.

"There's too much happening," I said. "I'm losing my way. You can't be here, Danny. This election is going to be close and when they're close they usually get dirty and I just don't want to have to explain you to anyone."

"Can you believe this?" Danny said to Caroline.

"He's upset," said Caroline, as if I'd suddenly left the room.

"I'm sorry," I said to Kim. She shrugged at me but I didn't know her nearly well enough to know if that meant she forgave me, or had expected as much, or hadn't any idea of what we were talking about.

"Are you worried it's going to reflect on you?" Danny asked.
"Yes," I said. "I absolutely am." There was a comfort in letting
the worst be known; it felt like unbuttoning a pair of trousers
you'd grown too stout to wear.

"Then we'll leave," he said. "But I think you're panicking. The
whole point is, I got in a little over my head, but now I'm working
it out. I found these two Romanian brothers, I think they're twins,
and they do all this factoring in the garment center. So I've sold
them some of the invoices we've sent out for money due us and
the Romanians are giving us forty cents on the dollar. I know that
sounds like a rip, but it's not that bad. And then I've got some
tax shelter deals lined up. That's really why we're here anyhow.
A lawyer here in Chicago's got all these rich surgeons who are
looking for tax shelters and we've worked out a book deal for
them."

"I've seen your tax shelter plans," I said. "All those doctors
are going to be audited and the deductions will be disallowed."

"Well, you haven't seen this one," said Danny. "This one will
work." He took a sip of his champagne and laughed. "And you
know why? Because it *has* to."

"How much money do you owe them?" I asked.

"Why? You want to loan me some?"

"Did you sell heroin, Danny?"

"I would never *sell* heroin," he said.

"What am I supposed to do about this, Danny?" I asked.

"Nothing. It's just that you're a powerful man. You've got
influence. *Access*. And in times like these, it feels luckier to be
around someone like you."

I felt a line of temper burning through me like the flame on
an acetylene torch. I wanted everybody to go away. I had gotten
this far essentially on my own, without anyone's fully understanding or even approving how I negotiated the curves. And now with
the finish line so close, it was beyond endurance to have them
crowding me like this.

"You're not in my district," I said.

"I *am* your fucking district," said Danny, jabbing himself in the chest. His face went scarlet. "And if you can't do it for me you can't do it at all. Who do you think made you what you are? You think you just made it up? Or read it in the *New Republic*? You're part me, you fuck, and when you turn away from me you turn away from yourself."

"So be it, then," I said.

"Are you saying you made Fielding what he is?" asked Caroline.

"Yes. Me. You. What would he be without us? Some repulsive combination of Harvard and the Coast Guard and the DA's office, stirred up by his pal Isaac Green and his tight-ass niece? He's worried about getting a few extra votes and he leaves it to us to worry about his *soul*. You know what? I think even Mom and Dad would rather him lose if all he wants to do is go to Washington and be like everybody else."

"Well, I don't know about that," said Caroline.

"Christ," said Danny. "You're getting sucked into it, too."

"Maybe I am," said Caroline. "Every family has to have a good son. He's on one side, you're on the other, and I'm the bridge between you."

"Right. With two black kids, three jobs, and eighty-eight cents in the bottom of your purse."

"I think of myself as a very normal person," Caroline said.

"Great," said Danny. "I'm thrilled for you." Suddenly, he was up and pacing. He dug his hand into his jacket pocket and felt for something in it. "Look, Fielding," he said, "I wonder if you at least could do me a small favor. I have to run an errand. Could you take Kim back to my hotel for me? It won't take but fifteen, twenty minutes."

"Fine," I said.

"You won't feel too compromised, will you?"

"I'll manage."

"Good. I'll know she's in good hands. You *always* accomplish what you set out to."

"Danny, if you knew what was going on in my life right now, you'd take it easy on me."

"I have a pretty good idea of what you're up against, Fielding. You always think you're such a mystery."

"You can't possibly."

"Let's not argue it, then," said Danny with a shrug. "You can't stiff me and then expect me to see it from your side." He took his black cashmere overcoat off the coat tree near the door. He had an Ecuadorian scarf shoved up the sleeve and now he wrapped it carefully around his neck and then smoothed it over his chest. When he was buttoned up, he put on one black leather glove. He must have already lost the other. Then he sat next to Kim on the sofa and put his arm around her. She buried her face in his overcoat and he stroked her smooth black hair. He seemed paternal, melancholy, and infinitely tender: I had never known more acutely than I did at that moment why women had always shown him such loyalty. There were few people more scattered, more irregular, but the sweetness of that touch and the way his body fit itself next to her, the sympathy and oneness expressed by the mere pitch of his hip, could not be duplicated by a more ordinary, reliable lover. My own embraces seemed by contrast grotesquely diluted by my own needs and as I watched Danny hold Kim and listened in the winter night silence of that room to the fragile reality of their breathing, I felt a thousand times over I would rather have been either of them than to spend another moment as myself.

I drove Kim downtown to the Palmer House. She sat as far away from me as the dimensions of the old Mercury would allow. I don't know much about fur coats but I doubt that the one she wore came from an animal; it was pinkish and gauzy, like fiberglass insulation. To our right, the lake was frozen and reached out toward the dark gray horizon like a field of moon-bright rubble. She turned on the radio and searched the frequencies until she found a song she liked. It was the Beach Boys singing "California

Girls" and she used the song to draw a curtain between us. I glanced once at her; she was silently singing along, moving her head back and forth twice as fast as the beat.

I couldn't send her up to the room on her own so I parked the car and went in with her. In the lobby, she linked her arm through mine and we took the plush, overheated elevator to the fourteenth floor. We walked down the long, dimly lit carpeted hall. A fellow from room service was wheeling a table toward the service elevator; he looked directly at us when he passed us in the hall and Kim gripped me harder. She opened up her little gold sparkling purse and gave me the room key.

They were staying in a suite with a view of the lake. The rooms had high ceilings, expensive-looking furniture. The walls were painted salmon and white. And it looked as if several frantic people had been living in that suite for weeks. There were open valises from which the clothes had been pulled and then left in a tangle on the bed, the chairs, all over the floor. There were the remains of a shrimp cocktail here—with a cigarette doused out in the little pot of cocktail sauce—and a virtually untouched chef salad there. There were two bottles of champagne and a copy of the *Sun-Times* that looked as if a puppy had been playing with it. There was tissue paper on the floor and the red roses that room service sent up with each order had been gathered into one vase and that vase had tipped over from the weight of those sweet American Beauties, shedding petals on the marble table and leaving a water stain on the carpet. Strewn everywhere were those European fashion magazines Danny loved and somewhere in his brief stay in this room he had found time to dismantle a small tape recorder completely, leaving its incomprehensible litter everywhere. And there were more ominous, familiar sorts of garbage: balls of cotton wool, broken wooden matches, a charred spoon abandoned in a glass of water—the barnacles scraped off the SS *Narcosis*.

"Do you want me to wait with you until Danny comes back?" I asked Kim.

"Soon come back," answered Kim. She covered a yawn with

her small, delicate hand. She wore a thin, childish ring on every finger; her nails were painted dark burgundy. "You want to drink?" she asked.

"All right."

She pointed to the telephone, which was draped over with a Palmer House towel. I stepped around the mess. I had yet to see the bedroom or the bath, though I knew they would be equally devastated. "I'm going to order some coffee," I said. "Do you want something, too?"

"OK," she said. "Me, too." She pushed aside Danny's striped shirt and some magazines and sat down on the fussy little sofa. She was still wearing her coat but she slipped her shoes off.

"Well, what would you like?" I asked her. I said it much too quickly and she looked at me, not understanding. She was exhausted and speaking English was an increasing strain. I repeated the question, slowly, with hand gestures.

"Tea and then Scotch in the little bottle. And a tunafish sandwich please."

I called in the order. The voice at the other end was very obliging and when he read the order back to me he said, "We'll get it right up there, Mr. Pierce." Danny tipped like mad to get that sort of treatment.

I cleared off a chair and sat down. I looked around the room and just then it struck me that Danny was probably someplace dangerous buying drugs. He never bought enough to keep ahead; he had to start from scratch wherever he was. He had so much to do, much more than he could handle. I didn't know why he needed to add this extra, insatiable demand to the mix. But how could I advise him? Should I have told him to buy his heroin supply so it would last a week rather than an evening?

"I was thinking about the night we first met," I said to Kim.

"In New York," she said.

"When we were leaving the place, you all of a sudden pretended you forgot your purse and you tried to go back upstairs."

Kim pointed to her purse lying beside her. "This is my purse," she said.

"I stopped you from going back up," I said. "Remember? You wanted to. But I just did what I thought Danny wanted. He didn't want you to go back and I really just went with my instinct. I didn't think what was best for you and now you're in all of this trouble."

"I'm sorry," said Kim. "My English is no good."

"No. It's fine."

"I sound like little girl. No brains. At home, everybody say I very smart. But here sound stupid. Very little words."

"Well, you speak better English than I speak Korean."

"You speak Korean?"

"No."

"A little bit?"

"No. Not at all, not a word."

She gave me a quick, sour look and I realized that my saying she spoke more English than I spoke Korean and then my saying I spoke absolutely no Korean had turned what I'd meant to be a compliment into a slight. But of course it wasn't a compliment in the first place. It was merely a bit of patronizing banter and as she turned her mouth down and glanced away from me I felt a surge of horror at myself—true horror—because it seemed suddenly that a sensitivity that I had always assumed was my second nature had turned into (perhaps had always been) something really rather coarse—a salesman's friendliness. Who in the hell was I to try and put Kim at her ease? She knew at least as much as I about the terrors of this world.

I felt a pain in the small of my back as if a blunted nail had just been driven in: the pain seemed to touch right into the marrow of my spine and then radiate out up to my shoulders, down toward my feet. I gasped and gripped the arm of the chair. I felt behind me and then I tried to get up, but the pain made me weak, willless.

"You hurt?" asked Kim.

"Nerves," I said. Lord, I thought, backaches: the sell-outs' disease.

"Your back hurt?" she asked.

"Yeah. It's OK."

"Danny, too. All the time. Too much worry. And then walk like this." She dangled her arms in front of her and shrugged her shoulders, simianesque.

"Really? I had no idea."

"Lie down. I give massage-y." She opened her purse and took out a piece of Juicy Fruit gum.

The fact was, my nerves along my leg felt as if they were being scraped with a fork. It was midnight. Juliet was gone. Isaac and Adele slept in their twin beds, on their backs, with black sleeping masks over their eyes. The election was slipping away from me. And Sarah. Like a shadow over the skylight, like a whisper in the dark, like footsteps in the snow that make a trail to the edge of a precipice . . . It struck me suddenly that Danny had sent me home with Kim so she could take care of me in some way. It seemed absurd not to accept.

"You want me to lie down on the floor?"

"Silly," she said, without any apparent amusement. "We go onto the bed." She pointed to the door into the bedroom. And then she sprang up, smoothing her skirt down, chewing her gum rapidly.

I followed her into the bedroom. All that remained on the bed was the bottom sheet; all of the other bedclothes were on the floor. There was more room service litter, more magazines, more clothing. The place *looked* like a slum but there was a spicy, elegant aroma in the air—probably one of Danny's imported colognes. They came in heavy obsidian cubes with golden caps, or else in little blue vials. They covered the heroin sweats, the days without bathing. He routinely anointed the bedsheets with them, like a priest sprinkling holy water. Kim turned on the lamp, which had been covered with Danny's plum-colored pajama top. And when the lamp was on, she closed the door.

"Take off your shoes, OK? And maybe your shirt."

It reminded me of the very best part of drinking—that overwhelming numb cool sense that it absolutely didn't matter what

I did next. I took off my shoes, my jacket, my tie, my shirt, and the gray tank top I wore beneath.

"You have big muscles," Kim said. She felt my biceps and nodded approvingly.

"Inherited and undeserved," I said. Yet I felt myself tightening them to make them larger. I felt a sense of self-pity suddenly go through me. After all those nights sharing my bed with Juliet, I had in essence forgotten I had a body. When we needed each other, I put my hand between her legs and she put hers between mine. Now I felt sublimely physical. Even the pain that went up and down my leg made me somehow more human than I had been in a long while. I gently eased myself onto the bed with my arms out. The bed barely registered Kim's weight as she got on it and now she was straddling me, leaning forward so her hands grasped the backs of my shoulders and her pelvic bone rested hard against the small of my back.

Whatever complexities of need and duty and desire that affixed Danny's affections to Kim, her brilliance as a healer was clearly not a part of it. Her touch was weak and then, as if to compensate for her lack of strength, she would now and again dig her lean fingers into some particularly painful junction of nerve and tendon.

I closed my eyes and turned up the heat of my inner concentration, trying to burn off the distractions and get to the pure nub of pleasure, like Danny burned off the superfluous ingredients in a spoonful of paregoric to get to the goo of opium. And there *was* pleasure in her touch—sensuality and danger and a comforting sense of utter abstraction: I knew she was barely even thinking of me. I was a child in a nursery, or, better, a man feigning injuries in a rehabilitation clinic, holding back the sneer of satisfaction as the therapist moved my arms, my legs.

If I could lie in this bed with my shirt off, if I could let Kim press herself against me and knead my flesh with her hands, then why could I not just roll over and take her in my arms? The pain that had driven me into the bed had disappeared as soon as I was horizontal. My life had been torn from all of its familiar meanings.

I could smell her perfume. Then why not fuck her? If she could touch my back then why not my cock? Wasn't it really simple-minded and perverse to say that one part of my body was all right to touch, but not another?

The doorbell rang and a moment after that I heard the fellow from room service wheeling in the table with our tea and Scotch and tunafish. I heard the scrape of the tongs against the ice cubes and the hellish music of the ice cubes falling into a nice heavy tumbler and then a moment later the waiter made his exit, closing the door behind him with a soft discreet click. And that click was my checkered flag.

I rolled over and reached up for Kim. Her face looked confused, uncertain, but, my perceptions caked over with the sludge of my loose, lazy desire, I took what was really a look of horror for a kind of quaint coquettishness and even as she leaned away from me I pursued her. I took her by the wrist and pulled her close to me.

"Stop it," she said. But even that was not enough. I rose up from the bed to kiss her on the mouth. In my mind I was taking this as a somehow gentle gesture, I was now making it all right. "No, no, no," she said, jerking away. I kissed her on the chin and even the hardness of that bone could not distract me enough. I still managed to hear the real fear and helplessness and loathing beneath the way she said no to me. In just the time it had taken me to roll from my stomach onto my back I had become the absolute embodiment of those pimps who had signed her up on the outskirts of Seoul for the long flight over on KAL with six other young women, all of whom had risen to the same bait—and who had then been spirited away in one of those cars that cruised as silent as sharks beneath the deep darkness of the American night. Kim pulled her hand away from me. I had debased myself beyond my wildest imaginings. I lay there and watched her scramble from the bed.

I felt much too worthless even to get up. I put my hands behind my head and stared up at the ceiling. I closed my eyes for a moment and went through my mind, looking for something to say. Finally: "If I win this election, Kim, I really will see if there's something I can do for Danny. I really will." I waited for her to say something but when I opened my eyes and raised myself up on my elbows, she had already left the room.

I had left Kim back at the Palmer House after Danny called from a pay phone in a bar on 44th Street to say he was on his way back. It was snowing again on the drive south. There was a pack of wild dogs running in double file along the side of the road; the powder their paws kicked up drifted through the headlights of the passing cars.

It was after two when I finally arrived back home. I was supposed to be at a breakfast club meeting in six hours: I didn't know how I could convince someone to throw a glass of water on me if my hair was on fire, much less inspire them to send me to Washington to represent them. It didn't matter; confronted with the situation, I knew I could improvise.

The apartment was empty when I let myself in. Everything was very tidy; there was even a whiff of furniture polish in the air. The ashtrays were empty; the glasses washed and put away. Caroline had left me a note on the coffee table. *See you tomorrow at the noon rally. I love you, Fielding. Caroline.*

I carefully folded the note and placed it in my wallet, as if it were a letter of credit. This would have been the most perfect time to have a drink; I would have gladly traded the liters upon liters that had been consumed before this moment for just one unencumbered glassful right now. This was the moment I had been waiting for. I went into the kitchen. The champagne bottles had already been tossed into the garbage pail. Juliet kept a bottle of Ballantine Scotch in the house to drink during menstrual cramps, but it was gone now. All I could find was a bottle of Cinzano sweet vermouth. It was not as bad as I would have thought. A thin line of heat jolted through me as I drank it down; there was a pleasing bitterness left behind. I poured some more into the glass and then tightly screwed the cap back on. I put the bottle into the cabinet beneath the sink, alongside the baking powder, the Devonshire Sesame Rounds, the bouillon cubes.

I patrolled the house, as if to make certain it was truly empty. Loneliness was falling through me like snow, but it seemed to be covering something far more disturbing than mere isolation and I welcomed it. I went into my study, now Caroline's bedroom. She was still circumspect about her presence; there was no sign she had been sleeping there—not a shoe, not a comb, not an earring —except for one of those picture frames that open like a book and hold two photographs. One was of Rudy and the other of Malik, artfully shot by one of Caroline's artistic downtown friends. I picked up the frame and looked closely at the boys: they both wore ski sweaters with a line of nubby pines across the chest. Rudy held his chin high and his lips were pressed tight in an aspect of virginal defiance. I looked for my face in his and though I could not locate any specific similarity there *was* something in him that reminded me of myself. Likewise in Malik, with his wide vulnerable eyes, the mouth that seemed to ask: Is it all right to smile now? I pressed their pictures to my chest and held them close. I wondered why fate had not led me to a real family of my own. I felt a sudden lurch within, as if I could suddenly sense the earth's lonely compulsive journey through the emptiness of space.

The phone rang. I put the pictures of Rudy and Malik down and looked at my watch. It was nearly two thirty. When you are my age a phone call in the middle of the night bodes only ill: there is no longer much of a chance that it's a friend offering to come over with a joint and his new copy of *Rubber Soul*. I sat at my desk and stared at the phone as it rang a second time, a third, a fourth. Was it the police after having found Danny dead in the sawdust of a ghetto bar? Or my mother from the emergency room of Rockland County Hospital while the medics shot electrical jolts into my father's chest to reawaken his dying heart? Finally, I grabbed for the phone.

"Hello?"

There was silence, brocaded by the buzz of the long-distance cables.

"Did I wake you?" asked the voice.

And though I didn't know why I would say it, I said yes. The silence returned; it seemed to wash over us like the tide. I listened; the silence laid its hands upon me and pulled me out of my chair. I was standing now, leaning across the desk, one hand holding the receiver, the other pulling at my hair.

"Sarah?" I whispered.

"Yes," she said. "It's me. It's . . . me."

I found myself sitting on the floor. The phone had slid off the desk but the wire tethered it so it dangled in midair.

"No," I said. "Who is this?"

"I'm sorry, Fielding. I'm sorry." She took a deep breath with a sob beating within it like a wing. "This has been so hard. Every day I had to decide whether or not to call you, to let you know. That was something I needed to do every day. I tried to bring you to me. I tried to conjure you. I wrote your name on a piece of paper and I pinned it to the top of my blanket."

"Sarah?" I said. "Is this really happening?" But even as I asked it, even as my heart swelled and raced within me, I knew it was her voice: she sounded exhausted, slightly frightened, and there was a distance, an involuntary strangeness that I had never heard before. But those were just passing clouds across the face of the moon.

"It's such a hard story, Fielding," she said. "I did what I had to. I needed to sacrifice. I couldn't stay where I was. I couldn't stay that person."

"Sarah. Where are you? Where are you right now? Are you far away?"

"Yes."

"Where?"

"I don't know . . . I called you up to tell you. But now I don't know. It seems like a vanity on top of a vanity to give you up and then come back."

"Where are you?"

"I just wanted you to know I was alive. It wasn't me in that car. It was so complicated. An ugly thing. It was one of the Chileans, the woman, but she was wearing my clothes. It wasn't my idea. But I didn't say no. I could do things I could never do otherwise."

"Where are you right now? I'm going to hang up if you don't tell me." I was not shouting; I was bellowing. I closed my eyes to picture her face as I had done so many times before, but now I could not see her: there was just blackness and a slow traffic of trembling dots. It struck me in a glancing sort of way that I was dying.

"Please don't," she said.

I stood up. I placed the phone back on the desk. I looked at the pictures of Rudy and Malik, the lamplight on the darkened windows, listened to the icy rustle of the falling snow.

"Was that you I chased into Stanton's church last week?" I asked.

There was a silence. And then she said, "No."

"You've been everywhere, Sarah. Christ. I don't even know who I'm talking to."

"I'm so proud of you, Fielding. You're so close to what you've been working for. You'll be in a position to do so much good."

"Oh Christ, I don't want to talk about that. You don't know what this has been like. You don't know what it's like right now. How can I know this is you? I've got to see you, Sarah."

"Maybe later. I want to see you, too, you know."

"Then right now, right *now*."

"I'm far away."

"Just tell me where. I'll be there. Tell me."

"I can't. I can't turn back and neither can you."

"Are you married?" I asked her.

She had to think about it. Finally, she said, "To a man? No."

"To a woman?"

"To no one on earth."

"What are you? A nun?"

"No, Fielding. No."

"But are you with someone?"

"Yes, I am," she said. "I'm with you."

The connection broke. This slight interruption of electronic impulse sent me hurtling back to the wrong side of eternity again. I placed the receiver into the phone's cradle and walked through the apartment, swinging my arms back and forth, talking to myself but not making the slightest bit of sense. A sob came up out of me and it felt as if an umbrella had opened up in the middle of my throat. I put my hand over my mouth; my breath was hot. And then the next thing I can remember is I was outside, dressed in overcoat, scarf, and gloves and the deserted street was its own frigid planet, separated from the rest of the universe by an eternal impenetrable darkness, illuminated only by a line of cool, dim moons.

14

I waited forty-eight hours for her to call again. Juliet did not come home, Danny and Kim went up to Toronto, I debated Bertelli in front of the local chapter of the League of Women Voters and he trounced me, beating me right back into the arms of my old childhood stammer and reducing my usual lilting logic to mere thrusts of half-believed notions. Then it was Friday, four days before the special election. Tony Dayton had done a nonscientific poll that put Bertelli and me in a dead heat. The money the Democratic machine had allotted me had already been spent and suddenly Bertelli was getting all sorts of fresh financing—from the national Republicans, the Teamsters, the Chicago Gay Alliance, and from that black preacher who was leading the anti-abortion campaign up and down Cottage Grove. Isaac and Adele caught up with me Friday night to tell me they were going to loan me $20,000 to take me through the last couple of days of the race.

They asked me over for a late supper, so they could present the check and talk about the campaign. They were clearly worried, though if my having lost Juliet during this sudden tailspin was a part of their concern, they gave no indication.

I appeared at the Greens' apartment about eight in the evening. Mrs. Davis let me in—she was wearing her fur coat and was on her way home. Her dark eyes threw off sparks of impatience like a tailpipe hitting the pavement at sixty. "They're in there," she said, "waiting for you." She walked right past me and into the hall. She was limping; she had an Ace bandage around her ankle.

"What's with Mrs. Davis?" I asked, walking into the dining room with my coat over my arm. The snowflakes were turning to little dots of water and then disappearing into the wool.

Isaac and Adele were at the dining room table. Places had been set and a platter of cold brisket was on display. All this was within the bounds of acceptable behavior but unfortunately they were not alone. Sitting next to Adele was Tony Dayton, with a thick computer printout next to his gold-trimmed plate, and sitting next to Isaac was Juliet, wearing a penitential black sweater and delicate ruby earrings (to say she wasn't really *that* sorry).

"Trapped," I said, trying to have it both ways by finishing with a smile.

"Sit down, Fielding, and eat," said Adele. "Then we'll talk."

"Your best friends in the whole world are at this table," said Isaac with a frown.

"Hello, Juliet," I said. "They put an all-points bulletin out on you?"

"Hello, Fielding," she said. "You look tired."

"Tossing and turning." A place had been set for me next to Juliet and I took it. No sense acting emotional about it.

"OK," said Isaac, "whatever problems of adjustment you two have been having can be put aside for a while. You two have been a team and an effective one and this is not the time to potchky around with that."

The others all had wine in their modern little goblets; mine had been filled with club soda. I took a sip; it was violently gaseous and salty. Like seawater after a nuclear war. "Are we really going to talk about this in front of Tony?"

"As if I didn't already know," he said, shaking his head. "What am I? Blind?"

"Oh God, I forgot to tell you, Isaac. Tony's been doing a great job."

"That you feel so divided from Tony is as good an indication as any how much trouble you're in," said Isaac. He raised his finger at me, but did not wag it. "How can we wage a successful campaign if you treat Tony as if he was an outsider?"

"Have I hurt your feelings, Tony?" I asked, smiling.

"Well," he said, looking down, "it *is* like trying to win a horse race while your horse is reaching around trying to bite your foot."

Isaac closed his eyes for a moment and touched the tablecloth with his open hand, looking for the strength of forbearance in the privacy of his own internal darkness, the feel of his own possessions.

"I doubt that's what you really meant to say, Tony," I said.

"You know what I mean," he said.

"Yes, of course. Do I have to take a saliva test after the election?"

Juliet reached beneath the table and took my hand. I squeezed her fingers hard until she let go.

"I thought you said this thing was a walk," I said to Isaac. "I thought I wouldn't lose."

"Are you really going to accuse me of making your mistakes?" Isaac said.

"So what does your latest informal poll tell you, Tony?" I asked.

"You've lost a tremendous amount of support," he said. "Fifteen points, more or less. But now we're hitting the bedrock of Democratic support and we seem to be holding. Bertelli's people are going to have to find a way of breaking that last support barrier—and if they do, then they can have the election."

"What are we talking about here?" I asked. "The people who vote Democratic no matter who's running?"

"Party loyalists," Tony said. "They're called party loyalists and if I were you I'd speak about them with respect."

Suddenly Isaac slammed his fist down onto the table. The china jumped. "What has been going on in this campaign?" he asked. "What has happened to our high hopes? Are we really going to lose a congressional seat to some nobody who runs a coffee-house?"

"He isn't beating us on issues, Isaac," said Tony. "On issues we cream him every time. But he's a very affable fellow and it comes across."

Finally, Juliet spoke. I'd been waiting for this. "When he wants to be, Fielding can be the most charming man on earth."

"You've got to be kidding me," I said.

"Well, it's true, Fielding. Maybe it goes against this—this self-image you have, of the rough guy from the poor family and all that—that *decoration*. But it's true."

"Why are you here, Juliet? How did they get you to do this?"

"I am here because I want to be. I've seen you through all the steps you've had to take to get this far. It seems wasteful to just let you throw it away when you're this close."

"Even if you win, Fielding," Adele said, "and I think you will, you're not creating an impression on the people you need to impress if you're going to continue with your career. I think we just need to focus our thinking. We're all jittery with the election so close." She took a deep breath and reached for the platter of brisket; it was brown, cold, an instant pathway to vegetarianism. "Why don't we all have a bite to eat and then get down to cases? It's brisket. Jeremy's favorite."

It was rare for them to mention Jeremy. He had escaped his parents' plans for him and now here I was eating his dinner.

"I wonder if you would all excuse Fielding and me for a moment," Isaac suddenly said. He took his napkin from his lap and rubbed his hands against it.

"That'll be just fine," said Adele. She had just served Isaac a slice of the brisket but she speared it again with the serving fork and put it back on the platter.

I leaned next to Juliet and whispered in her ear, even as she raised her shoulder and tried to protect herself from me. "I'd get out of here right now. Whenever you've been staying, whatever you're doing—it's got to be a better deal than you'll get here. The ship is sinking." And with that I stood up and followed Isaac out of the dining room.

We went across the corridor into his study. A small almost transparent fire was trembling in the hearth. The darkness that had settled into the corners of that room seemed heavy, like the darkness of another planet, a darkness that would take more than mere light to remove. Isaac switched on a lamp; it dropped a ring of light on the high polish of the table. I stood at the window and looked down at the view of streetlights and frozen lake. Though it had been only a few weeks, it seemed years before when I'd stood here with the governor and Isaac at my back. It was snowing then and it was snowing still. I wondered if on the South Side in my apartment the phone was ringing at this very instant. The thought went through me like a wheel of fire. I pressed my forehead against the window.

"Shall we get down to cases?" asked Isaac. He sat on the arm of one of his club chairs and crossed his legs at the ankle, folded his arms over his chest. He looked dapper, furious.

"I'm going to win the election, Isaac. Don't worry."

"Don't worry? What right have you to tell me not to worry? You know very little about this process. You are a neophyte. But I thought you had the instinct. I actually thought you were ready to take this step. And now I see how wrong I was."

"You're only wrong if I lose. And we don't know that I'm going to lose."

Isaac shook his head. "You see how upset Adele is. I don't like her to be upset. She is talking about Jeremy and she never does unless it's in private or she isn't paying attention. You don't seem to realize that when you enter into the lives of other people, they count on you. There is an obligation. A moral obligation."

"I think if Adele wants to talk about Jeremy it's fine."

"As you know, our son is a painful topic."

"For God's sake, why? He's not a criminal. He's not curled up in some room whispering into his own hand. All that's wrong with him is he didn't do exactly what you wanted him to. What's the tragedy? Especially since you found someone else to fill that spot and you went right on."

"And by that someone else, I assume you mean yourself."

"Of course."

"And do you feel you've been . . . victimized? In any way?"

"Not by you. No."

"I didn't come into your life," said Isaac. "You came into mine. You had all of your appetites before I ever laid eyes on you. And when we met, you saw in me a vehicle that could carry you more or less in the direction you wanted to move. You used my counsel, my home, my connections. So please don't suddenly pretend you were the victim of some diabolical plot on my part. What makes you so dangerous and so distasteful is how canny you are at imitating a gentleman."

"I already said I didn't feel victimized, Isaac. You've only been decent to me."

"Decent. You don't realize how goddamned lucky you were to have me. You think coming from a family like yours you had the slightest preparation for public life? We're talking about the real world, the big table where the big decisions are made. Not $4.85 an hour and going to work with your little lunch pail. We are talking about decisions of global proportion."

"Isaac, I want you to tell me something. What did you do for Governor Kinosis that he owed you such a huge favor?"

"Governor Kinosis is a frightened, sentimental Greek and you'd be surprised how little you have to do to make him feel in your debt."

"OK, then. Surprise me."

"It is not any one particular thing. He considers me an intellectual. It bolsters his confidence to think he and I are friends. From time to time, I write something for him, or look over some papers. Kinosis is a man of tremendous drive but he is very insecure and he takes my goodwill as a benediction."

"Yes. Well, this is the impression you gave me."

"Then what's the problem?"

"The problem is I no longer believe it. He doesn't give you a congressman because he's impressed with your letter to the editor of the *New Republic*. There's something more."

Isaac took a deep breath. He went to the little rosewood bar and poured himself a drink from one of the decanters. Isaac was a ridiculous drinker; I doubt he even knew what he was pouring into his glass. There were just times when his own sense of himself and the choreography of the moment told him he ought to have a drink in hand. He took a sip. I glanced at the decanter but didn't make a move.

"I have helped the governor with his investments and I've given him legal advice."

"What kind of legal advice, Isaac?"

"I resent—"

"Yes. I know. And I'm sorry. But I really do have to know."

Isaac finished his drink and placed the glass down on the table, glancing at it with what looked like disappointment, as if the liquor had betrayed him by not setting him at his ease. "He had some investments that could have been construed as a conflict of interests."

"Were they?"

"Technically speaking, yes."

"How bad was it?"

"He had a thirty percent share of a company that was getting state contracts." Isaac shrugged, smiled. "The idiot owned a chicken farm that was supplying chickens to the state prison. All very low level. But lucrative, of course."

"Well, what did you do for him?"

"A little of this, a little of that. You know." He was talking to me as if everything was going back to normal. He was summing it up, putting it into perspective; presumably this was something we would laugh about.

"I've got to go now, Isaac," I said.

"Go where?" His voice rose in anger and surprise. "Where do you think you're going? This is absolutely indefensible."

"I just have to go. If I told you the reason you'd be even more upset."

"I leveled with you, Fielding."

"You didn't tell me *anything*."

"Come. We'll go to the dining room. We'll have dinner. There's still ample time to put this back together."

"I can't do that, Isaac. I don't want it back together. Not the way it was."

"Pardon my gross insensitivity," he said, placing his hand over his heart, his voice rising beneath the swell of sarcasm, "but I'd be less than candid if I didn't tell you I have no idea what you're talking about. What are you? Finding yourself?"

"Yes," I said.

"We have three days before the voting begins, Fielding. Three days."

"I can't. Right now, the campaign would run better without me."

"What is happening to you?"

"I am involved in something, Isaac. I've collided—I don't know what to call it."

"What are you talking about?"

"Ever since I stood in this room and you and Kinosis asked me to run, something has been rising up. I see it, it's here."

"You've collapsed under the pressure, Fielding."

"That could be it. I don't know."

"What are you doing? Where are you going?"

"I'm going to find Sarah."

"Sarah? Sarah who?"

"Sarah Williams."

"You're going to visit her grave? Can't it wait?"

"No. Not her grave. That's not her in that tomb. They buried someone else, a Chilean woman. Someone Sarah helped get out of Chile. It was her in the car when the bomb exploded. She was wearing Sarah's clothing. Little shreds of it survived. I don't know. I'm thinking back."

"Fielding," he said, moving toward me.

"Wait. Listen to me. It wasn't Sarah. But they let us all believe that. They probably thought it would be good for Americans to think those bastards killed an American girl. They thought if it was only Latin Americans, no one would care."

"Why are you saying any of this? What's happened to you?"

"My mind is filled with white light, Isaac. Can you understand that?"

"I understand that you're in a great deal of trouble." He came next to me and took my arm. "I just want you to hold on for a couple of days, Fielding. After that, you'll have a complete rest. Please, you're like a son to me. You know that. I wouldn't be saying this if it wasn't for your own good."

I put my arms around Isaac and held him close. "I love you, Isaac," I murmured into his ear. I could feel him trying to pull away from me and I held him tighter still. "I'll never forget what you've done for me."

"For God's sake, Fielding," he said. "Let me go. You're strangling me. Will you please let me go?"

I waited through the night for Sarah to call and the next morning I showered, shaved, and packed a suitcase. I called a taxi and was taken to O'Hare Airport and took the noon plane out to New Orleans. I sat near the window and watched the ground crew de-ice the wings. It was a fierce blizzard but the runways were open. We were already a half hour late. I had the morning papers. Both of them had editorials supporting Bertelli, characterizing him as an independent, new voice, free from the alliances and solutions of the past. The great lie had dug itself in. The stewardesses served breakfast; the fellow sitting next to me picked his eggs apart as if he was trying to remove shards of broken glass. It was a rocky ride. The captain never turned off the seat-belt sign. We hit an air pocket. A woman gasped. I dozed off and dreamed about walking through Madison Square Park with Danny and I was wearing my Coast Guard uniform and then I was awake and the plane was just a hundred feet above the runway in New Orleans. It was raining hard.

I took a taxi from the airport to Sarah's parents' house. The driver was an enormously fat light-skinned black with freckles the size of rivets on his face. He was listening to a rhythm and blues station. The dj was the R and B singer Ernie K. Doe and apparently his health or mortality was in question because he continually repeated the phrase, "And you know Ernie K. Doe is *never* gonna die." And then there'd be a pause while you absorbed that and then he'd break in with something like, "You hear me, Martha? Now get yourself out of bed, girl. And come down here because I *need* you."

Soon, we were at the Williamses' rectangular brick house. It looked particularly cryptic in the rain. The cyclone fence was still there but the Chihuahuas it once enclosed were gone: now a sleek, red-eyed boxer paced slowly along the perimeters of the front yard. I paid the driver and took my overnight bag out of the taxi. As I approached the house, the dog got into position, as if it had just heard the bell signaling the next round. Its rib cage looked prehistoric through its soaked coat; its teeth were a dull pinkish white. But of course I'd come too far to be deterred by a mere dog. I figured I couldn't be the first person to approach the Williams house with this dog on duty and so I just opened the gate and did my best to project an aura of confidence. The dog pressed its muzzle into my groin and growled; the reverberations of his anger turned my spine into a tuning fork. He followed me up the narrow pavement, up the porch, right to the door, and he remained there as I rang the doorbell. The porch had a tin roof and the rain sounded like stones in a coffee can.

The door opened. It was Sarah's father, Eugene. His polar

blue eyes had softened and dulled until they looked like old denim. He was unshaved, wearing a robe. He'd put on weight. The sound of big band music was swinging and swaying behind him and he was holding a pair of drumsticks. He had no idea who I was. "OK, Rocky, get off," he said to the dog. The dog cringed, backed away. "Did he nail you?" Eugene asked me. He smiled and rubbed his chin whiskers.

"Well? What can I do you for?"

"Hello, Eugene. I'm Fielding Pierce."

His first reaction was fast, a reflex. "What did you say?" he asked, as if I were a child who had mumbled something disrespectful. But then the confusion rolled in, no longer held at bay by his familiar habits of aggression. The color drained out of his face and his whiskers looked like iron filings floating in milk.

"I'm Fielding Pierce," I said again. "Sarah's friend."

He nodded. He seemed to want to save face, as if showing too much surprise would put him at a disadvantage from which he could never recover. "That's right," he said. "What are . . . what are you doing here?"

"I need to talk to you."

"Talk to me?" he said, and his voice went suddenly jaunty, as if we were about to engage in something comic. "Well, there's no charge for that." He paused for a moment, as if to give time to the part of himself that was still reeling to gather in safety behind the front he was putting up. "Well, get the hell out of the rain, why don't you. Come in."

He stepped aside and I came into the house. It smelled warm, foul. The Music Minus One was lilting along, pausing now and then for a drum break—but the drummer was away from his post. "This is the third Saturday in a row my golf date's been rained out," Eugene was saying. "It's so depressing." I followed him into the living room.

His drum set was in the center of the room, next to the stereo console. And next to the drums was a female boxer with six pups on her. There were wet newspapers on the carpet. "Sorry about the mess. But the crazy bitch dropped her litter here and when

Dorothy tried to move her she almost got herself bit." With that, he went to the staircase and called up: "Dorothy? You decent? We've got a visitor from the past!" He turned back to me and smiled. "This ought to set her back a few paces," he said. And then he grabbed the bottom of the banister and shouted upstairs, "Dorothy, now, for Christ's sake, *now*." He shook his head and gave me a shrug that was meant to imply male complicity. "It's either that or be ignored," he said.

"I'm sorry to appear without any warning," I said.

"So what brings you to New Orleans?" Eugene asked. "Here for Mardi Gras?"

"No. I need to talk to you about Sarah."

"Great. My favorite topic. What do you want to know? The first day she decided to work against the interests of the USA, or the last?"

I heard the rustle of Dorothy Williams's chiffon robe as she wove down the stairs. She was wearing a proper blue dress and large amber beads. She was holding a coffee cup that I could tell from the curl of her fingers was carrying alcohol. Her face was in total disarray, smeared like a watercolor left in the rain. She saw me when she was halfway down the stairs and she gripped the railing; there was something strange in her movements, almost as if she were trying to be grand, trying to act as if her life was just a part in a drama.

"Oh good, Dot," said Eugene, "you're just in time. Look who's here. Sarah's old fiancé, Fielding."

"What is he doing here, Gene?" she asked.

"That's the beauty part, Dot. Come on down here and make sure you don't hurt yourself."

She made her way down the stairs. She placed her cup on a heavily carved table in the hall and then took her place at her husband's side. "Hello, Fielding," she said. "This is a surprise."

"Hello, Mrs. Williams," I said. "I'm sorry to drop in like this. I've been very busy and . . . I don't know. This is just how it worked out."

"Well, to what do we owe this pleasure?" she asked, taking her husband's arm and leaning on him. Eugene took the opportunity to walk away from her and turn off the stereo set. The room seemed to jolt forward like the passenger in a braking car.

"I have a question to ask you," I said. We were still standing and I paused, thinking they would at that point suggest we sit. I wasn't so far gone I didn't know what this was going to sound like.

"You know what?" Eugene said, tapping his forehead. "I just remembered. I *liked* you. You were just like a normal person. You weren't like—you know, the sort of boy I expected Sarah to choose. You were in the Coast Guard. You were going to law school. Did that pan out?"

"Yes, I'm a lawyer."

"What side?"

"I've been working in the Cook County Prosecutor's office. Now I'm running for Congress up in Chicago."

"Really?" he said. "Chicago? Dorothy has a sister who lived in Chicago for many years."

"Not really in Chicago, Gene. Emily lived many miles outside the city."

Eugene snorted contemptuously. "Well, that's a story that changes like the wind."

"Well, we're just standing here like a bunch of servants," said Dorothy. "Why don't we all sit down?" She put her hand to her throat and smiled.

Eugene walked over to his drum set and dropped the sticks on the snare and then we were all seated. The furniture I remembered from the time Sarah and I had stayed here was gone. I sat in a white wicker chair with lime green upholstery. Dorothy and Eugene sat on opposite ends of the lime and wicker sofa. Years ago, there'd been pictures of their daughters on the wall in this room. Now they'd been replaced by formal portraits of racehorses inherited from Sarah's grandfather.

"This is not an easy visit for me," I said. "I have something to ask you. It's about Sarah." A surge of exhaustion suddenly went through me. I covered my eyes for a moment.

"Before you go any further, Mr. Pierce," said Dorothy, "with your questions and your dredging up old memories, I feel I ought to tell you that you come at a difficult time. Eugene had a stroke a few months ago and he is no longer working for his insurance company and my own health, as you may have noticed—"

"Let's not go crying the blues, Dot," said Eugene sharply. "Our troubles are no worse than anyone else's. Isn't that right, Fielding?"

"I don't know," I said. "I suppose not. Look—here's what I want to say. I have reason to believe that Sarah is still alive." I looked from Dorothy's face to Eugene's. I don't know what I expected them to look like or to say, but they were looking at me as if I were something on TV.

Finally Eugene smiled. He raised his arms over his head and stretched extravagantly. "What do you mean by alive? You mean in your heart or something?"

"I don't know," I said. "Maybe that's all there is to it. There's no sense going into it if you have no idea what I'm talking about. She hasn't contacted you in any way?"

"Contacted us? What are you talking about?"

"Like in a séance?" asked Dorothy, furrowing her brow.

"No. Or yes. I don't know, I don't know. On the telephone. By letter. In person."

I could see perfectly well in Eugene's eyes that he was now regarding me in a different way: he was trying to calculate as quickly as possible if I was dangerous. He had large, carnivorous teeth and he showed them to me as he leaned forward. "This is a lot of goddamned nonsense, sailor. And I'm asking you once, like a gentleman, to leave this house right now."

Dorothy was patting her husband's hand, petitioning for the right to speak. "Are you saying you've seen her?" she asked me.

"I think so."

"Good-bye, Mr. Pierce," said Eugene, rising from the sofa.

I got up as well. "How about her sisters? Have they mentioned anything about this?"

"No," said Dorothy. Her eyes suddenly shifted and I glanced behind me to see what she was looking at: it was the cup she'd left on the foyer table.

"I'd like your permission to go to the graveyard and have that vault opened up," I said, as reasonably as possible.

The sextet of boxer puppies were sleeping now; the emaciated-looking mother crept away from them, her tail dragging, head down. Eugene watched the dog as she staggered into the dining room and then he turned back toward me.

"How can you come into this house and speak this way in front of my wife?" he asked. "You got your head up your ass? Is that it? You on dope or something? You think I didn't see you when we buried her? Sitting in the back of our church with your eyes half closed and your big ugly mouth hanging open? It just so happens, sailor boy, that I took a six-week course with the New Orleans Police Department on how to spot drug abusers so it's been your misfortune to run into someone who's aware of all the signs, all the little tricks."

"I know what it's like, Mr. Pierce," said Dorothy, "to love someone and lose them."

"Oh," said Eugene, "so we're back to that, are we?"

"All I'm saying is I understand his pain."

"Well, don't be so goddamned understanding, Dot." He pointed his finger at me. "If you get anywhere near that cemetery, any-where near where my family is buried, I'll have you arrested."

"Don't you care?" I asked. "I'm here to tell you the woman in that car wasn't Sarah. The body was so destroyed—no one could tell. Anyhow, no one stopped to think it could be someone else." I stopped and looked at Sarah's mother. She was staring at me, her face utterly passive, helpless, her mind blasted beyond any real usefulness. And as I paused I realized I had been shouting. My voice was not the voice of a strong person. Eugene was walking toward the table upon which was their telephone—a sleek, gray,

push-button phone with a built-in note pad. He rested his hand
on it and looked at me, nodding.

"OK, OK," I said. "You don't have to call anyone."

"You'd be doing yourself a big favor if you got out of my
house," he said.

"I'll go. I don't have time for any trouble." I put my hands
up, as if trying to appease a violent child. "But Jesus Christ, don't
you care? Don't you want it to be true?"

"It doesn't matter what I want," he said.

"She is your daughter."

"She was a fool," he said, and with that he picked up the
receiver and started dialing.

I walked the streets in the cool rain until I found St. Charles
Avenue and a taxicab. The driver took me to the airport and from
there I called Washington, D.C. I was phoning a fellow named
Richard Donahue, whom I had gotten to know a few years ago
while the investigation of the Minneapolis bombing was still on-
going.

Rich Donahue was an FBI agent. He and his partner, John
W. Walton, had been in contact with me off and on over the course
of a couple of years. The bombing was an act of terrorism and
they seemed reasonably anxious to find and arrest whoever had
been responsible for it. But they knew and I knew too that the
killers were probably no longer in the country and that the Immigration records would be of no use since there was no telling
when they had come to the United States, or if they had come
with false documents, or if they had gone through Immigration
at all. It was not a case receiving the attention I felt it deserved.
There may have been points in the development of the crime where
the paths of the assassins and the path of U.S. officials crossed.
Who knew? We had clearly lent a hand in the destruction of
Allende; perhaps our policy extended to the murder of Allende
ministers, no matter where they were, or with whom; or perhaps
the policy, once begun, knew no logical ending place, but just

gobbled up victims like a shark in a feeding frenzy. Neither Donahue nor Walton found much usefulness in my theories or my doubts, though they were always solicitous of my opinions and seemed to like drawing me out—as if they were jotting down notes for a future dossier, if I were ever to dare to become an enemy of the state. The truth was, I liked them. They were methodical, firm, seemingly uninterested in the ephemera of modern life—no fancy clothes, no up-to-the-minute attitudes, nice solid personal lives, modest homes with comfortable furniture, a sense of virtue, at peace with themselves. Walton had been in the beginning stages of multiple sclerosis; a year ago I got a card from him saying he was retiring from the FBI. "I'll be home watching 'Ironsides,' " the card said, "but Richie will still be handling the Minneapolis case and one day we'll have our man. Keep well and if you're ever in Potomac, Maryland, give me a holler."

I never was in Potomac and I never gave him a holler. Instead, I called Richard Donahue, first at his office, where the phone rang a dozen times without anyone's answering, and then at his home. It was early afternoon. A child answered the phone. A TV was blaring in the background. I asked to speak to Mr. Donahue and then Richie was on the phone. He didn't seem at all surprised to hear from me. I told him I was in New Orleans, that my plane to Washington was leaving in a few minutes, that I'd be there in two and a half hours, and that I wanted to talk to him about the Minneapolis bombing. I heard him snap his fingers and an instant later the TV set was turned off. Then he said he would meet me at his office.

A taxi took me from National Airport to 9th and Pennsylvania. I'd had nothing to eat that day but a cup of Delta coffee and a bag of Planters Peanuts. The sky was low, soft, and dark; the traffic seemed imbued with mystery beneath the indigo clouds. One by one the headlights came on, as if each auto was in its turn enchanted.

The J. Edgar Hoover Building found itself surrounded by

Washington's tiny pornography district, a little Toonerville of trashy books and peep shows and movie theaters showing double features with titles like *Box Lunch* and *Spurts Illustrated*. The headquarters were designed under Hoover's guidance and what was created was a contemporary fortress, a building that ended up looking like an enormous, gloomy Motor Vehicles Bureau run by civil servants who lived in dread the populace might come storming in to steal license plates. The Hoover Building was built without columns because Hoover thought Soviet agents might hide behind the columns. The windows closest to the ground were sufficiently high to be unattackable by thrown stones.

When my taxi pulled next to the curb I opened the door and it hit the cement. The FBI headquarters were so massively heavy that all the streets around it were sinking: the distance from curb to street had tripled in ten years.

I stood before the building. I heard the taxi pull away and after that there was a long deep roll of thunder. I seemed not to be able to move. The doors to the colorless building opened up and a big, fleshy, redheaded agent walked out, buttoning his raincoat, whistling to himself. He looked like a small-time college football player and he noticed me lurking in front of the headquarters. He gave me a quick, visual frisk and decided I was all right. He walked right by me, not so close as to make contact but close enough to let me know. Those guys all had a hunter's knack for dominating prey. I listened to his footsteps disappear and then I was still there, still standing in front of headquarters, unable to get a step closer.

And it was then I realized I would not be going in. Agent Donahue was probably already at his desk, with his boy's blue Crayola drawing behind him—Sean, yes, that was the boy's name, Sean—and the inscription proclaiming that "My Daddy is the Smurfiest." Why had he suggested we meet here and not at his house? Or in a coffee shop, a Roy Rogers? They were probably developing a case I knew nothing about, following leads, making connections, endlessly spinning out possibilities as complex as the circuitry of the brain. Until this moment, standing before that monolith with the thunder rolling around the soft obsidian sky like a madman in a padded cell, I had believed that I could walk into a place like this—a DA's office, a precinct—and have nothing to hide, nothing to fear. But all that had suddenly changed.

I had not come here to tell them Sarah was alive but to ask them what tests had been run to identify the body they'd taken out of that white Volvo in Minneapolis. But what guarantee had I that it would stop there? Donahue had specified that we meet in his office; clearly this was not a social call. He would want to know why I was asking. If they had developed any intelligence about Sarah or about the people she was working with, something I might say might fit in, or serve as a lead.

I didn't dare speak to them. Suddenly every person inside that building was my mortal enemy and it really did break my heart. It was just so unbearably sad to me.

And yet, even as I backed away and then turned on my heel, walking faster and faster, until my breath was coming in rapid, jagged gasps, I knew there was another reason I was fleeing. If Donahue could somehow show me real proof that it *had* been Sarah in that car, that meant I had burst through the membrane separating the rational from the irrational, and once you're through it, you are running free. I didn't want to know I had lost my mind. I didn't want anyone to prove to me that she couldn't possibly be alive.

I don't remember where I spent that night. It was in a hotel. The next morning, Sunday, I was on a flight to Minneapolis. The day was frigid and bright; the sky was a high blue tent pitched on poles of ice. I had only one more stop to make: I had learned that Steven Mileski was working for the state of Minnesota as a Catholic chaplain in a place called the Lake Omega Home for Older Boys, which was a sort of year-round camp for boys between eleven and eighteen. But the money had run out quickly and now Lake Omega was all that existed of the original impulse, and it was left with taking care of boys with problems ranging from retardation to petty larceny. A year before, *Newsweek* had run a story about Lake Omega calling it something like "Little Houses on the Prairie for Kids at the End of the Road." Accompanying the story was a photo of a staff meeting and sitting near the head of the table, right next to the mustachioed, ski-sweatered director, was Mileski, his long dark beard looking as heavy as a beaver's tail, his eyes so deeply black they showed on the other side of the page.

Lake Omega was a half-hour drive from the Minneapolis–St. Paul airport, near a town of Delft blue silos and yellow clapboard farmhouses called Center. The cab driver got directions to the place people in Center called the School. The roads were straight, the turns were sharp, the icy stubble in the cornfields stretched out and slowly undulated on to infinity. On either side of the macadam, the snow was piled three feet high. The driver was not a talker; he was content to drive and listen to the Andy Williams and Skitch Henderson on the radio and I was sitting in the backseat with my hands on my knees, looking out the window, with my mind feeling as impenetrable to the plow of reason as those fields that came flashing by, flashing by, and which were now giving way to dark clumps of forestland. Finally, we came to a sign announcing THE LAKE OMEGA SCHOOL—AN EXPERIMENT IN SUC-CESSFUL LIVING. The sign was burned into wood, lovingly crafted, rustic. Next to it, however, was an orange and black NO TRES-PASSING sign bought in the local hardware store. The narrow road turning in toward the school was plowed, but access to it was blocked by a chain-link fence hung between two giant maples. The gate was locked.

The cab driver stopped his car and turned around to face me. He had a long, soft face, droopy, rather mad-looking eyes, jug ears. "Do you have the key, sir?"

"I'll walk from here," I said. I reached for my bag and realized with a sudden lurch that I'd left it in the Minneapolis airport, or on the plane, or in the Washington airport, or in my hotel . . . It hardly mattered: my credit cards were in my jacket. I paid the driver and gave him a correct tip. "Can you wait here?" I asked him as I stepped out of the cab.

"I have to go back to the city," he said.

"I won't be very long. An hour at most."

"I got to get back to the city," he said. He opened his eyes wider for emphasis and they became perfectly egg-shaped.

"Look here," I said. "I'm a U.S. congressman from Illinois. And this is important."

He looked at me more closely, bringing me into focus with a few rapid blinks. I looked more like a fugitive from justice than a congressman. "Are you a Democrat or Republican?" he asked.

I only wanted to give the answer that would have the best result. "I'm a Republican," I said.

He shook his head sadly. "I'm late as it is. I have to get back," he said. And with that, he reached behind and closed the door. He made a U-turn. I stood there and watched as he drove away.

I climbed the fence and flipped over. The air was cold and dry; each inhale seemed to X-ray my respiratory system. It was a winter several notches more intense than the winter I'd left. I was wearing the comfortable brown walking shoes I'd had on since the campaign had begun and the earth seemed to pump waves of its own frigid reality straight through my soles. I dug my hands into my coat pocket, hunched my shoulders, pressed on. The road wound its way through the woods; the low boughs of the conifers were bent down to the ground from the weight of the snow they held.

It was a still, windless day; I could hear the busyness of the birds farther into the woods. I walked for perhaps a quarter mile and with each step I expected to be apprehended. But there was no sign of anyone. Finally, I came to Lake Omega itself, covered with ice and tracked-over snow. The sun was straight overhead and it seemed to tilt forward like a face over a crib. The sky was seamless and the trees around the lake were motionless, as if they had been sewn like the pattern on a sweater—pine tree, pine tree, pine tree.

I followed the road around the lake and then off to the right.

I came to the cabins where the boys and their overseers lived: cedar-shingled bunkhouses, each with a name over the door like Sunrise House or Rigor Hill, each with small curtainless windows, each with a potbellied stove hooked into a cinder-block chimney, each with eight narrow, militarily neat beds, each empty of people. I passed the basketball court. Someone had neglected to take down the nets and they hung there like thickly frozen lace, reflecting the sunlight.

In front of me was a large white building, with a sloping roof and a wraparound porch. It looked like a hunting lodge. There were cross-country skis and snowshoes resting against the walls and next to the wooden steps was a sign that said LAKE OMEGA HALL—BE RIGHT ON OR GET RIGHT OUT. And behind Lake Omega Hall was a smaller A-frame, painted brown, with double doors and one large, rather homemade-looking stained-glass window. Through the stillness of the winter air, I heard sounds coming from the A-frame and I walked toward it, and as I did I realized I was walking over the slight icy indentations of hundreds of footprints.

The double doors were opened and I walked into what was Lake Omega's assembly hall as well as its chapel. Sixty or so boys sat in gunmetal-gray folding chairs, and as I saw the backs of their heads it seemed they all had identical Spartan haircuts. Near the door was a cast-iron wood stove, bending and curling the air above it with immense waves of heat. I quietly closed the doors behind me. Not one head turned. The attention of everyone was on the makeshift pulpit, where Father Mileski was standing, wearing black trousers, black shirt, collarless, with a down vest, bright green, completing the picture. In the last row there was an empty chair on the aisle. I quickly sat down in it, next to a broad-faced boy about seventeen, with light hair, blue eyes, acne. He glanced at me as I sat down. "Hi," he said, with a quick smile. I said Hi back to him and he clicked his attention back toward Mileski while reaching over to shake my hand.

"And when we suffer," Mileski was saying, with his hands folded before him, standing without gesture, letting his eyes and his voice do it all, "when we suffer. As we have. As we do. As we *shall*. Do we suffer alone? Does suffering come and—*single* us out? No. *No*. NO! We are never so close to him as we are when we suffer. But what does that mean? Does that tell us to—to get high, to get drunk and drive Daddy's new car into a tree? Hey, Dad, like wow, I did it to be nearer to Jesus Christ our Savior. No. Of course not. We have to try and find our way. We have to try and live good lives. But we do it with the sacred knowledge that we *can't*. With the sacred knowledge that we will fall, we will fail, we will make a total royal mess out of just about everything. He does not reward our success. He rewards our *effort*. Let us harness our energies. Let us *use* some of that fantastic power and invention we've been using to foul up our lives, all those—*calories* we've been burning to make ourselves miserable. Let's take just half of it and use it for making ourselves happy. And peaceful." He paused and looked around at the faces before him. He took a deep breath and unclasped his hands. "I love you. And God loves you. He gave you his only Son. He let us nail his Son onto a cross because it was the only way he had to tell us how much he loves us. He has given us this earth. He has given us our lives. Let's not screw it up. Amen."

At the end of the sermon, everyone stood. I stood as well; I hadn't realized until coming into the warmth of the chapel how frozen I was. My face itched as it thawed. A boy standing to the left of Mileski began singing a hymn I had never heard before and everyone joined in. It was about wandering and finding your way home. There were lambs, there were shepherds, there were babbling brooks. It was awful. When the song finally ended, we all sat down. Mileski looked out at us. I slumped further down in my chair. He shook his head. "Guess what, guys? I don't have anything more to say." He clasped his hands together and placed them near his chin, bowing his head, closing his eyes. He stood like that for a few long moments until he said "Amen." And we said Amen and then it was all over. Almost in perfect unison, the boys and the staff stood up and began filing out.

I stood next to the stove. Each person who went by me tried

to make eye contact. Since slinging the law around in Chicago, I had somehow forgotten that boys in trouble could be this white. They were blond, Nordic, well-built kids; they looked like they ought to be attending hockey camp or playing in the school band. Finally a staff member walked by me and stopped dead in his tracks. He was a portly guy in his forties, with a Beatle haircut and rimless glasses.

"Who are you?" he asked, without the slightest attempt to put a friendly inflection on it.

"I'm a friend of Steven Mileski's," I said. "I came from Chicago to see him."

As soon as I was questioned by a staff member, the once friendly faces of the boys turned suddenly suspicious, as if now that my stock was sinking they needed to disassociate from me.

"Is he expecting you?" asked the staff member.

"I think so."

"You *think* so?"

"Yes," I said. "He is."

"Would you mind saying how you got in here? Do you have a visitor's pass?"

"No, I don't. I was in the area and I just came in."

The staff member nodded. He was satisfied to have proven his point, but he was uncertain where to go from there. I could guess from how he was leaning that he was considering taking me by the arm: his job had made him take the exercise of a certain petty authority for granted. "I think the best way to handle this is for me to bring you to Father Steve," the staff member said, narrowing his eyes and nodding in a way, I suppose, that was meant to look somehow threatening.

Mileski was surrounded by ten or so boys. A couple of staff members were standing nearby, looking on like secret service agents. One of the boys was saying, "Hey man, but if it's in my head, it's in my head, right?"

"There's a Frank Zappa song," Mileski answered. "Before your time."

"I know Zappa, man," the boy said. He was large, horse-faced, ponytailed.

"Good. Zappa says: 'What's the ugliest part of your body? Some say it's your nose, some say your toes. I say it's your mind.' " All the boys laughed and Mileski smiled with real pleasure. He reached out and put his hand behind the boy's head and said, "I knew you'd like that. You look like Zappa anyhow."

"Excuse me, Father Steve," said my escort. "Someone's here who says he's a friend of yours."

Mileski turned to face us. I was holding myself rigid, not knowing how he would respond to seeing me. It seemed to take him a moment to fix upon who exactly I was: I was far out of context standing in that iced-in homemade chapel. But then his eyes widened and even through the opaque mesh of his beard I could see his broad smile. "Fielding!" he said, his voice a sonic boom. "Fielding!" He threw his arms out to the side and walked slowly, ceremoniously toward me. I felt rather frail and unsubstantial as I watched his ursine bulk approach me, slowly filling my entire field of vision. And now his arms were around me and he was pressing me into his massive chest. "What a wonderful surprise," he said. And then, in a much quieter voice, almost a whisper into my ear, he said, "It just breaks my heart, Fielding. But it's so good to see you."

I clapped him on the back, like a vanquished wrestler pounding the canvas. "I've got to talk to you, Steven. Is there someplace we can go?"

"Sure, definitely. We'll sit, talk. Just let me finish up here, OK?" He turned back to the boys and staff members, the hard core of his following at Lake Omega. They seemed as if they were used to looking up to him—it was a safe sort of admiration because not one of them was interested in or willing to live his life and so they didn't really have to compare themselves to him. He was their unicorn. "Well," he said, facing them and rubbing his hands together, "I guess that about wraps it up." They smiled understanding smiles. Mileski saluted them and then turned on his heel and threw his arm around my shoulder. "My cabin's just across the way," he said. "You can join me for Twinkies and tea."

His cabin was the size of a small garage. It was painted the same dark pure blue that the farmers in Center chose for their silos. Inside, there was a bed, a table with four wooden chairs, an old shabby carpet, a wicker bookcase. In the center was a potbellied stove with a small stack of split wood and a bucket of kindling next to it. Stuck in one corner was a two-burner gas range that seemed more suitable for a weekend camping trip than an actual domestic life. As soon as we came in, Mileski threw a couple of pieces of wood into the wood stove and then lit the gas range with a match and put on an old cast-iron kettle that was already filled with water. I stood near the door and looked on.

"You know," he said, crouching down a little so he could see the flame beneath the kettle, "I've been sort of expecting you."

"Why?"

"I got a letter from Tim Stanton. Just two days ago. He told me that you appeared in his church. He didn't know what to make of it." Mileski turned and faced me. His smile was so broad, so easy and confident. "He said you seemed very upset, but you couldn't, wouldn't, talk about it. He always had a special fondness for you, as you know."

"No. That never occurred to me." I gestured toward the chairs and table. "Do you mind?"

"That's what they're for," he said, with a cheerful shrug. He watched me sit down with a curious sort of attention. When I was seated, Mileski strode across the room and sat across from me.

"It sure is good to see you, Fielding. As you see, I've been exiled to this little gulag. But. I'm trying to make the most of it. I'm not getting any support at all from the Church. Every two weeks I get a paycheck with the lovely seal of the State of Minnesota on it. All the Church does is allow me to do this. But. Things are changing. I may be able to serve as curate to a pretty interesting pastor in Joliet, Illinois." He snorted and shook his head. "I know what you're thinking. But after this place, Joliet will feel like the Bahamas." He ran his massive hand through his thick hair. I wondered momentarily if it was a nervous gesture. "Of course," he said, "you've had a lot of experience sending people to Joliet."

"How do you mean?"

"In your work. Isn't that where the prison is? Don't you have men sent down there in your work?" He furrowed his eyebrows and jutted his chin out, in that slightly humorous way people do when they mean to say, Are you listening to me?

"I'm running for Congress now, Steven."

He reached across the table and squeezed my shoulder. "That's wonderful, Fielding! I couldn't be happier for you." He nodded his head and squinted. "It's just like you planned."

"Yeah, well, we'll see."

"Father Stanton mentioned nothing about this in his letter. I wonder if he knows. Did you tell him when you saw him?"

"I don't remember. To be honest with you, I barely remember anything I said to him."

"What were you doing there? He said it was the middle of the night."

"Following Sarah. I saw her in a restaurant. I was with some reporters, my campaign manager—"

"Sarah? You mean . . . *our* Sarah?"

"That's right. Anyhow, I was sitting there. And I happened to look over and there she was."

"I'm not getting this. What are you trying to say?"

"Look, Steven. I mean, *Father Steve.* I haven't had a night's sleep in . . . I don't know how long. I've been flying all over the country trying to put this together. I haven't eaten. OK? I am trying to get this straight. Don't fuck around with me. Can we at least have that? Do not fuck around with me. It's too late in the game for that."

"What game, Fielding? You're ranting."

"I know I am. I can hear myself. For pity's sake, Steven. Help me."

"I want to help you, Fielding. But what do you want?" The water came to a boil and the kettle began to shudder over the gas jet. Mileski got up and turned off the flame.

"Just stop holding the truth back from me. That's all over now. It's just completely over. I want to know everything that happened. And I have to know where she is."

Mileski folded his arms over his chest and rocked back on his heels. I had always considered that a signal of an impending falseness. "You want to know where who is?" asked Mileski. "Are you . . . do you mean Sarah?" The incredulity in his voice lifted me out of my chair. I raised my hands over my head and brought them slamming down onto the table. The table leapt toward me, touching me on the legs. I tossed it onto its side and raced toward Mileski, reaching up and grabbing his throat with my stiff, outstretched fingers.

"Tell me where she is," I said through my teeth. I felt my own saliva on my chin. Mileski's hands were on my chest, pushing me back, but for the moment I was too strong for him. Now his hands were on mine, trying to unclasp them from his windpipe. "Where is she?" I screamed into his face.

"With God, Fielding," he said, choking. He ripped my hands off him and pushed me back hard, sending me stumbling, trying to keep my balance. "You crazy bastard," he said, rubbing his throat and shaking his head. "What are you trying to do?"

"I just want you to tell me where she is. I know she's alive. I've known it for weeks. Here." I put my hand over my heart. "And I saw her. And then she called me. She explained the whole thing to me. That it was Seny in the car. But then we were cut off before she could tell me where she is. And you see I have to find her."

"You don't get it, do you, Fielding. You never have. If what you're saying is true. If she is alive. And if I was aware of it, in on the plot, then why would I ever tell you about it? You were never really a part of what we were doing. You didn't understand it. It seemed—I don't know. *Inconvenient*. You mostly cared that someone might associate you with us. You felt only fear, Fielding. And you bred it in others. You wanted to take her confidence away. You tried to wedge your ego needs between her soul and her faith. You had no idea what she was."

"I love her."

"That doesn't give you a special claim. So many people loved her."

"Do you want me to get on my knees and beg you?"

"I think the real question is, Do you want to get on your knees and beg me?"

"You are so secure, Steven," I said. I moved toward him. He tensed slightly. I forced my body to relax and he relaxed, too. I stepped still closer to him. It was working. "I am much, much smarter than you are."

"I agree with you there," said Mileski. "You're brainy."

"You believe in resurrections. You believe in miracles. You believe in the fucking Red Sea parting and talking snakes and virgin births. But you haven't shown the slightest interest or curiosity in what I've been telling you here today. And that can mean only one thing."

"Yeah? What do you think it means?" he said. There was a slight film of huskiness in his voice. He was working too hard to keep his gaze steady.

"It has to mean you knew all along. You know she's alive. None of this is news to you. *And* you know where she is." I gave him a moment to respond but when he shook his head no that was all the waiting I could do. I lunged at him with all my desperate and insufficient strength. But he had at least sixty pounds on me and one of his fists was the size of both of mine. He twisted away from me, reared back, and hit me square in the face. There was a moment of wild, scarlet, throbbing pain and then all consciousness was gone like a dragon swallowing its own tail.

15

It was either evening or night. I really didn't know. The sky was black granite when my cab pulled in front of my apartment. I looked up. The lights were on and someone was keeping watch out of the window. The curtain wavered and a human form stepped out of view. When I paid the driver and added an acceptable tip to the fare, I was left with twenty-five cents to my name. It was weirdly exhilarating to be that broke. It made me remember a time in Boston, sixteen or seventeen years before, when I was in college and momentarily without a nighttime job. I had been plunged immediately into absolute pennilessness, as if the entire enterprise of my life was built on ice so thin that it wasn't really ice at all but more of a cool sheen. And until I got the job as night manager of the pool hall on Central Square (where jug-band musicians played nineball with local Irish hitters) I was reduced to patrolling pay phones in search of forgotten refunds, a degrading but strangely habit-forming enterprise that had me walking ten miles a day through that anemic Boston spring.

As I reached the third-floor landing, the door to my apartment opened up. I saw the wedge of light cast itself against the wall and then into that wedge came the shape of a human shadow. I stopped, holding onto the banister, and waited. I could hear my own heart beating, clanging away like a hammer against a radiator. The head of the shadow turned and then the shadow began to grow, and bend, and then it was indistinct, just a darkness. Whoever it was was coming forward, heading toward the railing to look down. I stood there, waiting. I looked down at my shoes. There was a latticework of white snow and salt stain on them. And then I looked up again and saw Caroline's face peering down at me.

"What happened to you?" she said, her voice a braid of annoyance and compassion.

"I'm all right," I said. "It looks worse than it is."

"Now you sound like Danny," she said. "Well, come on. We've been hysterical wondering where you were."

I came up to the landing and she put her arms around me. She winced as she looked into my face. "You're bleeding," she said, touching the whiskery indentation between my lower lip and my chin. "What hit you?"

"A priest," I said.

"A priest?"

"Who else is in there?" I said, looking at the half-open door to my apartment.

"Tony, Isaac, Juliet, and Dad."

"Oh Jesus, Caroline. Dad?"

"I'm sorry. Blame yourself, though. I called home, thinking maybe you'd gone there. Then he flipped out and flew out here. He got here two hours ago." Caroline sensed me about to back up and she caught me by the arm. "Come on. Whatever's broken, we'll fix."

"How is he?"

"Dad? He's said maybe two words to me. He's engrossed with Isaac. I think they're having a competition over who can take credit for the wonder that is Fielding Pierce." She tugged at me but I resisted and I gathered her close and held on to her with a desperation that hadn't much to do with what we normally call love.

"It's falling in on every side, Caroline," I said. "She's out there waiting for me."

"Oh God, Fielding," she said, holding me close. "You've got to stop this. You just have to let it go."

I shook my head but didn't say any more. There was very little point after all. We walked into the apartment.

"Tony!" Caroline called out.

At the sound of her voice, Tony came quickly down the narrow hall connecting the living room with the entrance foyer. He looked sloppy, unfocused; he was wearing a black and white T-shirt printed to look somehow like a piano keyboard. He was holding a glass of beer in one hand, a cigar in the other. "Caroline?" he said, with some real urgency, as if in his scheme of things she was always in imminent danger. Then he saw me and stopped. He took a swallow of his beer, a toke off his cigar. "Where the fuck have you been? You made me look like shit."

"That's something one man can never do for another, Tony," I said.

"Fielding," said Caroline, in her older sister accent.

"Why didn't you tell me before you wanted to blow this fucking election? I would have at least covered my ass."

"What's with this guy and all the excreta imagery?" I said to Caroline, putting my arm around her waist. (The truth was, I was wobbling and didn't want it to show.)

Just then Dad appeared, standing at the far end of the hallway with his legs astride and his hands on his hips, an aging colossus. "Are you OK?" he said, his full dark voice floating down the hall like ectoplasm.

"I'm fine," I said, breathing deeply, coming toward him. I could see him registering the disarray, the panic, the lack of direction, and even the slight blur of failure coming off me. He swallowed, looked me up and down, and then opened his arms to me. I strode toward him and accepted his embrace. His muscles tensed; like a high-school boy, he didn't want me to feel any softness.

Caroline, Dad, Tony, and I walked into the living room. Isaac was on the sofa and as soon as he saw me he reached for the phone. He quickly punched up the number and said, "He's here. I'll talk to you later." Then he hung up, crossed his legs, folded his arms over his chest. "Were you in some sort of automobile accident?" Isaac asked.

"No," I said. "I'm fine."

"You could have called," he said.

"Yes, that's right," I said. "I could have done a lot of things."

"Oh-oh," my father said, softly, involuntarily. He could feel things falling apart; he couldn't understand how I could talk to a man like Isaac in this way.

"Look," I said, "if we're going to talk, plan, then I have to get out of these clothes. I'll be right back."

Without waiting for an answer, I walked out of the living room and into the bedroom. I tore off my shirt. What I really wanted was a bath, but I couldn't make them wait that long. I opened the closet. Juliet's clothes were not *gone*, but it seemed there were fewer of them. They had been pushed to one side of the closet and I was certain if I had picked through them I would have discovered that some were missing. A shirt, a blouse, just enough to sustain the separation. And then a few days later, I would probably notice a few other things missing. And that's how it would go, until she was entirely moved out.

I went back into the living room with a fresh shirt on. I was barefoot and I saw my feet had been stained by my thirty-six hours in damp maroon socks. Everyone was standing around like rejects from a wax museum. "OK, I'm back," I said, rubbing my hands together. "Tell me what I've missed and then let's get this rolling again."

The next evening at eight, ten hours before the polls opened, Bertelli and I met before something called the Greater Hyde Park Citizens' Forum. The people managing my campaign and the folks running his had arranged for the mini-confrontation about a week before, when Bertelli's campaign was really taking hold. We were still leading at that time and Tony and the others took a gamble; but now Bertelli had pulled even or perhaps was a bit ahead, so my staff was weak with relief that the meeting had been organized.

The meeting was originally scheduled to take place at Ida Noyes Hall, one of the University buildings. But as the evening approached there were indications of twice, even three times the turnout they'd been expecting, so near the last minute the meeting was moved to a defunct movie theater in the center of the district, a gaudy, naive place called the Damascus. Sarah and I had gone to see *The French Connection* the week before the Damascus became the ornate tax loss it was to remain.

I was driven over by Tony, with Caroline next to him in the front seat. I was wedged in back with Isaac on one side of me and my father on the other. My father sat bolt upright, with his hands folded on his lap; Isaac had his legs crossed and he held his chin in his hand, looking glumly out the window.

"What do you think, Isaac?" asked my father. "Should he come on strong or act like an incumbent?"

"A little of both, I'd say, Eddie," answered Isaac, without looking around.

Dad shrugged and winked at me. "I see you're in good hands," he said.

"I'll take the alley around," Tony said. "That way we can slip in the back entrance."

"Absolutely not," said Isaac. He sounded weirdly languid, as if he'd taken sedatives. "This isn't a stage show. We'll walk in like everybody else."

"I think it's going to be a zoo, Isaac," Tony said.

"I don't understand you, Tony," said Isaac. "Have you been organizing Fielding's appearances so as to *minimize* contact between him and the voters? That's a rather unique concept."

"Tony's been working very hard, Isaac," said Caroline. "I don't think he deserves that kind of remark."

"I'm so relieved the Pierces are here to put everything straight." Isaac sighed. He began swatting the end of his nose with his fingertip, rapidly, back and forth, like a boxer working out on a punching bag.

"Who do you figure comes to a meeting like this?" asked my father. None of us knew whom he was asking and so no one answered. "Isaac," he then added.

Isaac stopped swatting the end of his nose and now was stroking it, as if to revive it after the punishment it had endured. "Who?" he asked. "Well, our people who've worked in the campaign. And precinct captains who'll be getting the vote out. And poll watchers.

And press, of course. And the membership of the Hyde Park Forum. They've got five hundred members on paper."

"But what I'm asking," said Dad, "is, you know, what about just regular rank-and-file *people*? I'm getting the feeling there's a large uncommitted vote out there."

"Where?" asked Isaac, suddenly turning his head with a kind of birdlike quickness. His eyes caught the light of a passing car.

"In the district," said my father. "People, just people."

"I mean, where did you get the feeling there was a large un-committed vote? Do you have some information the rest of us lack?"

There was silence in the car. Caroline slipped off her shoe and scratched the bottom of her foot—her most timeworn nervous habit.

Finally Dad touched my arm. "Don't you think there's a lot of undecided voters out there, Fielding?"

I didn't answer. I was suddenly and awfully aware of some-thing inside me. It felt as if my fear were patrolling my body, looking to grab at the lever controlling my nerves. And now it was getting close, closer; now it found it at last and had its hand upon it. I started to tremble.

"Don't you, Fielding?" asked Dad again. There was a burr of discouragement in his voice.

"Yes, I guess so," I said.

"That is just completely contrary to what we already know," said Isaac. If he'd taken a drug it was wearing off; his voice was sharp again. "I'd say there was at most ten percent undecided now."

"Does that mean we win or lose?" asked Caroline.

"It means we win, unless Fielding loses all ten percent."

Dad looked away. He blinked rapidly and folded his arms over his chest. I could feel him retreating into himself; his heavy feelings scraped like enormous pieces of furniture.

"I look at it like this," I said. "Every vote is essentially undecided until it's cast. I don't take anything for granted and I don't give anything up."

"The homos will never vote for you," said Tony, with a laugh.

"Perhaps they will," I said. "I hope so. I think I deserve their support."

My father smiled and nodded his head, very pleased with me, as if I'd said something that might make its way into some future biography. My knee knocked into his and he glanced down; I was shaking. He pursed his lips; he judged people as if he were a samurai when they betrayed weakness, not knowing how often his own showed through.

"I'm up for this, Dad," I said, pressing down on my legs to calm them down. I closed my eyes and took a deep breath. Tony turned the corner and started applying the brakes. We were there. I kept my eyes closed. It had crossed my mind a thousand times during the day that Sarah might very well be in the audience tonight and now that we were here I was all but certain of it.

"I know," he said, in as intimate a voice as he could manage. "You always come through when the chips are down."

We walked into the old theater. There was no time to look, no time to remember. Isaac was at my side, Tony was behind me. The Hyde Park Forum people had set up a literature table, selling pamphlets which were transcripts of the various debates they had sponsored. Isaac had me by the elbow, guiding me toward a side entrance to the auditorium, as if I were a blind virtuoso. Falling in with us was Henry Shamansky. He was with his wife, a dark-haired woman with a raspberry mouth and a pixie haircut. "Give 'em hell, Fielding," he said, balling his hand into a fist and grimacing, showing his square, nicotine-tinted teeth. Then came Sonny Marchi, the governor's son-in-law, who'd been using my campaign as a part of his never-ending pretense of having something to do. He looked certifiable tonight: his hair was slicked back; he smelled of coconut-scented hair conditioner, and the lapels of his plaid sports jacket were festooned with my campaign buttons. "Good to see you, good to see you," Isaac chanted to Sonny, meaning, I guessed, that Isaac took Marchi's presence as symbolic of the governor's surviving good wishes.

We walked through the lobby, into the theater itself, and down a side aisle toward the steps to the stage. The red velvet curtains from the old movie days still hung, still somber with dust, still gathered up by gaudy sashes that looked like swatches of Turkish pantaloons. The seats were just about filled. I noticed in the front row Adele sitting with Lucille Jackson. Lucille had Adele's attention like a moth on a pin; I could just about see the color draining out of Adele's face as Lucille jabbed her broad ebony finger toward the faint cleft in Adele's chin. There were three small wooden tables set up on the stage, each with a glass and a pitcher of water on it.

"Not yet," Isaac said, tugging at my elbow.

I stopped, nodded. I didn't want to be the first one up on the stage any more than Isaac wanted me to. And despite the speed of my devolution from young politician to dog howling at the moon, I felt a spasm of true surprise that I would have even considered taking my seat before Bertelli and the moderator. I had always assumed I had an innate sense of the best light in which to put myself, and any fool knew it would make me look eager and ineffectual to be sitting at my desk like a schoolboy waiting for the others. Isaac held on to my elbow and was saying something to me and I was standing there with one foot up on the stairs leading to the stage, and it must have seemed we were engaged in one of those quick, canny chats, one of those instant Yaltas, in which the powerful divide the spoils of the world.

A few moments later, Dr. Paul Brewer, who taught political science at the University and who had been named moderator for the evening, came down the center aisle. He was a small, stooped man, with shaggy brown hair and heavy spectacles. He wore a three-piece tweed suit and a spotted bow tie, and as he came toward the stage his large head bobbed up and down as if one of his legs were six inches shorter than the other. He bounced up to the stage and took his place at the middle table, setting his briefcase down next to his chair with a thud that was somehow as commanding as a judge's rap of the gavel.

Moments after that, Bertelli appeared on the opposite side of the theater. He was with a towering, slender black man with a small pointy goatee, à la Eric McDonald. The aide was holding a legal pad and was speaking with obvious animation. Bertelli walked with his small hands folded over his enormous taut belly. His eyes were hooded. He wore a voluminous brown corduroy jacket and a white turtleneck sweater.

Bertelli took the stage. He strolled over to Brewer and the two men shook hands. Then Bertelli shaded his eyes against the white footlights and looked out into the audience. When he found whoever he was looking for he smiled and made one of those annoying peppy pointing gestures, like a has-been in a Las Vegas floorshow. There was no need to give him the stage by himself and so I made it up the steps and walked over to Brewer.

"Hello, Dr. Brewer," I said, stepping around Bertelli, ignoring him, "I don't know if you remember, but I audited your class on constitutional crises six years ago, when I was in law school."

"Of course I remember you, Mr. Pierce," he said. His eyes were vague; he glanced down as if embarrassed.

"Well, Fielding," said Bertelli, clapping his hand on my shoulder. The velvet glove of fat-boy conviviality barely covered the iron fist of his animosity toward me. Since Bertelli had no record to attack I hadn't really spent much time on him during the campaign. When the audience was right for it, I attacked the Republicans, but Bertelli couldn't have taken that very hard. He wasn't much of a Republican—on his third marriage, with all those years squeezing out espresso to Sunday morning bohemians. He had bumbled into this race with some idea of himself as a token candidate whose main function was to keep the hinges of democracy oiled by making it a two-man race. But he had had luck and talent and, despite its seeming at first that my nomination was tantamount to an official appointment to the office, I had run a shitty enough campaign to make my defeat very possible. Now with just hours to go I could tell by the weight of Bertelli's hand on me that he wanted to win at least as much as I did. Perhaps more.

I took my seat, Bertelli took his. He poured water into his glass and drank it. The lights in the auditorium dimmed; the audience, the voters, the world, sank back into the shadows.

"Good evening, voters," said Dr. Brewer, folding his hands, "and welcome to this special, oh, I suppose . . . *town meeting* organized by the Greater Hyde Park Citizens' Forum. We have with us tonight the Democratic and Republican candidates for tomorrow's special congressional election. Both candidates have generously agreed to make this a freewheeling evening and to give us all an opportunity to ask whatever questions we wish to and to discover for ourselves what the real differences are behind the various slogans and speeches . . ." Dr. Brewer went on and the sound of his voice brought me back to law school, when I was all appetite with little on my plate and what was placed before me I could devour in two bites. I had spoken to Sarah about Brewer's class in constitutional crises; his name had passed between us and now he was here and this commonplace thought made me want to cover my face with my trembling hands. I was drifting—no, I was launched and I was sailing away, I was far off at sea, just about to dip over the hump on the horizon. I heard Brewer's voice but it was distant and empty and it was all I could do to keep my seat. The part of me that had kept me going was suddenly missing and in the inner space it had once occupied now rushed a torrent of sorrow.

And then the introductions were over and Bertelli slowly rose from his chair to the sound of what seemed to me alarmingly generous applause. He smiled, acknowledging the audience, and leaned forward, supporting his weight with his hands on the table. The wooden legs began to tremble and he stepped back—just in time.

"Thank you very much, Dr. Brewer, ladies and gentlemen. And the Greater Hyde Park Citizens' Forum. As you can all see, I lost the flip of the coin over who speaks first." He smiled, shrugged, showed his empty, guileless hands. Amazingly, there was quite a bit of generous laughter. "But with that loss out of the way, let me come right out and say that tomorrow evening, when all the votes have been counted, that I and all the people who've been working to make my campaign happen will be drinking champagne and making toasts. Because I know this district and I know the people in it. And I know that we are going to win this election tomorrow." What seemed like a spontaneous wave of applause washed up toward the stage and Bertelli took a deep breath, as if he were on the shore inhaling the renewing scent of the sea. "You see, Hyde Parkers they are a funny race. We don't like our elections to be foregone conclusions. We don't like the governor appointing our representatives. We have a habit around here. A habit the hacks down in Springfield and over Back of the Yards would like us to break. It's a habit called Thinking for Ourselves. When I first decided to . . . well"—he touched his mane of thick silver hair—"throw my beret in the ring, I believed what the so-called experts said. Enrico, you don't have a chance. Enrico, the fix is in. Enrico, the machine's got it all sewn up. But I love this neighborhood and the people in it. And I wanted them to have—you know the old saying: a choice not an echo. I thought, and, yes, think, the people of this district deserved something different than a freeze-dried, shrink-wrapped candidate sent to us by the fixers. And you know who the fixers are—the same snake-oil salesmen who gave us the crime rate, the war in Afghanistan, the shame of Iran, record interest rates, record inflation, and an economy that is slowing down to the tune of five percent every three months. The people of this district know me. Many of you have been friends and customers for years. This is my home. I'm not a newcomer. I'm not some fellow from New York City passing through and deciding to pluck himself a little seat in the House like it was some flower growing at the side of the road. I've made my whole life here and I think I understand what this district is all about. But what is more important—I'm willing to listen. I'm not part of some deal. I'm part of you and when I ask you to send me to Washington, what I'm really saying is, Let's all go there together. And get the job done. Thank you." Bertelli flipped the back of his jacket up as he sat, as if he were wearing a morning coat. The applause was fast and loud; it formed a bright undulating wall.

Then Brewer announced me. I didn't want to torpedo my confidence completely by noticing how much applause I got, but as I stood it did seem that just as much noise was being made for me as for Bertelli. My table had been placed unluckily. I was directly in line with one of the footlights and now that I was standing its intense beam was shining right into my eyes. I felt a wave of panic, as if it were a naked bulb in a police interrogation room. I forgot my control for a moment and put my hand in front of my face, but then I regained my wits and moved slightly to the left. The light rushed past me, over my shoulder, like a spray of bullets I'd managed to elude. And for a moment I could make out faces in the audience—but they were the faces of strangers. Middle-aged faces, a tapestry of furrowed brows. What kind of people trudged out into the bitterness of a winter night to listen to a debate like this?

"As an attorney," I began, and to my immense relief my voice sounded smooth, level, "whose job it was to make certain those who violated the rights of the people were punished, I often found myself having to confront defense attorneys whose only loyalty was to their fee. Attorneys like these—and I'm sorry to say there were many of them—felt no hesitation at shading facts so they became untrue, of manipulating the emotions. And I developed the habit of keeping a note pad at my table and writing down all the points made by the other side that needed refutation if I was to make my case. And then I would take those points and do my best to knock them down, one at a time. Well, I am not an experienced debater, so tonight I thought I would try to use that same method and as I listened to Enrico Bertelli's remarks, I kept a pad and a pen with me so I could write down whatever he said that needed some reply from me." I paused and took a deep breath.

The auditorium was silent and suddenly this silence seemed a wildly hopeful sign. I reached down and took my pad off the table and turned it toward the audience. "Blank," I said. "I could find nothing in his remarks that needed to be refuted. Nothing I care to argue. If he thinks 'a choice not an echo' is an *old saying*, when all of us know it is a slogan of the new radical right, then—well, it doesn't really matter. And if he thinks that his having lived in this district for more years than I have gives him some special claim—well, I don't think he would want that dangerous kind of thinking *really* to apply because then people might end up saying that candidates whose family's origins are strictly American are better qualified than those of us who find our roots overseas. Perhaps all those years selling coffee have led my opponent to believe the whole world operates like advertising. New ideas. Let's all go to Congress. Rah rah rah. But through it all there is an awful consistency. Not tonight, nor at any time during this campaign, has my opponent bothered to tell us what these new ideas *are* or what he would like us to *do* when we *all* troop off to Washington together. Either he has no ideas or he holds the people of this district in such utter contempt that he feels we don't really care."

I glanced down because I could feel my eyes were much too intense right now and in the wrong light they could look like the eyes of a madman. When you drive the nail in too hard, you excite sympathy for your opponent. I knew this. It was something I believed. But it was somehow relaxing to stop presenting myself as a reasonable person, as a gentleman; it felt good to—well, I wasn't really breaking the rules, but I wasn't sticking to them all that closely, either. It's awfully hard to speak honestly when there is a hope of somehow *winning* in the back of your mind. Winning calls for tactics, for a certain subtle and instinctual dissembling. But suddenly it didn't matter very much to me whether or not I won tomorrow. And that thought was like the tap of a little silver mallet triggering my keenest, most characteristic reflex: as soon as I let go of the idea that it mattered much if I won or lost, I felt a jolt of sheer, avid certainty that it was precisely *this* kind of attitude that would make victory more likely.

"I don't know how you run a campaign based on vague slogans and meaningless hints about having new ideas. I've tried to make my own positions clear. Human rights at home and abroad. A concerted effort to rebuild our cities. Massive job retraining for workers who are being displaced by technology and shifting world centers of supply and demand. Stiffer corporate taxes. A three-tiered simplified tax code, with a radical reduction of write-offs and the end of all tax shelters. A thorough reappraisal of the seemingly endless drift toward more and more expenditures for defense. Scrapping the B-1 bomber, scrapping the MX missile, the Trident submarine. I don't expect everyone to agree with me." I paused and smiled. "At least not right *now*." It didn't get a laugh but I didn't wait for one. "But I don't understand how you run for Congress and don't come forward on these issues—one side or the other." A lone pair of hands began to clap—three or four leathery bursts of applause and then silence. "Thanks, Dad," I said, "but I'm not quite finished." And now there really was laughter. I furrowed my brow in a way that indicated I had meant to cause this reaction. "I very much welcome this opportunity to answer any questions anyone has."

And so the questions began. The whole thing was chaotic and annoying. The Forum wasn't used to meetings of this size and no provisions had been made for microphones, or any other orderly way of posing the questions to us. In the beginning, the lights were kept dimmed in the auditorium and we on the stage had no way of knowing who if anyone was raising a hand, asking for the floor. A few self-actualized souls stood up and asked their questions (or made their remarks) without our calling on them and then it was like responding to an articulate but anonymous phone call— though, in fact, some of the questions were the political equivalents to heavy breathing: How about a Bill or Rights for the Unborn? Do you believe it should be against the law for homos to work for the government?

Finally, I demonstrated my leadership abilities by suggesting we kill the footlights and bring up the houselights. "I think the audience has seen enough of us. I'd like to take a look at you." There was a round of applause at this—it was probably the most winning thing I'd said all evening. After a small delay in which someone from the Forum looked for a maintenance man and Bertelli punctured the hull of his own ship by crudely implying that the maintenance man was not worth his salary, the lights came on—thirty or forty flame-shaped bulbs along the east and west walls—and the faces of the audience came into view like an image swimming up from the surface of photographic paper.

Tony Dayton had his legs tightly crossed and he was leaning over, whispering something into my sister's ear, the same ear into which I had for years hotly confessed to what I then took as secrets but which I now knew were merely dreams—preening, impossible dreams which, to my immense misfortune, I had now brought within my grasp. Caroline nodded and shifted slightly in her seat—away from him. I knew this pattern well: she felt him starting to fall in love with her and she was wisely backpedaling.

Isaac was a few seats in, near the center of the row. His eyes were closed and he was the very picture of despair. I had failed him; I had cracked beneath the pressure. He thought, I suppose, about the futility of turning a workhorse into a racehorse, an oaf into a true officer. He took this campaign as a rather easy test of character and it broke his heart to see how wildly I had failed that test, and it broke his heart even more irreparably to witness how the heat of these past couple of weeks had served to reveal an ugliness and, well, I suppose, *craziness* in me that he had not allowed himself to see before. He was, I felt, as angry with himself as with me, and what was more he was embarrassed.

Sitting next to Isaac was Henry Shamansky and next to him was Sonny Marchi and one seat over sat my father, right on the edge of his seat, his eyes fixed on me in a huge and undisguised stare. He felt my gaze touch his and he slowly shook his head and gave me a smile of such sly pleasure and such wonderful complicity that I felt at once elated and destroyed. I was pleasing him in some way but for the life of me I didn't know how. Was I winning? Or was I somehow exposing the emptiness of the game? It seemed all my life I had been dropping bones at my father's feet and now here I was doing more of the same, somehow able to concoct a magic that brought back spoils even from an unsucessful hunt. I was sinking, sinking, and he was nodding and pursing his lips as if I were knocking the world on its ass and he and I were sharing a marvelous, ineffable secret: the secret of my destiny; the secret of *his* destiny made manifest by me. This wasn't love. This wasn't even something as wholesome as ambition. This was fatherhood as fever dream, relationship as hallucination.

Bertelli was speaking now, something about how I had failed to address the central issue, which was that my candidacy was a part of a *deal*. I could barely hear him. My eyes went up one row and down the other, first east to west and then north to south. I had decided that if Sarah was out there I would simply step off the stage and go to her. I continued to look, deeper and deeper into the auditorium now, and the faces were smaller, less distinct, undulating behind a haze of human heat.

Dr. Brewer interrupted Bertelli, saying, "I think as a way of keeping some order here and, one hopes, encouraging a dialogue, it would be best if we gave Mr. Pierce a chance to respond to these questions now, Mr. Bertelli."

I turned quickly. Bertelli was making a little As You Wish bow in Brewer's direction and I was not so far gone that I didn't realize it was now up to me to say something. I cleared my throat and waited for a moment, hoping that perhaps I had been listening all along and all I needed was a beat to recall what had just been said and what my reply ought to be. But the silence brought nothing but the faint hum of itself.

"Mr. Pierce?" said Brewer, and at that moment his voice sounded patient, infinitely kind.

"Tomorrow is the election," I said, in a soft voice, and as I heard those words I realized I was simply speaking with no idea what I would say, no idea whatsoever. "And I am very aware of the presumption involved in my asking you to send me to Washington to represent you. I've been campaigning for this office, trying to make myself known, trying to listen to and understand the people of this district . . . and now tonight. The end of a short, but intense time. And it strikes me now that there are certain questions I never answer, certain questions I think we've pretty much forgotten how to *ask*. I worry about what sort of people we are becoming. Me. You. All of us. Why don't our marriages last? Why can't we educate our children? Why does public life become more and more uncivil? Why are the streets empty at night?"

I heard my voice as something coming from a long distance and the faces before me had sunk into a swirl, drowning in the turbulence of my own vision. Yet suddenly I did see a familiar face. Father Stanton was sitting about twelve rows from the stage and he smiled as my gaze touched his. I felt a rush of heat go through me and a stabbing, passionate pressure behind my eyes.

"I think we've come to a point where the *right thing* to do seems so obscure, or so relative, that we've excused ourselves from trying to do it. When I was offered this chance to run for office"—I glanced over at Bertelli and he looked back at me with his great cow eyes—"I accepted the opportunity because—" And then I stopped for a moment. A sadness was crashing down on me like the collapse of a wall. "Yes. I was going to say I accepted because it would give me a chance to serve my country. But it was a lot more complicated than that. I have wanted this opportunity for as long as I can remember. And when you want something for that long then just *getting* it becomes the most important thing, more important than all the reasons why you wanted to achieve it in the first place. We become like dogs chasing after a mechanical rabbit around a race track—and then what do we do with this thing once we have it in our jaws? And now with the race almost run, I can't help but ask myself: What will I make of the opportunity I am asking you to give me?"

I stopped. I felt suddenly so calm—and I knew what this meant. I had cut loose from my senses; I was just letting it happen.

Caution was like moral gravity and now that it was gone I was free-floating.

"Maybe it all comes down to vanity," I said. "But I have always believed and I continue to believe that I can make a difference. I feel a part of me can genuinely *hear* the voices of suffering. And I can feel the lack of opportunity, the lack of caring, the lack of . . . love that we have allowed to spoil our great national dream. And I don't think I'm alone in this. Others see it, too. You see it and feel it. But I am willing to live with it and try to move it and to try and direct our world toward justice inch by inch. I am willing to make the compromises and endure the boredom and paperwork and all the moral murkiness of politics and I believe that I can go through it all without really losing sight of the vision of *goodness* that I think many of us hold in common. Politicians make an awful lot of promises. But I want to make one more and I don't have the right to expect anyone to believe me. We've all been lied to so many times we've lost the ability to believe people in public life—lost the power to believe in the very idea of public life. But with that in mind, let me just finish here by promising always to believe in the democratic dream and to help others continue to believe in it, too, and to help protect what's left of the best of ourselves from the profiteers and the warriors and the selfish and the brutal. To make this world as close to paradise as we can make it—which may not be awfully close at all, in the end, but what better way have we to spend our lives than crawling toward it?"

I sat down. There was applause, though I can't say how much. I put my hand against my chin and rubbed it. I had a dim sense that I might have just lost the election. Bertelli was jotting down notes on his yellow pad. I finally took my hand away from my chin and looked at my palm. There was a little red mark of blood in it. The fissure left by Mileski's roundhouse had opened again.

It was a long wait for the results. A few hours after the polls closed we knew it was going to be close and it remained close all through the night and into the next morning. It was not the election night vigil of which dreams are made. There was no bunting, no gay vapor of champagne, no straw boaters, no band. It was just the hard core and me in the campaign offices, listening to all-news radio and making phone calls. As the night wore on a kind of informal system seemed to have taken shape and my staff took turns in waiting around with me, like a dutiful family spelling one another during a death watch. "I'm going to take Dad home," Caroline whispered to me about two in the morning, and no sooner had she left than Tony Dayton appeared, his hair still wet from the shower, his eyes bright from his quick nap.

About five that morning, Tony left, saying he was going to get some sweet rolls and coffee and run some errands, and a few minutes after he was gone Sonny Marchi came in with an off-duty cop, the two of them swapping stories about stolen cars. A woman named Doreen Fisher, who had been helping answer the phones during the campaign and whose husband was an outrageous bully, had decided to endure the long haul rather than go home, though now she was asleep at her desk, her head on her arm, her harlequin glasses still on. The sound of Marchi and the cop woke her up and she looked at me.

"Nothing yet, Doreen," I said. "Are you sure you want to stick this out?"

"Oh please, yes," she said. "I'd hate to leave."

I nodded. I knew how she dreaded going home; I didn't much care for it, either. Then I thought: If I win, I'll ask her to stay on. And the thought that I could offer her a job, take her to Washington, untie her like Pauline from the train tracks of her marriage vows, sent a rush of emotion through me.

Outside, the sky was lightening and the filigree of ice on the windows turned rosy for a moment. Kathy Courtney's car pulled in in front of headquarters. She got out, carrying the morning *Tribune*. The headline said IRAN ORDEAL CONTINUES.

Kathy came into the office trailing the winter cold behind her like a silver robe. She was wearing a black suit, a white dress with a high fluffy collar: it was another day on the job.

"Heard anything new?" she asked, coming next to me.

"Not really," I said. "Too close to call."

"Well, I wanted to say something, Fielding," she said. She took off her coat, placed the newspaper on an unoccupied desk, sat down on a folding chair. Stalling for time.

"What is it?" I asked.

"I don't want to sound presumptuous, because we haven't won yet and you haven't offered me anything," she said, folding her hands and placing them in her lap. "But I want you to know that I've decided not to go back to Washington after this."

"Why not?" I asked.

"That's just what I feel most comfortable with," she said.

"It's been pretty hard working with me, hasn't it," I said.

"It's not that. All you guys are hard, believe me."

"Then what is it?" I asked, though if I hadn't been so exhausted I probably would not have.

"It's just too complicated. When I came on with you, I figured my knowing Sarah might be a problem. So I thought about it and decided to tell you. But I think that just made matters worse. Don't you see?"

"I don't think it made matters worse," I said. I let my nerves settle for a moment; I had a decent instinct for when I had a fighting chance to get my way and I knew with some certainty that no matter what I said to Kathy she would not be coming to work for me.

"Do you have another job lined up?" I asked.

"No. Not yet. I was thinking of taking some time off. I haven't read a book in five years."

"I like you, Kathy."

"I know. And I like you too, Fielding. I really do. I think you might even do something in Washington."

"Then help me," I said. I took her hand in mine; it felt light, cool, smooth as soap.

"I am," said Kathy. "Do you think this is easy for me?" Her face colored; her eyes moved away from mine. "No matter what happens," she said, "last night was good. You know, hanging around politicians, I think I was starting to forget why I went into this business to begin with. Last night I started to remember again."

"Then stick it out with me," I said, with a sudden urgency.

"I can't," she said. "I'm sure of it, Fielding. I never should have told you I knew her—but I would have felt like such a liar. And that night you said you were going to call. I was home. And the phone rang and rang, but I just sat there and I just couldn't answer it. I mean, I wanted to be with you. But when the phone started ringing I realized you weren't coming to see me. You just needed to be with someone who knew Sarah."

"You should have answered the phone, Kathy," I said. "It might have been an emergency."

"I know," she said. "You're right. And that's why I can't work for you." She stood up and picked up her coat. "If you win it, there'll be a press conference later on. We'll be in touch and I'll see you there. And I won't leave you in the lurch. Not that you'll have any trouble finding someone, but I'll stick it through until you do."

I sat and watched her leave. She didn't turn around, but when she was unlocking her car she knew I was still watching her and she looked up before getting in and made contact with my gaze through the bright icy window. She put up her hand and wagged it back and forth and then she was gone and a moment later the exhaust was rushing out of her car, turning the snow behind it dark gray.

A short while later, the phone rang. "It's Isaac," Doreen called out to me.

I stumbled out of my chair and across the office, my hand outstretched for the phone.

"Hello, Isaac," I said. "What's the score?"

"Final tally's in," he said. "You won."

"What was the margin?"

"Six hundred and sixty-six votes," he said.

"Strange," I said.

"Why strange?"

"That's the devil's social security number."

There was silence on the other end. Then, finally, "Well, there's a lot to do. Will you be able to push on for a while?"

"Yes," I said. "My energy's fine."

"Good."

"And Isaac?" I swallowed, sat on the edge of Doreen's desk. She looked at me questioningly and I gave her the thumbs up signal. She clasped her hands together and brought them to her breast.

"What is it, Fielding?" he asked, wary.

"Thanks," I said.

I hung the phone up and started to shake, like you do on a highway a few moments after almost going over the side of the road. "I won," I said to Sonny Marchi, raising my fist.

Sonny and the off-duty cop had been sharing a laugh over a story about a kid from West Virginia, a stolen Plymouth Fury, and a backseat filled with tampon samples. The cop was oozing awful laughter like water out of a dirty sponge and Sonny flicked his reddish rabbit eyes toward me and gave a smile whose weakness was made poisonous by its unearned confidence. "We won," he corrected, smiling. "We won. And that is great news."

Four days later, I left Chicago in a light snow flurry and arrived in Washington in the afternoon, where the sky was a dome-shaped bruise and the rain was pouring down in huge windy flaps. Arrangements had been made for me to live in a residential hotel on Pennsylvania Avenue—steep tariff, but it was the best I could do. It was hard to say how long I'd last in Washington; there was really no sense in looking for somewhere permanent to store my gear.

The facade of the Hotel Manchester was somber, plain. It had that well-made gray suit feeling to it. Inside, maroon carpeting, an occasional urn filled with white pebbles—God knows why— an anemic philodendron beneath one of those bright lightbulbs shaped like megaphones. One of those new breed of men with round eyes and sly cabaret smiles brought me up to my two-and-a-half-room suite. Bed, sofa, chairs, kitchenette, bath, old woodcuts of nineteenth-century Washington on the walls, a scent of Windex in the air. The hotel employee (concierge: imagine!) welcomed me, congratulated me on my election, informed me that he had a sister who lived in Chicago, though stopped short of asking me if I happened to know her. He gave me a brochure describing the various services available from the hotel and then directed my attention to the complimentary bottles of champagne and Scotch that had been provided for me. I spoiled the moment for him by asking that they be removed.

I had an hour before dinner with my parents and Caroline. They had come to see my swearing in the next morning. Isaac and Adele would also be there, though they would not be joining us for dinner tonight. I was not focused enough to see that the Greens were now slightly uneasy with me. It was not that they could not forgive me for leaving Juliet behind, but they wondered if it was a prelude to my breaking with them. And so they were with me, but not in the spirit of celebration so much as the spirit of caution and subtly wounded feelings.

I lay on my new bed as carefully as I could, as if I wanted to leave as little evidence as possible of my having been here, in case I was suddenly recalled. My head was half on the pillows, half against the headboard; I took my shoes off, but nothing else. The light in the bedroom was grayish blue; the rain beat noiselessly against the thick windowpane. There was a glass-topped mahogany dresser on the other side of the room, with a large silver lamp on it. The lamp was segmented into three round parts, like an ant, and the shadow it cast appeared and disappeared from the smooth wall, as light came in and went out of the window, in and out, in and out, like breath. My mind was blank and for a few moments or more I fell asleep. I woke with a start and my face was slick with tears.

The restaurant we met at was called The Bengali. It was in Georgetown, with a bookstore on one side of it and a little shop selling pricey cooking utensils on the other. It was evening. The rain was still falling, though lazily now. I was wearing a tan trench coat, carrying a black umbrella. There were hundreds of men roughly my age wearing tan trench coats, carrying black umbrellas. We had to give each other a wide berth to keep the spokes of our umbrellas from tangling. I stopped for a moment in front of the bookshop. One of the books displayed in the window was something called *Black Socks in the Bedroom: A Sexual History of the Nixon Years*. I leaned to the side and bent at the knees so I could see the spine of the book and, as I suspected, it was from Willow Books.

Standing in front of The Bengali was a massive Hindu doorman, with clear plastic taped around his pale orange turban to keep it dry. Inside, the restaurant was lined in red fabric with dime-sized mirrors sewn into it. Sitar music was piped in; tall, dark waiters moved slowly around the restaurant, weaving in and out of the tables like ostriches. My family was waiting for me at a table near the back—my parents, Caroline, and Danny. It was the first I'd seen of him since he'd left for Toronto with Kim.

As I approached the table, my family all tapped their fingertips together, in a playful silent round of applause. I flashed my quick Pavlovian grin. "Danny," I said, "they've got one of your books in the window next door."

"I know," he said. "I talked them into putting it there right before I came here." He raised and lowered his eyebrows. There were dull purple-black sacks beneath his eyes. He looked as if he'd lost ten pounds since I'd last seen him. His golden hair was dirty, as were his pink shirt, his charcoal jacket.

"Sit down, Congressman," said Caroline. A place was waiting for me between Mom and Dad.

I sat. I leaned over and kissed Mom on the cheek and then patted Dad's arm. "How's it going?" I asked Danny.

"I'm here, aren't I?" said Danny, with one of those wan, existential smiles that were his specialty: he had known how to act brave and condemned even when he was ten years old.

"How are the boys?" I asked Caroline.

"Fantastic. Unbearable. Lovely. Grotesque. Moronic. And saintly. They are having an incredible time touring Africa with Eric. Sometimes I forget what a good father he is."

"Well then you'll just have to be a better mother," said Dad.

"It's not a contest," said Caroline. "I thank God Eric's a wonderful father."

"You don't want to end up losing those kids," said Dad.

"The prices in this place are *obscene*," Mom suddenly declared, closing the menu as if it were filled with smutty snapshots. "A family of ten could eat in India for a month for the price of one dinner here."

"Don't worry," said Danny, "this is a Willow Books party."

"Expense account money is still money," said Mom. "And anyhow I don't like being treated as if I was a sucker."

"I'll convince you to do a book for us," Danny said to me. "Like keep a journal of your days in Congress. Something like that."

"You know what?" said Dad. "That's not such a crazy idea."

"I'm not in business to have crazy ideas, Father," said Danny, without a trace of humor.

"My family," said Caroline, clasping her hands and batting her eyelashes. "I think I'll kill them."

"Caroline's right," said Mom. "We can't go off in a hundred different directions. Let's just concentrate on being happy for Fielding."

"And then after that we can go back to trashing each other," said Danny.

Our waiter came to the table. He asked if we wanted something to drink before ordering our dinner and Danny took over. "We'll have a Lillet with a slice of orange," he said, "a Canadian Club and water, a Johnny Walker Red, a Wild Turkey on the rocks, and a glass of—make that a large glass of club soda with lime." As he gave the order he pointed to Caroline, Dad, Mom, himself, and me.

"You know what," Dad said, leaning back in his chair, glancing up at the ceiling, "sometimes we *are* sort of rough on each other."

"Oh-oh," said Caroline.

"No, I mean it," said Dad. "I didn't mean to really say that Danny had crazy ideas. But we like to give each other the needle."

"Notice there's no remorse about saying I should be a better mother," announced Caroline.

"OK, OK, that's baby stuff, Caroline," said Dad.

"Love has no pride," she said with a shrug.

"I think what Dad's trying to say," Mom said, "is this family has got a lot to be proud of. And whatever we've been doing—I mean Eddie and me—well, it seems to have had a pretty nice result."

"I feel sorry for those parents who can't even stand to *think* of their kids," Dad added. "I mean, Jesus Christ, do you know what tomorrow means? Fielding's going to be sworn into the U.S. Congress. It's like a dream. And it gives meaning to everything we've all been doing."

"I didn't realize it lacked meaning before," said Danny, winking at Caroline.

"Well, this is the dream come true, the dream we all had," said Dad, oblivious. "I'm not saying you haven't done well for yourself, Danny. But it's not as if running a book company was what you wanted and we wanted from the time you were a kid. You see the difference, don't you? The whole publishing company thing just sort of happened. You and Caroline just sort of took life as it came, and that's OK. Don't get me wrong. But it's different from having a plan and seeing it through."

"Now you tell me," said Caroline. "I was always trying to figure out what you wanted from me, what you would have called success in my life. And now it seems all I had to do was make a plan and carry it through."

"You know, Caroline," said Mom, "when you're sarcastic like that, he doesn't even hear it. You just annoy yourself."

"How's Kim?" I asked Danny.

"We don't talk about that," said Danny.

"But is she OK?"

"She's fine."

"Who's Kim?" asked Dad.

"A Korean massage parlor attendant," said Danny, "and a real swell gal."

"Is he kidding?" Dad asked me.

"Of course he is," said Caroline. "God."

The waiter came with our drinks, calling each one of them off as he set them in front of us.

"I'll make the toast," I said, raising my glass. "First of all, to Caroline, for coming to Chicago and helping me get through the campaign. For Caroline—well, you know, service above and beyond the call of duty. And to Mom and Dad, for doing whatever it is they had to do to get me this far." I stopped. I had a sudden convulsive desire to simply stand up and walk away from the table, but I forced myself to let it pass.

"Ah, look at the destiny in those eyes," said Danny. "You lucky dog. You've got a career that you think is a cause. And now you can do anything—*anything*—for yourself and kid yourself into believing that it isn't really for you, that it's for what you stand for."

Just then, I felt a hand on my shoulder. I turned in my seat and there was a stocky black man with a handlebar mustache and a graying Afro. He had deep furrows in his brow, a wide gap between his front teeth.

"Hello, Fielding Pierce," he said. "I noticed you coming in and I just wanted to say hello." He had a deep voice, a slight stammer. "I'm Buddy Preston." He waited for me to recognize his name and then stepped back a little. "From the Seventh Congressional District?"

"Oh yes, yes," I said. "Hello." He was a Chicago congressman, in his fifth term. He was good at winning elections, though I couldn't remember what else he had done with his career. Isaac had once mentioned that Buddy Preston had the richest war chest of any of the Chicago politicians, with contributions coming in from milk companies, cement manufacturers, meat packers, the National Rifle Association—a crazy quilt of unrelated interest groups that he somehow stitched together with his own perseverance and charm.

"I don't want to bother you folks," he said. "I just wanted to welcome Fielding here to our delegation."

"Well, that's very nice of you, Mr. Preston," said my father.

"You all set for tomorrow?" he asked me.

"What happens in one of these?" Mom asked.

"Oh, it's no big thing, but it's nice," Preston said. "All the Democrats from the Illinois delegation walk up with him to the Speaker's chair and he's sworn in. You know. No big thing."

"I can see where that would be something to see, though," said Mom. There was something suddenly docile in her voice as she spoke to him, as if he were a cop, or someone who might be able to do her an important favor. Chances were, Preston was so used to that tone of voice, he couldn't hear it.

"Well, the Illinois delegation is just about the friendliest in the Congress," Preston said. "We really try to help each other out. And that's a good thing. We even try to socialize a little. The important thing is to keep talking and work together."

Preston chatted amiably for a few moments and then, his obligation fulfilled, went on. I watched him make his way toward his table, where a thin, exotic-looking woman with scores of bracelets on her bare arms sat waiting for him.

"You didn't even introduce us, Fielding," my father said, as soon as Preston was out of earshot. "What kind of way is that?"

"There's something I think I should tell you. Everyone." I picked up my glass of club soda; it felt as if it were made of stone. I heard droning, nightmarish music, melting voices, and then dimly realized it was a record piped in through the restaurant's speakers. I took a deep breath but it seemed to stop at the back of my throat. I placed the glass down again but not flatly and it tipped over: the carbonated water hissed and trembled on the white tablecloth. No one moved to sop it up. "I'm not feeling very well," I said. "I haven't been for some time now. I'm . . . I'm just not feeling very well."

"We can see that, Fielding," said my mother softly. She glanced at Dad, cueing him to say something.

"We didn't think it was our part to say anything," he said.

"No," I said. "I want to be honest about this. Something has happened to me. And it won't stop. It keeps coming on and coming on." I made a terrible, broken laugh. "This is very embarrassing, but you may as well hear it. Something inside me has jumped track. I'm very confused. I'm not sleeping right and I'm not thinking right and I really don't want you to think I'm complaining here or asking for help, because there's nothing anyone can do. It's just something that's happened and that's all there is to it. But I don't know what I'm going to say from one minute to the next and I don't even really know what I'm going to do." My eyes were open, but I couldn't see their faces. I didn't want to. "And I think the best thing—I don't know. Maybe the only hope I've got right now. I know it's coming at a bad time. But there's nothing I can do about it. I'm just very tired and I don't see things the way I'm used to seeing them. Everything is very strange and it all seems out of control. I feel very . . . I don't know. Frightened. But I don't think *you* should be frightened. It's not as if I was going to *hurt* anyone. Jesus. It's nothing like that. It's just that I know I'm not normal now and the best thing for me, if you wouldn't mind giving me a little help . . . what I think is, I better see someone. A doctor. I know I'm spoiling everything, but if I don't say it now, I may never say it. Tomorrow, it might be too late, because it's going very, very, very fast. And tomorrow I may be too crazy to even know how crazy I am. I think the best thing is for me to go to a hospital tonight. And get some help. Some treatment. Because something happened to me and I'm very lost and it won't get better. I just get worse and worse and there is nothing that can stop it."

The morning in Congress was taken with the tail end of a debate over farm subsidies. I sat in the rotunda and listened to the congressman from South Dakota drone on and on, with barely an inflection in his voice. He was just putting it on the record; there weren't ten people in that chamber listening to him.

At one point, the Speaker of the House came in and took his place. He was massive, eternal; his hair was as white as fresh Irish linen and his skin looked as if it had been scrubbed with a brush. He sat down and rested his face in his hands for a moment, looking at the congressman from South Dakota with what seemed like enormous pity; then the Speaker looked at some papers, glanced at his watch, and suddenly rapped his gavel against the table. He asked the congressman if he was near the end of his presentation and whether or not the matter could be brought to a vote. The congressman said he needed just ten more minutes to complete his statement and the Speaker nodded gratefully. A few pages left the chamber and in every office and in the corridors lights went on, informing the Congress that it was time to cast their votes. As the fellow from South Dakota continued to read his remarks into the Congressional Record, hundreds of representatives filed in through the doors, laughing, coughing, talking, taking their spots on either side of the great center aisle.

Buddy Preston took the seat next to mine. All twenty-four of the Illinois congressmen were here for the vote, fourteen of them on the Democratic side of the aisle. Sitting next to me a guy just a few years older than me, smelling as if he'd just splashed a half bottle of Brut on before coming to vote. He was Emil Z. Nichols from the Third District. He had gotten his power directly from Mayor Daley, but now with a new administration he was vulnerable and word was that the pressure of a possible defeat next election was making him unpredictable, like a man who's just been diagnosed with an incurable disease. The Third was a tough district to keep: half suburban, half urban, with some blacks and plenty of Poles, Germans, Swedes, and Lithuanians who had moved to get away from blacks. It was one of those places where people went as a way of proclaiming they were leaving the working class and then were besieged by lack of money, lack of decent housing, lack of safety—all of the things they had insisted would never happen to them again. It was a resentful district and Nichols had gotten three terms out of it only because the mayor had twisted enough arms.

"Hello, Fielding," he said, in an unusually slippery, dishonest voice, reaching over and shaking my hand. "Emil Nichols. Welcome to the zoo."

Buddy Preston put his hand lightly on my shoulder, as if warning me away from an evil influence. "We'll be bringing you up for the swearing in right after this vote," he said.

"Yeah," said Nichols, "you're lucky you don't have to vote. It's a ball breaker—especially for someone like you."

"How do you mean that?" I said.

Nichols laughed through his teeth, as if my question was a mere tactic. "Yeah, right," he said. "As if the governor didn't have you in his pocket. But try voting with the farmers and see what happens to you when you go back to your district."

Further into the aisle sat an old, loose-limbed, bald man wearing a brown suit and a red and white bow tie. It was Paul Germain, an old newspaperman turned politician whom I'd met at Isaac's a couple of years back. Germain was from East St. Louis—a burnt, scarred, smoking place, at once abandoned and frantic with the half-life of crime that reigns after the neutron of commerce dies. Germain was one of the few downstate Democrats; he had known Truman, Stevenson; he had a shattered leg from a parachute jump into Cologne in 1944. As he leaned forward, the light from the upper windows exploded in his glasses and his skin was so thin you could almost see the skull beneath it. "We'll talk," he said, and then leaned back, his narrow profile disappearing behind the human hedge.

The vote was taken. The measure was passed, but it didn't

make any difference because it was assured of defeat in the Senate. Above us, in the visitors' gallery, clumps of school kids were brought in to look down at us over the high railing, like a Sunday school class brought to a fissure in the earth where they could see the souls in Purgatory. It was not yet the time when Congress would be virtually closed to casual visitors, but security was still tight. You did not feel the invitation toward discourse as you walked those institutional green corridors. There were coolers of bubbling bottled water just like in any large office and bored-looking receptionists growing their rubber plants beneath fluorescent light.

In the committee rooms were round wall clocks like in old-fashioned classrooms and built into the faces of each of these clocks was a system of small electric lights—one to signal a quorum call, another to signal that a roll call was about to be taken, and yet another to announce a nuclear war had just begun and that it was time for the legislators to take cover. I didn't know yet where we were supposed to hide. All I really knew was where my offices were. After Carmichael's resignation, there had been a scramble for his rather well-placed, well-maintained, and spacious offices and as everyone who wanted a change of quarters had already shifted, the dankest, least convenient space in the Rayburn Building was left for me—a little ghetto up a back staircase, on its own half floor which it shared with the maintenance supervisor and a freshman congressman from Mississippi.

As the vote was taken, I sat with my arms folded over my chest and looked around. I was, on the whole, grateful my family hadn't listened to me last night and that I hadn't been taken to some hospital, shot full of tranquilizers, given a pair of paper slippers, humiliated. What I hadn't understood was that it wouldn't get much worse: in order to feel any crazier, I would need an entirely new mind to lose. I had topped off at the current level of sorrow and derangement. And if it would not get worse then perhaps, sometime, it would be better. I really had no clear idea anymore why I was sitting in the Capitol, why I had wanted this for so many years, or what exactly I had done to deserve it. But I had to trust that at some time in the past, when I had notched the arrow of my life onto fate's taut bow, I had known something that in my misery and hunger and utter apprehension I was forgetting now. The only thing to do was hold on—and hope that until I was myself again I could get away with the impersonation. My face would be a mask, my eyes opaque.

I looked up at the visitors' gallery, telling myself I was just trying to see if Danny and Caroline and my parents were in view. If I had taken this odd, compromising, confusing, and sad journey only to do my part in the greater magic, to sing the notes assigned to me as a part of the spell that would wake the dead, then perhaps she was here at this moment: as aura, as idea, or even as flesh. It suddenly made practically no difference: memory, when it is real, can well take the place of that jumble of conflicting impressions we call the present. Surely I loved her more than, say, Juliet, more, surely, than I could love myself: then in what real sense was she dead? Because she could not love me in return?

When the vote was over, the Speaker announced that the Ninety-sixth Congress would now welcome a new member to its ranks. He made no mention of Congressman Carmichael but instead confined himself to a bit of partisan joshing—professing relief that the new member was a Democrat, that sort of thing. Next thing I knew, Emil Nichols slapped his knees and stood up with a resentful groan and then on the other side of me Buddy Preston was also on his feet, tugging at my sleeve, smiling, saying, Up you go, Pierce. Down the aisle and into the history books. And after that, all the Democratic members of the Illinois delegation were up and we were going down the carpeted aisle toward the Speaker's chair and I heard the sound of static, as if the nerves in my inner ear were frying out, but then I realized it was applause, they were applauding for me, the entire House of Representatives, not because they liked me or knew anything about what I believed or hoped to accomplish, but because I had made it that far, like a fellow salmon who had made it through the torrents to this breeding ground where we could in relative tranquillity spawn more and more two-year terms. I had won. And they were applauding me and, of course, applauding themselves as well, because each of these men and women had beaten someone else out for this job, had made smart deals, said the right thing, known when to hang back and when to pounce, had convinced thousands of strangers that they truly cared about them, had grabbed hold of history's drag-ass tail and ridden it to Washington, had seen the crack in the door and worked it open until the light poured out and was golden.

And now I was a member of the club, too, and as I made my way toward Speaker O'Neill I saw Sarah's face among the dozens of faces in the gallery, looking down, and then I looked straight ahead and let myself be taken with the flow toward the podium where I swore to defend the Constitution and was duly admitted to the Congress of the United States of America.

After the day's adjournment, the Illinois Democrats had a cocktail party for me in Congressman Germain's office. He was our senior member and he had the largest, most comfortable offices: the Congress was definitely a place with good and bad neighborhoods—Germain was living on the Gold Coast while I had been given, say, an abandoned loft building to renovate, a dark little place huddling in the shadows of the El. Germain glanced at me from time to time, promising, I thought, to be a friend. I seized upon the possibility because except for him I felt astonishingly distant from my delegation. This was like the first day on the job and feeling the only way you'll possibly survive is if you keep absolutely secret the truth of your identity—an identity that was, till that moment, a matter of sublime indifference to you but which seemed to have bloomed beneath the alien fluorescent lights into a terrible secret. With the other congressmen were some of their staff, a couple of wives, my family, a small redheaded guy from the Washington *Post* who wanted to do a story about my first

month in the House, a woman from the AP who had done well
on the Carmichael story, and a lobbyist from the pharmaceuticals
industry who had been talking to Congressman Furillo, a guy from
the West Side who called himself Cookie Furillo and who looked
like a teen crooner twenty years later playing the oldies-but-good-
ies circuit. Furillo was a junior member of the Consumer Protec-
tion Committee and he was constantly besieged by lobbyists. Furillo
was so small-time in his corruption that he actually gave the various
and often handsome gifts he accepted to his sister, who sold them
to the public in her What-Not Shoppe on West Cicero Avenue.
Soon enough, Danny commandeered the pharmaceuticals lobbyist
and the two of them retired into a corner, where my clever brother
astonished the lobbyist with his encyclopedic knowledge of pills,
spansules, powders, solutions, and ampules. "You've got to look
at it from the point of view of the goddamned *consumer*," I heard
Danny say at one point.

It was the first day of my term and until I decided otherwise
I had quite a few people working for me. Carmichael's Washington
staff had remained for the most part intact, keeping as quiet as
possible in the hope they wouldn't be noticed and then fired. Of
course, they had been busy—frantic, really—looking for work,
sending résumés out to other congressmen, to lobbying groups,
law firms, newspapers. But in the meanwhile, they had been collecting their salaries. They ought to have been at this party, but
I think they decided that every day out of my sight was another
day's feeding at the federal trough. The only one of them to show
up was a tall, stout, boxy-faced, gray-haired woman named Dina
Jensen, who had been Carmichael's secretary for six years and
who rightly understood that she was, at least for quite a while,
wholly indispensable.

"This has been the worst week of my *life*," she said, coming
to my side, tapping her plastic cup against mine: we were both
sticking to the club soda.

"What happened to you?" I asked. She was a tall woman, just
about my height, with the solitary, intelligent gray eyes of a nanny
in a Victorian children's book.

"Oh, the *moving*. I despise moving. I've been living in the same apartment for eighteen years because I can't bear the thought of packing everything in boxes. It makes everything seem so impermanent. I don't know why that frightens me."

"I do," I said. "It *is* a total drag."

"Well, anyhow, all of Jerry's personal effects have been sent. He couldn't come for them himself, of course. And *tons* of God knows what have been carted over to your new offices."

"I hope you'll continue to work for the district," I said. "I really do hope you stay on."

"Well, I may as well," said Dina Jensen, allowing herself a small smile of relief. "After all that sweat labor."

The tall windows in Germain's office went cobalt as the day turned to evening. Isaac and Adele had left with Emil Z. Nichols. Danny, Caroline, and my parents caught the six o'clock shuttle back to New York. I felt unaccountably relieved to see them go. They were from another reality and I needed to cut away.

Caroline was the first to say good-bye to me. She held me by both hands and then looked around to make sure we wouldn't be overheard. "Are you OK?" she asked. "I know what you've been going through."

"I'm not OK," I said. "But I'm OK about not being OK."

"Ha ha?" she asked.

"I don't know," I said.

She looked at me with the peacefulness of family love and then squeezed my hands and kissed me on the cheek.

"I'm going to have dinner with Eric when he and the boys get back," she whispered into my ear.

"Good," I whispered back to her. "It'll help me with the black voters."

She stepped back and smiled and then, abruptly, held me in a fast, hard embrace.

Next, I said good-bye to Danny. He'd been drinking hard, but his eyes were sharp. "Maybe I can come to New York next week," I said to him, "and we can do something."

"I'm going to San Francisco," he said. "I met a guy in Toronto.

His family owns all this California real estate. And I've got him interested in investing some nice money in Willow Books. That's the fucking pain of this whole thing. I'm always one hundred thousand short of making a go of it. You know, if I could just push it over the hump, it would be so easy."

"The guy from Toronto's in San Francisco?" I asked.

"Yeah. Hey, Fielding. I'm sorry I've been shitty to you. I've been in a terrible mood. But, you know, the nice thing about long relationships is you'll have a lot of chances to get even."

"OK," I said. "Just make sure I do."

"What do you mean?"

"You know. Take care of yourself. Don't let anyone kill you. Not even yourself."

Danny smiled: it made all the oozy charm of the Illinois delegation seem like the gruntings of whores. Danny with a grin was a boy again; a true smile put him on the banks of the river with his bare feet in the cool blue water.

Finally, I said good-bye to my parents. They looked small and vulnerable in their overcoats and they both looked sleepy and shy, like children who've stayed too long at the party. Mom's hands were icy; Dad was looking at me as if I were suddenly a stranger, worthy of respect.

"Greatest day of my life," Dad said, with a serious, man-to-mannish nod.

"We're so proud of you, Fielding," said Mom, glancing over my shoulder into the hidden camera that she imagined recorded the precious moments of her life.

"Just don't forget who you are," said Dad, grabbing my hand as if it were something he had to capture.

"As if I ever knew," I answered, but with a smile so he wouldn't have to take it seriously.

The party was breaking up. Dina Jensen had delayed her going home to see if I needed anything and I asked her to help me get from Germain's office to mine. We took an elevator down to the ground floor and then found another bank of elevators and took one of those up to where we would be working for the next year or so. We were going against traffic; all the lawmakers and the office help were waiting for down elevators, on their way home. There were wheelchair-tire skid marks against the gray elevator walls, a scent of cigar smoke. Dina was softly humming to herself. Her features were placid. Her eyes seemed to be looking at nothing. The elevator went to the second floor, the third. Her humming sounded so pleasant; a warmth went through me, slowly, thickly, like honey out of a broken jar.

For some reason, I said her name to myself: Dina. DINA was the acronym of the Chilean secret police, the far-ranging death squad of the junta. It stood for Departamento de Inteligencia Nacional. Its leader was a madman named Contreras and it had probably been he who had called for Francisco and Gisela's assassination.

I must have begun to stare at Dina Jensen because she slowly turned and looked questioningly at me. Yet what could I tell her? Was she with me for a reason? Even as I stood in that elevator with my heart going cold and going fast and a smell of my own madness up high and back in my nose, like a faraway scent of rain, even then I more or less believed that her name was merely her name and had nothing to do with Chilean secret police, nothing to do with Sarah. My life was simply too heavy and it had struck that fragile, chaotic element called chance like a hammer smashing into a ball of mercury and sent it flying in all directions.

Dina Jensen led me to my offices. They were small, and looked smaller for the jumble of cartons and the overturned furniture, the ashen patches on the wall where the previous tenant had hung her citations and memorabilia. There was a small black sofa pushed up against one wall, a few reading chairs here and there, and two wooden desks, one resting on top of the other, face to face. The desk with its legs in the air had its drawers secured with masking tape. Masking tape had also been used to wrap the exit door of the ornately carved cuckoo clock that hung on the wall. As we came in, the hour was just striking and I heard the imprisoned cuckoo pummeling against the shut door, its call muffled and distant.

"Is your heart sinking?" asked Dina Jensen.

I shook my head no. And it wasn't. The squalor was oddly comforting.

"I didn't want to make any final decisions about how to put it all together until we had a chance to talk," said Dina.

"That's all right," I said.

"We hadn't even gotten the phones straight until yesterday," she said, shrugging.

Just then, one of the Capitol guards tapped on the open door. He was a man in his fifties with silver hair; the sole of his left shoe was built up four or five inches to compensate for a short leg. He carried a gun on one hip and on the other was a walkie-talkie.

"Oh hello, Harry," said Dina.

"Hello, Miss Jensen," said the security guard. He had an airy, wavering voice, as full of holes as a fishnet. "I thought I heard you here." He smiled and glanced at me and then shifted his watery blue eyes back to Dina: he was waiting to be introduced with all the slightly injured pride and propriety of a nineteenth-century suitor.

"This is Congressman Pierce, Harry," said Dina.

"Hi," I said, putting out my hand.

"Will you be working late?" he asked me.

"I think so," I said. "Tonight, anyhow."

"Oh, I didn't realize," said Dina.

"No, that's OK," I said. "You go on and do what you were going to do. I'd do better on my own right now, anyhow. I just want to go through some things."

"Are you sure?" she asked.

"Absolutely." I heard my voice as if it were echoing. Didn't know if it was the room or just nerves.

"Well, I'll be going off duty in an hour," said Harry. "I'll leave word that you're here and when you get ready to leave you just let us know. OK?"

A few minutes later, I was alone. I closed the door between the reception office and the outer corridor and with my back against that door I looked around me. Cardboard boxes from Mayflower Movers were in a druidical semicircle around the two desks, each one identified by Dina's bold hand: REFERENCE MATERIALS, SUPPLIES, CLIPPINGS, STATIONERY. There were framed maps on the sofa, newspapers piled onto the chairs, lamps with their cords coiled around their bases stuck in the corners. The wastepaper baskets were filled with white bags from a nearby takeout restaurant, each one printed with a picture of a steaming cup of coffee in which the steam dreamily takes the shape of a doughnut, a hamburger, a roasted chicken. The overhead lights were fluorescent and one of the tubes was dying, shuddering slightly and singing that insecty siren song as it went. I turned it off by the wall switch and the room leapt back and disappeared: I was in total darkness. I turned the lights on again and walked slowly from the reception office into another, smaller office that would be used for staff, and then, through that, into the larger of the offices, which would be mine.

My desk had been assembled and placed near the window—though the window itself, like a window in a desperate hotel, looked only onto the dark neutrality of a nearby wall. A bouquet of flowers had been placed on the glass-topped desk. Carnations, daisies: very affordable. I sniffed them but they had no scent. They were stuck in a green vase and there was a card taped to a sprig of the greenery. It said "Welcome to Washington!" and it was signed by Dina and four other holdovers from Carmichael's staff. I felt a flush of emotion, as if I actually held in my hand a genuine token of their goodwill toward me. When I realized how ridiculous it was to feel anything like that, I squeezed my eyes shut, as if the darkness within me was lesson enough. I shoved the card into my back pocket. I was wearing a blue suit, like any other defendant. Someone in the boiler room must have been defying the energy-conscious president because the radiators were pumping out heat and it was hellish in my office. I took off my jacket, loosened my tie, rolled up my sleeves. I sat on the edge of my desk. The desk was clean except for a small box marked COR-RESPONDENCE. That piqued my interest. Nothing like reading someone else's mail, though it did occur to me that if the box had been left on the desk it was probably meant for my eyes.

I was thirsty. The heat in that room. The inevitable dehydration of a long rolling journey to madness. I slid off the desk with the idea of finding something in the office to drink and then coming back and looking through the box marked CORRESPONDENCE. I wandered around, hoping to spy a can of Coke someone had forgotten. No luck there, but there was a small room off the middle office in which there was a tiny refrigerator and a sink. Next to the sink was a red plastic drainboard in which stood six plastic coffee cups, each bearing the Illinois state seal. I picked up one of the cups and felt an indescribable sense of unease, as if all my inner breath had suddenly become a storm. I placed the cup down next to the sink, as if letting it go would stop whatever was happening to me. But of course that did no good. I was aware of the earth's ceaseless pilgrimage through space and heard the sound of the wind that was displaced by the long hopeless orbit. I turned the faucet on and brownish water came thundering into the aluminum sink. I waited for the stream to clear and then put my hand into it. I couldn't tell if it was hot or cold; I could only feel the force of its beating against my palm.

I pressed my fingers against my face, hoping the wetness could revive me, but all I was really aware of was the weight of my hand over my eyes and nose, like the hand of an attacker. I had only one coherent thought: I've got to get out of here, and I believe what I meant was not to get out of that office, or even that building, or even that city, but out of my life, out of the maze through which I'd been walking with all that appalling confidence, as if will were a true compass and desire a true destination, but which now suddenly revealed itself as a path leading only to itself, a mere form of confinement, a path fate places you on when it has nothing better for you to do.

I turned off the water. The absence of that sound made things a little easier. I stooped down and opened the refrigerator. There was one can of root beer and I took it out. It was one of those pop-top cans, in which you pull a tab and a small aluminum circle goes down into the soda and lets you drink through the hole. It struck me as odd that a society that puts such a high value on sterility in its packaging would think nothing of drinking soft drinks into which had been immersed the outside of the can, without any particular thought that those little disks we were dunking in our soda might be covered with bacteria. I stared at the can of soda and wondered how it could be that no one had thought of this.

That was when I heard a slight dull tapping on the outer door. At first I thought it was just something else coming loose in my brain but when I listened closely it seemed clearly to be coming from without and so I moved into the reception office and stood near the cartons and listened again. And this time I was certain someone was at the door. I thought it was old Harry or his replacement, making the rounds. I turned around to see what time it was. It was just seven o'clock and the imprisoned cuckoo was once again trying to escape through the taped doors. Its mechanical nightmarish voice seemed to have gone hoarse with frustration.

"Who is it?" I said. But there was no answer. I waited for whoever it was to make the next move.

And then there was a knocking again, a shy tapping, a one-knuckler. Three fast taps and then two slow ones. I walked quickly to the door and opened it, thinking that now the best thing to do was to get them before they had a chance to get away—like an old solitary man trying to catch the neighborhood brats who've been pounding on his storm door and then running away.

And so I opened the door and Sarah was standing there and the first thing I felt was an overwhelming *calmness*. She was wearing a black wool coat and the wool was sparkling because there was rain on it and her dark hair was braided around her head and her dark hair was sparkling from the rain, too. She put her fingers to her lips when she saw me, the fingers of her left hand, and her right hand was in a red woolen glove and her right hand was holding the other red woolen glove. Her eyes were a lighter green than I had been remembering and they were larger, too. I looked at her and I was waiting for the calmness to turn, to break out into something fast and fierce, but the calmness only deepened, like the delicate color on a pale wall will deepen when you give it its second coat of paint.

She looked behind her and when she faced me again I saw she was afraid. She stepped into the office and I closed the door and something told me to lock it so I did. The smell of rain came off her, a wild smell, strange and inhuman. She had a scratch, a red line, in the deep crease between her chin and her lower lip. Her lips were pale; her teeth looked uncared for. And older. Of course older. A few more years than the actual years that had passed. She wasn't really beautiful. I remember thinking that. I jiggled the door to make certain it was locked and now we were facing each other and still neither of us had spoken. It was very grave and full standing there with her, but I needed to touch her and of course she understood that and did not move her hand or even her eyes as I reached for her and placed my fingers on her bare hand—so cold, but her hands had always been a little icy, even in summer, even when we made love and they touched the small of my back, my hips, guiding me.

It was not spirit. I will say this one more time. It was not spirit, it was flesh. It was flesh and it was bone and it was wool and it was rain and, above all, above every other thing, it was her, it was Sarah.

"You knew I would come," she said, looking at her hand where I had touched it.

I shook my head no.

"But didn't you see me? I was up there, looking down, when you were standing in front of Tip O'Neill taking your oath. I saw you look up."

"I didn't see you."

And then abruptly, as if I had fallen through a trapdoor in my

own soul, the calmness was gone and I had a terrible feeling that
what I was going to do next was strike her with all my strength,
right across the face, and this thought was so powerful that it
showed itself to me and I could see myself hitting her and see her
staggering back after the blow and even that was not enough to
express the anger I felt. I stepped away from her and looked down
at the ground. I was breathing heavily. I could hear my breath
and it was bringing me back.

"I don't know how I did it," she said, very softly.

"Did what?" I asked.

"I don't know how I stayed away from you for so long."

And then, as if by inspiration, I took her hand and pressed it
to my lips, her strong, cold hand, which still tasted of her glove
and smelled of her own specific mortality. I held her hand and
felt her fingers tightening around my hand, her grip going fierce.
It confused me for a moment: there had always been an element
of sheer strength in her most unguarded moments. When she loved
you most deeply she didn't melt in your arms but grabbed you
so tightly your breath broke in half like an icy twig. And feeling
those fingers pressing into me made me look into her eyes with a
question in mine. Her eyes seemed not really to be looking at me,
or at least not searching for anything in my face; they, instead,
merely presented themselves and invited me to know them. And
I did see what she wanted me to: she had changed. Suffering and
secrecy, assignations, too many nights alone, missed meals, broken
sleep, and the inevitable and irreversible lack of concern for her
own self, her own privileges, her own comforts, all that excess
baggage that had to be tossed over if the vessel was going to make
it through the turbulent waters—good God, I suddenly felt un-
equal to the task of gazing so boldly upon her.

"How did you get in here?" I asked.

"It's not as hard as they think it is. Anyhow, I've always looked
like a secretary."

"You don't look like a secretary," I said.

She pursed her lips, colored slightly. "Oh, I know what I look like," she said. "There's nothing to do about it." She smiled. Her teeth; it was the graying, broken smile of a poor woman.

We heard footsteps from the corridor and the cheerful tuneless whistle of an armed man, accompanied by the jingle of keys. Sarah put up her hand to silence me, as if I might do something stupid. This was between her and them and I was instantly reduced to a civilian observer. I indicated with my thumb that we ought step away from the door and go into my private office further in. And the act of walking, the feel of the floor beneath my shoes, the sight of the suddenly familiar things, brought me closer to my everyday self so by the time we were in my office and I was leaning against my desk I could face her and say, "Did you have to do it this way?"

"Yes," she said. "Yes." She had unbuttoned her black wool coat and beneath it she wore a slightly dingy white blouse with a high lacy collar, such as one of her sisters might wear. She was very thin now; she seemed to have no breasts at all.

"Why? I think I deserved better than that. We were *lovers*."

"It wasn't about you and it wasn't about me, Fielding," she said.

"It could have been." In all honesty, I don't think even then I knew exactly what I meant by that, but saying it was nonetheless ignited within me one of those wildfires that burn so deeply when we feel we have been *wronged*. My lips trembled and I wanted to turn away from her—yet I wanted, also, for her to have to witness my agony.

"It seemed to me," she said, in a perfectly level voice, a voice over which she had so much control that she could even shade in a touch of pity, "that we took it as far as we could."

"I don't think that. I don't think that at all. You tore my life in half."

"No, I didn't. You're just saying that because you think you have to. Look at you. Look what you've done with your life."

"You despise it."

"Of course I don't. I'm so proud of you. You did what you

set out to do. You know how rare that is? I didn't tear your life in half, Fielding. Perhaps I tore mine, though."

"Then we'll put it back together," I said, turning on a dime from emptiness to utter hope, like a child can.

She shook her head. "I threw the other half away," she said.

"I am the other half. I'm right here."

She smiled and put her hand on her chest, taking a deep breath, as if the force of my personality winded her, as if the demands of my heart were like a steep flight of stairs which she was required to scale while holding the unwieldy burden of her own life. She seemed at that moment an emotional coward.

"Are you afraid of me?" I asked, and now I smiled because if that's all it was then it could all be set straight.

"No," she said. "Not of you."

"How long can you stay? Here. Right now. With me."

"You're in a position to do so much good now, Fielding."

"Is that why you're here?"

"Can't we just talk?" she asked. "You don't *have* to question me." She took off her coat and then looked around for a place to lay it down. There was only my desk and the chair behind it, but she didn't want to walk past me so she turned and laid the coat down in a bare corner. She was on her haunches, folding the coat carefully over itself, as if she were packing it away and didn't want it to wrinkle. She was wearing a gray skirt and a broad, shiny black belt. The tail of her blouse came out of her skirt and a patch of bumpy spine showed. She was wearing black boots with worn heels; the backs of her boots were streaked with mud, pale spidery lines, as faint as fossils. It was odd to see her taking such care with her coat. I had been remembering her as someone who just let her things fly, content every week or two to rake them into a pile and sort through. But that was life in the material world, then. She now thought of her coat as something that would have to last her forever.

"I think you know a lot more about me than I do about you right now," I said.

"I don't know that there's anything really worth knowing about me you can find out by asking a lot of questions," she said.

"That sounds very, very wise," I said, letting a little of the acid out.

"Sorry. Occupational hazard."

"Are you here now? Here for good?" I asked, putting up my hands to indicate that I accepted in general the idea of no questions, but that I would just have to ask a couple of quick ones.

"No."

"You are with someone, aren't you."

"Fielding."

"I've been with someone. Isaac Green has a niece. I've been living with her."

"It's not a chess game, Fielding. I'm not going to match moves with you."

"I'm not matching moves. I'm asking you a question. My God, how can you not answer me?"

"Because every answer will only confuse things. There's nothing I can say one way or the other that can make much sense."

"Great. Then what should we do? Just stare at each other and communicate telepathically?"

"You have to stop asking around about me, Fielding," she said. "I beg you."

"What was I supposed to do? I didn't know where you were. I didn't even know *if* you were."

"It's not secure. You understand. If you create a lot of curiosity it could make it very hard."

"Who knows about this? I know Mileski does. Who else?"

"Please don't ask any more questions," she said, flushing with frustration. She closed her hands tightly.

And I thought to myself: Is this what you wanted her back for? To accuse and torment her? Where you really belong is on your knees. I stepped toward her and took her hands again and brought them both to my lips and then she slipped one of them out of my grip and reached around and softly touched my nape, brushing the hair away and touching the warm neglected skin, and I looked into her eyes and felt a thud inside, a solid, harmonious sensation, as if I were an arrow that had at long last hit its mark.

"Are you all right, Sarah?" I asked her, almost in a whisper.

"I'm good, Fielding. I really am."

"You know," I said, "I think I probably read about you in the newspapers, without knowing it's you. Those people who are bringing in Latin Americans and hiding them in churches, giving them sanctuary."

She looked at me, not saying anything. The dark pupils of her eyes expanded and contracted, as if keeping pace with the beating of her heart.

"It's a good thing you're doing, Sarah."

"There's so much that needs to be done," she said.

"Is it easier for you? I mean . . . now."

"It's never easy," she said.

"I miss you, Sarah."

"I miss you, too," she said. "I miss us." Her mouth looked very stern, almost angry, and she lowered her face. Tears tipped out of her eyes, but her cry was so silent I wasn't aware of it until she raised her chin and I saw the streaks on her face.

"We're going to work something out," I said.

"What I'm doing is very wrong," she said. "I shouldn't be here. I'm being irresponsible. I made my decision and I kept to it. It was never easy but knowing it was the right thing made it . . . *possible*. And I thought that wanting you would simply go away. I did think that. And others said it would." She took a deep breath and tried to smile. "They gave me a money-back guarantee that in six months I would stop thinking about you." She raised one finger but then her attempt at joking herself out of her feelings collapsed and she looked exhausted, devastated.

I put my hand on her face and kept it there and when she didn't move back or shake her head I came slowly toward her, slowly, and kissed her carefully on her lips. She allowed herself to be kissed and I kissed her more, hoping that something would happen and she would respond, but all she did was not prevent it and finally I pulled away. I stood there looking at her and my heart seemed to have gotten awfully large because not only could I feel it beating in my throat but in my legs, too. I wasn't angry about her lack of response. I wasn't even disappointed. Two months ago, could I have imagined having what I had right now? The terrible curtain of grief that had separated us for those years had been torn down and nothing—no separation, no conceivable *kind* of separation—could put it up again.

As I stepped back I seemed to draw her toward me. She reached out and grabbed me with a terrible strength. Her face suddenly loomed next to mine like a moon in a dream, a moon lured back to the warm miseries of the planet from which it had eons ago escaped. And now her lips were crushed against mine in a powerful, open kiss and I kissed her back the best I could, though I felt suddenly fragile and out of my element and her kiss continued and it continued until it was not really a kiss at all but some desperate stab at merging us, at putting my breath in her lungs and hers in mine: to turn us into twins joined at the soul, true lovers, sweet ineffable monsters.

When at last she stepped away from me, I couldn't help asking: "When you leave here, am I ever going to see you again?"

"I don't know, Fielding." She held onto my hand and pulled at me, leading me toward the window. It was dark; the lamplight in my office illuminated the raindrops as they hit against the glass. Sarah found the cord to the Venetian blinds and lowered them. They said *shhhhh* as they fell. Then she went to the lamp on my desk and switched it off. The entire room tipped into darkness and I blinked, fighting for a glimpse of her.

"Sarah?" I said, almost expecting her not to be there any longer.

She took my hand again and drew herself into me. I could feel the bones of her chest against mine. The pointed bone of her hip grazed against my cock and then she kissed me so furiously on the throat it was difficult not to start, not to push her away. I remember it passing through my mind that she had come all this way to kill me.

"I couldn't help myself," she said, laying her head against my chest, wrapping her arms around me. "You *are* my lover. So I got your phone number and then once I had it I had to call you. Sometimes when I thought of you living your life without me it would be like a knife in my belly turning around and around."

"You knew I was alive," I said into the darkness.

"Does that make it easy?" she asked.

I waited before answering. "No," I said finally. "Nothing makes it easy."

She was running her hand up and down my back and now my chest, my ribs, as if she wanted to make certain everything was where she had left it. She was on my stomach now and she grabbed the flesh and I was just holding onto her until she linked her fingers into my belt loops and then let them drop and squeezed my erection. Was I waiting for permission? I don't know. But as soon as she touched me sexually my passion, which until then had been distant, merely *possible*, was livid, almost insane, and I began to kiss her on the forehead, the eyes, the cheeks, the throat, her breasts and as I sank down I pulled her with me. I was just able to make out her outlines in the darkness but now that we were sinking to the floor she was lost in the blackness again. Yet I could surely feel her and hear her ragged, quick breaths, and feel them on my face, and taste them.

"I get so tired, Fielding," she whispered, and I knew that was all I would ever hear about the difficulty of the path she had chosen.

"Are we going to make love?" I said.

She was silent for a long while. I held on to her. Her ribs expanded and contracted as she breathed. "I don't think so," she said.

"OK," I said. "Oh God, Sarah. Are you really here?"

"I think I'd get pregnant if we made love. It feels like all the planets are aligned and that would definitely happen."

"I remember once we almost tried to make a child," I said.

"But then we stopped. Just at the moment. Or right before. We got so close. I surprise myself by how often I think of it."

"I think of it, too. You were already in me. All you had to do was arch your back and then come forward again. You know, just a little friction, a little movement of skin, and there would be another entire human being on earth right now."

"I'm glad you think of it," I said.

"Why?"

"Because I do."

"But why do you?"

She was on her back and I was above her. She was using my forearm as a pillow and I tried to keep it there as I lay on the cool floor next to her. "See?" I said. "Now *you're* asking questions."

"I wish you had a condom or something," she said.

"I don't have anything."

"Well, I didn't come very prepared."

"Maybe we could risk it."

"No. The forces are at work. Can't you feel them?"

"Well, then maybe God wants us to have a child," I said.

"God wants all sorts of things. He's totally indiscriminate in the things he asks for. It's up to us to negotiate intelligently."

We lay in silence. She must have felt my arm falling asleep because she lifted her head and then rested it higher, on my biceps, and then from there she moved still closer, until her cheek was just below my shoulder. She draped her leg over mine and sniffed. "It's you," she said.

"You don't have to leave me, you know," I said. "Anyhow, I won't let you."

"Before we were just sketches," she said, "and we could still imagine we could fit together. But now we've been painted in so deeply, you know all the lines are so dark. It seems wrong to think we belong together."

"But I think it."

"I guess I do, too. But I think I know why."

"Why?"

"Because it's what we want."

"You see?"

"Yes. But let's not forget how few people get what they want. And those who do—well, they're not really the lucky ones, are they?"

"They aren't? Then who are?"

"I don't know. The ones who do what they are meant to. Can we not talk for a minute? I would feel so happy if all you did was hold me. If you could just hold me and let me pretend that this is what our life is, that this is perfectly natural and no big deal at all. And then I can close my eyes and let everything else fall away."

"It's very hard, what you're doing, isn't it?"

"Yes. It's very hard. But the people we're trying to help—it's much harder for them. But please. Can't you just hold me?"

And so I just held her. I listened to her breathing and felt her growing heavier on me as she relaxed. I kissed the top of her head, stroked the side of her face, at first so I could feel her skin and then very lightly so that her down whispered against my fingertips. The feeling of peace, a deep serious peace, came over me again, just as it had when I first saw her an hour before. Sexual desire retreated, like a bear returning to its cave after having been woken by a false sign of spring.

And so I slept and when I woke a moment later, or an hour later, she was still next to me and we were still on the floor of that office, holding each other. And I drifted off to sleep again and woke some time later and still she was next to me, though now her leg was no longer touching mine and her breathing was quieter, slower, and the great bear of desire was stirring within me again, but I closed my eyes because it would have been awful to disturb her and I went back to sleep. My body was already starting to ache from the hardness of the floor, but I wouldn't allow myself to take the discomfort very seriously because she seemed to feel none of it. I imagined the hectic nights she must have spent in the years that separated us: asleep in the backs of vans, in church basements, in all the secret places she knew. She was a soldier and she was sleeping beside me and so I lowered myself into sleep, too, because that was where she was and I wanted to be with her. I slept deeply this time and I slept long. And when I opened my eyes again there was weak rainy light coming in through the window and I was alone.

I lay there, thinking she had just got up for a moment, perhaps to use the little bathroom around the corner. But it was too quiet. I was on my back and I raised myself up on my elbows and looked around. The coat she had folded so neatly in the corner was gone and at that point I was no longer merely alone. At that point she was gone. I stayed in that position for a few moments, looking around, waiting—thinking, I suppose, that if I stopped then time would, too. But it was so quiet. I let my head loll back and I squeezed my eyes shut, saying to myself: Get up, get up.

"Sarah?" I said, getting to my feet. I felt exhausted; my bladder was heavy. "Sarah?" I said again, and my voice died a few inches away from me, as if I were in a soundproofed room. It seemed foolish calling her name; she was so clearly not here. Nevertheless, I looked for her. What else could I do? And when I had looked around the office—for her, for any sign of her—I opened the door. It was unlocked. I looked down the corridor. It appeared cold and empty, uninhabitable.

I looked for her. But it was not a real search because I knew I would not find her. She had probably left hours ago. Before the day broke. I ran into a member of the Capitol police. He had no idea who I was, but I somehow communicated to him that I was Congressman Pierce. He asked me if I'd been in the building all night and I said I had. He didn't seem particularly surprised, but he did make it a point to walk with me as I went back to my office. He was a well-built black man. He wore thick eyeglasses that he kept snug on his flat, smooth face with a black elastic band. When we reached my office, the door was wide open.

"See you're just moving in," he said, looking over my shoulder and into the mess.

I nodded yes.

"Next time you spend the night," he said, smiling, "best you let us know so we know you're here. You don't want to make us look bad, do you?"

I walked into my office and closed the door behind me. I felt cold. I rolled my sleeves down, buttoned them, and found my jacket and put it on. I went to the bathroom and then drank a cup of tap water. I just wandered around, touching things, looking at the boxes on the floor. Suddenly, my heart began to race but then it slowed down to its normal beat and I felt very strange but in control of myself. I went back to the office where I had spent the night with her and looked at the floor, wishing it had been earth and the imprint of our bodies had been there for me to see. The window behind my desk was brightening and it cast a slanted box of light onto the desk. I touched the wood. It was smooth. Someone had waxed it recently. I felt a spasm of emotion and I stopped in my tracks, letting myself cry if that's what I wanted. But the feeling could not break the surface of the overwhelming sense of quietness I had just then. I walked around my desk and sat in my chair.

I picked up the phone, but it was so early and there was no one to call. I placed the receiver in its cradle and then reached for the box marked CORRESPONDENCE that Dina Jensen had left for me. It was a gray and white cardboard box, secured by a strip of masking tape. I peeled the tape off and opened the box. Inside, there were fifty or so letters, bunched in little groups by paper clips—some system Dina had worked out, I guessed. Attached to the front-most group was a handwritten note from Dina. "Congressman Pierce—These came after Mr. Carmichael left and so now they are for you."

The letters had been opened, probably scanned, and then placed back in their envelopes. I chose one at random, opened it, and read:

Dear Congressman Carmichael,

My son is nineteen years old. He was born with very low birthweight and has never enjoyed good health. Against my wishes, he joined the Army last July. I think it was a very bad thing the Army did to take him. When I got a letter from two doctors stating that Mark's health was poor and that he was a heart-risk, the man at the Recruiting Station (Sgt. Fred V. Colburn) said he would send these letters to Mark's Commanding Officer (Capt. E. M. Gomez). Mark is stationed in Hamburg, Germany, and Captain Gomez has not answered any of my letters. I called him international long distance and he would not even come to the phone! In the meanwhile, my son's health has gotten worse. He has been in the Army hospital with a very high fever and has had a blood transfusion. He is also having chest pains and has lost 24 pounds in the past eight weeks. If someone does not do something, I know as God is my witness that my son will die in the Army. He is all I have but he is very stubborn. No one will listen to me!

Yours truly,
(Mrs.) Laura Morris

Dear Congressman Carmichael,

Can you please send me any information about the rights of adopted children? Please mark the envelope Personal—Top Secret—Do Not Open. If the people here saw what I was doing they would kill me.

Thank you,
Steven Benardi

P.S. I don't know what my Real Name is.

Dear Congressman Carmichael,

Four years ago my best friend Andrew Rosen and I were in Marrakesh, Morocco. It was a vacation trip. Three days before we were due to return home to Chicago, Andy disappeared. The Moroccan police did nothing. In fact, their attitude was very offensive. The American Consulate in Rabat was polite on the phone, but when I went there to speak to someone, no one would see me. And it now has been four years and they have done no more than write a couple of letters. They seem to believe Andrew was involved in something he shouldn't have been. But I can tell you that Andy was doing nothing wrong. I am a waiter at the Blackstone Cafe and I have saved enough money to return to Morocco. If the police and the Embassy will do nothing to find Andy, I feel it is my duty to at least try. (The Rosens have given him up for lost and they don't seem to be very upset.)

If you will check your files, you will see that I wrote to you regarding Andy Rosen on September 9, 1978, March 1, 1979, June 18, 1979, and November 1, 1979. Although your office has sent notes acknowledging receipt of my letters, I have yet to hear from you, Representative Carmichael. I am planning my trip to Morocco for April 2, 1980, and while I am there will do everything in my power to find Andy and expose the people who have done whatever has been done to him. But I am only one person. My task would be much easier if I could count on some cooperation from Moroccan or American officials. Morocco is an American ally and I know strong words from a U.S. congressman would have a great effect. Please refer back to the letters I have sent you. All of the information about Andy is in them, including photographs, his school records, and statements from the many friends who loved him. If you could lend your name to our efforts, I know our chances of finding him will be greatly increased. If he is alive, he is in a living hell.

Thank you again,
Kevin Ertel

Dear Congressman Pierce,

Congratulations on your election to the United States House of Representatives. I want to say I proudly cast my ballot for you. My name is Samuel K. Smith. I am a retired member of the Brotherhood of Sleeping Car Porters. I used to live at the Belvedere Apartments on Cottage Grove and 60th Street, but since the fire I am living in a much smaller apartment on Cottage Grove and 54th Street. I am writing you now because I am having a bad problem with my Social Security. When I moved from my apartment after the fire, two of my checks were lost. Then some little crooks got their hands on the checks and cashed them. This caused a big problem with the Social Security and I was brought downtown to their offices and spoken to. When I left I thought it was all worked out, but I was wrong. It has been two months and I have not gotten a check. Also I have not been paid back for the checks that were lost. That makes four months with no Social Security. I have not had money for food. I have taken food out of the garbage in the halls. I have not been able to wash my clothes and I do not have money for bus fare. The people in the Social Security are taking their time. But time is one thing I do not have. I feel I am being treated very unfairly. I can't live without money. No one can. And this money they are holding from me is mine. I earned it. I have done everything I know how to do to get this problem fixed up. I know you are very busy but if I could come to your office in Washington I would be there right now and I would get down on my knees and take your hand and beg you to please please help me before it is too late.

A NOTE ON THE TYPE

This book was set in a digitized version of Janson. The hot-metal version of Janson was a recutting made direct from type cast from matrices long thought to have been made by the Dutchman Anton Janson, who was a practicing type founder in Leipzig during the years 1668–1687. However, it has been conclusively demonstrated that these types are actually the work of Nicholas Kis (1650–1702), a Hungarian, who most probably learned his trade from the master Dutch type founder Dirk Voskens. The type is an excellent example of the influential and sturdy Dutch types that prevailed in England up to the time William Caslon (1692–1766) developed his own incomparable designs from them.

Composed by Crane Typesetting Service, Inc., Barnstable, Massachusetts.
Printed and bound by Fairfield Graphics, Fairfield, Pennsylvania.
Designed by Virginia Tan.